"Futurist as provocateur! The world is sheer bat-shit genius . . . a truly hallucinatorily envisioned environment."

—William Gibson, *New York Times* bestselling and award-winning author

"The great American novel about the end of America. This book is marvelously propulsive, big hearted, and whip smart."

—Kelly Link, Pulitzer Prize–nominated author of *Get in Trouble*

"This vision of the future is violent, unforgiving, and bleak: Cormac McCarthy meets Philip K. Dick. It's disturbing because of how believable it is. . . . It's remarkably effective. Recommended for fans of Paolo Bacigalupi and China Miéville."

—*Booklist*

"Timely, dark, and ultimately hopeful: it might not 'make America great again,' but then again, it just might."

—Cory Doctorow, *New York Times* bestselling and award-winning author of *Homeland*

"*Tropic of Kansas* is like a modern dystopian buffet. It is, in this particular moment in history, frighteningly prescient. It is the nightly news with the volume turned up to 11."

—NPR.org

"This stunning novel of a time all too easily imaginable as our own highlights a few of the keen-voiced, brave-souled women and men who balance like subversive acrobats on society's whirling edges. . . . Read it to burn with the joy of realistic hope."

—Nisi Shawl, Tiptree Award–winning author of *Everfair* and *Writing the Other*

"A unique blend of Philip K. Dick, Kafka (just a smidgen), and a whole lot of Christopher Brown. Adventure novel meets political satire and the finest elements of realistic sci-fi, and it's so well written it goes down like a greased eel. It's hopeful dystopia. What a book."

—Joe R. Lansdale, author of the Hap and Leonard series

"*Tropic of Kansas* is savvy political thriller meets ripping pulp adventure—a marriage made in page-turning, thought-provoking heaven. It's a vision both frighteningly prescient and already too real, and a story of valiant heart and brain up against the worst architectures of greed and power."

—Jessica Reisman, SESFA Award–winning
author of *Substrate Phantoms*

"A real page-turner."

—Gavin J. Grant, Bram Stoker Award–winning
editor and author

Rule of Capture

ALSO BY CHRISTOPHER BROWN

Tropic of Kansas

Rule of Capture

A NOVEL

Christopher Brown

HARPER Voyager
An Imprint of HarperCollins Publishers

RULE OF CAPTURE. Copyright © 2019 by Christopher Brown. All rights reserved. Printed in the United States of America. No part of this book may be used or reproduced in any manner whatsoever without written permission except in the case of brief quotations embodied in critical articles and reviews. For information, address HarperCollins Publishers, 195 Broadway, New York, NY 10007.

HarperCollins books may be purchased for educational, business, or sales promotional use. For information, please email the Special Markets Department at SPsales@harpercollins.com.

Harper Voyager and design are trademarks of HarperCollins Publishers LLC.

FIRST EDITION

Designed by Paula Russell Szafranski
Frontispiece and part opener art © Fuse / GettyImages

Library of Congress Cataloging-in-Publication Data has been applied for.

ISBN 978-0-06-285909-9

19 20 21 22 23 LSC 10 9 8 7 6 5 4 3 2 1

For my brother Alex Brown (1966–2019)

Rule of Capture

PART ONE

Non-Compliance

IN THE YEAR OF THE COUP, DONNY KIMOE SPENT MONDAY MORN-
ings at the federal courthouse trying to help torture victims
remember what happened to them in lockup over the weekend. Judge Broyles liked having Donny in his courtroom to
take on-the-spot appointments. They had worked together in
the U.S. Attorney's office back in the day, before the country
went crazy, and relationships like that had legs. Even when
you ended up on different sides of what was starting to feel
like the beginning of a civil war.

More importantly, Donny had the security clearance you
needed to be able to appear in that court—a hard thing to come
by without having worked for the machine, and a harder thing
to maintain when you switched sides to work for the defense.
Not that having the clearance meant the prosecution would
share much of what they had compiled in their classified files
on your clients.

Getting justice at secret trials for people the government
wanted to disappear was not easy.

Especially when you had to show up on time.

"Late again," said Turner, laughing at Donny as he buzzed
open the bombproof main door. Turner was one of the four
beefy old marshals they had manning the security checkpoint:
one on this side of the machines, one viewing the screens, and
two on the other side waiting for their opportunity to shoot
someone. They looked like a gang of Shriners gone wrong.

"Donny likes to party," said the guy manning the machine, the one with the drone pilot eyes.

"Have you guys been watching my surveillance feed again?" said Donny. "Guess they cut off the cable at the home for old fascists."

All four of them laughed at that, a heartier and creepier laugh than you would have expected.

Then Turner took Donny's phone and his ID and put them in the lockbox. Somehow that was the most invasive part of the protocol, even more than the man-hands all over your body. It made you wonder if this was the day you would exit through the same door as the prisoners.

As Donny emptied the rest of his pockets into the plastic bin, he looked back through the window at the mothers of Houston crowded behind the barricade, holding up pictures and names of their missing kids as if it would help. You couldn't hear their chants through the soundproofing, but they still echoed in Donny's ears from his walk up to the building. One of them had called Donny by name as he squeezed through, but he pretended he didn't hear them. The tears of anguished parents couldn't improve the odds on those cases, or pay the fees for trying, and Donny already had his hands full that morning with deadlines past due.

"Come on," said Turner, brandishing his big electric wand. When it passed over the contours of Donny's tired body, it sounded like an old radio tuning in whalesong.

"You play me like a theremin," said Donny, as if being a wise-ass would keep the horror at bay. But Turner didn't laugh. He just shoved him into the body scanner.

A German shepherd stared at Donny from the other side, on alert. The kind of dog that wears a uniform.

Donny stood for the scan, looked back at his spectral avatar, endured the fat white hands groping his sweaty spots, and collected his stuff. That's when he noticed the little tin of breath mints he had left in his jacket pocket, the one that had something other than mints in it.

He looked at the dog, and was glad to confirm it only seemed to care about the kind of homebrew that could explode.

"See you on the other side, fellas," he said, grabbing his briefcase and hurriedly collecting his stuff. As he stepped toward the elevator, he noticed what it said on the dog's police vest.

DO NOT PET.

The Vice President John Tower United States Courthouse for the Southern District of Texas, Houston Division, had been built by the prior administration, which broke the budget on public projects to keep people working after the war. They also had the idea that justice should look nice, at least on the outside. The main corridor riffed some cross between a Greek temple and a museum of modern art, the way it opened up into these vaulting spaces of concrete and wood filled with light from unseen sources that highlighted the absence of people. They'd warmed it up a little with some timbers harvested from the building that came before, but when you knew that wood was from now-extinct forests, it kind of killed the feeling. And then you noticed the little domes of black glass in the ceiling and walls, and remembered this was a courthouse where justice was not blind, but all-seeing. There were cameras everywhere, except where they could do some good—in the courtrooms.

Especially the one Donny was going to.

Donny collected himself at the big wooden door, trying to summon a confident composure as he cued up excuses from his compilation of sins committed and lies told, the way a kid prepares to face an angry father. The only thing you could be sure of before you went in there was that the clients they assigned you to represent were probably guilty. It was the laws they had violated that were unjust—laws a government at war with its own people invents to make sure it wins. And to make doubly sure, they did everything they could to keep you from knowing what they knew about your case, often things even the clients did not know, things that only the electronic brains plugged into the eyes of the state could know.

As he reached for the door handle, the jitter in his hand reminded Donny he was guilty, too. He looked up at the government seal laser-cut into the door, an abstracted image of the eagle squeezing the snake, and remembered which one he was. And then he pulled the door open, assuring his slithering avatar the story wasn't over yet.

When he stepped through, he found the crowd. They were watching the prosecutor, Assistant U.S. Attorney Bridget Kelly, recite the state's coded reasons why the boy in the dock, some scrawny white kid with the hand-me-down clothes and homemade tattoos of one of the resettlement camps, should be detained on suspicion of membership in a rebel gang that had vandalized a FEMA command center.

Donny couldn't see the kid's face, but as he listened to

Bridget, he got the sinking feeling this was the case he was assigned to handle, and he'd missed it.

Fortunately, when he looked to the defense table, it wasn't empty. Loni Sandler was there, a veteran public defender whom Donny admired even though he could always tell the feeling was not mutual.

The gallery behind the bar was packed with feds waiting for their cases to be called. Government suits lined up like buzz-cut funeral directors, Coast Guard special operators in their blue-and-orange camo, Texas Rangers in their government-issue Stetsons, a pair of game wardens outfitted for hunting humans, and one Border Patrol agent in her dirt brown DMZ dungarees, no doubt preparing to testify about some dissident she had nabbed trying to escape the country and sneak into Mexico. Most were members of Counterinsurgency Task Force Foxtrap, though Donny knew some of the suits were also there to make sure the court did its job, ready to report back to Washington or Austin as needed. A few of them turned their heads and looked back at him as he entered their domain, with a judgmental group gaze designed to remind him he was on the wrong side. There was one friendly face, but even that one looked worried. Donny joined him in the front row, on the defense side of the aisle.

"Good morning, Miles," whispered Donny. "I thought you were supposed to be in Austin today with Mayor Chung."

Miles Powell was the smartest lawyer Donny knew, the most ethical, and the best dressed. All class, no flash, a black man in grey flannel. Where Donny got access to the secret court from having worked for the government, Miles got his from a career fighting it. That Miles somehow prospered in the process only heightened Donny's sense of moral inferiority.

"I am," said Miles, speaking under his breath. "This afternoon. Arguments at three. Heading out in an hour."

"They still have her in custody?"

Miles nodded. "Special detention in the brig at Camp Mabry. Live camera feed anyone can view."

Donny considered that as he watched the marshals escort Loni's client away, relieved to hear the name and learn it was not the case he had been assigned.

"That's messed up," said Donny. "I wish Mayor Barthelme were still around. He would know how to handle these guys."

"If Barthelme were still alive, he'd be too drunk to fight these guys."

"He might have the right idea," said Donny, looking around to see if he could figure out where the muffled squeal of pain came from. "So what did I miss?"

Miles just shook his head, put his finger to his mouth to shush Donny, and turned his attention to the court.

Which had now noticed Donny. And did not look happy to see him.

"Mr. Kimoe," said the voice from the bench, the voice of life tenure and final judgment.

"Your Honor," said Donny, standing at the bar. The honorific was reflexive, something they programmed into you in law school moot courts, and if you thought about it, about the system to which it kneeled, it made it hard to say. But Donny had learned to be part of the system before he learned how rotten the system is, and now paid his bills guiding people through it, a job that required a habituation to losing, or at least a rather compromised idea of what constituted winning. When she'd had enough of it, Donny's ex-girlfriend Joyce, a philosophy professor at Rice, told him it was like dating the riverman of the underworld. Donny said sometimes I bring them back, but Joyce was already gone.

"Nice of you to join us this morning," said Judge Broyles, looking down over the rims of the old wire-framed glasses he had been wearing as long as Donny had known him. Broyles was all grey now, and it showed in his eyes. The silvery grey of old money, from one of those blue-blood Houston families that had come down from the East way back when and made successive fortunes building the railroads and then the oil-and-gas business and now the commercial space business. The first lawyer in a long line of financiers, he had the demeanor of a prep school headmaster in charge of a secret prison. One that needed to turn a profit.

The stockholders were watching. Some were right there in the back of the room.

"I'm sorry, Your Honor," said Donny. "I was stuck on a call in another case. A matter of life and death."

"You look about half-dead yourself, Mr. Kimoe. Still trying to annul my sentence in the Hardy case?"

"Exhausting our client's rights of appeal, yes."

"As is your right, even if you are wasting your time and the People's money."

"We'll see about that, Your Honor."

"Yes, we will. Before sunrise tomorrow, if I'm right."

Donny looked at the clock on the wall behind the judge. The execution was scheduled for midnight, and would proceed unless Donny could succeed in getting a last-minute reprieve. But the law governing his service required him to be here this morning, taking whatever cases the court assigned him to defend—which made it hard for him to do a good job for any of his clients.

Just the way the government that called itself "the People" wanted it.

"Well," added Broyles, "fortunately for the client I was going to burden with you today, you were AWOL when his case came up, so I had Mr. Powell cover for you."

Donny looked over at Miles, who just raised his eyebrows.

"Mr. Powell proceeded to persuade us to let one detainee go free this morning. It will probably be our last. And so, Mr. Kimoe, I am going to give you the case I had assigned to Mr. Powell."

"Your Honor," said Miles, standing. "That's not fair to the defendant."

"Aren't you supposed to be in Austin trying to spring our scofflaw mayor, Mr. Powell?"

"Yes, Your Honor. But—"

"Please give my regards to Judge Leakey. And good luck getting her to invalidate the Governor's declaration of martial law. Though I have to say you have a better chance of winning that one than those avocado-sucking carpetbaggers they are flying in from San Francisco to help you."

"Thank you, Your Honor," said Miles, over the laughs from the gallery at the judge's derisive quip. "I'm happy to have all the help I can get."

"There's an election riding on the outcome, I hear." Broyles didn't mention it was the election of the President who had appointed him, one he had helped get elected the first time. "Go forth," he said, pointing Miles to the door. "I will help Mr. Kimoe wake up and provide our next contestant with an effective defense."

"Yes, sir," said Miles. He glanced at Donny with a face that shrugged. Then he grabbed his briefcase to go.

"Judge," said Donny, "I don't have time to take up—"

"America is waiting," said Broyles, cutting Donny off. "And justice is not." He hit the gavel with a hard knock, the forgotten call of some vanquished wood god, and then summoned the appearance of Donny's new client, spinning the Spanish vowels with Anglo-Texan inflection. "Bring in Xelina Rocafuerte."

A door opened in the courtroom wall, just a few feet away. Through it stepped a young woman wrapped in chains, with a black hood over her head.

She was sandwiched by a pair of marshals in their black-and-tan tacticals, one young and burly and the other old and wiry, but both with the eyes of trappers. Each held a stretch of the clanking alloyed link that encircled the prisoner's elfin body and locked onto the shackles around her wrists and ankles. You wondered how she moved, until you noticed the way the marshals held her.

Broyles made an imperious gesture with his hand. The older marshal pulled the hood from the girl's head. And suddenly you could sense why they were afraid of her.

They had clothed her in the red jumpsuit of non-compliance, a message that was also sent by her haircut, the kind of exclamatory coif that could get you pulled over in some of the outer suburbs. That and the way she carried herself locked in this steel sandwich of mean-ass white guys projected an aura of defiance so strong you could feel it roll through the room. She was barely as tall as the shorter marshal's shoulders, but she had her chin up, and after glancing at Donny she looked right at the famously temperamental Judge Broyles, making sure he could see the burn mark on her cheek, which matched her jumpsuit.

"Miss Rocafuerte," said Broyles. "While I have your full attention, may I ask if you know why you are here on this rainy Monday morning?"

He said that knowing she probably hadn't seen the outside for days.

"Because you are afraid of us," she said. Her voice betrayed the uncertainty she was trying to hide with her poise. They never told them why they had taken them in, because the not knowing made them more scared. And usually more glib.

"Your Honor—" said Donny, standing.

"Let us talk," said Broyles. "You're not her counsel, yet."

"You don't have to answer him," said Donny, speaking to Xelina.

"Sit down, Mr. Kimoe," said Broyles.

"He's just trying to trick you," said Donny, refusing to sit. "Save it until after you and I can talk."

The look in her eyes was an intense mix of anger, intelligence, and fear.

"Miss Rocafuerte," said Broyles, leaning forward a bit, to where the forelock of his wiry grey widow's peak flipped over. "You are here because the government has identified you as a rebel. A subversive. A conspirator against your own government. A traitor against the People. Do I have that right, Ms. Kelly?"

"That's correct, Your Honor," said Bridget Kelly, standing sharply at the prosecution table in her creased blue suit, blond hair pulled back tight. Bridget was one of the lawyers they had recently transferred down from D.C. to handle the case flow coming out of the crackdown. She was a true believer, with the Old Glory lapel pin to prove it, and a flair for the official narrative. "Our investigators have identified the defendant as a member of the Free Rovers Organization. She is a leading producer of their terrorist recruiting videos."

"I'm a journalist!" said Xelina.

"The defendant will speak when spoken to," said Broyles.

"The Rovers are not an 'organization,'" said Donny. "That's an invention of the government. It's like being an Astros fan."

The court ignored him.

Bridget approached the bench and handed a thick stack of papers to the judge. She then gave a copy to Donny. The top page was a charge sheet—a government form filled out with the defendant's name, date of birth, alleged aliases, and the laundry list of crimes with which she was charged. It was signed at the bottom by one of the senior prosecutors detailed to the tribunal, Deputy U.S. Attorney Jack McAuley, to whom Bridget reported.

"The defendant participated in the FRO's illegal infiltration, occupation, and sabotage of industrial properties in the Coastal Evacuation Zone," continued Bridget. "She documented their raids on several petrochemical facilities, including two on the national defense registry, and the drills in their paramilitary training camp."

Bridget was just getting started, and Donny was already having trouble keeping up. Attached to the charge sheet he had just been handed was a stack of exhibits. Almost all of them had been redacted with the thick black bars of the censor. Donny looked up at the court security officer, an executive branch employee who sat at a bench just below and to the judge's right, near the clerk and the court reporter. He quickly turned away, after being busted watching Donny digest his work.

"I believe I may have seen one of those," said Broyles. "Kalashnikovs, burning cars, and targets made to look like certain elected officials?"

"That sounds right, Your Honor," said Bridget. "Government's Exhibit A-17, at page 73, has some screen shots."

Donny's copy had no Exhibit A-17. It did have a red sheet where the index of exhibits was supposed to go, pre-printed with a notice.

*Defense Counsel: Portions of the document you are
trying to access are currently undergoing a security
review per the Regulations for Trial by Special
Emergency Tribunal, October 31 Revised Edition,
Rule 19.4. At the completion of the security review any
portions of the document deemed releasable to cleared
counsel will be made available. Please consult the CSO
in your case if you have any questions. Thank you for
your cooperation.*

"The defense has a right to see all of those as well," objected Donny. "But instead we get this." He tore the red page
loose and waved it like a flag. "What the hell is Rule 19.4?"

"If you would read the updates regularly sent by this court
you would know," said Broyles. "We are trying out a new process to better maintain security while facilitating more expeditious proceedings. I am confident Mr. Walton will be able to get
most of these submittals processed within a few days."

CSO Walton looked up at the judge and nodded. Walton
was one of those personally powerless but authority-oriented
guys who look middle-aged before their time, someone the ap-
titude tests said would make a great censor. In addition to his
redaction machine, the CSO had a button at his desk that allowed him to generate white noise to override any portion of
the proceedings that strayed into the garden of secrets. When
he did that, a small red light went on at the edge of his desk, so
everyone knew.

Donny looked over at his client. She looked terrified and
confused. And more than a little pissed.

"This is outrageous, Judge," said Donny. "I'm supposed to be cleared for this."

"I'm advised it's a sources and methods issue," said Broyles. "And we've had some leakage. Not saying it's you."

"That's correct, Your Honor," said Bridget. "And the copy provided to defense counsel is not entirely redacted."

Donny scanned what was there. Code names of confidential informants, dates, some fragments of investigatory narrative, a few screen shots that were only partly obscured.

"There is no way to mount an effective defense off of this," said Donny.

"If you would read the rule," said Broyles, "you would know that you are entitled to have the prosecution provide you a summary of all evidence that has been redacted. So you can work with Ms. Kelly to find a time when she can meet you in the SCIF for that purpose."

"Also correct, Your Honor," said Bridget, looking over at Donny and nodding. "We can do that at this morning's break."

The SCIF was the "Sensitive Compartmented Information Facility," a fancy name for a dingy little conference room downstairs that had been cleared for reviews of classified information. Technically, the courtroom they were in was a SCIF, but Donny saw no upside in arguing the point further. He sat down and looked back at his client. He gave her a reassuring look, but he could tell she wasn't buying it.

Probably because he wasn't selling it all that well.

"Thank you," said Broyles. "Please continue with your summary, Ms. Kelly."

The truth was Donny had already seen the training camp video. Everyone had. Outtakes from it had been blasted all over the media as proof of the government's claims that the isolated outbursts of political violence and eco-terrorism in recent years had coalesced into a revolutionary underground. Seeing its rainbow ensemble of young greens with guns made you realize the Second Amendment only applies to certain people. It also made Donny wonder if it was as real as the government said.

Donny looked again at Xelina. She seemed so young. She also looked tough, and angry, but more like a clever prankster than the revolutionary provocateur of Bridget's script. It dawned on him then that she might even be innocent.

"Your Honor," continued Bridget. "Many of the videos of these acts of terror and provocations to sedition were posted on public networks using an anonymous account, in violation of the Communications Freedom Act. See Exhibit 4."

Donny looked at the list of aliases on the first page of the charge sheet. They were all user names, which read like graffiti tags. X-Rok, Viridiana, gaia_llorona. The CFA mandated user transparency, in response to evidence that public opinion had been manipulated in recent elections by foreign infiltrators using fake accounts. Enforcement had been lax, but that was clearly changing.

"We have provided excerpted transcripts of the defendant's correspondence with her comrades in arms using these accounts," said Bridget. "All of whom also use aliases, and the defendant has refused to cooperate with our investigators in providing us their true names."

You could see the resolve in Xelina's face as Bridget mentioned her friends.

"Based on this information, defendant was detained by the Task Force," said Bridget. "Additional evidence of her involvement in these activities was uncovered in their search of her residence, along with unlicensed weapons, suspected explosives, scheduled narcotics, and fence-breaching materials."

"Fence-breaching materials," said Broyles, slowly, like a teacher reading an intercepted note.

"Our investigation reveals the defendant has been associated with this cell since last winter, with knowledge of their conspiracy against the United States and the State of Texas, and aiding in active concealment of their violent enterprise. She has been refusing to answer questions or provide access to the evidence she possesses regarding other members of her cell and their operational plans. The government recommends she be transferred to this Special Emergency Tribunal as a domestic insurgent and processed for denaturalization."

Denaturalization was the lawyerly way of saying take away your citizenship, even if you were born here.

"Your Honor," said Donny, standing. "A punishment that extreme can't be imposed without providing us full access to the information the government has collected in its so-called investigation. Not these crumbs." He waved the charge sheet again. "And not an executive summary in the SCIF that only includes whatever the government feels like telling us. How are we to prepare a defense if the evidence against Ms. Rocafuerte is kept secret?"

"You could start by getting her to give up the names of her associates," said Broyles. "That would solve a lot of problems."

"What bullshit," said Xelina, more to herself than to the court, but loud enough.

"Foul language in my courtroom will not do you any good, miss. How old are you?"

Xelina glared at the judge, shaking with fear and fighting her shackles at the same time.

"Twenty-three," said Bridget, answering for her.

"Old enough to be held accountable for your bad decisions,"

said Broyles. "And your dangerous ideas. Do you know what *misprision of treason* is?"

"Your lying name for journalism that criticizes the dead system you serve," said Xelina.

Broyles laughed. "If you know someone is committing treason against this nation, and you conceal it, or don't tell us about it, that's misprision of treason. A kind of aiding and abetting. I'm sure Ms. Kelly is ready to lay it all out for you."

"We are, Your Honor," said Bridget. "Chief Perez from the Guard is here if you would like her to provide any testimony on that."

"That won't be necessary," said Broyles. "Unless Mr. Kimoe is going to make me listen to more from this unkempt punk."

"Come on, Judge," said Donny, reddening now, just the reaction Broyles wanted. Broyles cut him off again before he could get his objection out.

"Meet your zealous advocate, Ms. Rocafuerte," said Broyles. "Donald F. Kimoe, Esquire. He used to have Ms. Kelly's job, until he decided to help us by helping your kind embrace the eyes and arms of justice. He is pretty good at his work, most days, and he is free. To you, at least."

"Who pays for him?" said Xelina.

"I do, with the People's money," said Broyles.

"No thanks," said Xelina.

"I am going to insist you at least talk to him. Because his job is to help keep you from ending up where you will most definitely be sent if you try to represent yourself. Do you know where that is?"

They all knew where that was, even though it was a secret. The kind of secret the government wanted you to know existed, and leave the rest to your imagination.

Broyles surveyed his audience with an almost-smile. "I

think we are all on the same page now. So I am going to let you meet with Mr. Kimoe, so he can explain the situation to you more patiently than I am inclined to do after he has already screwed up our schedule for today. We will reconvene at 9:30 tomorrow morning to decide your fate."

"Your Honor, that's ridiculous," said Donny. "That's not even twenty-four hours."

"You're lucky I'm giving you that," said Broyles. "It's just a preliminary hearing."

"But we still need time to get our arms around the case. And my day is already spoken for. I don't have time to—"

"You have time to meet with your new client," said Broyles. "And you know exactly how you can take care of this: in the expeditious and tidy manner we expect from you."

Donny could feel the sweat starting to find its way through the wool of his suit. He looked at the clock again. Then he looked back for Miles, who always had a better idea. But Miles was long gone.

"I know you will be able to persuade Ms. Rocafuerte that it is in her interests to help the government out," said Broyles, looking at Xelina as he spoke of her as an object. "Unless she wishes to find out where we send the wild creatures who cannot be housebroken. I hope I have made myself clear."

Donny looked over at his new client. She didn't look happy to meet him. Maybe because she could tell he didn't want to take her case.

"It'll be okay," he lied.

And for a moment there, it looked like she believed him.

"I'll see what I can do, Your Honor," said Donny, and before the words even got all the way out, he could see the change in her eyes.

Xelina turned to the judge. "I'm not doing this," she said.

"Don't—" said Donny, but she wasn't listening.

"Could you repeat that, Ms. Rocafuerte?" said the judge.

"You heard me," she said. "Obviously this whole thing is a setup, including this so-called defense lawyer whose job is to trick me into giving you what you want. Just so these monsters in the back of the room can round up my friends and lock them up for no good reason."

"You are out of order, miss," said the judge.

"Fuck you, you tyrant," said Xelina, slamming her shackles on the table. "Fuck you and every one of your genocidal colonist ancestors. You can chain me and you can send me off to your secret prison, but you know it is wrong and that a reckoning is coming and when it does all of you people will be the ones who get locked up."

That got the room's full attention. Broyles seemed momentarily at a loss for words—Donny was at a loss of air. He watched as the judge just glared at her. Then Broyles abruptly motioned with an angry thumb for her to be taken away, and turned his attention to the files on the next case.

As Donny watched the marshals put the hood back over her head, Xelina looked over at Donny and gave him the finger.

Then they took her away, through the door in the side of the wall, into the man-trap, to her cage.

2

THIS WAS DURING THE INTERREGNUM. WEEK TWO, TO BE EXACT, just days after they had an election and nobody knew who won.

Around midnight on election night, the last precincts came in from around El Paso, and they called Texas for the challenger. The pundits credited the hordes of Midwestern refugees who had resettled in the Lone Star State after fleeing the droughts up north. That tipped the Electoral College count over. Even California, one of the President's strongest bases of support, couldn't make a difference. When Donny left the bar that night, the crowd was ecstatic. President Mack was a one-termer.

When Donny got up the next morning, Mack was on TV declaring victory. Texas Governor Pat Jackson and his hand-picked Secretary of State said the popular vote could not be validated. Between the refugees and the Texans who had been relocated by that summer's storms—storms that had caused the evacuation of large portions of the coastal region and the decla-ration of martial law in an even wider area—it was impossible to have confidence in the polls. Citing the emergency powers the Legislature had given him, the Governor overrode the popular vote. He would pick his own slate of electors, pledged to vote for the President in the interest of maintaining the peace.

When Donny heard that, he knew the opposite was more likely. Small comfort that it also meant he would be a very busy guy.

Not like there had ever been much peace. When Donny was

younger, the country always had a war going on somewhere. They usually called it something else, but you could hear the guns and the bombs on the news, see the people fighting in ruined cities and scorched forests, usually fighting our own soldiers.

Then came the big war. The one we lost.

It happened right after Donny finished law school, when he was an associate at the firm. No one saw it coming, and it only lasted a week. But it broke the country. Mostly by revealing just how broken it already was.

The obliteration of the American narrative blew open the parameters of the possible. For a while, at least. There was a period of a couple years, after they signed the treaty that gave Hawaii and most of our Pacific possessions over to the victorious Chinese, when it seemed like something better was aborning. Economic and political chaos yielded opportunities for reinvention. The monolithic partisan divisions that had ruled for decades dissolved, replaced by a ferment of diverse new futures.

It didn't last. The new reel turned out to be an intermission. And now the war was coming home.

Defeat meant the end of empire. Economic sanctions, scarcity where there had been abundance, more people fighting over the less that was left. The rich hoarded what they had won in the years before, hiding in gated communities and shell companies guarded by privatized police and smart lawyers. The more irrelevant the American flag became in a time of worldwide crisis, the more some people started to wave it, on the news and on the job, trying to conjure the return of a past that had never really been.

The instability was compounded by deeper changes in the population, changes everyone had long known were coming, the same way they knew the heavy weather was coming, neither of which changes anyone could stop. The people who had the power saw that to keep it, they needed to use it to make sure those changes didn't take it away. So they went to war on the future.

Lately they were winning. The weather helped. Especially in Houston.

The Free Rovers, who made environmentalism a kind of religion, said it was a sign of divine judgment that the drought settled in over the heartland so soon after the end of the war. When he closed the Texas borders to inland refugees, Governor Jackson pointed out that most of them came from states that had voted for the president who lost the war. That excuse didn't work when Superstorm Zelda worked her way from Corpus Christi to Biloxi, made the weather wonks add two new colors to their storm maps, and turned a few hundred thousand Texans into refugees as well. That was when the Governor seized the opportunity to declare martial law, and asked his buddy the President for backup.

The President was happy to help.

Running on a platform of national restoration against the guy who lost the war had gotten him elected the first time. Declaring war on the people who opposed the whole idea of the nation would be a good way to get the people who preferred the mythic past to give him four more years. Four more years that, if they played it right, could be extended into forty.

It was working, but not well enough. He was swimming against a demographic current that was going the other way. And the President was not the kind of leader who accepts an electoral loss.

AMERICA IS FOR WINNERS

That was the big campaign slogan, on yard signs and bumper stickers and bright blue buttons.

So on Wednesday morning after the vote, as the talking heads equivocated, he sent his "peacekeepers" out to stop the protests before they could even get out the door. And then he lawyered up, to make sure his seizure of power could be papered over as the rule of law.

Like most people, Donny was sure he couldn't get away with it. That such a craven disregard of the popular will would be a bridge too far.

The problem was, it was legal.

THEY WERE TALKING about it on the TV as Donny waited for his escort in the courtroom security pod. A panel of pundits on Eagle News, strafing each other with bullet points on one of the screens behind Officer Wright as she filled out the morning's intake forms. The other monitors were tuned to closed-circuit feeds from the holding cells. Donny glanced at one, saw a naked ghost curled in the corner of a concrete cube, and decided to stick with the news.

The camera was on host Kathy Byrne, who had been the President's press secretary during the first two years of the administration. In the background played clips of people marching outside the Capitol the day before.

"They're not protesters," she said, in that voice that always seemed like someone had just cranked up the volume. "They're traitors."

"They're voters," said another one of the panelists, a guy Donny didn't recognize. "And they want their voices to be heard."

As they bickered, the camera switched to a much older guy. Charlie Graves, a veteran reporter who had looked old when Donny was a kid and the guy was always reporting from the

White House. Old Charlie kind of smiled, turned his head, and spoke, like some animatronic oracle earning the nickel that just dropped into his box.

"They can raise their voices and protest all they want, but the lawyers are in charge now."

And Donny thought he was half right. Certain lawyers were in charge, the lawyers who served power as their real client, at the expense of principle. The lawyers who write the memos that make it legal to end the rule of law.

Donny had been one of those lawyers, for the money, until they kicked him out for his politics, after they had already demoted him for following the law. They kept him down here in the basement of institutional reality, to keep up appearances, for themselves and for the system. That was the idea.

While wise media grandpa mused over the squawk box about what it was like to watch the kickoff of the big crackdown, the gathering of human wood that preceded the bonfire of civil society, on the next screen over you could see the grainy motion of what the memos that said they were lawful called an "interrogation enhancement." This one involved wall slamming.

That's when Donny talked back to the TV, as if by doing so you could complain to the gods on strike.

"Tell Aeschylus: Athena has left the building."

Wright looked up, first at the screen, and then at Donny. "Don't you mean Elvis?"

"He left a long time ago."

She gave Donny the look of someone trying to remember the last time they saw Elvis.

Then Turner came out, jangling keys and humming the melody to "Blue Christmas," even though it wasn't even Thanksgiving yet.

"Come on, Kimoe," he said. "Your new client is ready to chat."

As he followed Turner back into the jail, Donny imagined him and the rest of the guards in a Technicolor musical comedy version of a Greek tragedy, with Elvis as angry teen Orestes rocking the cellblock in the part where Athena traps the spirits of human vengeance inside the temple of justice, only in this version the Furies have shackled her for a session of enhanced interrogation that will never end.

The buzzer that blasted when the last door opened scared you every time, even when you knew it was coming.

3

THE WOMAN SITTING THERE IN THE INTERVIEW ROOM DID NOT
look like an insurgent. They rarely did. They usually looked
like kids, the kind of kids who in another time and place would
be experimenting with mind-expanding drugs or speaker-
busting music instead of world-changing politics.

The room was small and cold. Bare concrete walls painted a
plasmal shade of white, with a faint odor of bleach, a fainter odor
of whatever nastiness they had cleaned up from whoever came
before, and something like a steel picnic table bolted to the floor.
The last time Donny had met a client in there, he found the guy
hiding under the table. Xelina Rocafuerte was not like that.

"Nice suit," she said, sizing him up with untrusting eyes.

"Thanks," said Donny, knowing it was a put-down. "Don't
look too closely or you might see the holes."

"I guess selling out justice to the owners and their pet
police doesn't pay so good."

Donny smiled in grudging agreement and sat down across
from her. He'd made less money every successive year since he
left the firm, and now these court appointments were his only
reliable source of income. Enough to pay his rent and service
the loans that had paid for his law degree, without much left
over for the increasingly expensive extracurricular activities
that helped him manage the stress.

"Not enough to buy my independence," he said, wondering
if even he really believed that anymore.

"How much does that cost?" she asked.

"A lot more than they're paying me."

"You're supposed to say it's not for sale."

Everything is for sale, he thought. "I'll let you be the judge of that," he said.

It looked like she had already made up her mind.

Before he could even get his files out, Donny felt the buzz in his pocket, and pulled it out to see if it was the call he was waiting for.

"Is that a flip phone?" said Xelina.

"Yeah," said Donny. He held it up where she could see it but the surveillance camera could not. "My 'second line.' We're not supposed to have phones in here, but I sneak this one in sometimes. Like today, when I have to keep an eye out for an important call."

Then he looked at the number, and was surprised to see who it was. Joyce.

"Jesus," said Xelina. "You can't even pay attention for two fucking minutes. Why can't I get Miles Powell, like I was supposed to? He represented the Refugio Five."

"Sorry," said Donny, trying to banish the thought of Joyce from his mind. "You're right. Miles is the best. Not just the Refugio Five, but now he's representing the Mayor for her defiance of the Governor's decree. And he's not going to be back here in time for your hearing. Which means we're stuck with each other, unless you want to go talk to the judge again without me. Since that worked so well this morning."

She looked at him like you'd look at the dorky assistant principal of your shitty public high school.

"I want you to walk out of here tomorrow," he continued. "It's my job. My sworn ethical duty. Hand on the holy book and the whole deal."

She looked away, folded her arms, and shivered.

"Plus," he said, "I brought donuts."

She looked back at him without turning her head.

"And coffee."

Donny grabbed the cardboard caddy and pushed it across to Xelina. Then he pulled out his notepad and file.

"Go ahead," he said, watching Xelina warily eye the coffee as he got organized. "I figured you might be hungry. I'll have one myself, so you know it's not poisoned. And since it looks like I will be missing lunch again."

When she finally reached out to take one of the coffees and warm her hands, you could see the abrasions on her wrists.

"Hang on," said Donny. He reached back into his litigation bag, pulled out the old cardigan, and gave it to her. She accepted it, and as she pulled it on, Donny could see the tattoos on her upper arms. One side had images of animals that no longer roamed the plains, the other the flag of a country that did not yet exist, a flag with branching rivers instead of stripes.

"You can give that back to me when you're free," said Donny, setting unrealistic expectations in the hope of eliciting candor.

"Is this how I'm supposed to know you're the nice kind of white guy from the government here to help me, as long as I cooperate?"

"I think that was all cleared up in front of Judge Broyles," said Donny. "As you made our job about a hundred times harder, Xelina."

She kept her eyes on him while she sipped the coffee.

"Am I saying it right?"

"Shh," she said.

"Sorry."

"No. That's how you say it."

"Got it," he said. "Thanks."

She reached for the bag of donuts, pulled out the bear claw, and took a big bite.

"So while you're enjoying that, let me let you in on a couple of things. First," he said, pointing up, "they are watching us. Purportedly for my safety."

She looked at the camera eye in the ceiling and kept chewing.

"They are not listening," said Donny. "You probably won't take my word for it, but I know it's true. It's what their manuals say, and even in times like this, the bureaucrats stay inside their flow charts."

There was a CPR poster on the wall showing emergency resuscitation techniques for cardiac responses to interrogation. Next to it was a sign reminding prisoners of their rights, in bold black text spattered with old ink or maybe old blood.

"The other thing is, even though they can't eavesdrop on our conversation, they have the right to review my notes after I leave."

"So you really aren't my lawyer," she said.

"I am, but they treat everything you tell me as classified information until I convince them otherwise."

"What the fuck?"

"I know. It's a bogus system. That's why I do it all on paper, offline and unplugged. And that's why I won't write anything down I don't want them to read, and the things I do write down are written in a way that I understand, but they won't. So your secrets are not their secrets. And they're safe with me."

She shrugged. "If you think I'm going to give you that access code, it's going to take more than a donut."

"What access code?"

"To my phone."

"I saw that on the property sheet. A bunch of other devices, too." He looked at the file. "Laptop, two cameras, storage drives. All taken when they searched your place, I guess."

She nodded. "They think the phone code unlocks those, too."

"You can be pretty sure they already unlocked all those. They have your biometrics on file."

She shook her head.

"You know that's a felony by itself, not updating your passport or national ID."

"I burned my passport. We all did." She looked up at the camera, and talked right at it as if she were sure it had a mic, or could at least read her lips. "Fuck this country. Because fuck the whole idea of countries. I belong to the Earth."

"You sound a lot like a Rover," said Donny, hoping he really was right that they didn't listen in, and worried that she may have said similar things to her interrogators.

"What do you even think that means, Donald?" The way she said his name made it sound like a cartoon character.

"I think it depends on who you ask. The government says it's another word for eco-terrorist. Others say it means people who put Earth ahead of country. To me it usually means people who reject the idea of borders. Which I can almost buy if you're talking about nations, but not so much if you're talking about the fence around my house. Not that I have one."

She shook her head.

"I know for some people it means a way of trying to live free. Going wherever you want. Roaming instead of working. Which is cool with me as long as you're not another one who wants me to convince the judge trespassing is not a crime."

She smiled at that.

"I also know there are those who do more than just trespass. Who take a wrench with them. Or a bomb. And call it a prank."

Xelina looked like she was enjoying the bear claw. "Mostly wrong, but not bad," she said.

"I thought you said you're a journalist."

"I am."

"You just exclusively cover the Rovers."

"No. Most of what I do is just nature films. Or stuff about the destruction of nature."

"So that's how you can work without an ID."

"Don't need one. I'm independent."

"So I gather. You know they can just contact BellNet to get access to your devices, at least the ones that are on-network? I used to do that, back when I was on the other side. Now they don't even need a subpoena."

She made a face that suggested otherwise.

"Did you crack it?" asked Donny. "If you blocked their back door, that's another felony."

"It's my private business," she said.

"If it's so private," said Donny, "why are you uploading so much content onto these sites?" He pulled the sheet from the file and set it out so she could see.

"What is this?" she said.

"It's a list," said Donny. "Of every video you've posted in the past year."

"So what? Most of those are sites everybody uses. I'm just sharing my work. Letting people see what's going on around here. What they've been doing since the storms. Sometimes when you go looking for the wild things, you find other things."

"Gotcha. But they don't see it that way. First of all, you

posted most of these from anonymous accounts. Which is illegal under Burn Barnes."

"I heard they threw that out."

"They did, and then Congress fixed it, and made it even worse. By adding the provisions about media content they consider seditious. 'Incitements to rebellion.' Like everything on this list."

You could see her confidence drain out like air from a ruptured tire, as the fear grabbed hold.

"All of which they are trying to keep me from seeing. So if you have any other copies, it would sure help me convince them these are all as innocuous as you say. Because you will be amazed how good these government lawyers are at making your free speech look like revolution, when they feel like it."

She shook her head. She was starting to look a little freaked out. "All I did was film other people protesting," she said. "Shared it on these channels hardly anyone even looks at."

"You got them on crazy Mort Hanauer's show," said Donny, pointing back at the sheet. "A lot of people watch that, when he's not blocked."

"He's not crazy. The truths he tells are crazy."

"I hear you," said Donny. Mort Hanauer was a charismatic but eccentric conspiracy theorist with a show on the public access channel, best known for his obsession with trying to disprove the President's war hero stories—when he wasn't talking about the aliens from the future who are manipulating our present. Joyce used to watch it when they were still together, mostly for laughs. "He puts out interesting stuff."

"I guess you prefer the news with artificial blondes reading corporate scripts," said Xelina.

"Honestly, I prefer to read," said Donny. "But I'd like to see your work."

"So would they."

"They already have it. They just want that access code so they can get into your contacts and communications as well, and then talk to all your friends."

"After ripping them out of their homes in the middle of the night, like they did to us."

"Is that what they did? The red car treatment?"

"How did you know?"

"I get a lot of these cases. They want names, Xelina. They think they are oncologists, fighting a cancer that's eating the society. And each one of you and your friends is a cell."

You could see she got the metaphor.

"I guess the so-called Bill of Rights only applies to certain people," she said.

"Pretty much," Donny agreed. "Especially in times of so-called rebellion."

"Clint's right," she said.

"Who's Clint?"

"A friend. He says we need to take it to the next level."

"Which level is that?"

"Actual rebellion, instead of ineffective protest, or just opting out."

"Please don't talk like that. Actual rebellion is what they kill people for. Let's stick with the 'I'm just a journalist.'"

"I am. Doesn't mean I can't have opinions."

"What do you want to see happen?"

"I want us to take this continent back. Kick out the invaders, and bring back the wild."

Donny looked at her. This tiny young woman, so convinced of the possibility of her own idea of utopia, of justice, of something better, that you couldn't help but be momentarily infected, even as you were wrapping your head around the insanity of what she was suggesting. She still had the cardigan on, but with the sleeves pulled up now, both arms on the table as if guarding the remains of the bear claw, flashing those tattoos in a way that made them come to life, as authentic visualizations of the future she was trying to summon into the now.

"Can I stay?" asked Donny, only half-joking.

She shrugged. "We'll see."

"Unfortunately," said Donny, "what they are talking about is sending *you* off this continent. Do you understand that?"

"They can't do that."

"They disagree. They made it the law, that crimes of rebellion constitute revocation of citizenship. It kind of always was the law, but they sharpened the edge."

"I've heard the stories," she said. "I didn't believe them."

"I know, it seems crazy, but it's real. It started earlier this year, at least that's when we first started seeing the cases. And they don't even tell us the whole deal, even though we're supposedly cleared for classified information. So we hear the stories, too, and they're all different. But what we know for sure is that once they take your citizenship away, they won't have any other country that will take you, either. So they are keeping people someplace."

"In the resettlement camps?"

"A lot worse than those places, as bad as they are. The kind of detention facility where they put people who have no rights, and who the government deems the most dangerous threats to its existence. A halfway house to hell."

He waited for the reaction he wanted, but didn't get it. It looked like she wasn't buying it. He kept talking.

"But no one is going to die. So the easy way out of here is, if you know anyone who's *really* up to bad stuff—"

"I'm not going to give them any names. And I'm not going

to give them any passwords. You think you're so smart, and here you are sitting in the belly of the monster and you don't even see it's eating you, too."

Donny sat back. He had plenty of clients who lied to him. He was usually the one telling them the truths they wanted to evade. Not the other way around. He smiled, nodded, and then leaned back in.

"All right, then. You want to fight them? I'll fight them for you. But I need something to work with. I'll see if I can get them to let me see these videos, which have all been taken down already. See if I can convince Broyles they are harmless. And then maybe invalidate the arrest and the search."

"They don't have all of them, you know."

"All of what?"

"My videos."

"Really. Where are those?"

"I bet they'd love to know."

"What's on them?"

She looked at him. "What they really want to cover up. The real reason they are locking me up and all my friends. I can't believe they are getting away with this."

"*Tell* me," said Donny. He hadn't taken a single note.

A big cry came over her face, and then disappeared, like she had eaten it. Donny extended his hands across the table, palms up. She responded by crossing her arms and looking away.

"You can trust me," said Donny. "I don't want to know the password. I want to help you."

She looked back at him, resolved.

"I was with Gregorio."

"Gregorio Z? The opposition leader? He's been missing for three weeks."

"He's not missing." She looked down, as the tears tried harder to get out, propelled by memory of trauma. "They fucking lynched him. I was there."

"With your camera."

She nodded.

"Who did it?"

"I don't know. They weren't in uniform. But you could tell which side they were on. We took every shot we could that would help us dox them."

"Why haven't I seen the footage already?"

"We were too scared," she said, choking on it. "Mort's people said it was too hot. Like you said, some content will get you arrested. And then even without us getting it out there, people started disappearing."

"And now they have it," said Donny. "If they can crack the files."

She nodded. "We should have put it out there when we had the chance. But there's another copy."

"Where?" said Donny.

She looked at him. And then she told him.

"How do I get in there?" he asked.

She told him how.

"I'll go there tonight," he said.

He felt the buzzing in his pocket. She was watching him. He put the phone down on the table, trying his best to look at her instead of looking at the screen.

"What the fuck?" said Xelina.

"Sorry," he said. And then he looked.

This time, it was the number he expected. He checked the time. Then he put the phone back, but he could see from Xelina's face that it was too late. She made him wonder if she knew something he was hiding from himself.

"You want to be my lawyer?"

"Yes," said Donny, meaning it for real for the first time, even as he ran out of time.

"Get the footage. Get it out there. Show the world what they did to Gregorio. I already burned my passport. We all did. Because we're making a whole 'nother country. And then we're making a better planet, one where we all help each other. And if you want to help us, you need to prove you're on our side."

Donny was going to say something, but the sound of the metal truncheon tapping on the door told him his time really was up. And the truth was, even as he wanted to help Xelina, he wasn't sure he *was* on her side. Because he was one of the last ones left who didn't believe in sides.

4

DONNY HAD SEEN ONE OF THE BIG PASSPORT BURNINGS, THE ONE in D.C. The cops went in to arrest the protesters, because apparently passports are government property on loan to you—kind of like your Bluephone is property of BellNet on loan to you—and destroying them is a federal crime. First the cops made a line of armor, and then they all put on those crazy headphones and rolled in the sonic cannon. LRAD, they called it, and when they turned it on you couldn't hear it through the TV, but suddenly all these people were screaming and squirming. And like always, there was one guy who could handle it enough or just got mad enough that he got up and jumped on top of some of the other people and then leapt movie action hero–style toward the wall of cops. And they shot him, like hunters taking out a dove. The footage was ready-made for tragic slo-mo, add the cheesy soundtrack of your choice. But it didn't get a lot of playback. At least not like that.

They did play it back in the Special Committee, as one of the exhibits they rolled out when they passed the Burn Barnes Laws.

Burn Barnes was not the official name of the statute. On the books, it was 18 U.S.C. §799b, and when they passed it in Congress they called it the King-Bergen Act for the Prevention of Public Violence. As one of Donny's law professors who had worked in Washington once joked, the official title they put on a bill usually proclaimed the opposite of what it would actually do.

Donny had also seen the footage that was the reason they called it Burn Barnes. Everybody had seen that clip. You could play it back in your head every time you heard the name. This middle-aged white guy in a perfectly nice suit and tie kneels down and lights himself on fire in front of the Supreme Court. But instead of sitting there like some Zen priest of black-and-white memory, the guy starts running around screaming the way you would if you were on fire. And then these two cops come to try to deal with the situation and one of them goes to grab the flaming protester, who hugs the cop and takes him with him into the inferno.

"Protest is dangerous to public safety." Or can be. That was the basic idea behind the law, which passed easily—most Americans hated protesters, except when they were the protesters. And the statute only proscribed certain kinds of protest, namely the kind that a judge determined presented a "substantial likelihood of provocation to violence, riot, or injury." Given the number of demonstrations in recent years that had led to fights between opposing camps, it was an easy standard to meet. And the other thing was, the law had both criminal and civil elements. A prosecutor could file the motion, but so could a private party, and they did. Especially corporations, political operatives, public relations hacks, and activists looking to silence the other side. Further, the remedy was injunctive, meaning you could compel a law enforcement officer to shut down the protest or publication, usually before it even happened.

Pretty quickly, there were all sorts of standing orders for broad categories of public demonstrations and "inflammatory content." It had worked well to keep things quiet. Or at least keep things out of the news. Which was just as good for the people in power. People like Miles had been trying to get the courts to do something about this restriction on the supposedly sacred right of political speech, but they hadn't had any luck. Especially with a Supreme Court cowed by the impeachment of Justice Harrison the year before over trumped-up questions of his own loyalty.

To pass it, they tacked on a meaty package of enhancements to the existing treason, sedition, and citizenship laws, enabling them to shut down so-called conspiracies in which the violent statements of one person were imputed to all their friends. And to pass that, they added the denaturalization provisions, saying it was a more humane remedy for that species of rebellion.

America: love it or leave it.

THEY HADN'T YET figured out a way to silence the few remaining politicians who were unafraid to spout messages a judge might otherwise ban. At least not the ones who held elective office, because they were immune from the prohibitions of Burn Barnes. Gregorio was one of those. Just a Houston City Council member, but one whose district included one of the big refugee camps and a wide swath of the industrial neighborhoods that had been evacuated after the storms. He was one of those next-generation greens who married urban egalitarianism with radical environmentalism. Someone who figured out how to give voice to a generation of people like Xelina who were convinced the planet was dying and there was no future left for them. He even convinced some of them that by participating in the political system, they could change the future.

Donny had met Gregorio once, at one of those rubber chicken networking luncheons Donny almost never attended.

Miles had invited him to fill an empty seat at a table he had bought for the Harris County Criminal Defense Lawyers Association, along with Miles's half-retired dad, Milton, some toxic torts defense lawyer from Sikorski Walker, and County Criminal Court Judge Orzo and her husband, Harold, a divorce lawyer. This was before Gregorio had started to get attention from the international press, right after he got elected and was beta-testing the message that made him a target of much more powerful officeholders in Austin and Washington. Donny went to the event as a favor to Miles, and as an opportunity to hang out with the judge. He hadn't heard much about Gregorio. The lunch, where Gregorio was the keynote speaker, fixed that.

Gregorio was about fifteen minutes into his speech when the judge excused herself, dragging her confused spouse with her. The words Gregorio used to describe the Governor were not the kind you normally heard at the sort of events they hold in downtown ballrooms for a thousand bucks a table. A few of the lines were things that would be illegal to say on television, but somehow the way Gregorio wove them into his eloquent riffs on history, law, current policy, radical geography, and gubernatorial scatology made them sound like beats of erudite verse. By the time he was done, almost half the people had left the room, and two-thirds of the other half were hollering affirmation and already mentally occupying the Edenic post-racial eco-Texatopia Gregorio had managed to conjure. Donny, who was normally too cynical to be moved by the words of politicians of any stripe, joined in with a spontaneous hoot, caught up in the ballsiness of Gregorio's emancipatory proclamations and the way they co-opted the other side's core doctrine like a chop shop reworking some country clubber's Cadillac, even as he knew what an incendiary recipe it was. Only to see Milton, the dean of the local civil rights bar, scowling at him with probationary admonition and just a suggestion of a wink.

It's how it was back then. Donny cooled it. But he still went to shake Gregorio's hand. When he looked you in the eye, you could almost see the place he wanted to take you.

Follow the yellow brick road, y'all.

Of course they had to kill him.

Donny was no Rover, but he would do everything he could to expose what they had done. And save Xelina in the process.

But first he had to call a lady about another leader they had slated to die.

5

THE THIRD TIME HE TRIED, JANICE FINALLY PICKED UP THE PHONE.

"Tell me you have some news," said Donny.

"What if it's bad news?" said Janice.

"Then we will figure out another way."

"Donny, I think we're out of options. I was about to call you. We just got the order. The Supreme Court denied our petition. The Chief Justice himself."

The news made Donny immediately nauseated. As long as the odds were, he had convinced himself they had a good shot at a short stay of execution at least.

"That heartless old bastard. Why can't *he* die?"

"Probably because he takes so much pleasure in making sure our clients die. And the prospective nominees on the short list are worse than him. If Miles is successful, that'll change when the election gets called, but that doesn't do us any good tonight."

"The election results," said Donny, scheming another angle at relief. "That's what we go for. Executive clemency. It's a perfect moment for him to show some mercy, garner a little goodwill."

"Not really his style," said Janice. "And I don't think our board would let me do that."

"What do you mean, your board won't let you do that? We have a duty to exhaust every avenue!"

Janice was the Texas Deputy Director of the Capital Project, a group of lawyers who specialized in death penalty appeals.

"We talked about it at the outset of this case. We can't risk jeopardizing the chances of our non-political clients by taking that step. Jerome *is* a traitor, after all."

"He's not a traitor. He's a performing artist. And a political opponent of the President."

"He was convicted of a conspiracy to assassinate the President, Donny."

"All he did was teach some refugee kids how to hunt. He gave them those rifles to shoot deer, not dictators. If he were white they would be giving him awards."

She sighed. "We already exhausted those arguments, Donny."

"And you won't petition the President for clemency?"

"We view it as a conflict."

"You fucking cowards."

"Don't give me that shit, Donny. We have hundreds of hours on this file. And there's no way the President is going to give Jerome a walk. The President is the one who told DOJ to seek the death penalty, and his people helped them find the forum where they would get it. Asking him for it will only invite attention to the one who asks, guaranteeing prejudice in future matters, and a drying up of the funding to pursue them. I don't want Jerome to die, but I don't have any more options. I'm sorry, but we're done."

"Fine, I'll do it myself. Send me the form."

"There's no form for clemency, Donny. There are some precedents, but they wouldn't be useful, because they're all conventional criminal cases, mostly murders. Maybe the Rosenbergs would be close, but we know how that turned out."

"Well, those people were guilty," said Donny.

"This isn't about guilt or innocence, and you know it. It's about mitigating equitable factors, and Jerome doesn't have a chance. I wish you wouldn't do it."

"And I wish you weren't so chickenshit. I'm not an idiot—I understand the case is political. But so is the resolution. We just need to play it right."

"You're going to compel us to terminate our engagement, Donny."

"Knock yourself out."

The way she hung up the phone, it sounded like she wanted to knock him out.

Donny looked at his watch.

And then he wondered how he would pull this off.

He was standing in the so-called park across from the courthouse, the place he liked to go to make calls he didn't want to be listened in on. Turner was the one who told him it was a safe spot, because the way they had dug the memorial into the ground made it hard for the listening gear to penetrate. So that's right where Donny was standing, at the lowest point in the recessed corner of the block, close enough to the black marble walls of the Ares Memorial that he could read the engraved names of the three military astronauts who were killed in the first orbital conflict with the Chinese, the one that lost the satellites that lost the war that lost Hawaii. No wonder they hid it like this, hemmed in by a bus interchange, a freeway ramp, and one of those uglyass colored glass skyscrapers they had built back when they still built skyscrapers. Having conference calls among the dead usually felt like a violation, but today it felt right.

First, he sent Miles a message, asking him to call him when he was on his way back from Austin.

Next, he sent a message to his friend Lou, the only one of his former colleagues who was still at their old firm, Barker & Eames.

"5:15, the usual place? Urgent, not optional, will explain in person. My tab."

Then he figured out where he could go to get his filing done before he met Lou.

Then he called Percy, his legal assistant.

Thankfully, she answered.

"Where are you?" she said.

"The satellite office," he answered, looking at the orbital arcs engraved in the black marble.

"That's such a sick joke," said Percy, who knew just what he meant, because he had taught her to use the same trick when she was making courthouse runs on his behalf.

"Yeah, well, I'm learning the hard way just why they call it gallows humor. But it doesn't have me laughing yet."

"Jerome?"

"Supremes won't take the case."

"I'm sorry."

"It's not over yet. I have a plan. I need you to pull some clemency applications for me."

"You're crazy, they'll—"

"Don't you start with that."

"Don't you start dragging me into your suicide mission, Donny. I don't think I want to work on that."

"You need to work on what I tell you. I'm the one writing your paycheck."

"Not according to my bank."

"Listen, I'm sorry about that. We had some unexpectedly large client expenses to advance this month."

"Uh-huh," said Percy. "You mean you had some unexpectedly expensive 'study aids' you decided to eat this month."

Donny blanched, but there was no one there to see. Percy had the best bullshit detectors of anyone he had worked with, the by-product of training a seriously great brain in a seriously shitty neighborhood.

"I'm sorry, Percy," said Donny. "You're right. I've been letting the job get to me. That's going to change. I just need to get through this week. And to do that, I need your help. I have your pay. I just picked up my check from the court, fees for last month, so we're all good."

"Then when are you gonna get your butt back to the office and give it to me?"

"I can't get down there until tonight. It's almost 1:30 now, I need to file this thing by five Eastern, I have a very important meeting downtown at five local, and the traffic is already code red and only getting worse. I hear the checkpoint to get on 59 is running an hour plus. No way I can get there and back in time."

"Then you can wait until then for your precedents. I'll be here."

"I need them now!"

"Then get them yourself. Pay for play is where we are at right now, Mr. Kimoe."

"Fine. Fuck you, but fine. I'll be there as close to six as I can. Maybe in the meantime you can help me on this new case I just got today."

"Another political case?"

"I know you told me you just want to work on the regular criminal cases," said Donny.

"The people who actually deserve our help," said Percy. "Down at County, lined up to be put in cages for being too poor, too stupid, or too black, brown, or yellow."

Percy's father was one of them, one who died in the cage, and the reason Percy had gone to law school. Her full name was Persephone, picked by Dad, who knew how things worked.

"And the way we take care of those people is by changing the system," said Donny. He didn't mention the part about the rates on the classified cases being almost double.

"It hasn't changed in centuries, and you think you can change it by banging your head against the bench in that psycho-court? And now stretching your neck out on the block, sending flaming petitions to the man himself?"

"This case could change things. It's about what happened to Gregorio. Listen."

Donny told her the story. The condensed version. She listened. She got it. She said she would see what she could come up with. And suggested some things he might be able to get that would help her.

Donny checked his watch again. As he walked back toward the courthouse, he made a list in his head of what he needed to pull off in the next eighteen hours. He squeezed through the mob of parents still crammed behind the barricades, and when the guard checked him against the afternoon list and asked him what business he had back there, Donny said he had a meeting with Bridget Kelly. The guard waved him through, under the trellis of razor wire that canopied the main entrance.

6

"YOU READY TO GIVE ME THE STRAIGHT DOPE ON THIS ROCAFUERTE case?" said Donny.

"Sure," said Bridget, looking at her watch. "But we need to make it quick. I'm trying to get ready for a sentencing and the judge will be back soon."

"If you're too busy you can just give me the unredacted files. Because you and I both know what they are doing with this Rule 19.4 bullshit isn't going to hold up."

"I don't make the rules, Kimoe."

"You don't fight them when you know they're unjust, either," said Donny. You could tell she wasn't fazed by the jab. They were in the courtroom, but the judge was not there—just some of his staff working at their stations below the bench, and Bridget and a colleague with their files spread out at the prosecution table. "Mind if I sit?"

"I guess," she said, as if having a defense lawyer sit at the prosecution table would violate hygiene protocol.

Donny pulled out a chair, then set his litigation bag up on the table and opened it to grab his file. When he did that, a bunch of stuff he hadn't meant to grab spilled out on the table.

"Jesus, Kimoe," said Bridget. "Are you living out of that thing? You have more shit in there than I keep in my purse."

"Sorry," he said, sliding the portable office supplies and accumulated miscellany into a pile to the side. Then he opened the file, and reminded Bridget of the classified exhibits. "So what am I missing?"

Bridget reached for her own file. "Basically we have four things on this woman. The movies, chats and emails with her friends, physical evidence collected from her home, and the interrogation transcript."

"What about the details on the arrest?"

She flipped through the file. She stopped on a red page that looked a lot like the one in Donny's file. "I guess I don't even have that," she said.

"Sounds a little fishy, Bridget."

"I'll talk to the CSO." They both looked, but Walton wasn't at his station. "After my hearing."

"You working late again?"

"No, Kimoe. I have plans."

"I thought your boyfriend was still in Washington."

"I dumped him. Too whiny about me being away."

Donny smiled. "We should hang out sometime."

"Fuck off, Kimoe," she said. "No consorting with the enemy."

Donny laughed, and Bridget smiled.

"Is he a Coastie? I bet he flies choppers. Rescues children and disappears insurgents."

Bridget's father, Donny had learned, was an Air Force pilot, shot down and killed in one of the southern wars when she was a kid. The lapel pin she wore was an American flag in tones of black and blood blue, inset with a purple cross. Being the daughter of a martyred patriot gave her a privileged position with her law enforcement colleagues.

"The guy I'm meeting tonight is a real estate developer, if you really want to know."

"Now I know you are finally finding the real essence of Houston."

"And we're just going to a fund-raiser."

"The President's election defense fund?"

"No, that's week after next. But I'm going to that, too. You should come."

"You think it's a good investment?"

"Don't believe everything you see on TV."

"I don't. I know you're censoring it."

"I just help bag the trash and take it to the curb. Anything else?"

"How do I get the interrogation transcript?"

"You don't," said Bridget. "The confession should be all you need."

"What confession?" said Donny.

"Exhibit 21," said Bridget. "You want some Adderall?"

Fuck. Donny looked at his file. Exhibit 21 was a three-page recitation of admissions, signed by Xelina.

"Anything else?" said Bridget.

"You assholes. They used enhancements on her, didn't they?"

"They don't tell me if they do," said Bridget. "But I would guess not."

"How can you, Bridget?"

"She did it, Kimoe. All of it."

"All of what?" said Donny, scanning the confession's numbered paragraphs that described Xelina's social and online activity through the paranoid eyes of the state. "None of these things are criminal or seditious. All she did was bitch about politics with her friends and post some goddam amateur videos, like about ten million other kids do every day."

"She's a propagandist for the insurrection, Kimoe. Converting naïve young people to the cause. Turning them into new recruits for the FRO."

"By putting videos on Pinboard for her friends to see? Doesn't everybody do that?"

"I don't."

"Because you aren't allowed to," he remembered. "Unless you're one of the creeps behind a surveillance account."

She gave him a weird shrug.

"You *are* one of the creeps behind a surveillance account," said Donny.

"Maybe I was," said Bridget. "I'm too busy now with this." She nodded at the banker's box of case files.

Donny imagined a younger Bridget working her way up the ladder at DOJ by luring politically suspect citizens out through social engineering over the friendnets. Like high school, only with detention taken to a whole different level.

"Wow," said Donny. "Didn't you just try to link me on Breakroom?"

Breakroom was the workplace version of Pinboard, where people connected with their professional colleagues. Donny had an account, because you had to have one. He logged in an as little as possible, because he knew it was just another way they watched you, advertisers on government leashes making money off you every which way they could. But he got the messages whenever someone clicked his button.

"I don't think so," said Bridget. "Probably just the bot, trawling my contacts."

"When it's not busy monitoring kids for being too interested in saving the planet."

"Did you see how many views this little provocateur gets, Kimoe?"

"Not really. My legal assistant says every one of the links has been replaced with a government takedown notice."

"And I'll try to help you out with getting copies of those

when I talk to the CSO, because you'll see we're right. A lot of the content was republished on sites known to be associated with the underground."

"There *is* no underground, Bridget. Unless you mean the kids with no future Paxing their brains out in the tunnels under downtown. There's something else going on here. It's not about her videos. It's about what happened to Gregorio. They're even hiding it from you, for Christ's sake."

Bridget looked at the red censor notice she still had her file open to. Then she looked back at Donny. "I'll talk to Walton, like I said."

"How about helping me get Broyles to give us a postponement?"

"I wish. But you and I both know that would be a waste of time. He's all about the throughput, and not just because bonus time is coming. I'll see what I can do to get you more of the file before I leave today. And if you want my advice, don't spend all your time going after the legitimacy of her arrest and detention. The President and his Congress have suspended habeas corpus down here pending the end of the emergency. Or maybe you didn't get the memo."

"I got it," said Kimoe. "What I'm worried about is the memos they won't even give you."

She looked again, and closed the file. "We're all just following the rules, Kimoe. You should try it sometime."

"This would be so much easier if you weren't so likable," said Donny.

"Wish I could say the same," she said, smiling.

Just then the light glistened off her lapel pin, and it reminded Donny, and made him think about what she had said, about consorting with the enemy. Donny liked to think he didn't have a side in the big fight. That he was just a lawyer. It was a big part of what had torn him and Joyce apart. But the way the pin and what it stood for reflexively repulsed him made him realize he wasn't as neutral as he liked to think.

"Hey," said Bridget. "Can I bum one of those Mentodes? I love those things."

She was looking at the tin of breath mints Donny had moved to his bag after leaving it in his suit pocket on the way into the courthouse. It was now sitting there in the pile of stuff that had fallen out of his bag.

"Oh," said Donny. "Those aren't mints, sorry. I just like the tins. All that one has is some portable office supplies." He picked it up and shook it, wishing it sounded more like paper-clips and less like waxy nuggets of controlled substances.

"I have some gum, though," he added.

"No thanks," said Bridget. "I'll let you know what Walton says."

"Thanks," he said, putting the tin back in his suit pocket as he stood to leave, and then thinking it might be able to help him navigate his current predicament.

7

WHITE-OUT WAS JUST THE STREET NAME. THE ON-BRAND STUFF made by the German pharmacists of New Jersey was called Paxetrate. Donny could never remember the scientific name. It was developed as a stress management remedy that could be prescribed for diagnostic conditions clinically defined for just that purpose: Chronic Workplace Stress, Chronic Life Stress, and Sustained Performance Depletion. It first took off with people working high-pressure sales jobs, and quickly became popular throughout the corporate world, as a secondary market flourished among the year-end bonus crowd—people selling each other the free sample double doses the manufacturer had seeded so generously among the physicians, while building demand through a series of unintentionally hilarious and extremely effective commercials showing the freakouts of life in the productivity-credit-consumption grinder dissolving into medicated bliss. Once the patents were published, the high-quality street versions started to appear. Houston was good at inventing its own drugs from available materials.

The heavy users of White-Out were called blankers. Donny was one of them.

There is nothing wrong with wanting to concentrate and do your job better, he told himself.

They called it White-Out because it made your mistakes go away. The truth was, it didn't. It just helped your brain cover them up and stop worrying about them. The actual color of White-Out was usually a sticky black.

Some people said White-Out was the real reason we lost the war, but Donny wasn't buying it.

Donny had never really been a user before White-Out. He would go to the occasional pot tasting with Joyce after legalization, and drink a little, but no synthetics.

White-Out changed that. It was mildly euphoric, mildly hallucinogenic, and ephemerally antidepressant. The street had invented all sorts of variations that added other effects. Lights Out took the escape from sensory stressors to the edge of catatonic, aided by a douse in embalming fluid, and was the version that had really taken off in the poorest communities, leaving bodies zonked out on street corners. Love In was what they usually called the versions cut with virility drugs, only a few of which tripled your likelihood of an immediate heart attack and the most fun you had ever had getting there. Fear Off was the one the soldiers and gang bangers liked, often blended with performance enhancers and designed to turn you into something like a Viking berserker for half an hour. Closet Door took you on the longest trip, stimulating waking dreams of surreal insanity. Donny liked that one a lot, but his standby was Lights On, which helped you focus. It was cut with amphetamines and worked especially well for reading books, even hornbooks and case law, letting you dive deep into the material and stir up fresh ideas. Often the ideas did not seem as brilliant when you looked at the notepad scrawls the next morning, but Donny was convinced it had helped him come up with some of his most winning arguments.

The problem was the side effects. Most notably the cognitive gaps that would start to develop when you were technically sober, the extra sleep needed to recover, and the waxiness that would begin to develop in your skin, especially if, like Donny, you were of predominantly white complexion. The other thing was that most people, including Donny, quickly built up a resistance that required increasingly potent doses, which worsened the side effects, increased the likelihood of getting some unexpected toxin in the mix, and compounded the effect of rapidly depleting your available funds and making you want to do really crazy and stupid shit to be able to buy more.

But as he sat back out there in the open-air tomb of the dead astronaut heroes listening to the ambient sounds of the city burning up the organic sludge of the oceans that had once covered this land and were getting ready for their big comeback, facing two deadlines, neither one of which was reasonable to meet on its own, and one of which for sure and maybe both were a matter of life or death for his client, it seemed like the right thing to do. So he pinched off a nugget, ate it, and got to work.

8

FOR THE NEXT TWO HOURS, INSTEAD OF EATING LUNCH, DONNY camped out in the KopyKat and wrote a long public letter to the President of the United States, juiced by desperation, illegal performance enhancers, free coffee that had been sitting on the warmer coil all day, and a profound sense of fiduciary duty. He wished the latter were enough, and tried to remember the last time that it was.

The KopyKat Business Center #4 was an ancient office services place in a run-down 1980s building on Milam Street. Self-serve photocopiers, workstations, and printers. It smelled like old carpet, burnt paper, and workplace stress. The staff knew Donny, because he used the place a lot—in addition to being close to the courthouse, the machines were so old, and the business so obsolete, that the surveillance was minimal. He even had a preferred workstation, back in the corner. When he checked in, the young guy manning the counter sized him up like he could tell Donny was blanked, and then casually handed him the means of remote office production like he was in on the deal.

If it hadn't been for the White-Out, Donny might just have sat there and stared at the blinking cursor, not knowing where to start.

Because the truth was, there was no real form for a petition for clemency, just a kind of procedural wrapper. The administration had made pardons and commutations a bigger part of its program than its predecessors, with a widely known but rarely discussed transactional subtext. Turned out there was really no constitutional prohibition on selling such dispensations, at least not according to Justice Hatch writing for a 6–2 majority in *People for Ethical Government v. Mack,* on using the pardon power on behalf of those with whom the President had business, campaign-contributor, or personal relationships. The only real check was political, and so far it had not proven very effective. The President had pardoned one of his first-term girlfriends, the television actress Katrina Von, for selling classified situation room transcripts to the Peyton Report. He claimed she had done the public a service, since the transcripts showed how his predecessor had failed to retaliate against the Chinese when they disabled the Eris milsat on the eve of the war. He had pardoned the main ringleader of the NoDak biofuels scam, Weldon Bengtson, two weeks after Bengtson announced his billion-dollar endowment of a new investment fund to buy media properties critical of the administration. Most astonishingly of all, he had commuted the sentence of Walter Maughn, a Coast Guard Master Chief who was caught on camera hanging looters from a bridge after the New Orleans floods. "Justice is not always pretty," he said.

Donny looked at the precedents, and realized he did not have the usual currency with which pardons were purchased. Quite the opposite—he had a client who had been personally demonized by the President, by the Governor of Texas, and by the media, even what was left of the so-called opposition media. Jerome's was one of the first cases where the government sought denaturalization based on findings of treasonous conduct. Donny successfully prevented that outcome. They punished him for that by giving his client the ultimate punishment. So Donny dug even further into the death penalty precedents, and tried to make a better case on the merits than he had at trial.

It is true that Jerome Hardy provided weapons to occupants of Domestic Refugee Resettlement Center–Houston East. It is also true that he advocated for political change, in his musical performances and otherwise. But these two activities were unconnected. The rifles were funded by charitable donations and provided for sporting use to refugee student participants in the outreach programs run by Hardy's Big Tree Hunt Club. Hardy never disputed that the weapons used in the attack on the President were obtained through his youth charity, or that the alleged assassins possessed copies of Hardy's musical recordings, including the cassette releases HTX Bomb and Swamp Guerrilla. But no connection between Hardy and the attack was proven at trial. And mere advocacy by a public figure of a change in leadership, however hyperbolic, is protected speech, and even to be admired for

He erased that, and tried again.

The clock was ticking. More accurately, it was steadily spinning there on the wall, and the less time he had the faster the minute hand seemed to move. White-Out could bend time, but not always in your direction.

He tried to get inside the head of the President. It was a scary place, the mind of a person who thinks they should be able to exercise power over everyone else, including the power of life or death—a power whose exercise was guided entirely by the self-interest of one man. Re-arguing the weakness of the government's case was a road to nowhere. They didn't care about the facts, other than the fact of Jerome's opposition to them. When they couldn't nail him for the assassination, they went after him for treason—the only offense for which you could be killed without having killed anyone. Treason was an existential threat to the existence of the state itself, a state that had been birthed in revolution and knew how quickly the fuse could burn if you let someone light it. And the more the old order started to collapse as the climate degenerated, the economy cratered, and the geopolitical order inverted, the more the state worked to preemptively police unrest. Jerome's case was a loser precisely because Jerome's political posturing had been so artful, the way he leveraged his persona as a swaggering rapper into a nemesis of the ascendant authority. That the assassins had been playing his song "99 Names" on their way to shoot the President with guns obtained through a charity controlled by Jerome didn't help.

Donny needed an alternate pitch that would get the President's people to pay attention. A political angle. Mercy for his political enemies, even those he framed as terrorists. Even one who had supposedly tried to kill him. Subtextually, reminding others that life in the Supermax was in many respects a more severe punishment than death. And a demonstration of the President's capacity for forgiveness at a time when his power was being contested. To save his client's life, Donny needed to help the President—the guy he wanted out of office—to increase his chances of winning another term.

Donny tried begging. Words of supplication, words that licked boots, words that picked the toe jam out from the sovereign's feet and ate them like little pinches of black caramel. Words of prayer, seeking the mercy of the national father.

Donny threw in some legal arguments meant to give the administration cover that granting such mercy would not set a bad precedent, because the case was so unique. He whipped up a list of some of the most heinous things for which this President had issued pardons and reprieves. Things that Donny could make a pretty good case were more treasonous than what Jerome had done. Stealing from the people in the name of taking care of them.

He rode the wave of words that flowed from his fingers onto the screen, hearing the heavy jazz, surfing the rolls of cumulus riffs charged with the idea of real justice.

The White-Out had a way of opening the vein of insight. Or at least that's the way it felt when you were on it. He could really feel it when he added a section arguing the case from Jerome's point of view, laying out an impassioned defense of how someone could believe the only way to save the country is to kill the president.

It ended up longer than he expected, and he didn't have time to proof it. But he hit the send button at 3:37 P.M. Central time, twenty minutes before the deadline. And then, to bolster his odds by drawing public attention to the plea, he proceeded to jam up KopyKat's fax machines sending forty-three copies out to the press, using contact info for editors and reporters he tracked down on the workstation after making the deadline. The copy of the filing was accompanied by an even more hastily penned press release.

Donny had never written a press release before. So he erred on the side of writing something people would read. Bold claims, in big type.

It wasn't until he was done sending it all out that he started to wonder if maybe he had overdone it.

Not just because the tab for all of this required him to hand over a large chunk of the money he had promised to Percy. As he counted out the bills for the clerk, he could feel the crash like a tremor through the chest, the adrenaline and intoxicants draining from his body along with the exuberant confidence he had felt minutes earlier about the thing he had just done.

Fortunately, his next appointment was going to provide him with reinforcements.

If Donny could convince his friend to help.

9

THE WHITE-OUT HAD MOSTLY WORN OFF BY THE TIME DONNY GOT to the meet-up. The American Lounge was the lobby bar of the Mercure, a French five-star hotel on Polk Street that was popular with the international business crowd, visiting Californians, and locals who wanted neutral territory. The theme was mid-century Americana. Maximum lounge through a Euro prism, all streamlined aluminum, red leather, and neon. Now that the swing of the cultural pendulum had people wearing business attire again, when you walked into the American Lounge you could almost believe you had stepped into another time, a time when it was America that had just won the war for global dominion. Until you sat down at the bar and noticed the channel over the bar was tuned to CNN, the Chinese News Network.

The sound was off, but the captions were on, in Mandarin, English, and French, relaying a report on the Pan-Asian Summit about the Himalayan melt. During the recent campaign the President had proposed banning Chinese TV entirely from American frequencies. To do so would violate the Valparaiso Accords the prior administration had signed at the end of the war, the meat of which were more severe restrictions on military and astronautic activity he *also* advocated breaking. A lot more than the cases Donny worked was riding on this election.

Donny didn't understand any Chinese, but he liked to watch the Chinese channels once in a while. His favorites were the cooking shows and cop shows. It gave you a window into a different world, even if it was sometimes a bummer when the world you saw looked so much nicer than the one you lived in.

Donny had never been to China, but he had gone to Chinese Hawaii for a weeklong vacation with Joyce after he left the U.S. Attorney's office. Maybe it was the sun and the sand that made it seem so different. One evening when they left the resort and walked into town, the locals were having the town meeting. Donny and Joyce stopped to watch for a while, standing at the periphery out there in front of the little city hall, watching a community learn how to govern itself without any evident leaders. Donny suggested that perhaps the pair of Chinese facilitators standing there smiling in the background were more than that, only to have Joyce give him a lecture straight out of the Green Book about how the seeds of real change must be planted by people with a vision of how our best natures can be cultivated, and who know how to spot the weeds and pull them from the field as soon as they pop up. Donny said that sounds lovely except you left out the part about the giant machine intelligence that gets to decide who's a weed.

The symbol of the AI was there on the screen behind that beautiful CNN anchor Arlene Fong as she read the news, an icon that looked like a benevolent digital sun. Fong was giving her daily report on the national and global metrics, the ever-accumulating statistics that proved the national brain's success at centrally managing the economy toward sustainable and egalitarian ends. Donny wished he could share Joyce's faith in the dream, but he had never been able to believe in the infallibility of a machine programmed by humans. Especially if they tried to build a Yankee version.

As if on cue, they cut to Washington: video of the President's lead litigator, Fred Foust, standing at a podium with his baggy suit and saggy jowls, roostering about his plans to defeat the injunction just issued against the Governor. You couldn't really hear what Foust was saying through the Mandarin overdub, which could have been translating the statement, or, more likely, spinning the Mandarins' take. But the lawyer's body language said it all, to which Donny's self-interested response was to think maybe Miles would now have time to take back Xelina's case. He reached for his phone, only to be stopped by a hand on his shoulder.

"Don't believe everything they say," said Lou.

Donny turned and looked at the guy who did make you believe everything he said, the model of a hale and hearty middle-aged professional who hits the gym before sunrise every day before getting on the treadmill of billable hours. Lou had made partner at B&E the same year they pushed Donny out, and it suited him. There wasn't as much prosperity to go around as there once had been, but Lou knew how to get his respectable share, by helping the real owners of the world hold on to what they had, keeping their commercial and regulatory enemies at bay, and getting them out of jams without making any more of a mess than the eraser dust he left on the desk while marking up the pleadings. A natural-born trial lawyer, the kind who could point at a dog and convince you it was a cat.

"Don't believe the news, or don't believe the lawyers?" said Donny, smiling as he stood to greet his old friend.

"Neither, I guess," said Lou, running his hand to wipe the sweat from his brow.

"Good answer," said Donny. "I can count on you to remain an independent thinker, right down to the grey suit."

"It's blue, actually," said Lou, looking in the mirror behind the bar and straightening his party lapel pin.

"Must be the 1950s lighting in here," said Donny. "From a time when your clothing didn't need to match your politics."

"That's always been the rule, then maybe even more than now," said Lou. "But I'll know the new clarity has been achieved when you finally start showing up to court in bright green."

"Who knows, the juries might like me better that way."

"Who gets juries anymore?" said Lou.

"It's not easy, that's for sure. Another sign of the withering of democracy."

"Oh, spare me. Juries suck and you know it. They get it wrong every goddam time, just about, at least in civil cases, and the bigger the case the worse they screw it up. Kind of like voters do with elections."

"When they let them vote."

"Don't get me going about your supposedly disenfranchised traitors and nomads, Donny. Democracy belongs to people who love this country, and belong here. And law and order comes from jurists who understand the long game. You just like juries because the judges all hate you."

"They love me," said Donny. "They just don't like my clients."

"Can't say that I blame them."

Lou got the bartender's attention, and then got momentarily distracted by the news Donny had been watching. The bar was full now, with a healthy crowd of international disaster capitalists and some familiar local faces who liked the surveillance-free branding. The piano man was on the keys, tinkling a mellow lounge variation on "California Über Alles," the version that was popular during the three long years of the Green administration.

"Why don't you get with the program of getting our country back, Donny?"

"We have it. We broke it. You're the fixer, not me."

"You're making it worse, pal."

Lou was not a Texan. He was an import, from Queens, who had come down here during the boom-boom years, when Texas still set the price of oil and it still rained once in a while in the Midwest. His outer borough capacity for pinstriped aggression worked well with the big-money good old boys, who liked to sic him on the other good old boys, especially the ones who didn't have as much money.

"I wish they'd pay me for it," said Donny.

"Come back to the firm if you want to make some money. I could use a smart scrapper like you on these merger fights."

"Sounds like a blast, but you must have forgotten Freaky Friday."

Freaky Friday was what people at B&E called the day of the office purge. Donny was one of the Freaks.

"They didn't ask me," said Lou, drinking from his newly arrived cocktail. "And you know where I would come down if they had. Just like I come down here on short notice when you say you need something. Which I'm hoping you're going to tell me soon, because I have a place to be at seven and the traffic is backed up to Dallas."

Donny handed him a copy of the clemency application.

"What is this?" said Lou, looking the document over, and quickly seeing for himself what it was.

"It's a pitch," said Donny. "Why your brother's boss should cut my client a break, stay the execution scheduled for tonight, get some points for mercy, maybe help him win some goodwill with this election fight."

"You seriously sent this thing in?"

"About an hour ago."

"Jesus fuck, Donny. I thought you knew better." Lou handed the document back to him like it carried a disease he didn't want to catch.

"Zealous advocacy, Lou. They're going to kill him, and it's my fault."

"It's not your fault. The guy armed the rebels who attacked our leader."

"That's their version . . . and that's why I thought you could call your brother, Mr. Undersecretary of Commerce for the Restoration of Sovereignty. I don't have a chance unless it gets up the chain pronto, like before midnight."

"Donny, Bob left before the election. Went back to Ramco as their CFO."

"Oh," said Donny.

Lou shook his head.

"He still could make some calls," said Donny.

"For you and your scumbag client?"

"Life in prison, Lou. Not freedom. Show some beneficence to the opposition. Help calm things down."

"You assume they want calm. What if more violence is exactly what they want to provoke? The justification for a more severe crackdown."

Donny hadn't really thought about that.

"Lou, can you at least ask him?"

"No, you fucking fruitcake," he said, looking at Donny like he was crazy. "I can't ask Bob to call the President and do you and your worthless client a favor."

"Look at that," said Donny, noticing the new image on the TV screen: Jerome's mug shot. The bartender had switched to local news. "I didn't think that would work. And definitely not so fast."

"What the fuck?" said Lou, watching with him now.

"Maybe I overdid it," said Donny. "But I got them to pay attention."

"That's for sure," said Lou. "You're a dead man, Donny."

"Better me than my client, if it comes to that." Donny was surprised, when the words came out, that he actually meant them.

"They need your guy to be an example," said Lou. "This situation is already snowballing. You know better than me—you're down there taking numbers as they line them up, all these little copycat teen terrorist wannabes."

"You think state-sanctioned killing is going to make them behave, Lou? Is that really the direction you want to see things go?"

Lou looked at him. He looked at his drink. He jostled the ice. He sucked back a swig.

You could hear piano man over the noise of the crowd, singing about compulsory meditation.

"If I make that call," said Lou, "you have to promise me to clean up your act."

"What do you mean?"

"You know what I mean. Stick to booze. Everybody who knows you knows. Joyce made sure the word got around. And these days all you need is to get a look at you up close to tell what keeps you up nights."

Donny looked down. "We don't all have your gift for not taking the work home with us," he said.

Lou put a hand on his shoulder. "And I want you to talk to a guy I know about a job I think you'd be a good fit for. It's no secret you've been struggling. The other stuff is just a symptom of that. This defense work is bad for you. Not just for your bank account."

"I like what I'm doing. I help people who really need it."

"You're getting them killed," said Lou, with cold clarity. "And you're attracting a kind of attention to yourself that is a lot more unhealthy than that crap you put in your body."

"Is that a threat?"

"It's a word of friendly advice. This practice of yours is not a good business model. Remember those guys who were doing all those Cleanfund defenses before the statute got repealed? This is like that, only in this case after they get done locking up all the clients they're going to go after the lawyers. That's you, pal."

Donny wondered if that was a bad thing, or something to aspire to. He looked at Lou and tried to see if he really meant it. Lou was looking at the piano player instead of Donny.

"I'm exaggerating," said Lou. "And I know you provide an important service. An essential one. I just heard about an opportunity that could be a good fit."

"I'm listening," said Donny, checking his watch. The truth was he trusted Lou, who had always given him good advice, even if it usually wasn't the kind of advice he wanted to hear.

"You did international settlement cases before, right?"

"You know that. We worked on one together. Petroleos CPG."

"So after they get this election business sorted out, they're going to renegotiate the Accords."

"Even I could get behind that," said Donny. "But how do you think they'll pull that off?"

"With boldness," said Lou. "Fidelity to our independence.

He spelled it all out in the campaign, and they're already interviewing for the team. You'd probably spend most of the next two years out of the country."

"Now I get it," said Donny. "You want to save me by getting rid of me."

Lou shrugged. "Better than watching them get rid of you." You could see the truth in his body language. "And maybe I'd like to have my own contact on that team. One who can keep me up to date on how things are going. If I call Bob, I'll give him your pitch, which actually has some merit. But you also are going to let me tell him that if they work with you on this, you agree this is your last case representing their enemies. You have a long leash, from the work you did for our people during the trials. Don't run so far from home that you get flattened by a truck. And think hard before you turn down a chance for a fresh passport, because the old ones are all about to expire, and the new ones are only going to the people who deserve them."

Donny processed that. Lou kept talking, switching to pledge captain mode.

"We care about you, Donny. We're your friends. Your brothers. And we want you back on the team with us."

There was a reason Donny had never joined a fraternity, and not just because none of them would have him, though that was also true. Maybe one reason was because his mode of lying was different from theirs.

"I'm open to it," he said.

"Don't poke the dragon, Donny."

"Keep talking like your Chinese clients and you'll be next on the list, Lou."

"That's not a Chinese saying, dumbass, and I fired all my

Chinese clients a year ago. I'll do you this favor, and you will return it the way I tell you. There's only one side when this game is over."

Donny stared at the mirror behind the bar and wondered how much longer he could get away without having a side.

10

WHEN HIS OLD FIRM PUT DONNY ON THE PRO BONO CASES, IT wasn't entirely an insult. Many of the cases were matters the senior partners had brought in, the outcome of which they believed would impact the future of the entire nation.

"It's about saving heroes and patriots," said Mrs. Goodman, one of the retired partners who still came into work every day and ran the pro bono workload.

When the war with China ended, the international trials began about what had happened in the war that came before, the one that was really a series of wars with our neighbors to the south—several of whom were allied with China.

The idea that an American official could be tried as a war criminal was a risk they thought had been successfully buried under Pentagon-sized piles of paper. Everything the government did during the long war was reviewed by the lawyers, usually in advance. They memorialized the ways in which the actions complied with their interpretations of U.S. and international law. Sometimes the memos were made public, especially when the action produced a strong public response. Like the napalming of the eastern borderzone between Honduras and Nicaragua, the rounding up and resettlement of indigenous Guatemalans into "Integration Camps," the rendition of suspected liberationists into the arms of the Argentine and Chilean militaries, or the design and implementation of the new interrogation procedures to be used on the captives too valuable to outsource.

Donny read the memos when they were declassified. The first ones he read because they were assigned by law school professors who wanted to interrogate the idea of interrogation. Later he got one of the new professors who wanted to take soft-minded students and teach them to police reflexive sentiment in favor of a penal strain of reason. He taught them one of the formulas the economists had made for the judges to be able to assign a value in dollars to each human life, based on education level, projected labor value, and life expectancy. They threw in a little extra for what one of the footnotes called "hedonic enjoyment," but not much. Donny was happy not to be called on the day the professor went through an example of how a plantation could be worth more than the lives of the villagers who worked it.

The memos had long been filed away by the time the cease-fire was declared and the one-sided negotiation of the Accords began. The U.S. government was reluctant to accede to the idea of the trials, which was a submission of its sovereignty in some ways worse than the military and economic treaty concessions it was going to have to make, especially for the defendants. But the Chinese, with the enthusiastic backing of the Indians, Mexicans, Nicaraguans, Malaysians, Peruvians, Indonesians, and Greeks, and the reluctant backing of the French, Italians, Japanese, and Dutch, insisted, with the force of precedent behind them—all the similar proceedings the Americans had imposed on others in the century preceding.

And so Donny, as a junior associate, found himself defending war criminals as his employer's idea of charity.

The first one was for Major Kovacs, a friend of the head of the Dallas office of B&E. Major Kovacs was a former Army intelligence officer charged with a half dozen war crimes related to his interrogation of foreign civilians in U.S.-occupied territory. Donny was technically second chair on the case, with the Dallas partner running it and signing all the pleadings, but the reality was he did most of the work. Including the client interviews.

The first time they met was at Major Kovacs's corner suite out in the Silicon Prairie of exurban Dallas where most of the interactive TV start-ups and VCs had their offices. The richest suburb in America seemed like a weird place to meet a war criminal, sitting in modular chairs across a glass desk tidily cluttered with trophies. The name of the Major's company was Behavioral Outcomes Limited, one of the many businesses that had been started by military personnel who found themselves out of uniform and off Uncle Sam's payroll after the big muster out. Many of the start-ups had paramilitary business models, things like security, logistics, and communications. But Major Kovacs was fuzzy when Donny asked him what Behavioral Outcomes did. "Data-optimized predictive analytics," he said, with major global brands, including some political brands, as the lead customers. When Donny asked him if the case was impacting his business, Major Kovacs told him that's a stupid question. But then later when he was answering another question, he noted that, actually, with some of our customers, me fighting the charges helps.

The Major had a notebook ready for Donny, a black binder with the paper trail showing the legal authorities and military orders supporting his conduct in Suriname during the occupation. One of the memos was an analysis of each of nine proposed "interrogation enhancements" to be used on high-value suspects. The techniques were listed by their code names, and then by their clinical descriptions. Cigar Store Indian was the forced standing position for an extended period of time. The Mary Lou was hanging by wrist restraints from the ceiling with toes just touching the floor. Hockey Boards was what it sounded like. Midnight Express was a gratuitous rectal probe. Growler was the use of dogs. Dr. Strange Please Call Surgery was the one where the captive was locked in a small lightless box, sometimes with an insect. Jacques Cousteau was simulated drowning. The Major's favorite was Mary Lou. He even laughed when Donny said the name. He asked Donny if he was old enough to know who Mary Lou Retton was. He was not.

When Donny didn't laugh with him, Major Kovacs told him about some of the things the people he had interrogated had done. He told him what the scene looked like in Paramaribo after the bombing of the Méridien. A kid with a hole in her head big enough that you could palm her brain like a volleyball. Picking up the fingers of a Marine younger than Donny. A lady journalist screaming as they tried to pull off the reinforced concrete support column that had crushed her hips.

When Donny didn't blink and asked him if he thought what he did had worked, Major Kovacs said the only question you need to worry about is whether it was legal.

Donny convinced him he needed to be ready for tougher questions than that. Major Kovacs asked Donny if he was ready to help take the country back from the weaklings who have sold it out to foreigners, taken our tax money to support parasites who have no place on our land, installed as their supposed leader a man who desecrates the People's house with pagan love-ins, and made the flag we served one the rest of the world laughs at. Donny said I'm happy to have a job, and the Major laughed, like that was okay, and maybe he had been too serious.

Donny got him a deal. The partner loved it, and got Major Kovacs to love it as best he could. Two years of climate cleanup labor at the Chinese territorial prison on the Big Island, a former Hawaii state correctional facility repurposed as hoosegow for the war criminals who had lost it, with an opportunity for commutation after the first year.

Even with the deal, they made the Major take the stand for the sentencing. When they gave him his chance to make a statement, he disregarded Donny and the partner's advice and went off on a rant. Like the one he had given Donny in private, but longer and better, richer. Cinematic, full of feeling, delivered in crisp language that evidently foreigners found easier to follow than typical American accents. So cinematic and global in its clarity that it went viral, in a piece of footage with Donny briefly visible sitting there next to his client. Donny's friends who thought the trials were a good thing, or at least real justice that made up for our own failure to prosecute such crimes, gave him a ton of shit when they saw him. He took it, because the work was interesting and the pay was good. And because he foresaw that such associations could serve as nice insurance to have if and when the pendulum swung back, as it always did.

Lately he was wondering what policy limitations that insurance had.

They locked up twenty-seven Americans and executed three. None of them were the lawyers who wrote the memos that green-lighted the torture.

And while the international authorities permanently banned use of the special interrogation techniques, they couldn't ban their domestic use. Or maybe they just didn't want to bother, figuring whatever the Americans did to each other could only help hasten the collapse that would really open things up for redevelopment. So, like so much of the innovation that had been created to fight faraway wars, the techniques of psychiatrically designed and legally vetted "human information collection" came home. For a while after Donny started his solo practice, he would get calls from guys defending civil suits about prisoner abuse. His reputation preceded him. Now that the precedents were clearly established, he spent most of his time defending the people who still wouldn't talk. Them, and a few weird operators who mediated the zone in between, just like him.

DONNY'S OFFICE WAS IN AN ABANDONED BRANCH OF THE TEXAS
Commerce Bank on a stretch of Bissonnet that was now domi-
nated by payday lenders, used car salesmen, and martial arts
studios. The branch had been constructed in 1976, the year of
the American Bicentennial, eleven hundred square feet of corner lot brutalism that used concrete forms to hide the bankers
from the sunlight. When the bank failed, the branch sat idle
for a decade, and then housed a series of random businesses
including an insurance agency, a camera repair shop, and a ho-
listic healer. Sometimes when he worked late Donny thought
he could sense the ghost of the healer, Dr. Birdsong, who had
died in the clinic. Maybe that was why the rent was so cheap.
But it was not an adequate excuse for the fact that Donny was
a month behind.

When he finally pulled into the lot after fighting his way
through the remains of rush hour, Ward Walker was standing there waiting by the front door. Ward was one of Donny's
oldest clients, and definitely the guiltiest. And where most of
Donny's clients were only really guilty of pissing off the government, Ward was the real deal. At least if you believed that
selling designer drugs to the rich was a bad thing.

"Hey, Donny, I've been trying to reach you all day," he said,
fidgeting there in the shadows.

"I've been kind of busy, Ward, and still am."

"I just need a minute."

Ward was a skinny white guy, maybe a couple years older than Donny, balding and with the sort of moustache that made him look more like a carny than a pharmaceutical sales rep gone to seed. It was hard to see his eyes, because he was wearing those yellow-tinted aviators he always had on, even at night. The dim fluorescence of the vintage door lamp didn't help. But you could tell he was going to be hard to brush off. Donny checked his watch, making sure Ward could see it.

"You can come in, Ward, but you're going to wait until I'm ready, okay? I'm staring down two deadlines and it may take an hour."

"I can wait," said Ward.

"And I'm not looking to buy anything tonight," added Donny.

"I know," said Ward, hands up. "I'm not selling, either. Just need some quick advice about this pinch I seem to be in."

"I bet," said Donny, unlocking the door.

Percy was inside, working in the office next to Donny's.

"I told him to go away," said Percy, looking up from her desk and glancing at Ward. "The doctor is out."

"It's okay," said Donny. "Any progress on that new case we talked about?"

She held out her hand, reminding Donny of their deal.

Donny told Ward to wait for him in his office, and then shelled out the bills for Percy.

"This is short," she said, as she counted it herself.

"I know," said Donny. "I had some unanticipated expenses."

"I bet," she said. "He cut in line ahead of me."

"Not him, and not even like that," said Donny. "Cost me more than I expected to file the petition. Check it out." He handed her the copy Lou had declined.

"Wow," she said, scanning it over. "Another reason why I am quitting."

"You can't quit."

"Hell I can't. I got a new job."

"You haven't even taken the bar yet."

"Real law firms hire you while you're still in school. Help cover your expenses while you take the bar."

"What part of that am I not doing?"

"The part about the six-figure salary and the sweet bonus program."

"Don't tell me you're selling out."

"Powell & Shah, the people's lawyers."

That hurt. But Donny knew it was good for Percy.

"In that case, you have my full support, even though you are seriously screwing up my situation. Miles is the best lawyer I know, and a good friend. And old Milton isn't too bad, either. You can learn a lot from those guys."

"Thanks, Donny. I appreciate that."

"Got anything for me on Gregorio and co.?"

"Not much. Pulled some of her chats. Reverse engineered the true names of a couple of her associates, but no luck reaching any of them. Found a few videos they haven't taken down. A few as in two. Nothing on Gregorio. Not even stories about him being missing, even though I swear I read about it a week ago. Can't even find many stories about the occupation, which I feel like was big news for a while. It's like they're jamming it."

"Burn Barnes takedowns," said Donny.

"Feels like more than that to me. I put what I found on your desk. Red folder."

"Can you stay until I see what Ward needs?"

"I can't, Donny. I have a street law clinic tonight, and I'm late."

"You're already a better lawyer than me."

She was standing now, with her bag packed and ready to go.

"One more week," said Donny. "I really need the help."

She looked at him with the determination of a protégée about to lap her mentor, and shook her head. "Call me when you have the rest of my money, and we can grab lunch."

"Come on," said Ward, leaning out from Donny's office.

"Oh, one other thing," said Percy, halfway out the door now. "You had a call, someone at the Justice Department. Wouldn't tell me what it was about. I put the message on your desk, on top of the file."

Donny hurried to his desk to look. It was in the bank's old vault, which was the coolest thing about the building. It wasn't a big vault, which made it a tiny office, but the thick walls kept out the snoops. Or so Donny liked to believe.

"How can you work in this mess?" said Ward, surveying Donny's setup.

"Like I told you, I'm busy," said Donny, picking up the message and noting the name and time. That's when he noticed the blinking light on the phone, indicating he had eleven new messages. "And my filing system is unstoppable."

Ward pulled out a cigarette and went to light it.

"You can't smoke in here," said Donny.

"Got any coffee?"

"It's after seven at night. If there's any coffee left, you don't want it. And who the hell still smokes cigarettes?"

"People who can see that the world is ending," said Ward. "And that it's time to take some risks."

"You sound like my other clients."

"They do it for politics. I do it for money."

"They do it for a better future for all of us," said Donny.

"Excuse the fuck out of me, Senator."

"And I am busy helping two of them right now," said Donny. "People who are each better than the both of us combined, and are counting on me to keep their worlds from ending. One tonight, and the other in the morning. So make it quick. You can light up when you leave."

"Sure, Donny." He looked back at the door. "Is your assistant gone?"

"For good. I think you scared her off."

"Just as well. You'd be better off with someone more plugged in."

"That woman is smarter than any lawyer I know."

"I just mean somebody like you, with clearance, some inside access."

"I like to hire people who have skills I don't. Now spare me the human resources consulting and get to the point."

Ward looked around again. Maybe he knew about the ghost of Dr. Birdsong. "You do contracts work, right?"

"No, Ward. I do criminal defense work. A little bit of civil plaintiffs work."

"But you could look at a contract, right?"

"I guess. I mean I took the class like everybody else. And I dealt with a couple of breach-of-contract disputes back when I was at the firm, but those were part of white-collar crime cases."

"This is totally white-collar," said Ward.

"I bet," said Donny, looking at Ward's eyes through the yellow lenses. They looked more lucid than Donny expected.

"Seriously," he said. He handed Donny a manila envelope.

"Can I look at this tomorrow?" said Donny. "After my hearing in the morning?"

"You don't even know what it is."

"It's a contract, I'm guessing."

"Right."

"So tell me what you need me to look at."

"You've heard of Texical?"

"Sure," said Donny. "I even know some folks who work there." Texical was the kind of company that Major Kovacs would like. They had started as an oilfield services company, and branched out into paramilitary logistics, disaster relief, and natural resource extraction. His former colleague Trey, who had been at B&E with Donny and Lou, had gone in-house and was now Texical's General Counsel.

"They have some bad hombres over there."

"Can't be that bad," said Donny. "They got that big contract to clean up the Evac Zone."

"Exactly," said Ward. "That's got them going from bad to worse. And kind of how I got hooked up with them."

"I guess that means they're doing business with you now."

"Seemed like a good idea at the time. A way to go legit. Make even bigger margins on totally legal deals."

"What are you selling them?"

"I'm not. I'm buying."

"What kind of stuff?"

"Drugs, mainly. Botanicals, from the jungles. The good shit. But it's legal. Grey market stuff."

"You and the feds must be using different color wheels."

"Nothing wrong with getting people what they need to feel good."

"Yeah, cut off their supply and they might realize they need to change the system."

"How's that working out for you?"

"Kind of shitty, today. Just the drugs?"

"No, that's the thing. These guys I've been dealing with, they bring their stuff in through the Evac Zone."

"No customs."

"Not really, not right now, the way they have it set up.

That's the whole idea. These companies operating the leases are like their own customs bureau."

"So they can bring in stuff that's banned under the Accords. Evade the sanctions."

"Bingo. And the crazy thing is, they say it's legal under U.S. law."

"What about international law?"

"They say it's unenforceable, at least for what I'm doing."

"As long as you don't take any foreign vacations."

"No, seriously, they say they have an angle. It's all covered in that contract."

Donny peeked in the envelope. The document was thick, but not as thick as he expected. "Looks like you already signed this," he said. "Who's Fredonian Enterprises?"

"That's me," said Ward. "My LLC. The other party is the outfit I'm dealing with. Patriot Logistics."

"They sell flags, too?"

"Yeah, right," said Ward. "That's a new company set up by these Texical guys. But the relationship is evolving into other stuff now. Like pirate stuff. Foreign cash, narcotics, black market smokes, some bullion, some scary porn, and a ton of guns. All of which they still insist is legal, since it's just for re-export. But I'm not taking their word for it, which is why I really want to make sure I'm covered on this contract."

"Where do the guns go?"

"I don't know. I don't deal with stuff that can kill you."

"Not that quickly, at least. What else are they bringing in that's above your pay grade?"

"I shouldn't even tell you."

"I'm your lawyer."

"I mean I don't think you even want to know about this."

"Try me."

"Your funeral," said Ward. "Aerospace stuff. Mostly Russian, some German, via transshipment through Namibia and British Honduras."

"Of course."

"Space program is the number one ban."

"And they want their milsats back."

"I think it's about water."

"Water from space."

"Yeah, dude. Fucking giant planetoids of ice, ready for capture. Make it rain like Bible rain."

"Getting high on your own supply again, Ward?"

"Whatever. What I know is I saw them rolling a big-ass rocket engine off a tanker there in the port. In the closed-off part of Corpus. Middle of the night, straight into a big hangar."

"Rockets."

Ward nodded.

"Texical isn't doing this," said Donny.

"I don't know. Definitely some of their people."

Donny could tell Ward was giving him the straight dope. "You could do a lot with this information," he said.

"I guess," said Ward. "Makes me not want to go back in there."

"Into Corpus?"

"Into the Zone, period. Any part of it. I'm afraid what else I'll see."

"So they even got you a pass to work in there?"

"Yep," said Ward, holding up his phonescreen so Donny could see. "It's an app."

"Just like the new passports."

"Yeah, but this one doesn't make you do citizenship quizzes or any of that bullshit. This is like the passport to the place no one wants to go."

"What's it like in there?"

"In the Zone?" His eyes lit up, even behind the yellow lenses. "It's the goddamned petrochemical Chernobyl out there, man. I try to not even get out of the car if I can manage."

"Cleanup's going to take a long time," said Donny, imagining. He remembered the maps that came out in the weeks after the storm, showing the areas Zelda left too polluted for human habitation, like a densely packed archipelago of islands from the East Side of Houston down to the Gulf and along the coast.

"Cleanup?" said Ward. "I don't think that's the real business plan."

"What do you mean?"

"I mean maybe, but that's not the priority. This is about liberated territory, bro. Place where you can make your own rules. Like this whole state used to be."

"Now you sound like Gregorio."

"Who?"

"The guy who occupied that park out there. City Council member."

"Oh, right, that idiot. The one who thinks no one should own anything. Took all those kids out there camping on the banks of a benzene river."

"He's dead," said Donny. "One of my clients witnessed it, and now they have her locked up to keep her from talking about it."

"Heavy," said Ward, shifting like he didn't want to hear any more.

"I guess that means I'm fooling myself thinking you might have some information about what happened to him."

"You would be correct."

"How about if I look at your contract tomorrow, you make some calls and see if you can get some intel on that tonight."

"You got that in the wrong order, Donny."

"You're the one coming to *me* for help. You get me some info, I'll get you squared away on your contract for free."

Ward still looked shifty as he considered that. "I know one guy I could call. Hopefully without getting dragged into whatever mess you're sticking your nose into. But if he can't help, you still need to look at that. I'll just pay your normal deal."

"Or maybe we call my guy at Texical, and see what they'd pay to keep you quiet, rocket man."

"You scare me sometimes, Donny," said Ward as he got up to leave. But you could tell he kind of liked the idea.

"Thanks . . . I guess," said Donny, looking at the red folder Percy had left him, and then at the clock on the wall. "Wish I could scare the people I need to scare."

"Well, if you need any study aids, I left something in that envelope to help you see things more clearly," said Ward. "Especially good for late-night brainstorming."

"See you, Ward," said Donny, turning to his work and trying not to look inside the envelope. He was proud of himself that he waited until Ward left to slide the contract and the contraband out onto the desk. Then he put the cellophane-wrapped treat in his suit pocket, and reached for the phone.

12

THE MESSAGE PERCY HAD LEFT WAS THIS:

Elizabeth Corley
Justice Dept
(202) 555-6070

Donny called the number. He got voicemail, with a prompt identifying Ms. Corley as someone from the Office of the Pardon Attorney. Donny looked her up, and learned that she was not the Pardon Attorney herself, but a member of the staff.

He searched the BellNet directory for a personal number, but it was unlisted. He tried all the other numbers he could find for the Office of the Pardon Attorney. He got an answer with the fifth one.

"Perkins," said the voice at the other end, a man.

"Hey, Perkins," said Donny. "Is Elizabeth still there?"

"You mean Liz? No. Who's calling?"

"Donald Kimoe. I'm a lawyer in Houston. It's urgent. She was calling about a clemency application."

"Oh," said Perkins. "That one."

"Yes, that one. Any news?"

"I can't really say."

"Come on, dude. They're scheduled to kill my client in like three hours. If I need to call somebody else, tell me."

"I think Liz just called you to ask who all you had sent this to, because we have been getting all sorts of press calls."

"I covered some bases. Hoping His Leaderness will see the potential goodwill he can generate by locking my guy up for life instead."

"I really can't talk to you."

"Don't you have a professional—"

Click. Bastard hung up on him.

Donny checked the other messages on the phone. Five spambots, two impatient clients, and four reporters calling about his press release. They would have to wait.

He called Lou. Straight to voicemail.

He called the White House. Main switchboard, the only number listed. The answering service was a robot. He tried to make it comply, and then he tried to make it cry, and then he tried to make it scream. There was no limit to how long a message you could leave.

What he should have been doing was preparing for Xelina's hearing in the morning. But instead he recorded an unsolicited oral argument with an unintelligent AI, improvised on the fly, that he knew no one would ever hear.

When he was done venting that rant, he hounded Lou again, until he finally picked up.

"Sorry, Donny. No dice."

"Shit."

"I tried, for real. I wish you had let me see what you had written."

"I did."

"I mean before you sent it, you crazy fuck. I think you're done."

"I'm just getting started."

"Whatever. Tell that to your client."

White noise.

13

EVEN BEFORE HE ATE THE NUGGET ON HIS WAY TO WATCH THEM
put his client to death, Donny got a little wiggy. Literally,
because he was thinking about dudes in wigs. The Founding
Fathers, specifically, the ones who made treason one of the
three crimes defined in the Constitution, along with piracy
and counterfeiting. As he hauled ass down the highway to
get there by midnight, he saw this old dude with long stringy
white hair in a weird coat with his socks pulled up over his
pants pushing a shopping cart loaded with loose paper and
found objects along the shoulder, and for a minute he was
sure it was old Publius 1.0 himself, James Madison, as ghost
or time traveler. And as he drove on Donny's mind drifted
into this almost dream where the two of them were hanging
out drinking PBR by a fire behind the liquor store, Madison
talking about the kinds of changes in government that would
be allowed and the kinds that weren't, Donny asking him
what the fuck's an antirepublican, and all this other crazy
shit that was like a mix between *Federalist* No. 43 and a drunk
poetry reading, both of them laughing and then Donny crying, partly because of what he was about to go see happen all
because Donny had not been able to prevent it, and partly
because he realized that, contrary to what they taught you in
school, especially law school, James Madison was an asshole.
They all were, every one of those slave-owning old bastards,
except maybe Aaron Burr, the first one who had the excellent

idea to start his own new country. The feeling was so real that Donny looked back to see if he could still see the guy, and even wondered if he had time to swing back. Maybe Madison could tell him how to get the last-minute clemency that would happen in the movie version. Or maybe he would tell him the truth: that Donny better get used to it, because they are just getting started.

When he exited at Mannheim for the facility, Donny finally pulled over and ate the thing Ward had given him, just chewing it and swallowing it down fast instead of licking it slowly like Ward suggested. It looked like weird candy but it tasted like one of those synthetic air freshener cakes. As he put the car back in gear and approached the checkpoint, he decided that taking an unknown hallucinogen on the way to an execution was either a really good idea, or the worst idea he had ever had. And as he talked to the guard in what felt like slow motion and started to feel the paranoid coming on, he checked it by willing himself to remember how much worse his client had it.

They had an impatient lady guard waiting for him, at what once had been the door to the emergency room. The only established federal death chamber was in a maximum-security facility in Indiana, and the feds didn't have a properly equipped prison in the Houston area, so they were repurposing this old community hospital they had commandeered the year before as a refugee medical clinic. The guard escorted him down a long corridor past closed clinical doors until they came to a little portal at the end, unmarked. She knocked, unlocked it with a big key, and ushered Donny into a room the size of a walk-in closet, one wall of which was a window into another, bigger room—an operating theater repurposed as execution chamber. And already strapped to the table not more than four feet away was Jerome Hardy, Donny's client.

Donny assumed the window was a one-way mirror through which the people on the other side could not see, but then Jerome turned, as if sensing commotion, and made eye contact with Donny. Or at least that was how it seemed, but Donny wasn't sure whether his senses were still trustworthy. He returned the gaze, and tried to convey a sense of apology, sorrow, and farewell across the chasm, while the reptilian trio of suits clumped together in the closet with him murmured about who he was.

"Fuck off, lizardman," said Donny to the one closest to him, who was taller and balder than Donny.

The guy laughed at him and turned away.

Jerome's head had been shaved. By him or by his captors, Donny didn't know. They had dressed him in something like white pajamas. A big white sheet was draped from his ankles to his chest, and a crazy thick leather strap pulled across it at his waist, holding his center of gravity to the table, which was more like a crucifix than a bed, with drooping branches for his arms extending off to either side. Intravenous tubes ran to each arm from translucent bladders of lethal chemicals hanging off wheeled metal racks. The bladder on the rack that was closest to the window had a purplish fluid in one and another the yellow of beer or piss, and when Donny looked at that he looked into a spot where a lightbulb was shining through from the other side and it made a weird grey portal into which he was momentarily certain he was about to fall, into the place where he deserved to go more than Jerome. But then he noticed the way they had both of Jerome's hands all wrapped up in Ace bandages, and remembered Miles telling him how they do that not for medical reasons but to keep the prisoner from giving his executioners or the attendant watchers the finger.

In the role of the warden was Ned Szabo, Assistant Attorney General in charge of the Gulf Region, a black-haired ideologue with the blood blue suit to match, the bright red tie a somewhat tasteless touch. He looked to the crowd, looked to the pair of executioners in their red scrubs and black surgical masks, looked at the clock again, then turned to the prisoner and asked if he had any final words.

Jerome was breathing kind of quickly, giving off the energy of a small animal that knows it is trapped and has a pretty good idea of its imminent fate, but is not yet quite sure. For a moment Donny saw him as an actual animal, the way we all are. He noticed for the first time that Jerome's feet were bare, and that the big toe of his left foot had been painted gold.

The last time the death penalty had been administered for disloyalty to the nation was long before Donny had been born. Another tradition they were reviving in the name of the flag.

General deterrence was the general idea.

It wasn't until Jerome looked up at it that Donny noticed the camera there in the ceiling, red light illuminated to indicate they were filming this. Outtakes would probably appear on the morning news shows, between the perky weather forecasts and celebrity interviews. The premonition of that, and the names and numbers of reporters he had written down from his answering machine, gave him more bad ideas.

"Water," said Jerome with difficulty. You could see how parched he was, and you could hear the barely contained sense of horror in his voice.

"Guy needs water!" yelled Donny. The suits in there with him looked at him like he was crazy. He tried the door, but they were locked in. He went to bang on the window, but then he saw Jerome was looking right at him.

One of the executioners offered him some ice chips, but he shook his head like that wasn't what he needed.

"Tell them," said Jerome, more audibly now, looking at

Donny as if he were the only one who could hear. "Tell them to follow the water."

He no longer looked pained. He looked relieved.

Jerome had opted for the opioids to be administered before the procedure. Donny knew, because he got copied on all the morbid memos.

"I didn't try to kill that son of a bitch," said Jerome. "But I wish I had. Because if I had, he'd be dead." He took a few long, slow breaths. "I am here because I decided to talk back. And teach others how to stand up and take care of themselves. Not fighting each other like they want us to, tearing up our own streets and hurting our own families and neighbors. Fighting the city, the state, the whole country. Standing up for the people, for real democracy, against the people with the power and money who know democracy is no longer on their side. Standing up for the land they brought our ancestors here to steal from our other ancestors, and then to make the whole place their slave the way they made people their slaves. The only rebellion I called for was mental. Teaching people how to take care of themselves and their people. Now I know it really is time. Time to make our own new country with our own rules, based on real democracy and human rights and love for the land that feeds us. So my only crime is that I am the future they want to abolish. You are that future, too, a future they can't stop any more than they can keep the sky they have poisoned from drowning their mansions, or the bodies of their grandchildren from carrying the seeds of a whole planet finally coming together to build a new model of community. It's coming, and they can't stop it. See y'all in the future. The real future. Not the one these assholes are trying to kill by killing me. They don't know they're just making it come sooner."

You could see the exhaustion in his eyes, but you could also see the pride, the courage. Donny tried to project his admiration, through the overpowering shame of his failure. They held each other's gaze for what seemed a very long time, and what Donny felt through the mostly vicarious stress of the moment and the unexpected evocation of Jerome's words and the layers of simultaneously clarifying and clouding intoxicants Donny had ingested was the sense of some tenuous mental connection through the space between them, almost like a handoff had just occurred. Jerome's case wasn't over. The price of losing was that Donny was now bound to carry on Jerome's fight, on his own terms. If he could discharge that duty, it could make everything that had happened to this moment worth it. Acts of liberation, Jerome once said to him, are illegal until the liberators win and rewrite the laws. The feeling of forgiveness and purpose that came over him did not make what followed any easier to watch.

Szabo recited the sentence in the rigid prose of the state. He read the time on the clock on the wall, checking it against his wristwatch. Then he authorized the executioners to proceed. Each released a catch valve on the I.V. bladders on either side, one the real deal and the other a placebo so no one would know who was the true executioner. Death by medical science and industrial chemistry dripped into Jerome's veins.

The minute it took for the concoction to effect its seizure of Jerome's corpus felt like one in which the forward movement of time had stopped. Even the aiding and abetting assholes standing there in the viewing chamber with Donny seemed to sense it. And then Jerome grunted, convulsed visibly in his tight restraints, and finally snorted just as the essence of his life left his body.

Just when you thought it was done, this insane belch emitted through Jerome's mouth, and then the discolored spittle dripped down his chin.

They stood there watching the dead body for ten minutes, in a kind of funereal trance, until the doctor came in, checked Jerome's vitals, and pronounced him dead. Szabo noted the time of death.

When the lady guard came to escort them out, Jerome's eyes were still open, but he was not there. Except for the words he had said, which were still echoing in Donny's head, a spell whose incantation he did not yet understand.

14

WHEN HE GOT IN HIS CAR AFTER THE EXECUTION, DONNY WASN'T
sure where to go. So he just went. The traffic was light at 2:00 A.M.
on a Tuesday morning, and he could really open up the throttle.

He had gotten halfway to the airport when he realized he
had someplace to go other than nowhere. Maybe it was the lin-
gering effects of that thing Ward gave him, but somehow the
plane icon marking the route reminded him of his promise to
Xelina. The way the plane looked like a bird. A free bird like
Xelina. Or like she had been, before she got caught in the net. It
was Donny's job to get her back to that. Her and all the others.
That's what Jerome would want him to do.

He had seven hours until her hearing. It had been a while
since he pulled an all-nighter on a case. Time to suck it up.

He got off the freeway and found the nearest Pronto Mart.
While his thirsty Geely sedan drank the dinosaur juice from the
pump, he went inside for provisions. They had everything you
could need in there: food, oil, water, beer, wiper fluid, booze,
hardware, antifreeze, edibles, pornography, money cards, phone
cards, burner phones, rubber boots, ponchos, chewing tobacco,
lottery tickets, weird movies, weirder art, and guns. The guns
were kind of a new thing, part of the suspension of the licensing
laws that had been justified by the general breakdown in law
and order as local police forces ran out of money and people got
used to never leaving the house unready for a gunfight. That
suited most Texans. Donny wasn't one of them.

Jerome was.

So was Joyce.

As he stood there looking at the guns in the case, most of which were the cheap-ass 3-D printed plastic disposables popular at the corner stores, Donny wondered if maybe this was the time to break his no guns rule. Especially where he was going.

"You need to get yourself one of those," said the clerk, whose worn Cornhuskers cap and the vowels that went with it marked him as a member of the Midwestern diaspora. The Nebraskans of the Platte River plains had taken over many of the corner stores in recent years, relying on kinship networks and the informal credit systems they had brought from back home and refined in the resettlement centers. The Texans loved the way they brought their foul-weather self-reliance into the shops, even if they talked a little funny and were not always super friendly.

"Thinking about it," said Donny. "Just afraid that if I start using it I won't be able to stop."

The guy gave him a weird look. Maybe he could tell Donny meant it.

"Do those things work?" asked Donny, pointing at the little metal phone cases next to the guns.

"Guaranteed," said the clerk. "Block all known modes of electronic surveillance. And all incoming signals."

"I'll take one."

At that moment, it was a more powerful weapon than a gun would ever be.

The loot Donny loaded in the car ten minutes later included a big metal flashlight that could work as a blunt instrument in a pinch, extra batteries, latex gloves, one of those super-detailed Houston road maps, a shrink-wrapped bean burrito with Day-Glo salsa, a red-eye coffee, a Rebel bar, a cheap face mask, a cheaper folding knife with the logo of the store, a five-pack of money cards pre-loaded with twenty dollars each, and a crowbar that was probably too small for the job but better than nothing. He wondered if there was a joke already about the lawyer with the crowbar. But that only reminded him of the lawyer jokes Jerome used to tell. The memory cut, maybe because of the way the jokes did, especially in the hindsight of that moment.

He spent a few minutes with the map locating the address Xelina had given him, and then figuring out a good route, one that would avoid the known checkpoints. The destination was close to a section of the Evac Zone, so armed checkpoints were likely, as were unexpected road closures and the kinds of potholes you don't come back out of.

As he sipped the coffee before starting the car, he saw the attendant in there under the fluorescents watching him and talking on the phone. It made Donny wonder if, on second thought, he should go back in and buy one of those guns. Jerome probably would have teased him and told him he wasn't cut out for shooting, just for talking. Joyce would not have given a shit what Donny did, but she would totally have bought herself one if not two of those guns.

That's when Donny remembered she had called earlier that day, which was now yesterday, and he had not had time to call her back. So he sent her a message saying "sorry I missed you." Then he put the phone in its new case.

He looked for the attendant again but couldn't see him. Then the lights went out inside the store. Donny put the car in gear and hit it, taking side streets through industrial zones and bombed-out neighborhoods to avoid attention. It was Houston, so you never knew when you might stumble upon a couple of blocks of higher-end uses, the kind of blocks wired with surveillance and maybe even private paramilitaries on patrol. If it came to that, he would have to talk his way out of it.

As he brainstormed possible cover stories and evasions, he opened the windows to the stench of the industrial swamp, and heard the distant booms in the direction he was headed.

15

AFTER JOYCE BOUGHT HER FIRST GUN, SHE STARTED DRAGGING Donny to target practice with her. They went most Thursdays, as a date night.

"Bullets and barbeque," she'd called it.

Big Red's Maximum Range was an old warehouse off I-10 that had most recently served as the meeting place of the Assembly of the Rapturous Ascension, until Pastor Roger Loving's TV show went national and he moved to a former basketball arena closer to downtown. When he first started tagging along, Donny asked Big Red Jr. if they had any images of Satan or Caesar left over as targets, but no one else thought that was funny, if they even knew he was joking. The targets they had were traditional bullseyes, and if you wanted to pay a few bucks extra you could have a street hoodlum, a Central American soldier, or one of the new domestic terrorists, who looked a lot like a farmer.

Donny stuck with the bullseyes, which made him appreciate what a very bad shot he was. Joyce liked the hoodlums. Her favorite was the guy with the fedora. She said it made the experience more noir. It worked, because Big Red himself started coming to watch her, saying you're pretty dang good at this, Professor, and encouraging her to sign up for some competitions. Joyce modestly credited the quality of the Austrian equipment she had invested in, but you could tell she liked the compliment.

Big Red did not ever think to talk politics with Joyce,

which might have changed his opinion. If he could have understood her. Joyce tended to speak in fully formed scholarly paragraphs, complete with footnotes. Donny told her it was a shield from feelings, and she didn't argue. He thought maybe that's why she found the pure tactile intensity of shooting a gun so refreshing.

"Bullets have their own language," she said. "America's true language."

One time Big Red set up one of those cubes of ballistic gelatin for Joyce, after Donny asked him if he had any. It was what the crime lab guys used to re-create shootings, and Donny had learned about them while working as a prosecutor. The gelatin was designed to replicate human flesh. When you heard the sound of one of Joyce's hollowpoints hitting that block of goop, you never forgot it.

When they went for their walks after dinner, Joyce would open carry in this crazy designer holster she bought. Armed and probably more dangerous to themselves than any assailant, they strolled places you were told to avoid after dark, and talked freely in the unsurveilled open air about the kind of things that were normally kept coded. Or never discussed at all.

Joyce developed a philosophy of the gun, a crazy variant of the radical theory she wrote about in academic journals that many libraries were increasingly scared to even carry on their shelves. It was a theory of revolutionary empowerment, charged with phrases like "the sovereign body," "zones of autonomy," and "cordite-based consent." Donny said the only thing scarier than a philosophy professor with a gun is one who talks about actually using it. But when the time came for him to defend Jerome giving guns to the refugees in the resettlement camps, Joyce's theories came in handy.

Now he wondered if maybe he should have kept the far-out

Second Amendment arguments out of it. It obviously hadn't worked for Jerome.

Donny was thinking about that as he sat there at the end of a dark dead-end street trying to figure out which turn he had missed when the phone rang.

As he opened the case that was supposed to block all signals, he cursed the clerk who sold it to him. But then he was glad, when he saw who was calling.

"Hey," said Donny, holding the phone to his head.

"Hey," said Joyce.

"Sorry I missed your call," said Donny. "I was at the courthouse."

"I saw you on the news. Your picture at least."

"Is that what you were calling about?"

"No. The news was later. I called about something else."

"I'm driving," said Donny, as he turned around and headed south. "Let me know if the noise gets too bad."

"I can hear you," said Joyce. "Are you crying?"

"They did it, Joyce. They fucking killed him."

"I saw that, too. I'm sorry."

"I blew it," said Donny.

"You can't win, Donny. It's like I keep telling you. There is no real law. Just raw power, dressed up in a tie. It's always been that way. And it's starting to get a whole lot worse."

"I know, but I have to do something for these people. There's still some law, and so there's still some hope."

She sighed. "Look, I didn't call to rehash our favorite argument."

"I thought maybe if I gave them a political reason to do it, to stay the execution, they would bite."

"Yeah, that's what I saw on the news. Good idea. Too bad

they spun it the other way. Now they're talking about you the way they talk about your clients."

"What do you mean?"

She paused. "It's late, maybe you should just watch it yourself after you get some sleep. Are you fucked up?"

"No," he lied, telling himself the effects had mostly passed. He drank another sip of coffee.

"Well, keep it buttoned up, Kimoe. Because you seem to have gotten their full fucking attention."

"Good," said Donny.

"Just remember those of us who get tagged by the algorithms whenever they look you up in the database, counselor. I had two of those goons come see me today. Before the latest news, even."

"That's why you called."

"Yeah. They came by my office on campus, no less. Not good, Donny."

"Shit," he said.

"Not exactly what the tenure committee needs to see," said Joyce.

"Sorry. Who were they?"

"Feds. In suits. Said they were updating your background check, but the questions they were asking seemed like more than that."

"What kind of questions?"

"Loyalty questions, like they always have. But a lot more specific. Questions about your cases. The kind of questions you'd ask about a co-conspirator, more than a lawyer. I told them to fuck off."

"Joyce—"

"I was polite at first, since it was at school, but I lost my patience."

"It should be over soon," said Donny. "Once they call the election for the candidate who actually won."

"God, for someone who sees the things you see, how can you be such a sucker?"

"Miles is on it. Him and a bunch of other good, smart lawyers from around the country, including in government and on the bench. They won't let that happen. They won't let someone steal the presidency."

"You really believe that, don't you? I guess the White-Out is making you forget all that history you used to read. You better keep those smart lawyers' numbers handy for when they lock you up. I'm outta here."

Donny laughed.

"I'm not joking," she said. "I'm leaving."

"Leaving the country?"

"Absolutely," she said. "What do you think I'm doing awake at 2:30 in the morning while you're driving around wasted texting old girlfriends? I'm packing."

Donny processed it.

"It's just hard going through all these fucking books," she continued.

"Where are you going?"

"Someplace I can drive," she said.

"Vamos a la playa," said Donny.

"No beach. I need Metropolis. Mexico City. I have friends there. It's where everybody's going."

"Who's everybody?"

"Jesus, you're so wrapped up in your work you don't even know what's going on. You better get one of those new passports while you can."

"With the biometrics?"

"Yes, on your phone. Super creepy. Makes you take a little

patriotic quiz every time you open it. Go ahead, ask me the names of the presidents."

"So I guess you didn't burn yours with the kids after all."

"Sorry, no, I'm too selfish in the end. But you already knew that."

"When are you leaving?"

"My travel pass is for a week from Friday." There was a pause on the line. "You should come with me."

It surprised him. And caused a flutter in his stomach. Just not one of anticipation.

"I can't. My clients—"

"You can't help them, Donny. The system is rigged. You're banging your head against the wall. It's hard to watch. I'm not saying we should get back together. Just share the ride."

Donny considered it. "You just want a lawyer with you when you cross the border."

"Wouldn't hurt," said Joyce, and he could hear the shrug. "But I would enjoy your company."

Donny looked out at the landscape around him. A helicopter was moving low over a tank farm in the near distance, searchlight scanning the ground.

"Can I think about it?"

"Sure," she said. "But don't take too long. I'm leaving on Friday with or without you."

After they hung up, he turned off his phone. Then he turned around and took an alternate route to his destination.

When he saw the car turn around behind him, he drove faster.

16

FORTY MINUTES LATER, AFTER A FEW DETOURS TO SHAKE THE tail or the paranoia, Donny finally found Xelina's house. It was way out east, on the south side of Pasadena, in a part of town that had looked like the end of the world long before the storms put the oil back in the ground and made big swaths of the area uninhabitable. Pasadena, Texas, was not a place you would ever confuse with its California cousin. No flowers, just flareoffs.

Except in front of this place, of all things, the first things Donny noticed in his headlights *were* flowers. The yard was full of them. Yellow flowers, not too big, but wild and tall, sticking up out of the weeds that looked like they were about to swallow the front porch of the little house.

The house didn't look like the headquarters of a terrorist conspiracy. It looked abandoned. One of those little shotgun shacks that are so common in mostly winterless Texas: wood frame with a pointy roof and a little more insulation than your average cardboard box. There was purple warning tape across the front. Not crime scene tape, but the kind they used to seal off contaminated sites.

Donny looked around. There were two other houses on the short block, some more the next block over. Behind the house was a patch of woods. Farther back you could see a tall fence around what looked like a warehouse, with one lonely security light where the bugs were dancing. Next door all the way to the corner was empty, and almost as overgrown.

Probably razed, since at the end of the street there was fencing blocking off the road and everything in that direction—the beginning of the Evac Zone. Donny wondered how people could live so close to cancer land. But it had always been bad around here in these residential neighborhoods sandwiched between the chemical plants, mostly occupied by people who worked in those same plants. The weirdest thing was, when he turned off his headlights and rolled down the window to listen and look more clearly, it seemed so nice. Not pretty, but real. And not quiet, but quietly alive. You could hear the bugs and frogs out there mixed in with the machine hums and thunks of the factories and the buzz of the electric lights, a little corner of tranquility hiding in plain sight. A different kind of hideout than he'd had in mind.

He put on the gloves, put the knife in his pocket, grabbed the flashlight, and stepped out into it.

He didn't get far before he caught his sleeve on the thorns of a mesquite, puncturing skin and cursing as he tried to pull it loose, and then screaming when the flashlight roused a snake that lay in the branches. It wasn't a big snake, or a venomous one, and the tree was really just a bush, half hidden by the weeds. But he screamed anyway, pure reflex, and that got some dogs barking across the street.

At least they sounded small.

Donny scrambled through the weeds as fast as he could around the side of the house, hoping to get out of sight before the pit bulls woke up.

When he got to the back, he could already feel little prickly things on his ankles, something from the weeds poking through the thin socks he wore with his suit pants and wingtips. He shined the light on the back wall. The windows had the bright FEMA stickers on them but no tape. There was a door, like Xelina said. And there was the big oil drum that had been made into a planter, with some kind of yucca growing out of it. He went in close, and found the fake rock that had the key.

Turned out he didn't need it, because the back door was already open. The flimsy screen door made a loud noise behind him as he stepped in.

The place looked vacated in a hurry. Dirty dishes in the sink, muddy rain boots on the floor by the back door. No sign of anyone there now. Flashlight on, he looked for the cache.

The long hallway was papered up like a big collage. Photos of wildlife mixed with industry. A hawk sitting on a telephone line, humongous storage tanks looming behind it. A family of deer crossing the interstate, blocking four lanes of traffic. A coyote in front of a suburban office building. There were posters, too. A campaign poster for Gregorio, young, handsome, pan-racial, and hopeful, one fist raised and the other holding some little kid's hand. The kid was the one holding the flowers. An older one farther down, the famous one of Tania, before she was martyred, with her beret and the AK-47, the one they said started it all. Donny remembered his mom had a smaller version of that image on the wall of her study when he was a kid, before she quit the people's clinic and went to work for the company.

The front room looked like a storm had blown through, furniture upended and stuff dumped all over the floor. He didn't have time to go through it, but his eye was drawn to one thing, maybe because it was hanging from the ceiling, slowly turning in the flashlight beam. Some kind of art object, almost like a chandelier, but made from animal bones and human trash instead of glass. Antlers and teeth and rebar and valves, a few dashes of color from the severed heads of plastic toys, all attached to one center piece, a piece of driftwood that looked like it probably floated up the Ship Channel from some primordial ocean on the other side of time.

He scanned away from that, following the ceiling back down the hallway until he found the thing that Xelina said covered the access to the crawl space where he would find the backups of her videos. It was a band poster. Electric Hephaestus, the original album cover for *Back to Pishon*, where the musicians and their friends were all skinny dipping in a mountain stream. Donny had smiled when Xelina told him what to look for, because he had a copy of that album as well, with the censored version of the cover, and without the backmasking. In a way, it was the first thing they had really shared in common.

It probably still was, until suddenly lights from outside filled the house, and he heard the voice of the machine calling his name.

"DONALD KIMOE. WE KNOW YOU ARE IN THERE. THIS IS THE TASK FORCE. WE HAVE YOU SURROUNDED. COME OUT. NOW. HANDS OVER YOUR HEAD."

He looked to the window to see, but the light was so bright he couldn't see anything. And when he looked back at the poster, he only saw white. He reached up anyway, looking for the pull cord with the idea that maybe he could get up there and get it in time, but then he hesitated when he heard the chopper blades, thinking he better wait until he could come back, and not tip them off now.

Then he heard the three hard knocks, and before he could say anything, he heard the splintering of the door, which sounded like it was his own head.

17

"YOU CAN'T ARREST ME," SAID KIMOE. "I'M A LAWYER."

"Shut up," said the officer who was watching Donny be cuffed. The guy wore a blue windbreaker that said POLICE FEMA on the back and had the name "Coats" on the front. "Martial law means we don't need any more fucking lawyers. We are the law now, pal. And you broke it good."

"I represent one of the residents of this house," said Donny. "I have every right to be here."

"Sit down," said Coats, and the guy who had just cuffed Donny pushed down on the chain between the cuffs like he was yanking a dog's choke collar. Donny didn't fight it, and kneeled in the middle of the street between the headlights of a half dozen patrol cars and one big green police truck. He looked up at Coats, who had turned to say something to one of the guys up at the house, but the chopper was so loud he couldn't hear what the guy said. Then Donny felt the rotor wash and his tie slapped him in the face.

Coats turned in time to see that, and pointed and laughed.

"I'll be in court in the morning," yelled Donny. "And we'll see about who broke what law."

"Let me play you something, smartass," said Coats. "Hold him good, Garrett."

Garrett got down behind Donny, grabbed both arms, put his knee up against Donny's back, and pulled. It hurt. When he tried to resist, the guy pulled harder.

Coats pulled out his phone, messed with the buttons, and then put it to Donny's ear. The volume was all the way up, which hurt even more than the knee in his back. But what hurt the most was that what he heard over the noise of the chopper and the hollering cops and the barking fucking Chihuahuas who had probably gotten him in this mess was the sound of his own damn voice.

What was playing was the message he had left on the White House voicemail.

It was not the kind of message your lawyer wants to hear.

Donny knew each provision of the federal criminal code that those sorts of threats on the life of the President violated. He had defended his fair share of cases involving less imaginative and more profane versions.

He looked up at Coats, who was giving him the stern father, angry good old boy edition.

"I meant every word," said Donny.

Now Coats got a different look in his face. Those eyes.

The eyes of frontier justice.

"Light it up," hollered Coats, turning to the squad at the house and flashing a hand signal.

A couple of the guys went over with hand torches from the truck and did as Coats commanded, hitting spots inside and then around the outside of the house.

And then they watched the house burn. So hot Donny could feel the scorch on his face from out there in the street.

Razing damaged buildings in the disaster zone was part of the job description for FEMA cops. They had a reputation for getting a little carried away with it sometimes. Gentrification by fire, people called it. What amazed Donny was how fast they worked.

He was in the back of the police truck looking through the

bulletproof glass when the whole frame collapsed in on itself. Right around the time the tow truck came to take away his car. It was an old car, but a nice one, the fancy Chinese import he had bought with his severance money from the law firm. And because it was Chinese, they started abusing it before they even got the chains on.

For some reason it was the car that finally made him lose his shit. Maybe the way it reminded him of some of his other epic fails.

18

"YOU SHOULD BLAME HIS PREDECESSOR, PRESIDENT GREEN," said Broyles, as he teed up on the fourteenth hole one Saturday morning that summer. "He's the one who started turning our own people over to the tribunals."

Donny had tried to reply, to make a distinction between war criminals and political dissidents, but Broyles signaled him to shut up and wait while he addressed the ball.

This was in August, right after the political conventions, as the campaigns got their frenzy on for the final stretch. It was a beautiful morning at the Cypress Bayou Country Club, the third Saturday of the month, when Donny's former colleagues played a round followed by lunch and cards at the grill. The other three were members of the club, and Donny was their guest, filling in for their regular fourth, a deal lawyer named Alan Massey who had to spend the morning with a merger agreement—the Pendleton Services acquisition of Bolan Corp. they would read about on Monday before market open. The fourth hurricane of the summer was supposed to blow in from Africa that night, but the skies were clear and the air surprisingly cool. Trey and Lou were still sweating through, probably because they were wearing the blood blue, as was the judge. Almost-black polo shirts and slacks—black madras shorts in Trey's case, a Southern preppy variation on fashion-as-politics that some boutique menswear store out of South Carolina had come up with. It was the first time Donny really appreciated the dark turn politics had taken that year, in no small part because of the case he had before Broyles. Only the most strident radicals ever called American patriots "fascists," but seeing those three standing with their clubs that morning made him wonder. Like maybe if he said the wrong thing Trey would hold him down while Lou shoved a ball in his mouth and Broyles brained him with the sand wedge. They used to joke about shit like that back in the day. Maybe they meant it more than Donny realized.

Inviting Donny along was Lou's idea, and the reason was a case Donny had before Broyles—the Jerome Hardy case, which was about a lot more than Jerome Hardy. Lou was worried it was destroying their friendships. That maybe some time together on the course would help bridge the gap, maybe even help clear a path to working out a deal. Donny figured it couldn't hurt to have a chance to work on Broyles outside the courtroom. He knew the good the guy was capable of from the years they had worked together. But those years were starting to feel like a whole different reality, one that was lost forever to the rapidly distancing past.

At his convention the week before, the President had announced the suspension of habeas corpus in thirteen counties in Texas and Louisiana that he had designated in an earlier executive order as "zones of insurrection"—areas where law and order had failed after the storms. Earlier such declarations had included mostly rural areas in the drought-ravaged Midwest, but this one included most of the Houston metroplex, with exceptions for downtown and some of the neighborhoods that had been cleared. Houston was ground zero, in a way, for problems in other parts of the country that had migrated here. Literally, in caravans of pickups and station wagons and sometimes tractors, to the resettlement camps that included the big one by the airport not far from where they were that morning. The one the President had been visiting when those refugee kids, four originally from Wichita and one who had walked all the way from Kearney, Nebraska, tried to put a hole in him.

They got themselves shot in the process, and took three Secret Service agents with them. Their pictures were everywhere, and the domestic refugee problem became a whole different kind of crisis. The resettlement camps became a whole different kind of camp—the kind you never leave. And then they started looking in the cities and towns for other homegrown enemies who needed to be excised from the population to keep the political disease from spreading.

It was a phrase one of the kids screamed as he pressed the detonator, a lyric from one of Jerome's songs, that got the investigation focused on just what Jerome had been instigating in the tapes he had been selling kids in the camps, and in the bombed-out storm zones of the metroplex. Donny, being a fan of Jerome's music, was happy to take the case. He hadn't really thought about the politics of it, or the personal consequences, until he was all in.

The trial had been expedited, and short. Donny's part, at least. Broyles gave the prosecution as much time as they needed to build an error-free record, and gave Donny a day and a half. After being name-checked by the President in his big speech, complete with a scary photo of the "terrorist ringleader" holding a rifle in one hand and a political tract in the other, Jerome had been convicted that week after Broyles did his best to preempt the jury. Donny had been working on his sentencing brief the afternoon before when Lou invited him to join them.

"We all need to stay friends," was all he had said.

And for half the course, they had followed the rules and talked about a lot of nothing. A few fishing stories, one adulterous confession, and the world's longest lawyer anecdote about a screwy case Lou and Broyles had worked on. Until they got in the carts at the thirteenth flag, and Donny finally called out the elephant on the fairway.

"I can't believe we are playing golf while you all are shredding the Constitution," he said.

Broyles was immediately aggravated, but the only way you could tell was by how quiet he got. It didn't show in his play, when they got to the next tee. He hit the ball hard and straight. They watched it sail.

"Nice," said Trey, the voice of a forty-something pledge captain.

"He's been taking lessons," said Lou.

"Just clarity of mind," said Broyles. "It comes with age."

"And the power to lock up anyone who bugs you," said Donny.

Broyles gave him a look normally reserved for the worst defendants, and then changed to a mean smile. "Don't be bitter, Donny," he said. "Stick with sentimental."

Trey and Lou laughed. All four of them had worked at the same law firm, though not all at the same time. Broyles had left the summer Donny clerked, to take over as head federal prosecutor for the region. Trey and Lou had been the senior associates Donny worked with right out of school. Trey was now the GC at Texical, more of a corporate fixer than a lawyer, and Lou was still at the firm, a senior partner handling big corporate disputes.

"Donny is good at sentimental," said Lou. "Remember the Helios Industries case?"

Donny remembered. That was the case where it became

clear he would never make partner, after he disclosed incrim-
inating documents he found in their own client's files, documents revealing the client's knowledge of defects in their heat
tiles that had caused a corporate orbiter to flame out on re-
entry and crash into a Mexican village. What Donny did was
required under the rules. They rewarded him by putting Lou
on the case instead, and making Donny the lawyer who handled the non-billable pro bono cases—the charitable work
the rules also required, the subject of public admiration and
private derision. That lasted a year, until Donny and a half
dozen other lawyers were terminated for what they said were
economic reasons but in fact was a political purge. At least
they made it a soft landing, getting Broyles to bring Donny on
as an Assistant U.S. Attorney. And then President Mack took
the oath for the first time, Broyles went on the bench shortly
thereafter—the prize for prosecuting cases that helped take
down the prior administration—and Donny switched sides.
And things between them were never quite the same, even
as the cabling of collegiality persisted across the divisions of
politics.

"He cares," said Trey. "We all care. Donny just lets the
scales balance all the way over to where the old blind lady's
about to fall and not get up."

"Apparently His Honor finds me sentimental for thinking people should not be detained without a legally defensible
reason."

"Then blame Abraham Lincoln," said Broyles, pulling his
tee, also black, and then using it as a pointer to aid in the lecture. "He was the model. Not for the reasons people usually
cite. The model of iron-fisted strength in service of nationalist
principle. First president to hire his own elite mercenary corps
to do his bidding."

"Pinkertons," said Donny, looking at Trey and Lou. "For 'protection.'"

"A convenient rewrite of what was really very common back then, and one we are right to be reviving. Lincoln would admire what we have done in the last four years."

"Including the last ten days," said Donny.

"Exactly," said Broyles, ignoring the irony in Donny's voice. "This habeas business. He was the one who set the precedent, rounding up half the officials in the state of Maryland to keep the supply lines from the North open. Martial law is underrated as a tool to make democracy stronger. The trick is getting enough people excited about its exercise."

"Who can argue with arresting politicians?" said Trey.

"Seems to be working pretty well for our Governor," said Lou. "I think he's the one who gave the President the idea."

"That doesn't make it constitutional," said Donny.

"It does if no one stops him," said Broyles, making it deliberately unclear if he was talking about then or now.

Donny knew the story, and he was annoyed the judge was right. They both knew how the country really worked. The difference was how they thought it should work.

"They did," said Donny.

"And he went ahead anyway, pushing them to exercise a power they had, by exercising it for them until they finally papered it over. Do you know why?"

"Yes," said Donny, without elaborating. He knew Broyles liked to deliver the lesson.

"Because it was necessary to protect the security and integrity of the Union, and everybody knew it."

"You understand we're talking about a political campaign here," said Donny. "An election, not a civil war."

"Said the last dumbass in America naïve enough to believe

122

there's any difference left," said Trey, taking the judge's side and then some, as usual. "We have foreign powers dictating how we run our country, and so-called Americans trying to tear what's left into pieces and taking up arms against our own government. We need a leader who is going to make people earn their citizenship, and make that citizenship worth what it should be again. And you should be happy about it, Donny, because we are going to keep you a very busy man."

"Let's play golf, guys," said Lou. "There's another foursome coming up behind us. Your shot, Donny."

Donny set up while the others stowed their clubs and got in the carts. As he shoved his tee into the turf, he wondered if it had really always been this way, and he was just starting to see it clearly for the first time. Then he saw an egret flying through the frame of the wide green fairway, tinted orange from the morning light. And just as he got ready to swing, the judge broke protocol, and character, and talked.

"You do know we are talking about the future of the country here," he said, in the tone of a pissed-off dad. "These people are like the early Christians. They seem like a fringe movement now, but they are the seeds of something much bigger. We need to be lions. Or watch our whole way of life collapse into ruin."

Donny sliced the shit out of it, and watched the ball land way off in the trees, almost at the fence along the road. He remembered the time when country clubs didn't need razor wire or armed guards at the perimeter.

It wasn't until Jerome's sentencing, which no one saw coming, that he really appreciated what the judge meant.

19

THE JAILERS LET DONNY CALL MILES, AND THEY LET MILES COME
pick him up, after a few hours of questioning. Miles offered
him a ride to the courthouse, after saying I should make you
ride the damn bus.

"You're a mess, Donny. You want to swing by your place on
the way, get a change of clothes?"

"We don't have time, Miles. This will have to do."

He looked himself over sitting there in the front passenger
seat. There was a grass stain on his white shirt, which he tried
to rub out with his handkerchief. Then he noticed the rip in
his left pant leg. He reached into his litigation bag, which they
had returned to him upon release, and looked for the Scotch
tape.

"You should get a postponement," said Miles. "Broyles would
give you that, under the circumstances."

"Broyles is probably the one who did this to me, Miles.
Things are getting crazier faster than I ever thought possible. I
need to just show up."

"I think you'd have better luck with a safety pin," said
Miles, watching Donny fumble to suture the rip.

"You always know better than me, don't you," said Donny.
It had been a while since he had experienced the shame of detention, a shame you felt no matter how unjust the arrest.

He pulled down the sun visor and looked at his face in the
little mirror. He straightened his hair, assessed his whiskers,

noted the little scrapes and nicks, and then used his finger to try to clean his teeth.

"Some days it's hard to convince yourself you're not an animal," he said.

Miles just glanced at him and kept driving.

"Did I see you won in Austin?" asked Donny.

"Yeah," he said. "It was good. She invalidated the martial law decree, other than the areas that are still too contaminated. And the Governor has ten days to provide updated testing data to back up those."

"Well done," said Donny. "Maybe this really is going to go the right way."

"If we keep fighting them every day, it will," said Miles. "Sooner or later."

Even though he had just suggested it, Donny wasn't sure he agreed. A few hours in a cell had a way of changing your outlook.

"Do you have a copy of the judge's order? I think I can use that this morning. Might be just what I need to get this kid home."

"Absolutely," said Miles.

"Thanks," said Donny, noticing Miles was still looking at him, like he was trying to decide if he should take him to the mental hospital instead of the courthouse. "You should watch the road."

"It's not far," said Miles, reaching for the radio. "Let's hear what's in the news."

"How about let's not," said Donny. "The real story is never on the news. And that's the one we need to figure out. Figure out and tell."

Miles nodded. They sat there at the light quietly for a minute in the clog of morning rush hour, watching the slow flow of a fat and sclerotic society about to learn the bill has come due.

"You ever wonder if the Indians will come back?" asked Donny.

"Can't say that I have," said Miles. "Maybe their ghosts."

"The ghosts are everywhere," said Donny. "Wait till the Comanches ride in from Dallas and raid the Galleria."

"I don't know if the Comanches came down here much," said Miles.

"They will when they have pickups and Harleys," said Donny.

Miles smiled. Then he turned right onto Rusk Street.

"What happened, Donny?"

Donny was unbuttoning his shirt to inspect the pained spot on his ribs he had just noticed. He looked over at Miles.

"Xelina Rocafuerte happened. You never met with her, before Broyles transferred the case to me?"

Miles shook his head.

"You really want in on this?" said Donny. "Because I could use the help, but I don't want to pull you into my mess."

"Just tell me."

"She says she saw them kill Gregorio."

"Oh."

"Says she got it on film."

"Wow. Who did it?"

"She's not sure. They weren't in uniforms. Plainclothes, street wear, masks."

"Have you seen the footage?"

"No. Not sure anyone has. She blocked her devices, and won't give up the code."

"If she gave it up she could go back to her life."

"I told her that. She doesn't want to rat out her friends, Miles. She wants to rat out the ones who killed Gregorio."

"Good luck with that."

"She's right. That it's the right thing to do."

"Is she a bona fide insurgent?"

"I don't know. Maybe? Probably? Does it matter?"

"It matters, Donny. Violence is not the answer."

"No," said Donny. "But I can't even remember what's the fucking question anymore."

"What happened last night, Donny?"

"They burned her goddam house down, Miles. I went there looking for backups she said she had, stuff that would make our case. And they knew. Maybe didn't know what I was there for, because I honestly don't think they know she has footage of the deed—they just want to find and lock up all the witnesses. But whatever she had is gone now. Torched."

"You're lucky they didn't burn it with you in it."

"Right," said Donny. "End up like old Njal."

"Who's Neal?"

"Njal. Viking lawyer."

"Oh, right, that Icelandic saga. Never read it."

"Great book. I wonder what he'd do in this situation? Some arcane procedural gotcha, I bet."

"He probably wouldn't leave psychotic threats on the White House switchboard."

Donny shrugged. "Everybody should do that once in a while. It's cathartic. And cheaper than therapy."

"Not at my hourly rate."

"You're billing me?"

"I should be, the way you're pulling me away from the case that needs all my attention. Don't you understand what's at stake? I swear you'd give the whole country away just to save one client. Or your own ass."

"I'm doing my job, Miles. Sorry if I can't do it to your standards."

Miles just sighed, and pulled up by the concrete bollards that blocked the road leading to the courthouse.

"So what are you going to do?" he asked, looking at the courthouse looming over the barricades. There were some words about justice chiseled into the frieze across the top of the building, but you couldn't make them out through the barbed wire.

"Don't you mean we?" said Donny.

"I have my hands full with bigger fights, but we'll see."

"Well, if you're right, I just need to keep her from being denaturalized before the election makes all that insanity moot."

"I hope so," said Miles. "I think so."

"So this morning I'm going to use that decision you got to attack the whole thing from a legal angle."

"It's worth a shot. If nothing else, it could create a good basis for reversal on appeal."

"And for delay in the meantime. Beyond that, I have to work with what I've got."

He held up his scuffed hands for Miles to see, like a magician showing he has nothing up his sleeves.

"You know there's Listerine in the men's room by the judge's chambers," said Miles, thinking that would help.

But nothing was going to get the bad taste out of Donny's mouth about where this case was going. This case, and everything else in his world.

20

BRIDGET DIDN'T MAKE DONNY'S MORNING ANY EASIER.

She started with the confession, which would have been enough by itself. She then offered excerpts from Xelina's communications with her friends, in which she expressed her desire for a change in government and some of the more imaginative ways in which she thought that could be achieved, a couple of which made Donny's White House voicemail sound tame. The logs evidenced discussions of various "infiltrations" people in her network had planned under the cover of the storms—some groups breaching the border fortifications while others broke into industrial and government facilities with big talk of the damage they could do to "the Machine." Most of these were pulled from chats Percy had also found for Donny, and when you had the full context they all showed Xelina wanting merely to tag along with her camera as a documentarian. Donny was sure he could use that material to counter Bridget's characterization of Xelina's conduct and intent. That was before Bridget got around to showing what was on the videos Xelina had made while tagging along.

Donny had managed to get there on time for the hearing, but not with enough time to prep, or to meet with Xelina. He was stuck telling her the bad news when they brought her in right before Broyles. He hoped his appearance conveyed how hard he'd tried, but he also knew coming close was the same as not even trying. Before she could vent her anger and disappointment, he told her he thought he had another way he could get a copy, which was mostly true. But first, he said, we need to get through this morning. He also told her it wasn't too late to try to make a deal with the prosecutors—give them some names of the people in your network and they will let you walk on little more than a trespassing charge. Xelina thought about that for a long minute. Then she asked if he would get a copy of what they said in court that day. He told her yes, a transcript. I guess that'll have to do, said Xelina. And then she made Donny promise her he would publish it.

He promised, even though doing that would be a crime.

I guess that means you want to testify, he said. And then he told her how risky that would be.

So as the opening frame appeared in the wall-mounted monitor opposite the jury box and Bridget's assistant went to press play, Donny wasn't surprised that Xelina looked like she was eager for Broyles to watch her show.

Donny objected to the way the prosecution had cut the videos, knowing, as with his objections to the selective declassification of Xelina's communications with her friends, that it would not do him much good today, even if it was important to build the record for subsequent appeal.

As he saw Xelina's work through the government's eyes, he got a better understanding of why they wanted to silence her.

The way they cut their montage, they were trying to show people taking up arms against their government. And there was some of that, of the so-called self-defense clubs and people's militias. Armed patrols asserting the sovereignty of bombed-out neighborhoods. Footage from the occupation of the refuge that Gregorio had led. The clip they called the recruiting video, with the kids learning to blow up cars and aim for the head.

But even when they showed the girls field stripping their machine guns blindfolded, they couldn't keep the scenes from being through Xelina's lens. And what that showed, if you paid attention, wasn't people fighting back. It was nature fighting back.

Mostly, it was in the backgrounds, or in little interstitial cuts:

A burning-down sun silhouetting the petrochemical arcade of industrial Houston.

Light and ozone, machines pumping, traffic jamming, toxins leaching.

A deformed pigeon eating trash. A nest of parakeets in a cell phone tower. An osprey fishing in a flooded river of trash.

Montage in silence at first, then the sound of Shatter beat slowly coming up. A mix that riffed the sounds of the city and the sounds of the field, ambient dissonance.

Scenes of the Tropic, the drought-blighted North, from a car in motion. Highway through dead brown going to grey, a thousand acres of dust.

Scenes of the Evac Zone, from an intrepid traveler on foot, right after the storms. A freeway underwater. A huge tanker, capsized in the Ship Channel, bleeding its contents out. A well on fire, half contained, half rogue, looking like it will burn forever, or until everything in the earth below is gone.

A butterfly on a prairie flower, smokestacks in the background.

A factory robot, lured out from its post and decapitated by a primitive axe that looks designed for that purpose.

A raccoon crawling under a fence, followed by a refugee white boy with a rifle.

Vines and fungi growing up along the side of a petroleum

storage tank. Camera eye climbs to the top edge. Inside, soil and new foliage flowering, like some secret valley in the world's biggest accidental planter.

A huge sinkhole, devouring the business end of a polystyrene plant.

Buffalo, a big herd, coming down the interstate, eating the median as they go.

An old Chevy sinking slowly into the bog of a wetland, tall grasses growing up through the busted windshield. A fox moves through the background.

A map of Texas, dissolving into green.

Pan out to the whole nation, then the continent, then the hemisphere, lines of political demarcation coming to animated life, then disappearing, replaced with topography.

Broyles looked less impressed than Donny. "Mr. Kimoe," he said. "Do you still wish to challenge the authenticity of this footage?"

"I don't dispute that the videos are real," said Donny. "But the connection to my client has not been established. Unless we are allowed to review and challenge the classified foundation that has been provided, this material should be excluded."

Bridget started to respond, but Xelina beat her to it. "I made them," she said. "And I'm proud of it."

Donny looked at her, but she didn't look back.

"I'm going to suggest you let your lawyer do the talking," said Broyles. "Unless I ask you the question."

In a normal court, the judges rarely asked the witnesses or the parties any questions. But this wasn't a normal court. It was a civilian version of a military tribunal, where the presiding officers often acted more like inquisitors. It suited Broyles.

"Ms. Kelly, do you have anything else for us this morning?"

"No, Your Honor. Just summation."

"Let's save that until we hear what Mr. Kimoe has to say."

"Your Honor," said Donny. "I'd like to make a motion to dismiss the government's case."

"I was afraid you would say that."

"The evidence they have provided this morning is insufficient to meet the standard in the statute and rules for the classification of Ms. Rocafuerte as an insurgent combatant."

"The standard for this initial determination is a reasonable belief that the accused has engaged in or advocated armed hostilities against the United States or any state or subdivision, or the secession of any territory. I'd say we have more than enough."

"There's a big difference between generalized political advocacy and bona fide calls to action," said Donny.

"There is a difference," said Broyles. "But not one we can afford to quibble over in a time of insurrection. At least not at this preliminary determination. You'll have time to argue those nuances at the denaturalization proceeding."

"What if we could establish that the real reason the government has detained Ms. Rocafuerte is to silence her as a witness to the murder of an opposition politician?"

Broyles perked up. "That would be a different matter," he said. He looked like he meant it. "If you could provide solid evidence to support that."

"I need more time to do that, Your Honor."

"Then you'll have to save that for trial as well."

"How about I let my client tell you about it?"

"You want to put her on?" said Broyles, in a way that suggested he thought it was a bad idea.

Donny was pretty sure he agreed.

■ ■ ■

As they swore Xelina in, looking almost too small for the witness box, Donny glanced back at the gallery to see who was watching. It wasn't too crowded that morning, but there were two suits sitting together in the back row taking copious notes, a bald man and a dark-haired woman. Donny recognized the woman as someone he had seen in there often, but never known who she was. They were always watching.

Court Security Officer Walton was watching, too. Sitting there at his station below Broyles, with his hand on the button. So Donny decided to start out far away from anything that had anything to do with the government. He might even catch Walton off guard.

"Ms. Rocafuerte," Donny asked, after laying out the basics. "Where were you born?"

"Here in Houston."

"In a hospital?"

"Memorial."

"How about your parents?"

"My dad was born in Mexico, and then lived in Honduras on and off. But my mom is from here."

"And her parents?"

"Same. Not Houston, but Texas. Corpus Christi."

"How far back does that go?"

"Forever, just about."

"Do you know how many generations?"

"My grandpa says nine generations on paper, but it goes back further. Because we were here before there was paper. Before people had to write their names and birthdays down in books to be tracked by the government."

"Before the Americans."

"Before the Anglos, you mean. Yeah. Before even the Mexicans, really. Just like a lot of people that so-called Americans call Mexicans."

"You're saying your family was here long before European settlement."

"Yeah, on both sides. On Mom's side, Grandpa says we were Penatekas. The Honey Eaters."

"The honey eaters."

"Yeah. Tougher than that sounds. We were the ones who came down from the north and pushed the Lipan across the border."

"'Indians.'"

"Yeah. I guess they called them Apache. I just learned about it when I was in middle school, and I'm still studying it. But when you realize you are an 'Indian' and you are not extinct, you see things differently."

Percy had flagged correspondence between Xelina and her friends talking about these subjects, giving him the idea to lay this foundation as a left-handed way to invert the government's narrative. Actually hearing it in person was different than he expected. And you could see Broyles was surprised. Maybe in a good way.

"Did your family have to go live on a reservation?"

"Some probably went to Oklahoma. Some to Mexico. But there weren't really any reservations here, in Texas."

"They took it all?"

"Grandpa said the family had to adapt when Mirabeau Lamar took over as President of Texas from Sam Houston and said he was going to bury every last Indian in the ground."

"President Lamar, the one the street a couple blocks over is named after."

"He didn't know we are seeds, said Grandpa."

That raised Broyles's eyebrows. Donny wondered if it was a bad idea, but he was already in the water.

"Is this part of what your work is about?"

"Yes, exactly. Once you understand that everything that you thought had been erased by the conquest is actually still here, waiting to grow back, it changes how you feel about the future."

"Growing, not fighting."

"That's all I'm trying to show in my videos," she continued. "Show the parts of that future that are already here, hiding in plain sight. Help us nurture it. Maybe if I was better at what I do, there would be less confusion about what I stand for."

"You're young, and these are confusing times. Am I correct that most of your videos are nature documentaries?"

"Yeah. I mean, most of them are too short to call 'documentaries,' more like just cool shots. But they try to show the remnants of the way this place was before, remnants that are still here, waiting to reclaim what was taken."

"My vision must be worse than I thought," said Broyles. "I thought those were bullets I saw, but they must have been butterflies."

"Banana clips, maybe," said Xelina. "If you mean the clips the prosecutor called the recruiting videos, that was a joke. Like a hoax."

"A hoax?" said Broyles.

"Yeah. You know how all those militia groups used to make their videos, back when they were calling for people to get rid of President Green, take our country back, all that stuff?"

"Like the People's Border Patrol?" said Donny.

"Exactly," said Xelina. "The Brownsville Boys, the Bellaire Rifles, all those dudes showing off their guns, helping round up refugees, police the border. I was just like, how would they like it if we did that?"

"Who do you mean by 'we'?" said Broyles.

"People like me, I guess," said Xelina, not falling for the trap. "People who aren't like them. Brown people. Black people. Poor white people, like those kids from the camps, the farmers and workers who lost it all to the drought. We're all 'Indians' now, and we're tired of being colonized."

"Then the guns weren't a hoax, were they?" said Broyles.

"They were real guns, but the people holding them weren't soldiers, or guerrillas. Not yet, at least."

"Were they 'Free Rovers'?"

"Some of them were Rovers, for sure."

"So you don't believe in countries, am I right?"

"Right. We don't believe in borders, or property lines."

"You just go where you please."

"When we can. It's more important that the animals get to go where they need to go. But we reject the legitimacy of boundaries in the land made by men."

"And all you did is make films trying to illustrate these ideas, right?" said Donny.

"I did that. And to do that, I went where I wanted."

"With your leader Gregorio."

"We don't do 'leaders.' And I don't follow any man. I go where I want to go."

"Tell us about Gregorio, Xelina," said Donny. "Tell the court what happened to him."

And then suddenly her voice sounded like she was talking backwards, inside a barrel, underwater.

Donny looked over at CSO Walton. The red light was on.

"Your Honor," said Donny, waving at Walton. "You already agreed this is relevant."

"I did," said Broyles. "But I don't get to decide what's secret. Mr. Walton?"

"Judge," said Walton. "This subject matter is off-limits. Top Secret, Grade Alpha."

"Oh," said Broyles, looking surprised at the designation. Grade Alpha was as high as it got for domestic operations. Donny had never seen anything at that level in this court. Maybe Broyles hadn't, either.

"Are you going to let them cover up a political murder, Judge?" He looked down at his cheat sheet, shorthand for the court's rules on classified evidence. "Why don't you have Mr. Walton give you the in camera review you're entitled to under 9.2? Then you can decide for yourself who has the facts on their side."

"Good idea," said Broyles. "Mr. Walton? I'd like to know what you have on this topic."

Walton looked at Broyles. Then he looked down at his notes. Then he looked at Donny. Or so Donny thought, until he realized Walton was looking at the suits in the gallery, behind Donny.

When Donny looked at them, only one looked back. The guy. He had the eyes of a predator, one that was controlled by machines.

"I'm sorry, Your Honor," said Walton. "You are not cleared for that."

Broyles raised his eyebrows. "Would you repeat that?"

"It's in the rules," said Walton.

Broyles didn't like that. No judge would.

"Turn on your noisemaker and get over here," ordered Broyles. "Or I will let this woman walk right now."

Walton looked at the back of the room again. Then the red light went on, and he got up and approached the bench from the side.

Broyles leaned over as Walton spoke to him, hand cupped

over the judge's ear so you couldn't even see his lips. Donny tried to read Broyles's expression. He kept a poker face. But then he looked at the man in the back of the room, and noticeably whitened.

"Very well," said Broyles. He cleared his throat. "Mr. Kimoe, I'm afraid you are going to have to try a different line of questioning."

"You know I'm right," Donny persisted. "What happened to Gregorio Zarate-Taylor is the real reason the government is keeping her."

"You have no idea what the government knows," said Broyles.

"They know how to pull your strings," said Donny.

Broyles reddened as he looked down at Donny. "Look at you, Kimoe. Seriously. You're an embarrassment."

Xelina was looking at him, too. It looked like she agreed. She was the one sitting atop the trapdoor, while Donny showed what happens when you think you can outsmart the referees who've already rigged the whole game.

"What happened to Gregorio is also the reason the government kidnapped me last night," said Donny.

Broyles shook his head. "No, it's not. Everyone but you seems to know why that is. They sent me a copy of your recording to listen to on my way into work this morning. You're lucky I allowed you to appear."

"It wasn't the way they make it sound," said Donny.

"I think it was," said Broyles, taking the face he usually saved for sentencing. "I can see as much looking at your disheveled and half-drugged mien here before me right now. A desperate man. Maybe even a bit deranged."

"Does this mean you're going to give me a new lawyer?" said Xelina. "Because I kind of agree."

"Not today," said Broyles. "Because you will be happy to hear I am satisfied, thanks to Mr. Kimoe's surprisingly and probably accidentally lucid line of examination, that you are not a combatant, but an advocate."

"Your Honor—" said Bridget.

"Hold on, Ms. Kelly," said Broyles. "I have also heard quite enough to be persuaded that Ms. Rocafuerte has revoked her citizenship, and qualifies for denaturalization on *that* basis."

"Your Honor," objected Donny. "That has not even been charged by the government."

"You forget that in this court I *am* the government, Mr. Kimoe."

"Could have fooled me," said Donny, looking at the suits in the back.

Broyles ignored him. "I am also persuaded by her admissions, which you so handily served up, that the defendant participated as a conspirator in the illegal occupation of United States government facilities in the Coastal Evacuation Zone, an act of insurrection." He held up a document. "All of which is substantiated by her confession, which is all we need."

"Obtained through unlawful means of interrogation," said Donny. "But I suppose your master Mr. Walton wouldn't let us talk about that, either—"

"In light of all this," said Broyles, talking over Donny, "I find that Ms. Rocafuerte's denaturalization should therefore be handled under the expedited procedures and interim detention authority of the Special Emergency Tribunal."

"You want to take away the citizenship of a woman whose family has lived here longer than this has been a nation?"

"To that I would remind you of what Justice Marshall concluded in such matters," said Broyles. "'Conquest gives a title which the courts of the conqueror cannot deny.'"

"A title stamped in blood," said Donny. "Perfected with cover-ups and lies. And cured in the cowardice of spineless jurists."

Broyles finally lost it. "Gregorio Zarate-Taylor was a traitor!" he yelled, the veins in his temples engorged with his anger. "And if he was killed by government agents, it was not murder. No more than was the execution of Jerome Hardy."

Thank you for getting your real feelings on the record, thought Donny. He wanted to keep pushing Broyles's buttons, but Xelina beat him to it.

"When we take over, we know who will be in the front of the line for execution," she said.

"And there we have it," said Broyles. "An aspiring Robespierre represented by an aspiring Oswald. I am afraid, Ms. Rocafuerte, that you will find my property lines rather harder to cross than the ones where you live, or in the abandoned quarters of the Zone where you like to go help your animal friends."

"You'd be surprised," said Xelina.

"Not as surprised as you will be as to the even harder time you will have getting through the barriers that will contain you in the place I am sending you now."

"I'm not afraid," said Xelina, not looking entirely convinced.

"You should be," said Broyles. "Because you are going to find out, too late to do anything about it, why they say it is the only sentence worse than death."

She definitely looked scared now.

Donny started to interject, but Broyles banged the gavel and ordered the court reporter to cut. Then he called the marshals to bring back the hood, and take the prisoner away to the prison so secret they didn't even let you know the name.

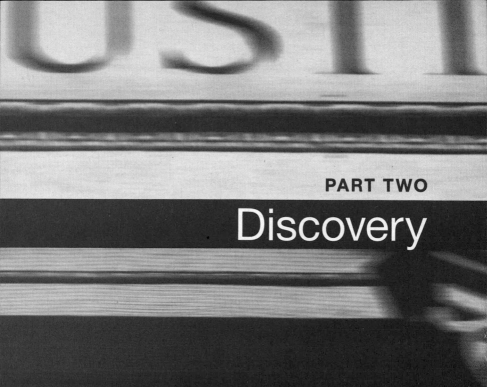

PART TWO

Discovery

21

THE MORNING AFTER THE HEARING, AS XELINA WAITED IN A COLD prison cell for her transfer to the insurgent detention facility, Donny went fishing in a concrete creek.

Houston was a city built on a swamp. A place where the pavement was either on top of the water or underneath it. Most of the homesites along the bayou were empty now, the idea of their occupancy ceded to the inevitability of the next flood. People who could afford it had been elevating their houses, as armies of entrepreneurial good old boys with pickup loans to pay and a will to conquer got into the business of adapting real property to the environmental future their grandfathers had endowed. People who could afford more than that started tearing down their old houses and building entirely new structures on stilts. The best of those were beautiful lattices of fractal steel rising up out of ferally landscaped tropical foliage, the kind of innovation Houston's zoning-free development culture fostered, beautiful and also sad in the message they sent about what was coming. The banks were behind it all, keen to believe in a viable future for the business of asset-backed securitization.

The irony of living in a city that was partly underwater for a good chunk of the year was not lost on Donny. He wondered how the quants in the skyscrapers did their present value calculations, in a world where the historical weather data the nerds had so studiously compiled over the years had lost almost all of its predictive power. Maybe someone was teaching the bots how to make their models factor in alligators sunning on the on-ramps of submerged freeways.

On mornings like that when he woke up early and sober, Donny would crack the books with a cup of coffee and do his best work, taking advantage of that hour after dreamtime when the big fish of the subconscious were still swimming close to the surface, ready to yield glimpses of the unconsidered possible. And as dawn began to seep through the flyover, Donny would grab his fly rod and walk down to the water where the real fish were waiting.

The first few casts in the morning were always the best, especially when they hit, when the lure would land right there for some big boy ready to bite. This stretch of the bayou was not paved in the channel, part of old Mayor Barthelme's awesome but unfunded plan to restore the waterways to a simulation of their natural condition, but there were roads running along the curve of both banks, and bridges in sight upstream and down. That time of year a lot of waterfowl were on the move, headed south or settled into the Texas tropics for the season, and it never got old to hear the quacking and flapping of a flock following the routes of the urban rivers. The herons and egrets were always out there, fishing alongside him as the planes took off in the distance and the Coast Guard choppers set out on their morning patrols. Sometimes Donny would see a big owl in this one tree on the opposite bank, watching the weird hairless ape do his loopy string-and-hook dance. And once in a while an osprey would show up, cruising over the creek, sharing intelligence about where the big fish were loitering.

The fish in that urban water were not beautiful, especially not the gar, and the way the water sometimes made your skin tingle was a good reminder not to eat them. The trash that showed up on the banks after the floodwaters receded—tires and lawn furniture and backyard toys, plastic bags filling the trees like toxic fruit, and a million plastic bottles bearing their invisible messages of the absence of human care—made you wonder what less visible pollution lurked in the dark channel. But those fish were fighters, hardy survivors adapted to this fucked-up place we made, and when Donny reeled one in on the barbless hook he would eyeball it, check for mutations, then give it a little massage and let it swim off. Catch and release was a concept largely alien to Texas, the only state Donny knew of that had included the right to hunt and fish and "harvest wildlife" in its Bill of Rights, a place where coming off the water without filling the cooler with your limit was a species of failure, but it made sense here. At least until the food in the stores ran out. That hadn't happened yet. But it had come close after Zelda, especially in the poorer parts of town.

Exercising his constitutional right to hunt was the root of how Jerome got into trouble with the law. When Donny first got the case, he already knew who Jerome was. He even had some of the old tapes, which were collectibles now. The first exemplars of a homegrown genre: Shatter, a jazzy avant-hip-hop that mixed found sounds from radio and TV and the noise of the city with fractured beats and electronic screech. It was regionally popular, but too edgy for radio. And too political, especially as Jerome got better at splicing up the words of the pols to sound like they were rapping their own funerals. Jerome started the Big Tree Hunt Club out of the back of his little record store on the East Side. Initially it was just him and his buddies doing the kind of stuff they had done as kids with their dads and granddads, trapping varmints and noodling big catfish in the interstices of the city. It morphed into a youth group, first with neighborhood kids, then with the kids in the resettlement camps.

Donny had failed Jerome in a lot of ways, but the one that really nagged at him as he tried to untangle his line from a truck spring embedded in the shallows was the way he had been unable to crack the government's theory that Jerome was part of the conspiracy to kill the President. Because it was too easy, and too convenient. But he never got to the bottom of it. And the way they rigged the rules against the defense was no excuse.

Maybe, though, it wasn't too late to prevent Xelina's case from being added to his list of failures, and, more importantly, to prevent another life from being stolen.

As he put the line out again he remembered what Xelina had said when they first talked, about how the real answers to our problems, the things we fight about and kill each other for, are in the land. In the way we treat the land as territory, the source of our security, our sustenance, and even our identity. You could see it there standing in the ancient river from which the twenty-first-century city rose, a city that had been made from the idea of the things you take from the ground you seize, a city whose ethos had been the motive engine of the wars and deals that had kept it alive, even as much of the country around it began to wither from the way that model had drained the fuel tank of the future.

The next steps for Xelina's case were clear. First, try to delay. Delay her transfer to insurgent detention, delay the denaturalization proceeding to follow, delay any aspect of the case that he could. Second, use that time to properly investigate her case. Build the evidence for Xelina's status as an observer rather than a participant. Find the footage, find other witnesses, and expose the killing of Gregorio. Maybe even find out who the killers were. It wouldn't be easy. He had maybe a week to work with before the machine would be grinding his new client up beyond the point where any legal remedy could help her. He had other clients whose cases also required his attention, clients he had neglected over the past weeks in his failed efforts to save Jerome. And he was broke, in a city where the fastest way to get information and aid was with cash in the palm.

What he really needed was a line of attack that would change the game for *all* of his cases. And the answer was there in front of him, in the way Xelina suggested, but in a way maybe even she couldn't quite see. The way the city, if you looked at it right, revealed the source code of the whole system. The way the towers and the pipelines and the power lines and the strip malls and the gated blocks and projects and the rivers and the freeways all grew from the law, from the way the system allocated access to the land, air, and water, and the other resources they contained. What you needed to do to really change the game was to hack that source code. It would take a smarter lawyer than Donny to rewrite the operating system—probably a whole army of them. But he might have a shot at extracting a nice ransom—and saving some people in the short term.

Conquest gives a title which the courts of the conqueror cannot deny.

That was what Broyles said when he unloaded at the end of Xelina's hearing. Donny knew the quote. Old Chief Justice Marshall, the venerated ur-father of the American judiciary, in one of those cases where he demonstrated his capacity for jurisprudential contortion to provide legal cover to take land from the first peoples of the American continent by force. The case Broyles quoted was the first big one like that, *Johnson v. McIntosh*, the one where the guys who had actually paid the Indians who lived there for most of the land that later became Illinois and Indiana, under a negotiated contract, were found to have inferior title to the developers who got it from the sovereign that had captured the whole continent—Marshall's "conqueror."

Donny knew why Broyles had quoted that, too. It was his answer to the idealism of Xelina and her Free Rovers. The thing was—and you could tell even Broyles knew it when he said it—that case was wrong. It was like the *Dred Scott* of real estate law. But nobody ever had the balls to say so, because if you did, it would break the whole American model.

He wondered if he could explain it to Xelina, who *wanted* to break the whole idea of America, in a way she would understand. Maybe. But first, he needed to focus on keeping her from being taken to wherever it was they were putting the people they decided no longer qualified as Americans.

He knew one thing: if he could protect her until the election fight was over, odds were good that the whole game would change. In the meantime, he needed to move fast. Because they knew that, too, and could be counted on to finish what they started before it was time to crank up the shredders.

22

AFTER SPENDING THE MORNING POLISHING UP HIS PETITION OVER a second pot of coffee and a very small dose of White-Out, Donny went down to the courthouse to file it in person. That was an inefficient way to do something that could have been done with a click on his office screen, the way the rules preferred things now be done, but he had his reasons.

The feds still had his car in evidentiary impound, and the soonest he would get that back would be the following day, when the initial hearing in his own case was scheduled. Miles told him he hoped to dispose of the matter without even having to do that. Donny wasn't counting on it, and he doubted he would ever see the car again. He wished he had time to take the bus. But he was stuck taking a cab to his office, where he had been keeping the ancient Oldsmobile he had accepted as payment in lieu of fee for guiding a friend's father's estate through probate.

The car's expansive hood was caked with six months' worth of Houston air pollution, but the engine underneath it started right up. The wipers scraped the gunk from the windshield like some old geezer rubbing the sand from his eyes, and when he turned on the radio it was still tuned to the easy listening station old Mr. Felcher had probably been blissing out to when he had the heart attack. Donny left it on there, hoping they'd have the midday news monologue from Harvey St. Cloud out of Omaha, the syndicated show that had been on the air longer than Donny had been alive and always finished with a wry twist that made even Harvey's most antiquated nationalist riffs seem clever. But then he remembered Harvey was dead, and Omaha was half-abandoned due to the drought. He turned off the Muzak and popped in one of Jerome's old tapes, which was a better motivator, even though the backbeat sounded like someone trapped in the engine trying to hammer their way out.

When he got to the courthouse, he looked for Turner. Cleburne said he was offsite that day. Donny asked why, and Cleburne said he wasn't sure, but he'd heard there was some kind of special training all the senior deputies had to go to. But he'll be at the bar tonight.

The clerk's office was on the ground floor. The files were mostly electronic, but the clerks were still buried in paper. Some of them were even armed with old-school stamps.

There was a window you walked up to for the regular cases, and a door you knocked on for the secret cases. Sometimes when you knocked on the door, you had to wait a very long time. But if you knocked a second time, chances were you would wait even longer.

Wendy came to the door after about five minutes. She was cranky when she opened it, and crankier when she saw who was standing there.

"Whatcha got, Kimoe?"

"Kind of an urgent filing, Wendy." He pulled the duplicate copies of the document from his briefcase.

She made a face. "Is that paper?"

"Yes," said Donny.

"We don't take those. You know that."

"Actually," said Donny, "there's a provision in the rules that allows it, in this type of proceeding. But I can file it electronically if you want. I just need to talk to you about how it's going to be routed, and if I leave you a hard copy it might help."

She made a different face.

"Trust me," said Donny.

"I don't know about that," said Wendy. "But come on back."

She waited until they were at her desk before she accepted a copy of the document.

"What's a Section 23–2 motion?" she asked.

"It's new, part of the Burn Barnes Laws that created the Special Emergency Tribunal."

"Gotcha," said Wendy, leafing through the pleading. "How do you say 'Xelina'?"

Donny told her.

"I hear they're processing a bunch of these cases a day now up there."

Donny nodded. "Afraid they're about to run out of time. It's scary stuff, Wendy. Most of them are kids."

"Dangerous kids."

"Not that dangerous."

"I hear they made a new camp to put 'em in," said Wendy. "Some emptied-out old petroleum storage tanks, out there in the Zone."

"I've heard that," said Donny. "I've heard other theories, too."

"I think this one's legit," said Wendy. "You know Bobby Kirk, in Facilities? His wife works with a guy whose brother helped build it. Says they already have like a thousand people out there."

"Could be," said Donny, half meaning it, and trying to use what she said to enlist her support. "That's why we need independent-minded judges looking into this stuff. Before they put us all in there."

Wendy raised her eyebrows, and looked back at the document. "And so you're appealing Judge Broyles again."

"Yes, ma'am."

"I heard how that worked out for you last time." She meant Jerome.

"This is different," said Donny, hoping he was right.

"Yeah, maybe this time it really will be your funeral."

Donny let that pass. He was worried about Xelina.

"Sorry," said Wendy. "You need to file this on NESTOR."

"Okay, but if I do that can you help me get it in front of the right judge?"

"Let me guess."

Donny nodded. She knew which judge he had in mind, without either of them having to say the name. It was better that way, since what they were talking about doing was prohibited.

"And why would I do you that favor?" said Wendy.

"Because you believe in justice."

She rolled her eyes.

"Because I'm your favorite lawyer."

"You're way down the list, son."

"Because I took your son Andre on a tour of the jail."

"That's actually true. And it worked."

"And I'm glad about that. But you should do it because it's the right thing to do. Read it if you want."

She did. Scanned every page, at least. When she was done reading she looked at the cover page again, then set it down and pulled out her rulebook. She opened it, found the section she was looking for, and read.

"So where's your new evidence?"

"It's in there. See the first exhibit."

"I saw that. That's like, nothing. Like a summary of nothing. Not even a page."

Sometimes the non-lawyers had better bullshit detectors than even the judges.

"I plan to supplement that before the hearing."

"Uh-huh."

"Seriously, Wendy. Cut me a break here. They make most of the evidence secret. Doesn't even matter that I have a security clearance. The game is rigged. I need to buy some time, and get in front of a judge who will give me—who will give my innocent client—a chance to show the truth of her case."

"You are so full of shit, Kimoe. Tell you what. You go file this thing on NESTOR. I'll take a closer look, and I'll keep an eye out, and see what I can do."

"Imagine if this was about Andre," said Donny.

"I already did, honey. And nothing is that simple."

23

THAT NIGHT DONNY WENT TO DETENTION, LOOKING FOR INFORMA-
tion for sale.

Detention was not what it sounds like. It was a nightclub, on the frontage road of the American Martyrs Highway south of downtown, with a theme that varied between after-school S&M fantasies and darker variations on prisoner and guard. It was a law enforcement hangout, especially popular with guards from the camps, FEMA cops, correctional officers, certain Coasties, and an assortment of other freaks who liked to pay to be locked up in cages and served drinks by naked people. It was a nasty place by any measure, and because this was Houston it was across the street from an elementary school, next door to a gun store, and around the corner from a child care center and one of the illegal abortion clinics that had been popping up with names like "Women's Health Center" since Governor Jackson signed the ban. Detention at least was coed, maybe because in its bones it was a place dedicated to hacking the usual power dynamics, or at least pretending to.

Donny had learned of the place from Joyce, of all people, who learned about it from a visiting colleague. They went in a group, Donny and a little posse of slumming theoreticians interested in documenting niche variations on human perversion the way biologists seek out weird bugs. One of them tried to show the others how he was not afraid to go native, and it got weirder from there.

Tonight the doorman was a posable action mullet with a corporate tattoo on one hairy forearm, the morale logo of a military engineering brigade on the other, and an off-brand automatic pistol that looked like it had seen some hard use sitting there between his hands next to the cash drawer. The proprietor was standing behind him, a tall lady with big white Texas hair who looked like a candidate for the sexy grandmas calendar and also reminded Donny of his third-grade math teacher, Mrs. Winterberger. This lady was packing, too, a snub-nose revolver tucked into the waistband of her shiny hip huggers. She sized up Donny while the doorman checked his ID, reading over his shoulder to see the details that matched the face. Donny wondered if maybe he should have changed out of his suit.

"You're that lawyer, aren't you?" said the lady.

"Which lawyer would that be, Mrs. D?" Donny had never met her, but he had heard the stories. The full name was Dombrowski.

"The defense lawyer. The one who helps terrorists."

"I guess you saw my ad in the Yellow Pages."

"You seem more like a Black Pages kind of guy."

"My reputation precedes me."

"Don't he, Andy? He looks a little off for a lawyer. A little bit of a blanker."

Action Andy looked at Donny and nodded, then went back to counting money.

"Some of the guys here were talking about you the other night, is how I know," said Mrs. D. "Saying how you used to be such a great lawyer, then you got soft and started working for traitors. And then you started using. Maybe it's just a rumor."

"Are you going to let me in, or is this an intervention?"

She laughed. "I'm just fucking with you, honey. But if you

157

want an intervention, I can hook you up. Just let me know what flavor of new friends you have in mind."

"Any chance I'll find Mac Turner in here tonight?"

"Not as a hookup."

"Gross."

She smiled. "You should have seen him back in the day, when we were all working for the General. He was a stud."

"Is he here?"

"At his usual table, over there in the back."

Donny stepped into the main room and found his way to the bar. The place was about half-full, under a throbbing strobe that alternated between red and white light at the same rhythm as a fire alarm, probably on purpose. Around two-thirds guys, but a fair number of women as well, including a table of lady prison guards confiscating their server's six-pack in violation of the no-touch rules. Maybe they were inspired by the live tableau on the stage, which looked to be a gender-inverted musical fantasia on the theme of the strip search.

Over the bar hung Old Glory, the Lone Star, the Coast Guard pennant, and the Gonzales Battle Flag—the one with the big fat cannon and the binocular-friendly legend daring the Mexicans to COME AND TAKE IT. Next to that was a hurricane-warped wooden plaque salvaged from the original resettlement camp in Memorial Park, with the Detention Corps motto.

HONOR BOUND TO DEFEND FREEDOM

Donny ordered a twelve-dollar tonic and lime and looked around the room until he spotted Turner, at a table near the wall laughing with two of his buddies.

"I hope Mrs. Turner knows where you are," said Donny as he walked up and put a hand on Turner's shoulder.

Turner smiled. "Just waiting for the traffic to die down."

His buddies laughed.

"Didn't think I'd ever see Donny K in this place," said Turner, looking at Donny but talking like he was addressing his crew. "I guess he just needed to have an extra shitty couple of days to need to blow off some steam the right way. Maybe get somebody to lock him up in the big chains, like his clients."

His buddies laughed, harder.

"Just wanted to see you in your natural habitat, Turner," said Donny.

"Well, then come on and have a seat," said Turner.

"Thanks," said Donny, grabbing the free chair. He shook hands with the other two guys. He didn't recognize either one, but they both seemed like they knew who he was.

Donny looked back at the stage. He recognized the emcee introducing the next act. It was a local rich kid turned silver-haired eccentric named George. He was the main investor in the place, according to Ward, who numbered George among his clients. With his disheveled blue suit, manic party mae-stro enthusiasm, and bow tie on the edge of untying itself, he looked like the coke dealer at the Yale Club. Which, according to Ward, he was.

The next act George brought out was a man wearing noth-ing but the collar to which his leash was attached. Donny turned to Turner.

"You come here every night?"

"Nah," said Turner. "Usually just on Tuesdays when they have the specials. Diane's husband and I served together in Iran, during the cleanup. May he rest in peace."

Donny tipped his drink.

"Everybody goes sometime," said Turner. "Speaking of which, I hope we're gonna see you at Judge Elwood's memorial."

"TBD," said Donny. "They've been keeping me pretty busy."

"So I heard."

"I'll definitely try to make it to the afterwake."

"Gotcha," said Turner. "They don't invite the help to those."

"Trust me, you're better off," said Donny. "Let me buy you guys some skin. And another round." He signaled the server, who was dressed in a barbed-wire bikini.

"That's real nice of you, Donny," said Turner, saying it like he meant it. He raised a glass, and the guys joined in.

"You doing as shitty as you look?" asked Turner, looking right at Donny.

"Shittier," said Donny.

"Not as shitty as your clients, sounds like."

Donny returned Turner's gaze. Those cold blue eyes glowing through flaps of pink middle-aged skin and government-issue plastic spectacles were not without sympathy. They reminded him of his high school cross-country coach standing there while he was puking after the first race, telling him "pain is weakness leaving the body."

"Nope," said Donny. "I'm the guilty one. They're innocent. Were, in Jerome's case."

"I can't believe they really did it," said Turner.

"Midnight Monday night," said Donny. "I was there."

"I heard you went a little loco," said Turner, raising his white eyebrows. "Loco enough for them to pick you up for questioning."

"Did you hear what they did?"

"Above my pay grade."

"Bullshit, Turner. You seem like you know everything that's going on."

"Just some of it. I hope they didn't give you any of the special treatment." He looked at the bondage scene onstage when he said that.

"They probably wanted to, but were afraid of blowback. They won't start torturing lawyers until they get done stealing the election."

Turner smiled. "Sounds about right. But doesn't sound like that's going to happen. No way they'll let the Governor call the election all by himself."

"Not if Miles Powell keeps beating him in court," said Donny.

"I figure that's why they went ahead and executed your client."

"For the elections?"

"Yeah, getting folks all amped up about how dangerous it will be if they lose. People love executions. Especially of traitors."

"He didn't kill anybody, Turner."

"He wasn't innocent. None of those people you represent are."

"Look around," said Donny.

Turner scanned the room, and smiled. "I getcha," he said.

"They just want a future that includes them," said Donny.

"Then they can fight to get our country back."

"There's like ten states north of here that are already dying, Turner. We can't fix that kind of broke all by ourselves."

Turner shrugged. "Whatcha gonna do about that little firecracker that popped off in the judge's face?"

"I'm gonna get her out, that's what. And make sure she's the last one, if I can."

"You got a few days, at least," said Turner.

"Before the elections get sorted out?"

"No, before they transfer her. They only take 'em out there once a week. Friday night flights, they call it."

Donny considered that, and wondered if he could figure out a way to get Broyles's order invalidated before then.

"Is it true what they say?" he asked. "About the ship?"

"Fuck if I know," said Turner. "They got so many levels of secret now in so many compartments, I don't even try to figure it out. I just want to get through the next three years, take my full retirement, and hit the road."

"In that trailer you bought?"

"Goddam right."

"Mac's gonna be one of them R.V. swingers," said the younger of his buddies, a wiry bald guy. "Hooking up in all forty-nine states."

"Sounds disgusting," said Donny. "No offense, Turner."

Turner laughed. "What're you looking for?" he asked. "I know you didn't come here for the show."

"You should be a psychic," said Donny. He leaned in, to where the others wouldn't hear him over the noise. "You really want to know?"

Turner nodded. Donny wondered if he was for real, or just luring him in.

"I need to examine some evidence they have on my client. Physical evidence, some of her personal property they confiscated. Just so I can have a shot at giving her a fair trial. It's not a secret, and I have a clearance anyway, so they're just playing bullshit games rigging the rules and you and I both know it. I was about to collect some duplicate copies when they picked me up, and made me watch while they destroyed it."

He looked for Turner's reaction, but he was just listening.

"Imagine if it were your kid," said Donny.

"My kid died," said Turner. "Fighting revolutionaries like

her on the other side of the border, before they infected our own country."

Donny shook his head. "This isn't like that, Mac. I'm telling you, she really is innocent, and I just need a quick look at this thing to be able to show it."

Turner nursed his beer.

"Think about it," said Donny. "Like you said, everyone can see how the election is going to be called. The curtain is about to come down on this whole dark episode. And trust me, I know what it's like when a political flip like that happens. I represented guys before the tribunals after the last one."

"I remember."

"So trust me, Turner, you're better off helping me than helping them. Having me owe you one could come in handy when the new regime comes around looking for scapegoats."

Turner looked at him with eyes that had seen the military detention camps that got some of those officers hauled in front of the tribunals. Then he looked down at his beer while he processed Donny's postulate, as if the label encoded the answer.

"I know a guy you could talk to," he said.

"I'm listening," said Donny.

Turner leaned way in, talking in Donny's ear. He wore the same cologne as Donny's great-uncle Vic, the one who smelled like dead flowers and Barbicide.

While Donny listened, some fat guy in his underwear was breaking out of the cage they had put him in on the stage, while George the emcee crooned that old Bobby Earl Lee song about how Freedom Isn't Free.

24

DONNY'S APARTMENT WAS IN MONTROSE, ON THE SECOND FLOOR of an old commercial building. His front window had a view of the bar across the street, a place called the Submariner. When Donny went to open the blinds and crack the window, he could hear the music from the bar. "Ebb Tide," the Tom Jones version, extra loud, one of Donny's favorites from the Submariner's well-curated jukebox of cheese. He sat there at the window and listened to it for a minute, momentarily forgetting his troubles as he imagined the water washing over, washing over them all. He looked down the street, remembering what it had looked like that summer when he woke up the morning after the first big deluge and saw that dude paddling a canoe toward downtown.

Right about where the canoe had been was where he saw the car. A red GMC Metron, just like the one he had been sure was following him after his meet-up with Turner, only to convince himself he was being paranoid. He had taken an alternate route just in case, cruising through the hospital district and then around the gated-off sections of River Oaks.

The car was empty, parallel parked there among the other cars in front of the bars. He couldn't see the license plates, or if there were any. The only people he saw were the guys hanging out at the tables in front of the Submariner.

He closed the blinds, and then looked out the back windows at the alley. He saw motion at the edge of the light, then looked more closely and saw it was a little screech owl sitting on the power line. Donny's Oldsmobile was there under the lamp, undisturbed. He checked the locks on the door, looked through the peephole at the empty landing, then checked the view from the bathroom window, and decided to stop worrying and see if he could get some work done. The Metron was an exceptionally common car, not just in the fleets of government agencies—perfect fodder for the kinds of urban legends people invent to explain strange times.

Donny kept a bigger law library at home than at the office. Part of the reason was many of the volumes in his collection were ones you weren't supposed to have—precedents of the secret court that were never supposed to leave the courthouse, documents from the underground, and his collection of banned books.

One of the banned books was sitting there on his armchair, underneath the liner notes from one of Jerome's old tapes that he had been reading Sunday night, which now seemed weeks in the past instead of days. As he put the notes back in their little plastic case, Donny morbidly wondered whether the value had already gone up. He went to get the tape from the deck, and thought about playing it again, only to decide he wasn't ready yet.

He had forgotten what book it was he had been reading as he stayed up that night sleeplessly waiting for news until he fell asleep in his chair and then overslept for morning call. *Stay Hungry* was one of the newest and craziest tomes in Donny's collections, a chapbook of free verse by an American transient known only as Benjamin O. The energetic and explicit riffs on outlaw sex under freeway overpasses and in convenience store restrooms were what had gotten it banned, but the page Donny had had it open to when he zonked out was the thing that should have gotten it banned—a poem titled "Beautiful Boys," a not-so-coded ode to the refugee kids who tried to kill the President. There was a passage that floridly traced the bullet that got blocked by one of the martyred agents, and another that envisioned the buttered popcorn paradise that awaited the boys.

Donny closed that as the melancholy flashback came on, and put it back on the shelf where it belonged between *Horizonte Verde,* Brigada's novel of eco-revolution that got him locked up in a Panamanian prison for seven years, and *The Free Rebels,* a rogue translation of *The Aeneid* by some high school Latin teacher who had reimagined the story of the retreat from Troy and the search for a new national home as a prescient allegory for the founding of the American republic—an allegory infused with the ultranationalist ideas that had taken fire after the loss of the war. On the next shelf, Donny found what he was looking for: the notebook he had labeled MARTIAL LAW.

The document he was looking for in there wasn't about martial law per se. It was a government memo outlining the basis on which large swaths of the state could be declared off-limits based on bad weather. Donny hadn't printed all the appendixes that detailed the damages to the area they had fenced off—just the list at the end of the memo ran almost thirty pages of single-spaced text listing chemical spills, poisoned groundwater, failed bridges, power generation and transmission systems destroyed beyond repair, indefinitely fouled municipal water supplies, whole subdivisions of housing stock rendered uninhabitable due to water damage and rerouted tributaries. There was a map that showed the locations, islands in red scattered densely across the state east and south of Houston. And out in the Gulf, the much bigger zone where the spills were still spilling, like someone had slit the wrists of the Earth in the warm bathtub of those turbid waters.

The message they had given the public was that those areas would be off-limits until the necessary repairs had been made. The problem was, the state and federal governments didn't have the money to pay for the repairs. So the memo, written by a committee of lawyers supporting the interagency task force charged with coming up with a plan, went in a kind of unexpected direction. It started with a lengthy distillation of the governments' emergency powers and how they provided a sound basis for temporarily seizing any properties as reasonably deemed necessary for public health and safety. It noted the state constitutional authority of the Governor to declare martial law in those areas where normal government could not be administered and the courts could not be kept open. But then there was this footnote that ate up a couple of pages all by itself, going off about how the governments could use their power of eminent domain to permanently seize the properties and sell them as-is for "rehabilitative redevelopment."

First the eviction, then the auction. And you could bet with public officials on one side and real estate types on the other, it would be a process rife with opportunities for corruption. Especially when you considered the value of some of those sites. The majority were industrial, and most of those related to the nation's energy supply, places whose restoration to full capacity was urgent. Some were parklands, mostly along waterways, slivers of habitat that had never been amenable to development. And then there were the huge acreages along the coast that had been devoted to commercial and military space launch operations and already closed down long before Zelda by the treaty that ended the war.

One of those, the HKBR Space pad just south of Galveston, was next to the national wildlife refuge where Gregorio had led his weeks-long illegal occupation. Donny thought about what Ward had told him, and wished he had been more specific about where.

There was a second footnote in there, almost a footnote to the footnote, and that was the one Donny had really been looking for. A succinct recitation of how it was that all real estate in the state, and the whole country, was ultimately owned by the government, and everyone else just had a kind of permission to occupy it or extract resources from it or both. An idea at the base of American law that went all the way back to William the Conqueror divvying up England among his victorious warlords. But one that, when you dug down to the roots, had no principled basis—just whatever force had been able to take it and keep it. If you could expose the flaws behind that premise, it would upend the whole system.

Donny must have been there an hour taking notes at his kitchen table before he heard the yelling outside and went to look. And when he peered out at the street, that red car was still there, and he still couldn't see if it had plates. He decided it was time to go take a closer look.

He walked down the block like he was out for a stroll, looking down the long straight sidewalks for signs of suspicious characters, but seeing none. It didn't help that the street lighting left big stretches of shadow.

When he got to the corner, he cut back toward the car and the bar. A couple of guys were walking in his direction, laughing, then they cut between the cars and jaywalked over toward the other side of the street where Donny's apartment was.

Donny slowed when he got to the car. No one seemed to be watching.

It had plates. Basic Texas plates, not government. The windows were darkly tinted, which was not unusual in sun-scorched Texas. He looked around again and then used the flashlight on his phone to peer inside. It was tidy, almost too tidy, but for the air freshener tree hanging from the rearview mirror. That and the plates made him conclude it was probably just some civilian's generic car, and he could relax.

The blue neon of the Submariner beckoned, close enough that you could hear the crackle of the lights out front.

The Submariner was Montrose all the way, a place that combined a superhero fetish theme with a sense of climate-change languor. Like it was always last call at the end of the world, the superheroes had given up the fight and decided to get drunk instead, and that was a good thing. The summer before, Donny and Joyce would hang out there on hot nights when the power company had started imposing rations, staying up too late shooting the shit with friends at the sidewalk tables under the misters. The place had been converted from an old gas station, so they would throw open the big garage doors and even from the outside you could sit there and watch the beautiful men swimming in those giant aquarium tanks they had installed. Joyce liked that so much that Donny half-expected to see her there as he walked up. She wasn't, so he grabbed a stool at the bar.

"Hey, Donny," said Vonda, the bartender. "Haven't seen you in here since election night."

"Geez, that seems like a memory from another reality now."

"It'll be over soon."

"I hope you're right."

"What are you having?"

"How about one of those Atlantean Dreams."

"You want that all the way?"

Donny wrestled with that proposition, but not for long. "Yeah, why not. It'll help me finish the work I still need to get done tonight."

"Gotcha," she said, with a friendly wink. "Back in court in the morning?"

"Yeah, but tomorrow I'm the defendant."

"Whoa," said Vonda. "What happened?"

"I got a little carried away arguing another case."

"Sorry to hear that. Let me get you your medicine."

The swimmers had the night off, and without the back-light the aquarium glass let you see the reflections of the bar behind you without having to turn around. Donny checked out the crowd that way, and saw only a sparser version of the usual scene—a few of the neighbors and some coupled-up dudes. So when the cocktail came, he felt safe enough to see where it took him.

Vonda's mixology was not always entirely legal, but it was usually safe.

The brain bomb went off pretty quickly in this mix, like the soft distant boom of the explosions you sometimes heard at night at the edge of town, sounds some people said were demolitions of storm-damaged buildings and others said were signs of fighting with the emerging underground. Donny could feel the ends of his neurons light up just a bit, while the stress of the week started to bleed off like a hearty sigh.

The jukebox was playing "Iguanas of London," while the TV screened a grainy old video with the sound off. Some dude in a chain-mail Speedo, free swimming like a man-porpoise down to the ruins of an ancient city at the bottom of the sea.

That got Donny wondering, if you found Atlantis, who would own it?

He thought about all the wild theories there were about

different groups that had "discovered" America, from the lost tribes of Israel to the Chinese admiral to Frank Dodd and his Front Range Vikings. About the fights governments had about who owns the moon. About the Honey Eaters, who pushed the Lipan across the Rio Bravo. About who really owned the land on which that bar sat. Behind the myths of discovery were the truths of violent conquest and colonization, justified by force rather than law. It was there in the place names, some given by the people who lived there before, others by the soldiers who first secured the territory. Someday all of that history would be up for a fresh legal reckoning.

Donny thought about how you would make that case. Then he looked at the TV and decided it was about as likely as a man being able to breathe underwater.

That was when he looked back at his own home, which he didn't even own, thinking about the unfinished work that awaited him, as quixotic as it was. And in the window, he saw the silhouette of a guy standing there in his living room.

He looked for Vonda to see if she saw it, too, but she was in the back.

When he looked back, the figure was gone.

Donny ran from the bar, straight across the street, up the stairs to his door. It was locked. He turned the deadbolt and the knob, then put his keys in his fist so the edges stuck out between his fingers like claws, the way he'd seen somebody do in a movie once.

Then he opened the door, slowly.

"Hey!" he yelled. "What the fuck are you doing in here! I just called the cops!"

Nothing.

It was empty. The place was easy to check, just the living room, bedroom, and bath.

He looked out the window, and the red Metron was gone.

The light bent for a second as he scanned down the street, and he cursed the enhanced cocktail.

It was only when he sat back down at his table with a fresh cup of coffee that Donny saw the note. It was there marking the page of the notebook he had been reading from. A business card, but with no identifying information, just a printed image of a cartoon wolf in a tuxedo.

Someone had written a message on it in ink pen.

"Don't forget your oath."

He was looking up the Texas lawyers' oath, wondering if they meant the part about upholding the law or the part about demeaning himself honestly, when the phone rang.

"Hey, Donny," said the voice on the line. "It's Walker."

"Hello, Ward."

"Sorry I didn't get back to you sooner."

"Right," said Donny. "It's okay. Honestly, I got so busy I forgot all about it. I can try to take a look at your contract tomorrow. It's been a rough week."

"I heard."

"What do you mean?"

"I talked to my guy, like you said. About you know who."

He meant Gregorio.

"He said anyone who even asks about that must want to go on a trip. The kind you don't come back from."

"Who's the guy, Ward?"

"A customer."

"Law enforcement?"

"Nothing like that at all. A businessman. Local, one of my oldest and best customers."

"A real pillar of the community."

"You'd be surprised. Point is, this guy is super plugged in. And I think he knows what's going down."

"So who did it?"

"He wouldn't say. Instead, he started asking me questions."

"You didn't tell him about me, did you?"

"He already knew all about you, dude. Or so it seemed."

"Jesus, Ward."

"Shit's getting dark out there, Donny. A whole lot of self-help, if you know what I mean."

"Frontier justice. So I'm learning."

"'We don't need no badges' kind of justice. You follow?"

"I'm starting to get the picture."

"Call me tomorrow after you look at that contract. And be careful."

"I'll try."

When they hung up, Donny looked again at the card the intruders had left. He thought about all the modes of intimidation the human species had invented. He figured it was the combination of Vonda's Atlantean Dream and the silent recitation of his duties as a lawyer that got him to grab his laptop, crack the books, and use the fear to fuel the new claim he had in mind. If they were going to read what he was working on, he might as well see if he could scare them back.

25

MILES HAD DONNY MEET HIM AT THE COURTHOUSE EARLY, BEFORE
eight. Donny waited on one of the benches in the main hallway,
just past security, watching the eye watch him. Miles was late.
Miles was never late.

"You get stood up again, Kimoe?" said Turner.

Donny looked over at Turner, who was sitting at his station
watching the closed-circuit feeds. There was a red blinking light
on one of the monitors, and you could see a prisoner transfer in
progress on the black-and-white screen, as four guards carried
a shackled guy wearing a hood and headphones out one of the
basement doors into a waiting armored car.

"Only by you, Turner," said Donny.

"Hang tight, big mouth. I'll be in touch."

"Today would be good."

Turner looked at him and rubbed imaginary bills between
his finger and thumb.

Donny thought about giving him the finger, but opted for a
thumbs-up. If he got lucky with his petition, he might not have
much time to get together the new evidence his filing promised. And if he blew that shot, he would likely never get another. Xelina would be gone.

There was another screen there on the lobby wall, running
the live feed from Eagle News Net, in that new ultra high resolution that made everything look realer than real life. They had
a clip from the President, touring the scene of a bombing the

night before at the federal building in New Orleans. Donny tried to tell if the guy was wearing makeup, or if he really looked that good. Donny hadn't heard about the bombing, but those kinds of incidents were as common as mass shootings these days, maybe even more so, and he was only slightly ashamed to find himself watching to see if they identified any potential suspects he might be able to represent. But they didn't give any names. Just the President saying whoever did it were terrorists, and answering the question about the election fight by saying his only focus was protecting the American people from "the enemy within."

The elevator pinged, and out stepped Miles, almost smiling.

"I expected to see you coming from the other direction," said Donny, meaning the front door security checkpoint.

"I got here early," said Miles. "And you are all set."

"All set, as in postponed?"

"As in no charges. I talked to Broyles. Caught him as he was coming in to work."

"You stalked him outside his chambers?"

"I don't stalk people. Especially not members of the federal bench. He was happy to talk about it."

"Ex parte?"

"He got the prosecutor to come down and join us in his chambers before we wrapped."

"You are untouchable. Broyles loves you."

"Actually, he loves you. Or at least cuts you a lot of slack."

"Could've fooled me."

"He said you pissed him off in court this week, but he knows you didn't mean any actual threats on the President."

Donny looked at the President's face still talking on the screen, and wondered if that was really true.

"Motive, not means."

"Come on, Donny."

"Sorry."

"The AUSA agreed. No charges."

"Bridget?"

"No, that new guy that just came in from Washington. McAuley."

"Haven't met him yet."

"Kind of a hard-ass."

"More than Bridget?"

Miles nodded. "He initiated a review of your security clearance, Donny. And said he's recommending you be added to the Secret Service watch list."

"What?"

Miles held up his hands. "Be glad they're not going after your license. Broyles had your back."

"You had my back. Broyles just feels guilty for being party to the insane shit that is going on in his courtroom."

Miles looked at the screen behind them. "Just when we thought we couldn't get any busier," he said.

Donny nodded, but his mind was on other things. Like whether it was a good thing to be protected by Broyles, or a sign of his own moral failings. His failure to pick a side. His willingness to serve a corrupt system moving rapidly into shadow.

"Broyles is going to be pissed when he hears what I pulled in that detainee case you got the free pass on Monday."

"Oh, yeah," said Miles. "I was going to ask you about that."

"He screwed us over, so I filed a Section 23–2."

"I know," said Miles, his mood changing. "I'm glad you reminded me. I was going to ask you what the hell you thought you were doing putting my name on that."

Donny had meant to tell him, and forgotten.

"How did you find out? Tell me Broyles didn't tell you."

"I just got a notice from the court this morning, on my

way down here. Telling me I'm supposed to be here tomorrow afternoon at 2:30 in front of Judge Jones."

"Awesome!" said Donny, standing.

"The hell it is," said Miles, pointing a thumb at the screen. "I have oral arguments in front of the Fifth Circuit tomorrow."

"They're already hearing the appeal in the election case?"

"A piece of it, yeah, the martial law issue. How else do you think you get things moving that fast? At least somebody else wrote the briefs. And at least I don't have to go *there*." He pointed at the TV. The smoldering bomb site on screen was across the street from where the Fifth Circuit heard appeals out of the region, until the storms and the fighting caused its recent relocation to Houston.

"Well, I don't need you tomorrow," said Donny.

"I might be better off staying home. Between the threats from the President's supporters, and you signing me up to represent insurgents I haven't had a chance to vet, I'm starting to regret taking on these political cases."

"Sorry, Miles. I should have asked first. But this one is not like those bombers. And I figured it was okay to put your name on her case, because one, you were already on it and they hadn't taken your name off even though Broyles reassigned it, and two, the client actually asked for you instead of me—"

"Really?"

"Yes, she was fangirl raving about your handling of the Refugio Five case."

"We got lucky on the coverage on that one," he said.

"The third reason is, you owe me after stealing my paralegal."

"She came to us, Donny."

"Fine, poacher man. Just help me on this one. Because I have an even crazier thing I want to file. One of those world-changing

Hail Marys we used to talk about when we believed changing the world was possible. I sent you the brief. Kind of a work in progress. If you could just look at that, it would be a huge help. It's all I ask."

"Okay, but you need to promise me the same thing Broyles told me to make you promise."

"What's that?"

"Remember your oath."

Donny was stunned. It took a minute to react.

"Broyles said that?"

"Yeah," said Miles. "Those exact words. I told him it was excellent advice, right on the money."

Donny looked at the electronic eye above the TV. Then he looked over at Turner, who turned and smiled.

"I need to get out of here," he said.

"Me too," said Miles.

They got up and walked for the exit. As they stood there at the waist-high barriers waiting to be buzzed out, Turner looked at Donny and held his thumb and pinky to his head. Call me.

Miles had his driver there waiting in the Town Car, just past the barricades. Donny thanked him again, for real this time. As Miles drove off, Donny got his phone out to check for messages, and then wondered if he should toss the thing in the sewer. And then he looked up in the sky to see if he could spot the helicopter he heard.

When you started looking for the eyes, there were a lot more than you realized.

Maybe, Donny thought, there was a way to use that to his advantage.

26

THE DOGS WERE STILL THERE WHEN DONNY DROVE BACK TO XE-
lina's place. Three Chihuahuas, taking turns charging into
the middle of the street thinking they could scare him off.

Donny did his best to ignore them, and shuffled through
the ruins looking for things that might have survived. The
smell of smoke was intense. He found an old coin, some cheap
jewelry, pieces of plates, and a glass bottle. He was standing
there holding a melted video disc wondering if he might be
able to salvage any of the data when he felt the chomp on
his leg.

He yelped, then kicked the little dog with his other foot.
It yelped back, not as bad as Donny. He saw when it was on its
back that it was an intact male. Then it got back up and charged
him again, stopping short this time.

"Fuck off, Cujito!" yelled Donny, doing his best to be
scary.

"Hey!" said a woman's voice from across the street. "Stop
hurting my dogs!"

Donny looked. "This little bastard bit me!" he said.

"Well whadja expect snoopin' around in other people's
yards?"

She was a white lady, late sixties maybe, with hair the color
of cigarette smoke.

The presence of their owner gave all three dogs more

confidence, and suddenly they had Donny surrounded. He tried growling, and it seemed to have some effect. He walked out to the sidewalk to meet the lady, who soon had two of the dogs in the pocket of her robe and the one with the cojones in her arms.

"Look," said Donny, pulling up his pant leg and pulling down his sock so she could see the wounds. It looked like he had been attacked by the world's tiniest vampire.

"Sorry," she said, after taking a minute to size him up. "They've been real jumpy since what happened. Especially Aldo, 'cause he's so protective." She stroked the monster. "Aren't you, Aldo." It licked her back.

"It's okay," said Donny, pulling his sock back up. "We all get a little jumpy these days."

"Who are you?" she asked.

"I'm a lawyer. I represent one of the girls who lived here. Xelina Rocafuerte."

"You look like a lawyer," she said, like it wasn't a compliment.

"Good, because lately I feel like I'm faking it. You live here?" he asked, pointing at the house across the street.

She nodded. "Nineteen years."

"Wow," said Donny. "A real survivor, sticking it out so close to the Evac Zone."

They both looked at the fence at the end of the street. In the daylight you could see what lay beyond. A bridge over a creek that had been washed out, old warehouses on the other side, and some derelict LNG tanks in the distance, like the broken eggs of some Japanese movie monster.

"I don't know where else I'd go. Everything else is so dang expensive with all those damn people coming here from every other part of the country."

"I hear you," said Donny. "But you know they closed the borders to try to get that under control."

"Too late if you ask me. They oughta put some piranhas in the Red River. See how they like that."

"You should write the Governor and pass along the idea. You might be surprised."

"Is Xelina the one with the crazy hair?" she asked.

"Yes," said Donny. "I mean, I think so. I haven't met the others."

"If you came here looking for her, you're wasting your time. She's gone."

"So I see. The whole house is gone."

"I know. Woke me up. Took forever for the fire trucks to get here. But they still got that trailer in the back there."

"Where's that?" asked Donny.

"Down that drive," she said, pointing at some parallel tracks that went around the far side of the yard into the trees behind. "That lot's real big. Backs up to the creek."

"Gotcha," said Donny. "I'll try back there. Maybe her friends are still around."

"You can try, but they all cleared out."

"You know where they went?"

"Hell no. Off to make trouble someplace else. Or jail, it sounds like."

"Something like that," said Donny. "Did you see any of this happen?"

She looked at the scorched site. "No," she said, looking at the dog in her arms.

"You mean to tell me Aldo there didn't set off the alarm?" said Donny. "If he went after me like that, I'd hate to imagine what he'd do to some guys with guns."

She stroked the dog more intensely. You could see the feeling coming up.

"You know what they did? They Tasered him! Tasered a little sweet dog!"

She ran her hands over the welts on Aldo's shoulder, which Donny hadn't noticed. They were bigger than Donny's bite.

"Tough dog," said Donny. "Glad he's okay."

Somehow knowing that he had recently been electrified made the dog's crazy eyes seem more likable. They looked extra crazy when she kissed him again.

"So did you see that?"

"I don't want to talk about it."

"When did it happen?"

"Thursday night."

"When they came for Xelina."

She nodded.

"Police?"

She shrugged, and got a weird look on her face.

"What kind of cars?"

"Government cars, I guess. Red. Smaller than cop cars."

"How many people?"

"A bunch. Maybe eight. Just the two cars."

"No uniforms?"

"Nope."

"Weird."

"It's because those girls were terrorists, isn't it? That's what kind of cops those were."

"I don't think they were terrorists," said Donny. "I think the government is looking for terrorists, and thought these young ladies might have some information."

"Well, they took that Xelina one with 'em. Carried her out. I couldn't even tell which one it was because they had her wrapped in some black blanket. Then I saw the other two after."

"Did you talk to them?"

"No. I minded my own business. Then in the morning I saw them leave. The one boyfriend came and got 'em in his truck. The one who used to always be up to whatever kind of no good back there in that trailer."

"You know his name?"

"Nope. Don't care to."

"You mind keeping your dogs in for a while so I can go check back there?"

"I guess, if you're really her lawyer."

Donny pulled a business card from his pocket and handed it to her. "What's your name, ma'am?"

She read the card, then sized him up again. "Nina Pritchard," she said.

"Okay, Mrs. Pritchard," said Donny. "Thanks for talking to me. If you see any of those girls, or the guy, or anything else you think I might want to know, will you call me?"

He had a hundred-dollar bill in his hand when he said that. She grabbed it before Aldo could.

"Sure," she said.

"Thanks," said Donny.

There was a loud boom in the distance, off in the direction of the Zone. They both looked, but didn't see anything.

"What was that?" asked Donny.

"I don't know," she said. "I've been hearing noises like that since summer, seems like. I just figure they're blowing up the stuff they can't fix."

"Maybe," said Donny.

He looked back at the scorched yard of the ghost house. "Hey, look at that," he said, squatting down to the burnt grass. There was a green sprout just emerging from the black earth, a few fuzzy little leaves he recognized. "Bluebonnets. There's another one, over there. They'll be blooming before you know it."

He looked up, but Mrs. Pritchard was already headed inside.

27

HAVING ALREADY SUFFERED ONE DOG BITE FOR THE DAY, DONNY
decided to drive down the path through the trees. He was glad
he did, because it was farther than he expected.

It only took a couple of minutes, but by the time he got into
the little grove where the trailer was, just like the lady said, it
felt a little like he had passed into a different time. Maybe because the old aluminum camper looked like it had been parked
there for decades, and somehow at the same time looked ready
to run for the border at a moment's notice. But maybe it had
been left behind, after Donny had drawn the vengeance of the
state back to this spot.

The trailer wasn't the only thing hidden in that grove.
There was an ancient German military truck sitting in the dirt
with the hood off and the engine out, for what looked to have
been a long time, a couple of empty parking spots with fresh
tracks in the gravel, and a foldout table in the yard with four
chairs and one coffee cup, but no other sign of people. It was
only after he got out that Donny noticed the dog bowl, and the
bone that looked about the size of his femur. But not a bark or
a rustle, just more dull noises in the faraway distance and a
couple of cardinals alerting the woods behind the trailer to the
arrival of a stranger.

The name on the front of the trailer above the hitch was
ARGO, spelled out in squared-off letters cut from some lumi-
nescent material long past its half-life. It was boxy and angled,

leaning forward over the hitch, and when you peeked through the cloudy old glass you could see the warm patina of wood paneling from old forests, warmed up further with hand-woven draperies in the colors of a happier culture. Donny stepped up onto the entry block made from flotsam wood and knocked, not expecting an answer and not getting one. Through the porthole he saw plates stacked to dry, a little portable color TV hooked up to some weird old deck, almost like a cross between a VCR and a ham radio, a vintage assault rifle with a wood stock and a banana clip leaning up against the table, and a kitchen cart set up with a gunsmith's reloader. Donny looked toward the back of the trailer, but saw only darkness.

The gun was the most likely sign that whoever lived here was coming back.

Behind the trailer toward the woods was a little shorty storage container, white paint turning green and blue paint turning the color of the polluted sky. You could still read the faded-out brand of BREMEN OST. Donny was about to walk back there when he heard another vehicle rumbling down the lane, and decided he better wait in his car.

He watched the Ford pickup roll up in the rearview mirror, and wished he'd thought to park facing out. The driver was a white guy with a ball cap, and a big grey dog riding shotgun. Donny stayed in the car, which was a good idea because about fifteen seconds later the dog had jumped out of the open window before the truck even came to a stop, jumped up on the door, and started to see if it could get through the glass to Donny, who grabbed his briefcase from the seat and held it in his lap ready to serve as a shield. When he looked up again the guy was standing there looking down at him with hard eyes. Then the guy almost smiled, knocked on the window, and put a calming hand on the dog.

"What do you want?" said the guy, Texas all the way down. Young, but older than Xelina, with longer hair and wily eyes.

Donny cracked the window just far enough to properly converse, but not far enough for the dog to get through.

"I'm looking for family and friends of Xelina Rocafuerte."

"Is that right," said the guy. "And who the fuck are you?"

Donny noticed the guy's belt buckle, cowboy brass embossed with the image of a barbarian riding a unicorn. Hanging from the belt was a knife, fixed blade, with what looked like a hand-tooled hilt. Donny wondered where you go to find the rodeo where they lasso unicorns, but thought maybe he should wait to ask about that.

"I'm her lawyer. My name's Donny Kimoe." He pulled a business card from his suit pocket and slipped it through the gap. "You must be Clint."

The guy didn't answer that. He just read the card, looked at Donny, looked back at the card, then looked up at the road. "Guess that explains the suit."

"Yes, it does," said Donny. "I just came from the courthouse."

"Where is she?" said the guy, a different look in his eyes now.

"Let me come out and tell you," said Donny. "If Fenrir there will let me."

"His name's Wayway," said the guy. "He's Xelina's dog. And yeah, I'm Clint. I'm Xelina's roommate."

They shook hands as Donny stepped out of the car and Wayway—or maybe it was Huehue, Donny thought—took an inventory of the scents on his trousers and shoes, and the accumulated intoxicants sweating out through his fingers. He wondered if the dog could pick up any trace of Xelina.

"Grab a seat," said Clint, leading him to the outdoor table. "The place is kind of a mess. I've been going a little crazy trying to figure out where the fuck they got her."

"Well, she's alive," said Donny. "They brought her in for questioning. And accused her of being an insurgent."

"I knew it," he said. "Those motherfuckers." He had two fists out on the table, clenching tighter.

"My job is to get her home. And maybe you can help me."

"I'll help get her out, all right. But I betcha talking about it isn't going to get the job done."

Donny decided to be honest. "Well, it didn't work for me this week, partly because Xelina decided to give the judge a lecture."

Clint looked at him. "Sounds about right," he said.

"But I have another shot. Different judge. Nicer judge."

"Uh-huh," said Clint. "Is that kind of like good cop and bad cop?"

"No. It's different. It's about the possibility of getting a fair shake. Of justice." He raised an eyebrow at the word.

"Where do they got her now?"

Donny paused. "She's still in federal custody. Currently at the annex downtown, but they're getting ready to transfer her to this new detention center they have set up for denaturalization cases."

"They gave her to the fucking Coasties?"

"Not yet," said Donny. "I'm hoping to keep it from happening."

"With words. The 'nice' judge."

Donny nodded. "Tomorrow afternoon. Before the Friday evening transfer is scheduled."

"Uh-huh. You know where that place is they want to send her?"

"Not exactly, and if I did I wouldn't be able to say, because it's secret. I know it's new. This whole system is new, and hard to keep up with, because they change the rules every day. But yes, you are probably right that the Coast Guard is part of it. Them and other agencies on the Task Force."

"I'll tell you where they want to take her," said Clint. "They got a fucking ship. Right out there." He pointed off toward the Zone, in the direction of the coast. "Just far enough you can't see it, which I betcha means just far enough that lawyers like you can't do anything about it."

"It's a secret, like I said. So secret they won't even tell lawyers like me where it is. But I've heard the rumors. That one and other ones. They already have people behind the wire in those resettlement camps. It's not a big stretch. And it's happened before. It's just been a while since they did it to Americans."

"They're more than rumors, pal. I know a guy who talked to some guys who make deliveries out there. Seen the prisoners lined up on the deck, eyes and ears and the whole fucking deal, just like those JSOC mothers used to do to the enemy when I was in Panama. Sensory deprivation, they call it. You got to be fucking kidding me."

"I'm sorry," said Donny. You could see the raw feeling welling up in the guy.

"How'd she find you?" asked Clint, his tone turning toward the accusatory.

"She didn't," said Donny. "The court appointed me."

"You work for the court?"

"No, they just pay my fee, on cases like this."

"Well that's fucking great. No wonder she ended up where she did with a setup like that."

"The system is rigged, but she ended up where she did because I screwed up," said Donny. "And I need your help so I can fix it."

"What if I prefer self-help?" said Clint.

"Live the Seven Habits?"

"More like the Seventh Son."

"Can you see the future?"

"I know what I want it to look like. And sitting around watching won't make that happen."

"Xelina told me you think making movies to show what's going on isn't enough."

"Not unless you want to rot on some prison ship or eat government cheese in some suburban concentration camp."

"We have a system in place for fixing those things. There are a whole lot of us working to change it. The law is on our side. And once this election gets sorted out, it should be a thing of the past."

"I thought you had to be real smart to go to law school," said Clint.

"Not so much," said Donny. "But your guns are not the answer to our political problems."

"You telling me the law is? A bunch of guys like you, arguing inside the air-conditioning until the power runs out? If you want freedom, you gotta make 'em give it to you. You gotta take it."

"I agree. But the way you do that is through the power of democracy. Like the election. No way they can deny the power of the people. They do that, there'll be riots in the streets."

"You'd think a guy like you knows how the system actually works. I served the flag, because I didn't think I had a choice. I saw what we were doing down there, on the other side of the Gulf. No matter what the laws and the lawyers and the judges say. The law's just the rules they make up to keep themselves in power. Keep taking what they want. And it only applies to us, not them. So if they don't follow the law, why should I? They gave me skills. Now they can't come bitchin' if I use them to protect my people. My family. My country."

"All by yourself? Didn't sound to me like Xelina's entirely persuaded."

"There are a whole lot of people who agree with me. And we're more organized than you think. Or they think. Change is coming."

"Okay," said Donny. "In the meantime, I just want to get Xelina out. And all I need from you is some information. Can you help me with that?"

"Sure."

"Where are Xelina's friends? The ones who were with her when she got picked up?"

"I assume the secret police or whatever got them, too. I was gone the night they came. Can't you find out from the court?"

"I can try, but it's hard. The feds have suspended habeas corpus—the right to not be unlawfully detained—and they say they don't even have to tell us who they have, let alone why."

"So messed up."

"It is. But I have sources. Where were you that night?"

"Let's just say I was hunting."

"Uh-huh. Can you think of any other people that I could talk to? Ideally people who were there at the occupation with Gregorio."

"She told you what happened."

"Yes. And if I can prove it happened, I think I can convince a judge that's the real reason they are holding her."

He looked away, thinking. You could hear a helicopter nearby, flying pretty low.

"There's one gal you could try."

"Who's that?"

"Tara. I don't know her last name."

"Where would I find her?"

"I think I have her number. But she's probably at the camp."

"Which camp?"

"The resettlement camp," he said. "The big one."

"Iowatown."

"Yeah. She said she was going back there until things settle down."

"Great. Now how about Xelina's recordings? She told me where she kept her backups, but—"

"But you're a little late to that party." He looked Donny over afresh. "I may have kept one disc with some stuff you'd find interesting."

"Yes, please—anything like that should help."

"Make it count," he said, holding Donny's gaze.

"I'm on her side," said Donny. "And I'm going to get her out."

"Here's my number and Tara's," said Clint, scribbling on a piece of an envelope and handing it over. "Anything else?"

"Just one other thing," said Donny. "What's Xelina's password?"

28

AS HE HEADED BACK IN, PERCY CALLED.

"Hey," said Donny. "I didn't expect to hear from you."

"And I didn't expect to be calling you. I haven't even officially started work and my new boss says I need to help you on a project."

"Your new boss is a hoss," said Donny.

"Please don't try to talk redneck to me or I might change my mind."

"Sorry. Spent the last hour hanging out with a cowboy."

"Yee-haw."

"Did he tell you about the case?"

"Yeah. Same one you were working on Monday."

"Except now it's a lot harder. The train has left the station."

"Yeah, but sounds like you have a shot at putting the brakes on."

"You in? Even though it's a political case?"

"Yes. Sounds like the government is making it a political case, when it's not. It's a free speech case."

"Did you read my filing?"

"Yes. You need some better precedents to cite."

"Can you help me find them?"

"Already did. More than cases, though, you need some better evidence."

"That's what I've been working on. Where are you now?"

"At my new office."

"Great. I'll meet you there this afternoon. I have a couple of meetings lined up in the meantime."

"Hey, Donny. I'm sorry about Jerome."

"I know you are, Percy."

"Maybe we can still prove him innocent. That would be worth something."

"Yeah. After we get Xelina back on the street."

29

WHEN DONNY GOT TO THE SATELLITE OFFICE, TURNER WAS THERE
sitting on a bench taking his coffee break. As they had agreed.
They acted surprised to see each other anyway.

Donny stood while Turner stayed seated, smoking a cigarette and drinking coffee from a styrofoam cup.

"No donut?" said Donny.

"Doctor's orders," said Turner, taking a long drag.

Donny remembered what Ward had said, how smoking
makes sense once you understand the whole world is dying.
He just wasn't sure he agreed.

"What's the news?"

"You should be all set. I told the guys how you wanted to
make a donation to our benevolent fund, and they really appreciated it. So if you want to take that tour you were asking
about, you can meet our treasurer, Richie, over at the annex
tonight."

Donny didn't know yet what was on the disc Clint had
given him, and he couldn't take chances.

"That's good news, Turner."

"Richie said meet him at the loading dock. Seven-forty-
five."

"Got it."

"He can process your donation, too."

"Remind me how much I said? I was distracted by the floor
show."

"Five."

"Right," said Donny. Five thousand cash was four thousand and change more than he had immediately available.

"You've got it, right?" said Turner, watching him closely.

"Of course I've got it," lied Donny. What he had was half a day to get it. But hopefully he wouldn't need it.

"Want one?" said Turner, holding out the pack of smokes.

"No thanks," said Donny.

"You look like you could use it."

"If I do that I'll only want something stronger."

Turner laughed, but Donny was already thinking about something else.

"You think your friend Richie would be interested if I told him I had the code?"

Turner gave him a long look. "I knew you didn't have the dough."

"I can put it together. Just thinking about a way to really wrap the whole thing up with a bow. Maybe I should just talk to Bridget Kelly."

"That sounds like a real smart idea."

"I just want this girl to see another sunrise."

"She will," said Turner. "Just maybe not in this hemisphere."

There was a sunrise right there behind them, gold metal inlay in the black granite of the Ares Memorial, image of the sun peeking out from behind the moon.

"You ever wonder if maybe it was a bad idea privatizing NASA and sending corporations into space?" said Donny.

"Nope," said Turner. "It was the best thing that happened to this town since Spindletop."

"Until they shut it down."

"That won't last forever. Trying to keep Texans off the

moon is like trying to keep the Sooners from rushing Indian Territory."

"Nice analogy," said Donny.

"Except there aren't any Indians on the moon."

"Are you sure?"

Turner smiled.

"I think that's where the Comanches are hiding," said Donny.

"Well, I was up there for a year working security, right at the beginning, and I never saw no Indians, Donny. Least not that kind. And now the Chinese are running it."

"Yep," said Donny. "That's what I was thinking. That if we'd never made space into real estate, we never would have needed to militarize it, never would have let so much of our security rest on that satnet, and wouldn't be grounded down here now eating austerity pie. We should've stuck with 'For All Mankind.'"

"You think too much," said Turner, standing up. "If you had seen it, seen the mines when they were running full steam, you wouldn't be asking that question. We'll get it back. Quicker than you think."

"Maybe you're right."

"You call me before five and let me know if this deal with Richie is on."

"Thanks, Turner. I owe you."

"Yes, you do. Don't fuck it up."

As Turner walked off, Donny looked up at the actual moon there in the daytime sky and wondered if it was watching him, too.

30

AS GOOD AS SHE WAS AT KEEPING INFORMATION FROM DONNY that he had every right to have, once in a while Bridget Kelly helped him out. It was usually unintentional.

When he accepted the friend request she disclaimed ever sending, the link took Donny to Breakroom. Donny hated that site, like he hated all the others. They always made him feel like he was trapped in the mall, modeling the clothes the department stores sold, but never getting paid for it. Break-room was a Dallas company, of course. Some of his former colleagues at B&E worked on the deal. His own former client, Major Kovacs, was one of the investors. Maybe that was the red flag, the foreknowledge that if you got out of line on there one of the virtual mall cops would give you the Midnight Express. Any deal like that where the users don't make the rules seemed like a bad deal to Donny. Some days it made him think about whether the country should work the same way, like that wackadoodle Maxine Price used to say when she was Green's Vice President.

The consequence was that Donny did not have many friends on Breakroom. Just the ones that had found him, most of them former workmates or people he had gone to school with. But he had a few, and when the page opened up to cel-ebrate his new connection with the lady in charge of locking his clients up, it told him what one of his other friends had been up to lately.

Donny, would you like to congratulate Amanda Zorn for being selected as lead financial advisor for the Governor's Texas Gulf Region Reclamation and Restoration Fund?

Hell yes, said Donny. And then he figured out how to do it in person.

AMANDA ZORN'S OFFICE was on the eighty-first floor of the Jupiter Energy building on Louisiana Street, a purple-looking high-rise that was one of the newest towers in the skyline and one of the last to be built before they stopped building new skyscrapers. The main lobby was all polished stone, with a big point of light coming from somewhere on the other side of the elevator bank. To get to the elevators you needed to get past the security guards at the fortified desk, who dressed in fancy uniforms like doormen of the future but carried the gunmetal and mien of privatized paramilitaries.

Machine guns at the front door were something you got used to after a while.

The investment bankers of Manaugh Feldman & Co. occupied two whole floors of the building, connected by an internal stair that created an atrium out of the reception area, where they had Donny wait on the sort of couch that was so comfortable it made you uncomfortable, in front of a table holding four unread newspapers. On the opposite wall was a huge screen streaming the financial news with the sound off and the captions on. The anchor was interviewing some expert about the boom in catastrophe bonds, which sounded like complex bets on permutations of apocalypse. Donny wondered how much money you needed to get in on that—and if you could even collect if you were right. And then a skinny young guy in a suit that looked too expensive for a secretary walked up and said Ms. Zorn can see you now, and escorted him up the stairs, past the young bankers at their open floor plan desks monitoring complex trajectories of capital on multi-screen boxes and working deals over headsets in a polyphonous murmur that filled the room with unexpectedly soothing white noise.

"Mr. Kimoe," said the secretary, announcing his presence as they crossed the threshold of the corner office where Amanda was working at her big glass desk, then closing the door on them.

When she turned to look at him, before she even stood, you could see the welcome of an old friend in her eyes, even as you could also see how far their paths had diverged since school.

She still had that inky hair, but now with a distinct tuft of early grey, all styled perfectly at the edge between fashionable and businesslike. She wore one of those trendy new power suits that looked like a cross between the topcoat of some Victorian gentleman and the oracular robes of an ancient cleric. Her jewelry had the signature patina of lunar platinum, rarer than rare earth, with one big diamond sharp enough to cut through that desk should the situation require.

The diamond was not on her ring finger.

"Donny fucking Kimoe," she said, stepping around the desk to greet him with a smile and a hug.

"It's great to see you, Amanda," said Donny. "You look amazing."

He meant it.

"How long has it been?" she asked.

"I don't know," said Donny. "Maybe one of those parties after the bar results came in?"

"I feel like I've seen you at some of the alumni events, across the room."

"Not likely," said Donny. "I still owe them money."

That drew a patronizing smile. "And I've never even been to a courtroom, where you real lawyers hang out. Come on, sit down." She pointed at the small sofa as she sat in the armchair across.

For a long moment, she just looked at him across the coffee table, still smiling, almost squinting.

"Oh my God," she said. "Now I remember that party. At that place Pooji rented, out in the country."

Donny smiled.

"What a bacchanal," she said.

"At an actual winery, if I remember right," said Donny.

She nodded and smiled in agreement. "With Pooji's pharmaceutical tasting notes blended in," she said.

"And that September weather."

"Oh God, yes. I remember that moon."

And then you could see the shock come over her face as she must have just remembered what Donny remembered the minute he saw her profile pic on Breakroom—that they had made out that night, at that crazy party after they passed the last exam they would ever take and before they would get on the hamster wheels that would pay for their heavily indentured educations. He couldn't remember what kept them from getting more intimate than that, but he recognized her smile. A smile she now seemed to have lost, as she looked across the table resizing the man before her.

Donny adjusted his suit coat, and noticed a new frayed spot at the cuff. Then he noticed one of the translucent cubes that were set out on the coffee table, and picked it up, initially so he could look at something other than her appraising gaze.

Inside the cube was what looked like a tiny relief map of some little island, etched with a date, and a number that had enough zeros on the far side of the dollar sign that Donny wasn't sure which multiple it was.

"Isla Perdida," said Amanda. "In the South Atlantic. Held at various times by the French, Spanish, and Argentines. Very tiny, rather barren, and likely to be underwater in a couple of decades, but very strategic and perhaps capable of being elevated through geoengineering."

"Is it for sale or something?"

"Already sold. Last year, for our client the Argentine government, which needed the money. It was a very nice deal."

"Who bought it?"

"Who do you think?"

"Beijing?"

She shook her head. "Good guess, but no. It was a group of wealthy Africans, together with two Texans. Forward-looking entrepreneurs who understand where the growth will be in the long game."

"Is that what you do? Buy and sell countries?"

"I hope to buy or sell a whole country before I'm done, but for now I'm happy to put together deals for smaller slices of sovereign territory. In a world that is changing so much in so many ways, it's a valuable intermediary service, one that helps what wants to happen happen transactionally, not through force of arms. Win-win instead of win-lose. I'm working on another island deal right now, one that will be a brand-new territory on the map. Rather close to home at that."

"How close?"

"I can't say."

Donny thought about that as he looked at the world map that covered the wall next to them. The color coding showed how the world had changed in their lifetime, mostly through the win-lose of war. The central Asian states resurgent in the territory between China and shrunken Russia. The German-dominated bloc of central Europe. Lonely, loco Britain and its handful of far-flung chartered colonies. Chinese Hawaii, and the other territories conceded across the Pacific Rim.

"It's not one of those islands, is it?" said Donny, pointing at the blots across Texas that marked the Evac Zone.

She looked at him with less friendly eyes than she had at first. "Who was it you said you were representing?"

"I didn't," said Donny. "I'm working on a case that involves the Rovers' occupation. And I'm trying to get a better understanding of what's going on out there in the Zone."

"Creative destruction," she said, relaxing a little at his lie. "The petrochemical economy was already struggling when the storms delivered their blows."

"Not exactly a knockout punch."

"No. There are plenty of people, especially around here and in Washington, who still think fossil fuels are a big part of the future. I'm not one of them. But the mess we are cleaning up presents some other interesting strategic opportunities."

"I hear the state is condemning huge swaths of real estate all through there."

"They are, and wisely so. Time for a fresh start."

"I don't understand how they can afford it. Texas may be doing better than the Midwest, but we're still pretty broke. Too broke to rebuild that whole industrial corridor, you'd think."

"Well, we can't afford not to fix it, right? And just because eminent domain is a public power doesn't mean it has to be funded with public money. These deals they are doing now involve simultaneous sales to private investors."

"Like when the Soviet Union finally collapsed and they auctioned off all those state-owned businesses."

"Kind of like that. But more like strategic sales than auctions."

"Subsidized by a lot of free refugee labor."

"Not free, Donny."

"Close enough. Do you work any of these deals?"

"This office is proud to be involved in most of them. We are the state's advisory firm in the project."

"I read about that. When did they have the election for that gig?"

"Oh, come on, Donny. Don't walk into my office and give me that sour bullshit. The world is changing. Physically changing. Maybe you can't read our legending of it, but that map shows what our models say about what's coming. Not just sea level rise, but other changes in weather patterns, agricultural productivity, animal populations, and the mass migrations of humans. Our machines tell us it could be decades before things start to recover in the Midwest, and they're going to get worse before that. There are other blighted regions emerging across the hemisphere, and beyond. We're helping clean up the mess to make room for new blood, here in a place where we at least have work, plentiful housing, and rain."

"Looking for water in a drowning world."

"Exactly," she said. "That's pretty much our business model, helping put deals together that build a viable future."

"Viable for who?"

"Good stewards, we hope."

"How much do they pay?"

She shrugged. "It varies, but usually about seven and a half percent of the gross proceeds, plus expenses."

Donny looked at the deal trophy again, the one with all the zeros, and tried to do the math.

"Glad to know someone figured out how to properly leverage their law degree."

"I've been very lucky to work with some visionary people who helped me see the way."

"Will the election make a difference in any of this?"

She looked at him with rising impatience. "Sounds like the political unrest pays your bills," she said.

"It does," said Donny. "And that's why I asked, because I think a lot of the work I'm doing now is about to dry up."

"I wouldn't worry about that," she said. "Some trajectories cannot be altered."

Something about the way she said it made it seem like she knew. Especially when she stood and looked down at him.

"Nice to see you," she said, sending him off along with the memories of past lives you could tell she had already banished.

31

MILES KEPT HIS OFFICE IN THE 1920S VERSION OF A HIGH-RISE, one of the last such buildings left in downtown Houston. It wasn't as nice as the Gulf Building or the Esperson Buildings, but it was pure Miles, a remnant of a mellower time that was also the era of a different kind of injustice, or at least an earlier version. Donny had been to the open house when Miles first got the space, and still remembered the remarks Miles had given to his gathered friends about what the civil rights regime was when the building was first opened, at a time when the law mainly served to enforce racial oppression.

Miles's suite was on the ninth of twelve floors, with views to the north and west. Miles had done well on his own, building a solid trial practice with a mix of criminal, civil rights, personal injury, and occasional commercial work. He had a partner, Cheryl, who helped share the load, and a team of reliable associates that now included Percy, two paralegals, and a secretary.

But what Donny really envied was the corner office Miles had scored, a place that suited a guy who spent most of his time at work—one of those expansive executive spreads that the prior century indulged before the spreadsheets took over, furnished with period pieces, including bookshelves stuffed with the lawyerly portion of Miles's extensive library and half of his history books. The wall space not taken by books was covered with photos. Most were of Miles with his clients, but a few with judges and politicians—many of them now out of power, including two in exile, and one in jail.

"I feel like the one thing missing in here is a hunting trophy," said Donny, sitting in one of the big chairs and admiring the antique globe next to it, full of countries that no longer existed.

"I don't hunt, Donny," said Miles. "White guys in the woods with guns and me don't go together."

"Maybe you need one of them on the wall. Some old judge or cop."

"I guess that's basically what some of these photos are, if you know the stories."

"No kidding," said Donny, thinking about what stories he had hidden in the fabric of his own office. "How's the Mayor?"

"Glad to be home. That was crazy."

"I still can't believe they put her in a military brig."

"You know what the sign says when you enter that place? 'Headquarters, Texas Military Forces.'"

"I know. Straight out of the state constitution. What's scary to me is how they've been reviving that part about the Texas State Guard—the all-volunteer militia 'organized under the Second Amendment' or however they put it. That's how the Governor's been deputizing all these local parade clubs. It's like telling everyone they're a cop."

"It's a lot worse than that. And you want to talk about parade clubs, you should see them out there at the base in Austin. They're building another temporary detention camp, right there on the MoPac freeway, so all the locals can see."

"So much for home rule," said Donny. He knew just the spot Miles was talking about.

"No kidding," said Miles.

"Are you really going in front of the Fifth Circuit tomorrow?"

"Not just me. I'm on a team."

"Nothing like a constitutional crisis to get you a speedy trial."

"This one's too speedy."

"They can't get this done fast enough, if you ask me."

Miles raised his eyebrows. "Don't assume it's going to go our way."

"You're about the only thing left I believe in, Miles."

"Said the guy who's high half the time."

"Didn't you get a good panel?"

"Yeah," nodded Miles. "This stage should go well. It's what comes after that that worries me."

"There are six Supreme Court Justices who definitely love executive power. But martial law? Maybe in the absolute disaster areas. Not to overturn an election."

"I don't know," said Miles. "The Constitution lets the state legislatures decide how to pick electors. The real remedy is political."

"Maybe it is," said Donny. "But that doesn't work if they throw out all the ballots."

Miles nodded. "Good point."

"Thanks. And speaking of good arguments, did you read that thing I sent you?"

"That crazy brief?"

"Not as crazy as trying to deal with Broyles."

"True. And I guess now you're dealing with Judge Jones, which is a whole different flavor of unpredictable."

"I'll take those odds."

"Agreed," said Miles. "Too bad your motion reads like some nutjob pro se thing. The kind some jailhouse lawyer writes up in ballpoint pen and mails to the court from prison."

"Tell me what you really think."

Miles laughed. "I think you may be on to something, actually. But it could use a little refinement."

Miles handed Donny the document. He had marked it up heavily in red pen. On the back of the last page he had written down the citations of a dozen cases.

"Look that over, read those, and then let's talk."

"Does this mean you're all in?"

"Not necessarily," said Miles.

"I'm starting to see how all these cases are connected."

"You just figured that out?"

"Yeah, well, I've been distracted."

"You mean you've been wasted."

"A reasonable response to the current climate, you have to admit."

Miles nodded, but didn't laugh.

"Do you think we can stop it?" asked Donny.

"Of course not," said Miles. "It's the natural course of American history, five-hundred-plus years on. We just need to survive it, and see what advancements we can make when the cycle comes back around."

"You think that's going to happen?"

"Yes."

"You think it's true what they say, that they're going to turn the Evac Zone into a Texas-sized gulag?"

"It will be, if we let it."

Donny looked at his old friend, looking back at him with eyes older than he remembered.

"I think I may have something that will really help."

"What's that," said Miles, not really a question.

"I think I have a shot at proving they killed Gregorio," said Donny. "I may even be able to prove who."

"Do I want to know how?"

"Sources," said Donny. "Sources who may have access to the footage my client shot at the scene of the crime. Footage the government doesn't even know it has, or at least I don't think they do. If I get that, I can get it to the press, and blow this whole thing open."

"That's a terrible idea," said Miles. "And not just because I know you have some shady angle to get that evidence."

"It's a fucking great idea," argued Donny.

"Donny. Listen to me. There's no way any press outlet will run that material. It's all under a Burn Barnes ban. I already checked. Why do you think there's been almost zero news, not just about the disappearance, but even the whole occupation, at least since the first couple of days? They have successfully scared the press into submission. No one is going to do anything like you think, at least unless we're lucky enough to win our case and have a new administration come in. So the only thing that's going to happen is the powers that be will hear you have stolen from them, and you'll be calling me at four in the morning again to bail your ass out."

"So I tell them I have it, and use that to negotiate a deal."

"They don't negotiate with terrorists. Remember? Even if there are hostages. This is 3-D chess, not poker."

"Very funny," said Donny. "Maybe I'll just buy some TV time myself and put it out there that way."

"Now that I would pay to see," said Miles. "That's one arena where you would be a fierce competitor: to make the most outrageous lawyer ad on Houston TV."

Donny warmed at the idea.

"You'll need a good nickname," said Miles. "Those guys always have one. The Hammer, the Hawk, the Bulldog. Maybe you can be the Snake."

"Very funny."

"The Cottonmouth."

It wasn't as funny as Miles thought, but it was a good opening.

"You want to help me buy some slots?"

Miles stopped laughing at his own jokes when Donny said that, and then gave Donny a long, penetrating look. You could almost feel him reading your mind, like some kinder and gentler but ultimately tougher version of the cop stare.

"Classic," he finally said, after divining what Donny was really asking for.

"I need five thousand bucks, Miles."

"Not from me, Donny."

"I've got to get that footage."

"I know you believe that, Donny. But I'm not giving you any money. Especially not for whatever corrupt deal you've cut. And it's not even that much. Surely you can put that together."

Surely.

"Why don't you work here this afternoon," said Miles. "Grab a conference room. Use the library. Get ready for tomorrow. You have good arguments, if you can polish them up. Use my secretary, get help from Percy if you need it. And I'll be here working, happy to look at the next draft."

"Okay, thanks," said Donny. "Some help sounds good."

"Good," said Miles. "In fact—" He reached into his desk, pulled out a pair of keys on a ring, and handed them across to Donny. "Why don't you keep these until we're done. That one opens the main entrance, and the other one this suite."

Donny reached for the keys. Miles didn't let go just yet.

"Now just promise me," he said, "if you're going to keep putting my name on things, that we're going to play by the rules."

"Okay," said Donny, grabbing the keys. And it wasn't really a lie, because as far as he could see, there were no rules. They had suspended them.

Like they said, it was an emergency.

32

"YOU'VE GOT TO CHECK THIS OUT," SAID PERCY.

Donny was in Miles's conference room, hitting the books. Percy did a double take when she saw the mess—dozens of printouts of cases, old hardbound federal reporters open to selected cases and arrayed in a pile that looked certain to topple at any moment, Donny's black notebooks compiling obscure precedents and the week's new rules for the secret court, half a sandwich, and four empty soda cans stacked on the credenza.

"Whatcha got?" said Donny.

"Corporate charter for a new company."

"Why do I care," said Donny. "There must be a hundred of those every day."

"Not like this. This one is special. Read it for yourself."

She handed him the printout. It was thicker than those things usually were. The cover page had the stamp from the Texas Secretary of State's office, and the all-caps declaration of what it was.

CERTIFICATE OF FORMATION
OF
PALLANTIUM CORPORATION

Donny scanned the pages. He didn't read a lot of those things, and when he did it was usually with the eyes of a plaintiff's lawyer, figuring out who to sue and how to serve them.

212

They were mostly boilerplate, maxing out whatever liberties the state statute gave them, sometimes detailing more complicated aspects of the capital structure—which investors got what percentage if the company shut down or was sold. This charter was different. There wasn't any boilerplate. It was a custom job.

"What is this?" he asked.

"Read the purpose clause," said Percy. "Article Two."

Donny looked at the section she was referencing.

"This is like a giant legal description of some real estate or something. 'Beginning at the mouth of the Sabine River then south to the marker of the southeast corner of the del Vago League blah blah'—"

"That's exactly what it is," said Percy. "But it's also more than that. Do you see the part about the powers?"

"'. . . shall have exclusive dominion over the territory heretofore described beginning on the effective date of this charter and until the ninety-nine-year anniversary thereof,'" Donny read out, "'including the right to make such ordinances and impose such levies as may be deemed appropriate in the business judgment of the board of directors, the right to maintain an independent private militia . . .'"

Percy nodded.

"What the fuck?" said Donny.

"It goes on."

"So I see," said Donny. "How much land is that?"

"Most of the Evac Zone," said Percy. "The contiguous portions, including the coastal section and both sides of the Ship Channel from Baytown down."

"Jesus. That's like the equivalent of a whole county."

"More."

"Like a little country."

"It's exactly like a little country. Complete with its own laws."

"And army."

"Militia, technically," said Percy. "But yeah. And the thing is, if you keep reading, and also read the enabling statute, I think the idea is to make it exempt from the treaty strictures. At least for the ninety-nine-year period of the charter. Because the Accords only apply to the territory of the United States and its subdivisions. And this basically carves off a chunk and makes it independent."

"Corporate sovereignty, in other words."

"Yep."

"And wait, did you say 'enabling statute'?"

"Yes. The Legislature created this. Through a private bill."

"What do you mean, a private bill?"

"As in, not a public law. A special law just to benefit one citizen."

"Right. Like when Congress gives someone citizenship even though their adoptive American parents screwed up the paperwork and the deadline's long gone, or when they extend the patents of some big pharma company so they can keep gouging monopoly prices after having had to spend all those years of the original patent term proving the drug was safe."

"Uh-huh. In this case, at the state level."

"Where's the money in this deal?"

"In the statute. They pay a share of their annual profits, ten percent, devoted to the climate crisis restoration fund, and a chunk for the election fund."

"So they just sold a chunk of the state to one company, and let them make it their own corporate country."

"Basically."

"How is this not all over the news?"

"I think, one, because they buried this in the Zelda emergency spending bill, and two, maybe they got a news ban on it."

"Or maybe no one's paying attention. That's how most of this stuff happens, especially when the opposition has been so completely neutered. And you kind of have to be a lawyer to make heads or tails of it."

Percy nodded. "You might be right."

"Who's behind this? The company, I mean. Board of directors, shareholders, all of that."

"That I don't know."

"Don't they have to put the names in here?"

"Just the name of the incorporator. The lawyer who filed it."

Donny flipped to the back pages to find that section.

He was surprised to see it was someone he knew.

"Motherfucker."

33

DONNY TRIED CALLING TREY, THINKING MAYBE HE COULD SHAKE
him down on short notice with the information he had. But that
was a bad idea on a lot of levels, and Trey was already gone for
the day by the time he had it. So he pursued an even worse idea,
but one that he was pretty sure would work.

Global Auto Mart, which Donny always remembered because of the size of the huge red neon letters that spelled the
name out on each side of the little building, was not far from
his office. It was at the heart of a three-block stretch of used
car dealers, but where the others specialized in high-mileage
rides for people who lived outside the gates, the Mart had a
different business model: buying classic American cars for re-
sale to wealthy foreigners. With a particular specialty in the
mega-cruisers of Donny's youth, when Detroit ruled the world.
The kind of cars that had fouled the planet, and became illegal
to manufacture even in the U.S. In most other countries they
were even illegal to drive, unless you were one of the rich col-
lectors who could afford to pay the freight—and the carbon tax
the global remediation authorities imposed on members of the
Pact, which would often be double or triple the price of the car.

For people of Donny's generation and older, holding on to
and taking care of cars from before the Accords was a point of
pride, of tribal identity. One of the few left that transcended
even politics. Selling your car to be stored in some tycoon's
garage in Melbourne, Mumbai, or Seoul was worse than the

usual flavors of austerity pie. It was a sellout, like pawning the family furniture to your landlord. Almost as bad as trading in your passport for another, richer country.

Even worse, it meant Donny would be stuck without wheels. In the congested sprawl of Houston.

But Donny was out of options, and as Lou had reminded him, his standards had been slipping for a while. It was already getting dark when Donny rolled into the lot. He had hit the drive-through car wash on the way out there, and cleaned his trash out of the interior, and the car looked good, if a little crazy—like its owner. He parked it right in front of the office where you could see it from inside, and headed in.

There were three people working there, one older guy on the phone at a desk and two younger ones taping down a cherry red Pontiac to be loaded on the boat. Donny preempted chance and went and sat right down in the chair by the older guy, as if he had a meeting.

Perhaps because of the suit and the briefcase, or maybe the edge Donny was giving, the guy looked at him with eyes that registered low-level alarm. He held up a finger to signal he would just be a minute, and moments later told whoever was on the phone that he had to go.

Hanging on the wall behind the guy was a framed photo of the Governor and the President waving from a convertible Eldorado in a July Fourth parade.

The name on the business card Donny helped himself to was Bob Cregan, CEO. Bob had an Australian accent, which made sense—most of the buyers were Asian, and the Aussies made good business inventing new niches in trans-Pacific trade.

By the time Bob got off the phone, the two guys who looked like they were probably his sons were outside gawking at the Oldsmobile.

When Donny proposed his deal, Bob didn't like it. "The market's getting soft," he said. "Only thing I'm buying is Cadillacs and muscle cars."

"This is better than a Cadillac," said Donny. "It's a Double Ninety-Eight."

The 1998 model Ninety-Eight Millennium Edition Cabin Cruiser was the car they called the last Oldsmobile, even though it wasn't the last, just the biggest.

"I can see that," said Bob. "And that's cool, but like I said, I'm not really looking for that right now. Maybe come back after New Year's."

"Believe me," said Donny, trying to play it cool. "I wish I didn't have to sell it."

Bob laughed. "You guys always say that." He smiled, then sighed, and got up to do a walk-around.

Watching Bob treat that beautiful relic like an ugly mule was rough.

Watching him get into the driver's seat and start it up was worse. It sounded good. Like a warbird ready for the runway.

Bob raised his eyebrows and nodded. "I guess I could give you three."

"Come on," said Donny. "It's worth twenty grand at least."

He got him to six.

As he suspected, Bob had plenty of cash on hand. Because the other thing Donny knew about Bob, from a case he had worked in the U.S. Attorney's office, was that Bob was a node in a totally global and totally informal money transmission network. And that sometimes the cars were used to ship other things.

After Donny signed over the title and Bob counted out the cash, Donny asked him if one of his sons could give him a ride.

Bob smiled. "Getting colonized is a bitch, eh? The boys will call you a cab."

34

THE EVIDENCE LOCKER WAS IN A BUILDING THAT HAD FORMERLY
served as the main post office, at the edge of downtown near
the federal building where most of the Task Force members
had their desks. Turner's guy met Donny there after sundown.
The building was secure, not even designed for public visitors,
but it still had a partially covered parking area in the back
where the mail trucks had once loaded up. As Donny walked
into the loading zone he remembered it had been a popular
spot for skate punks after the post office closed and before they
remodeled it for packages that would never leave. You could
still see the wheel burns along the raised dock where Donny
saw Turner's guy staring at him through the face-sized window
in the reinforced metal door.

"Richie?" said Donny.

The guy nodded his head in a way that said come on. The
high-pitched klaxon startled Donny when Richie opened the
door to let him in, but it cut off as soon as the door shut behind
them.

"Follow me," said Richie, after quickly sizing Donny up.
No handshake or niceties, not seeming nervous, but ready to
get Donny out of sight. The hallway was long, but they didn't
walk far before Richie opened the door to a small conference
room. When they were in, he closed the door behind them.

"You got something for me?"

"Right here," said Donny, pulling the envelope from his

jacket pocket. He thought five thousand dollars would have felt thicker, but watching Richie count it, he was reminded that it wasn't that much money anymore, even if it had been a struggle for him to pull it together.

Richie nodded. He turned to the evidence box on the table. It didn't have Xelina's name on it, just the number. He pulled the inventory sheet from its sleeve and set it down. Then he dialed the code into the side of the box and opened it.

"Use these," he said, handing Donny a pair of latex gloves.

Richie pulled a clear plastic bag from the box, unsealed it, and pulled out a beat-up black plastic Bluephone. He then pulled a cable out from the power port in the center of the table and plugged it in.

"Just this one, right?" asked Richie.

"Yep," said Donny.

"I am going to leave you alone in here now," said Richie. "I'll be back in fifteen minutes."

"Can we take a little longer than that?"

Richie shook his head.

"Any cameras I need to worry about?" said Donny.

"That question is both indiscreet and stupid," said Richie. "All taken care of." He pointed at the ceiling, where two nodes in opposite corners had been taped over.

Donny nodded.

Electric buzz and the sound of steel on steel as Richie locked the door from the other side.

Donny looked around the room. There was a photo of the Attorney General on the wall, just two cold paper eyes watching over him.

He grabbed the phone, flipped it open, and dialed the power button on the side. The Bluephones had the design logic of tiny televisions, even in the way the screen came online.

Unlike BellNet's interactive TVs, they had the keyboard integrated, in the bottom half of the clamshell.

The password prompt came on.

Donny punched the code Clint had given him, and he was in.

What came up was a notice from the system.

FACTORY SETTINGS RESTORED

"Bastards!" he cursed.

He tried everything he could to find backups. No dice. The phone was clean. Where she would have kept the videos, Donny found stock photos of happy families and enhanced landscapes.

Maybe they suspected something from Donny's midnight visit to Xelina's. Maybe Xelina had told them more than she said, or more than she remembered, when they interrogated her. But they knew that they already had enough to lock her up the way they wanted, and the only thing on her devices was downside for them.

And Turner, that lying son of a bitch, was in on it.

He went to the door, but there was no getting out. He pounded on the little window, but no one came.

He waited there for a half hour, which seemed a lot longer. He saw Richie looking in through the window. Richie had company with him this time, another guy. A suit.

It was the bald guy from the hearing. The one Broyles and Walton both seemed scared of.

He watched Donny like you'd watch an animal in a zoo, wondering why it's not doing anything, while Richie talked to him. Donny couldn't hear a word they said.

And then they were gone. This time for longer.

It must have been another hour before they were back. Richie opened the door. The suit came in alone and sat across the table from Donny.

"Find what you were looking for?" he said.

"Who are you?" said Donny.

The guy was hard to peg. The suit seemed almost too nice for a fed, but it covered a physique that had a military bearing. And the shaved head made it hard to assess his age. He could have been anywhere between thirty-five and fifty-five.

"Someone who's been wanting to meet you," he said.

"There are easier ways to make that happen."

"I like this way. More private."

Donny wondered if Richie had locked them in. He'd been so distracted by the suit that he hadn't thought to listen for it.

"Are you the one who destroyed the evidence on there?" said Donny, pointing at the phone. "You know that's a felony."

"You're one to talk about felonies, Donny."

The way the guy said his name made it sound like something sleazy.

"What do you want?" said Donny.

"Honestly, I just wanted to meet you."

"Right. What agency are you with?"

"It's not important. What's important is that you listen to the advice of your friends. Your recklessness could do much more damage than you realize. And the only reason you're here talking to me, instead of where you could be, is because your friends vouched for you. Pointed to your patriotic service in the past. Said they could manage the situation."

"Which friends would those be?"

"It's a short list, because you don't have many."

"Not many of the kind you're talking about. And not by accident."

"Well, I'm definitely not one of them. And the people I work for feel even more strongly about it. Part of my job is to mediate the situation. Mediate, and monitor."

"Can I go?"

The guy stared at Donny like he was making up his mind. He looked at his watch. Then he looked at his phone. He seemed to be reading something.

"Sure," said the guy. "But this is your final notice."

"Whatever," said Donny. "Where do I get my five grand back?"

"I don't know anything about that," said the guy. "And Richie already left."

Bastards.

35

THEY'D HAD A REGULAR MEMORIAL FOR JUDGE ELWOOD EARLIER that week, in the church his widow chose, but the real funeral was that night at midnight, on a closed-off overpass west of downtown, part of one of the private freeways reserved for the wealthy elite. More than a hundred friends gathered, more men than women, with their best old cars lined up in long rows, all tuned to the same private FM feed, blasting border metal at the city below while the judge's body lay there atop the hood of his 1989 Cadillac Conquistador, which in turn had been raised on a pyre of rebar and mesquite doused with high-octane fuel drained from the tank of the car. The boys had gotten good at building those pyres in a way that you could drive the preferred chariot of the deceased right up there at the beginning of the fest and not need a crane or a bunch of floor jacks.

The judge was dressed in a chalk-striped charcoal flannel suit with a green foulard tie, white handkerchief, and the snake boots he wore for the hunt. His party lapel pin glistened like black gold, reflecting the moonlight. His favorite Ruger was holstered right there in the waistband of his suit pants behind the sterling belt buckle monogrammed with an etching of an eagle clutching a rat in its talons. The nine-inch knife with its hand-carved handle hung from the belt in its handsome Brooks Brothers scabbard, and folded into his arms was the Remington double-barreled 12-gauge with the inlaid silver image of Robert McAlpin Williamson, the Republic of Texas–era judge known as Three-Legged Willie for his primitive prosthesis, and for the Bowie knife he always wore under his judicial robes.

The judge's friends lined up to pay their respects, leaving gifts with him to take off to the beyond. Cactus flowers, black-and gold-jacketed bullets and shells, flasks of fine tequila and whisky, cigars, antlers, and condoms. People talked and told stories about him, and then they turned off the music and his wife walked up with her bold blond hair done up in a vintage coif with a fresh streak of silver through the bangs that matched the platinum sequins of her dress. She gave a talk about what her husband stood for and what he believed the future would be if they continued the fight to which he had committed his life, a patriotism made from blood and dirt and the melding of the Anglo and Spanish traditions of law, property, and the enjoyment of the life of born leaders. Then the mistress got her turn, talking about some of the things he liked to do for fun, including an anecdote about the trip they had taken after the last diagnosis had come in, which involved three extramarital couples on a private jet loaded with spirits and firearms and a big tent you could put up in the desert after you landed. His daughter talked about his most important decisions, listing some of the most dangerous enemies of the state he had incarcerated. And then they each kissed him in turn, intense goodbye kisses to warm dead flesh. They stood together after that, arms locked, and sang the Song, a cappella, so crisp and clear that it carried far from that vaulted freeway even though you could hear the tremors of loss in their chorale. When they were done, the men took the torches they had been holding and put them to the pyre, as the feed came back on with "Judgment Day," the last instrumental duel between Page and Gibbons before they went their separate ways. Somehow the flames engulfed the Caddy just at the part where the drums and guitar find their shared harmony and then the bass joins in and then the screaming wails, the unofficial anthem of twenty years of flag-draped victory celebrations, and you could almost believe in the mythic past these people accepted as true heritage.

Donny, who was the only one who had gotten there by cab, took it all in from the edge of the crowd. He was enjoying a tall boy of Alamo Martyrs wrapped in a black koozie printed with the judge's fanciful coat of arms when he finally saw Trey alone and available to harass.

"Pretty amazing ceremony," said Donny.

When Donny walked up next to him, Trey didn't even notice him at first. He looked pretty tranced out on the fire, as the light flickered on his face and conjured weird shadows from within.

"He was a great man," said Trey, looking over at Donny and tipping his glass.

"Shame to see that car go with him," said Donny.

"You always know the wrong thing to say," said Trey. "I can't even believe you're here."

"I worked with the guy almost as long as you, and had a half dozen cases with him after he went on the bench. We may have different ideas about some things, but it was hard not to like the guy."

"You fucking weasel," said Trey. "You never could stand him. I remember you telling me as much, when we were at the firm."

"And you agreed, so don't give me that shit. I'm here to pay my respects."

"You came to make fun of us. And then to bug me. I saw you called me at the office earlier."

"I thought it would be easier to discuss in person."

"Then make an appointment. This is not the time or place."

"It's kind of urgent."

"It's always urgent with you, because you are so fucking sloppy. Sloppy in your thinking, sloppy in your work style, sloppy in your politics, and sloppy in the way you live."

"I guess that means you won't be recruiting me for your little corporate space program."

That got his attention, no matter how hard he tried to mask the initial reaction that came over his face.

He took a drink, half-smiled, and looked back at the fire. The smoke was pumping thick and black now, burning rubber and leather.

"One of my clients has been helping your guys develop their import market," said Donny. "Asked me to look over his contract."

"You don't do contracts," said Trey. "That's what lawyers who want to be wealth creators do. You just help terrorists work out plea bargains. When you're not helping out your drug dealer buddies."

"Well, what I'm working on now kind of involves all those things. And Pallantium Corporation. Which is a great name, by the way."

"You son of a bitch," said Trey, grabbing Donny by the lapel and baring his teeth as he spoke.

"Ease off," said Donny, putting his hand over Trey's. "I already got bit by one dog this week."

"Sorry they didn't get your throat," said Trey, backing away.

"Come on, Trey. This is just business. Like you always say."

"What you are screwing with is about more than just business, Donny. It's about the American future."

"Sounded more like a wholly independent corporation's future to me."

Trey looked back at the fire. Like it was a mirror.

"But you would probably tell me those two are the same thing," said Donny.

Trey shook his head dismissively.

"So in the spirit of interests-based negotiation, I thought I would reach out to you about how my clients and I can help you if you help us."

"Blackmail, in other words."

"No, not that word, Trey. And maybe it doesn't even involve money."

"You always need money," said Trey, in a way that suggested that was the worst of all.

"How about I send you the details, and maybe we can talk at a better time. But pronto. Like mañana kind of pronto."

While Trey digested that, another guy walked up. A younger guy, with dark hair, wearing a black technical jacket.

"Everything okay over here, Dad?" he said.

"All good," said Trey.

"Is that Charlie?" said Donny, recognizing the kid now.

Trey smiled, looked at his son, and put a father's proud hand on Charlie's shoulder. Charlie was a little bit taller than his dad, a little whiter, and in a lot better shape.

Charlie wasn't smiling. He was standing there, backlit by the raging fire, registering contempt for Donny like a fraternity brother blocking the door from an unwanted party guest.

"You got bigger," said Donny. "Last time I saw you, you had braces and zits."

"You remember Donny Kimoe," said Trey. "We worked together at B&E."

"I know him," said Charlie.

Donny reached out to shake Charlie's hand. Charlie was slow to reciprocate, and when he did he gave him one of those grips that feel like if you make the wrong move you'll end up with your face on the pavement and no chance to tap out.

"What are you up to these days?" asked Donny.

"Charlie just graduated from the Institute last summer," said Trey.

"Congratulations," said Donny. "One of those dual MBA and public affairs deals?"

Charlie tipped his chin up at Donny in a nod.

"They say that's where our new generation of leaders will come from," said Donny, not mentioning that the Institute was where they trained leaders of a very particular political bent.

You could tell both father and son thought he was being sarcastic, even though he had tried not to be.

"You headed to Washington, then?" he asked.

"Staying right here," said Charlie. "My hometown needs me. This is where we shape the future."

"Working on the cleanup?" asked Donny.

"You could say that," said Charlie.

"It's okay," said Trey, speaking to Charlie and then turning back to Donny. "Charlie's getting into real estate. Spent the summer interning at Atlas Group on a couple of the remediation projects, and now he's putting together his own deals."

"Nice," said Donny. "What's the name of the company? I'll keep an eye out."

"New Frontier," said Trey. "And as if that weren't enough, they just named him deputy squad leader in the San Felipe Street Parade Club."

"Really," said Donny.

Charlie nodded. He had the eyes of a hunter.

"We're going to get back to our friends, Donny," said Trey.

"Look for my note, and let me know when we can meet," said Donny.

"I'll be in touch," said Trey. He paused, and then looked right at Donny. "You be safe."

Donny smiled and raised his beer at the two of them. Charlie waited a while before he took his eyes off Donny to turn away. And as father and son walked back to the fire you could see them conferring.

You could even say conspiring.

36

IT WAS LATE WHEN THE CAB DROPPED HIM OFF AT HIS OFFICE, BUT
Donny wanted to finish pulling his work together for the morning. But when he unlocked the door and stepped in, it didn't
take long to see that he had a new pile of work to deal with.

It looked like Xelina's house after the raid. Maybe a little
tidier. Someone had been there, going through his work. File
cabinets had been left open, banker's boxes out on the tables,
everything obviously rifled through. His private office was a
bigger mess, with furniture moved, drawers unlocked and ajar,
his little desktop trophies out of place. They had tried to stack
things back neatly, but not the way Donny or Percy would do
it. They didn't want to hide that they'd been there. They wanted
him to know.

For a lawyer, there was really no more unthinkable violation than the confidential files of your clients being ripped
open. Even by law enforcement, if that's what had happened. It
was sacrosanct. The judges who had to authorize such searches
were lawyers, too, and very reluctant to breach that line. If they
gave a warrant like that, it almost always meant they suspected
the lawyer was the real criminal, or in on it with his or her
client.

Donny could feel the fresh fear taking hold. He looked out
the windows, half-expecting to see suits in government sedans
waiting for him to come out.

He took a closer look around the office, and tried to figure out what they had been looking for. He decided he didn't have much time—every minute he stayed here increased the likelihood that they would be back to take him. But he could see enough to assume they had looked at almost every one of his case files. And spent most of their time looking at the classified cases.

The files he'd had out on his desk regarding Xelina's case were gone. And when he looked for them, so were Jerome's. All he had left on either of those were the files he'd been carrying in his litigation bag.

As he stood there in the dark of his office entrance waiting for the cab, he finally put it together.

"Fucking Turner," he said out loud. But the face in his head was that chrome dome from Washington looking at him through the window in the door after Turner's contact stole his money and locked him up.

He wondered what windows they were watching him through at that moment, real or virtual.

So when the cab finally got to his apartment, and he saw the lights were on, he told the driver a different place to go.

And he left his phone in the cab, on purpose, after he paid the driver and said I know it's weird, just promise me you'll drive there.

On foot, the streets were dark that night. For the energy capital of the universe, they sure didn't spend much on streetlights. Maybe because they didn't believe in the idea of pedestrians.

More likely because they didn't like the idea of *anyone* outside at night.

37

WHEN JOYCE CAME TO THE DOOR, SHE HAD HER GLOCK IN HAND.

"Jesus, Kimoe," she said, opening the wooden door but not the screen. "What the fuck are you doing? I nearly shot you."

"Sorry," he said. He had come to her back door, the one that opened onto the kitchen. He had been banging on it for five minutes before she came. "Can I come in?"

"No! Are you wasted again? Get off my lawn."

"Joyce, I'm totally sober, I just—"

"Just because I invited you to share the ride to Mexico with me doesn't mean you can come around here in the middle of the night like some crazy fucking stalker, backdoor man."

"I just need a place to hide, Joyce. I need a safe bed."

"You came to the wrong place, Donny. I'm serious. This is so insanely uncool. Your friends are right about you. You've lost it."

A light went on at the house next door.

"What time is it, anyway?"

"One-thirty," said Donny.

"Are you kidding me? And look at you. You even brought your goddam luggage."

She was looking at his litigation bag, which looked like a cross between a briefcase and a steamer trunk.

"That's not—" he said, the hostile reception making him realize he was getting too tired to form complete sentences. "This is just work stuff. Files. I came from the office. They raided it.

Stole my files. And when I went to my apartment, there were people there, too."

"Well, you better go kick them out. Because I only have one bed and you aren't sleeping in it."

"I just thought maybe I could crash on your couch for a couple hours."

"No, Donny. If you can't go home, get a hotel."

"That's not safe," said Donny. "They're looking for me. I can't risk missing this hearing tomorrow. It's my one real chance to save this woman from being sent to the camps."

Joyce sighed. She didn't have much sympathy for him, but she always felt for the clients, especially the politicals. They took action she only ever had the guts to talk about in the faculty lounge.

"I'm sorry, but you are going to have to figure something else out, Donny. The feds already came here once this week tagging me with whatever it is they have on you. If they're after you tonight, then you've already put me at risk. And I'm on my way out of here, and I'm not taking any chances that will screw up my plans. So please leave."

She had a point. She also had a gun.

Then she closed the door on him, locked it, and turned out the lights.

The light was still on next door. Donny looked, and saw a man watching him from a bathroom window.

"Fine," he said, looking at the man but talking to the sky.

38

WHEN THE RECEPTIONIST OPENED THE OFFICES OF POWELL &
Shah for business the next morning, she found a man sleeping
on the lobby couch, and screamed.

Donny woke like a startled animal at the sound, lost deep
in a paranoid corner of dreamland and not even remembering
where he was.

"Hey," he said, after coming halfway into the world and sitting up. "Hey, Linda. It's me."

"Mr. Kimoe?"

"Yes. Donny. Sorry to scare you. Miles gave me a key. And
I was in here working late, so I decided it made more sense to
just crash here. Since we have a big day today."

He looked at the look on her face, and then looked at himself, and realized he had no pants.

"Jesus, sorry," he said, pulling on his suit trousers, which
somehow made it even worse. "Let me get it together here. Guess
my alarm didn't go off."

They both knew he hadn't set any alarm. Only he knew
that part of the reason was that he couldn't, because he had
tossed his phone the night before to evade the law.

Linda had taken a more secure position, behind her big
desk. He wondered if she kept a gun in there. That wouldn't
be Miles's style, but it might be hers. Especially as someone
whose job description included greeting the felons as they
came through the door to meet with their lawyer.

"Let me get out of your hair," said Donny. "Is there a shower around here?"

"There's a locker room in the basement," she said, clearly heartened at the idea of him leaving. "Part of the gym."

"Great. Any idea where I can get a toothbrush?"

WHEN HE CAME back through the front door forty-five minutes later, feeling clean and refreshed despite having to put back on yesterday's clothes, he said good morning to Linda like it was the first time they had seen each other that day. And then he reclaimed his little conference room and got back to work. He had a hearing to prepare for, and some calls to make.

He closed the blinds in the conference room, just in case. And then he turned on the TV, partly as monitor and partly as company. It was when he was tuning the thing through BellNet's five hundred channels looking for news that wasn't government-approved that he got the idea he wished he'd had at the beginning of the week. It was an idea that Miles would definitely not approve of.

Fortunately, Miles was out of the office that day.

39

THE STUDIOS OF RADIO FREE HOUSTON TURNED OUT TO BE
not far from Donny's office, in a converted warehouse behind some old train tracks that ran parallel to the Southwest
Freeway. The door was black tinted glass, with peeling decal
lettering that said SUITE 203-NEW SUN PRODUCTIONS
INC. It was locked, and there was no doorbell. So Donny
knocked.

No one came.

He knocked again.

He looked around. There were a few cars in the lot, including a black Corvette and a Chevy Mammoth, one of the last
of the souped-up pickups with race-grade engines. The Mammoth had a bumper sticker Donny had seen before.

REFUGIO WAS AN INSIDE JOB

He walked around the side and looked for another door.

He saw a guy back there standing in the shade of the building smoking a cigarette. The guy was big, a little older than
Donny, wearing one of those fancy print collared shirts designed to be worn untucked.

As Donny approached, the guy looked up at him and blew
a cloud, the look on his face that of a man who wants to be left
alone.

"You're Mort Hanauer," said Donny.

The guy didn't say anything. Just kept smoking.

"I have an appointment with Paula," said Donny. "Tried the front door but nobody answered."

"I don't think she's back yet," said Mort.

"Maybe you can help me."

A flash of recognition came over Mort's face. "You're that lawyer, aren't you? I saw you on the news."

"It's not like they make it sound."

"No kidding. I work with one of your clients. Xelina knows the truth."

"Probably better than any of us. And that's kind of what I wanted to talk to you guys about."

"Maybe you better come inside," said Mort.

THE OFFICES WERE modest, a first-floor production suite made from repurposed warehouse space. Mort walked Donny past a short row of cubicles piled with papers, and showed him the recording studio where they did the program. It was weird to see it in the dark.

"You watch our program?" asked Mort.

Donny nodded. "My ex turned me on to it. You're a brave man."

You could tell Mort liked compliments. Behind him was a poster promoting one of his specials with a life-sized picture of an alien.

"Let's grab the meeting room," said Mort, leading him to a door down the hallway.

Donny grabbed a chair at the conference room table. The whiteboard on the wall was covered with scribbles, an elaborate chart mapping unlikely connections between names.

"Got a phone?" asked Mort.

"Yeah," said Donny. He had bought it that morning at the drugstore, along with his new toothbrush. Prepaid, under a fake name.

Mort grabbed a metal box from the middle of the table and slid it over to Donny. "Put it in there, will you?"

"Sure," said Donny, distracted by the chart.

"See anybody you know up there?" asked Mort.

"Yes, actually. I mean, I think so. It's hard to read." But that definitely looked like Lou's name down by the lower right corner.

"We've been trying to map local connections to the administration. Trying to reverse engineer what really happened last summer."

"I saw the poster in the hall. I'm embarrassed I haven't seen your report. Especially since I've been working that case."

"I know you are. And it hasn't come out yet. We're still finalizing a few things. Sorry about Hardy. That was just wrong."

Donny nodded. "Thanks. When's your release date?"

"Hopefully by the end of the month."

"The election will be a done deal by then. Could be good timing for reopening the investigation."

"Would've been better timing if we could have gotten it out before the election. But we just weren't there yet."

"Hard to get people to talk."

"I know some guys you could talk to. In Iowatown."

"Really?"

"Really. This one kid seems to have the missing link."

"You gotta give me their names."

"I don't know how they'll feel about talking to a lawyer, but I can see if they're open to an intro."

"That would be great."

"I'd also like to talk to you," said Mort. "How about we tape an interview."

"Now?"

"As soon as Paula gets back."

"What about?"

"Jerome Hardy. How they false-flagged him for Refugio. And Xelina Rocafuerte, too, if you want."

"Let's talk about her first. She told me she gave you some footage recently. Hot stuff. So hot you wouldn't run it."

"Have you seen it?" asked Mort.

Donny shook his head. "Trying to get my hands on a copy."

"If you see it, you'll understand. I need to stay on the air."

"So make me a copy. I've got a judge who wants to see it." He didn't mention his promise to Xelina to put it out there.

"Sure. Give me an interview and I'll burn you a copy."

Donny nodded. He had some things he wanted to get off his chest. Most of it was illegal to talk about in public, but it looked like they were getting ready to arrest him anyway. And if he played this opportunity right, he might be able to hasten the imminent regime change that promised to solve all of their problems. Once you started to realize you had to fight the system to make it work the way it was supposed to—really fight it, maybe not the way people like Clint had in mind, but with every non-violent means you had at your disposal—it changed how you played the game.

And it got him Xelina's footage, finally.

"Just as long as you don't air it until after five today," said Donny.

Mort gave him the thumbs-up.

AFTER THEY FINISHED the interview, Mort was so happy he gave Donny some free ad time. When Donny said he didn't have any commercials to put up, Mort said his team would hook him up.

40

WHEN THE CAB PULLED UP TO THE JERSEY BARRIERS OUTSIDE
the front of the federal courthouse, Donny saw a posse of feds
standing there at the main gate. Four uniformed marshals,
only one of whom he had ever seen before, and three suits, all
with earbuds and activated eyes. They didn't look like a welcoming committee, and he assumed they were there for him.
So he had the cab take him to the back, and snuck in to the
other entrance between the armored trucks waiting to pick up
their freight of live humans headed to new cages.

Cleburne was in charge of that checkpoint that afternoon. He told Donny some guys from Washington wanted to
talk to him. Donny said tell them they can come find me after
my hearing, because if I don't show up in her court in twenty
minutes Judge Jones will be ready to hang me and anyone else
she finds out wasted her time. Cleburne didn't argue.

Then he asked Donny if he'd heard what happened to
Turner the night before.

"That asshole?" said Donny. "He screwed me over big time.
And owes me some money. A lot."

"Turner's dead, Donny," Cleburne said harshly. "Drove
right off one of those unfinished sections of the Mayor B. I was
with him right before, at the bar, but he didn't seem drunk."

He probably wasn't, thought Donny.

Donny could see how upset Cleburne was, and gave him a

hug, the kind of hug you give a man who is ready to shoot you or handcuff you if you make the wrong move.

"Can we talk after my hearing?" said Donny.

Cleburne nodded.

Maybe Turner wasn't such an asshole after all.

"There you are!" said Percy, hollering at him from the other side of the checkpoint. "Come on! They're almost ready."

"Go on," said Cleburne, holding open the gate to let him bypass the scans.

"Thanks," said Donny. He turned to Percy and grabbed her shoulder. "Did you get the footage from Hanauer's people?"

"Yes!" she said.

"And?"

"What?"

"I haven't seen it."

"Come on! I have it on my laptop. You have to use it. Miles is wrong. He would agree if he were here."

"If Miles were running this case, it wouldn't be our only option."

Percy hit the elevator button.

"No," said Donny, looking around. "Let's take the stairs."

41

THEY AVOIDED THE MAIN HALLWAY AND SNUCK INTO THE COURT-
room through the judge's chambers.

"Hope you don't mind, Dennis," said Donny to the clerk,
turning to Percy. "I brought our new associate with me today,
and I wanted to show her the Batcave. She's a big admirer of
Her Honor."

Percy nodded. It helped that it was true.

"Okay," said Dennis. "But make it quick, and don't disturb
the judge. She's reading all that stuff you sent."

"We'll be very quick," said Donny. "Thanks."

They walked straight through, down the hall and into the
courtroom. You could see the surprise on Bridget's face when
Donny stepped around from behind the bench.

"Can we talk?" asked Bridget.

"Give me a minute," said Donny.

They took their places at the defense table. Then Percy
opened her laptop, gave Donny her headphones, and opened
the file.

THE FOOTAGE WAS a long clip, and only the last part had the
scene they needed.

It started with fragmentary scenes of the group of activists
packing up at the camp and heading into the Evac Zone. Personal shots more than documentary footage. Behind the scenes.

Friends screwing around. Swappable fails, mostly of the guards around the refugee camp before they headed out. One longer one of Gregorio giving an impromptu pep talk and homily about civil disobedience and the impossibility of trespassing on the land of your ancestors. Shots from inside a van, people chatting, smiles and hand signs, signs of nervousness, sights outside the window.

A crossing into the Zone, at an unmarked spot, on a gravel road. Looks like far outer Houstonia, dead end at a gate, camera eye on construction debris and used tires dumped at the shoulder, heavy metal compost slowly sliding into the woods. A hard stop there and another Gregorio stand-up, giving everyone a last chance to bail. And then the bolt cutters to the chain holding the gate closed. Cheers all around, and a little bit of clanking.

A checkpoint tower rising above stubby trees, blurred from zoom. A flag of unknown provenance. Probably a company.

A green lagoon. It looks coastal, swampy, verdant. Then you notice the abandoned buildings in the background. The lagoon is a pit, an old dig site working its way back to wild. In the distance, three tall structures, lattices of steel.

Those booms, the same ones Donny had heard, but much closer. Like the sound of explosions underground.

A campfire. Someone brought a guitar. Thankfully no bongos.

Tents. Sleeping bags inside what looks like an old office.

An inventory of salvaged items. Rusty tools. Shotgun shells and the jackets of pistol cartridges. A beat-up metal locker. A barricade of salvaged tires.

A young woman plucking some red fruit from a wild tree. She peels it, shares it, eats it. It's a pomegranate. Exotic gone native.

Clint, smiling at the side of a creek. The sound of birds.

A Coast Guard helicopter, coming over close.

More nature. A government cutter, out on the open water through the trees.

A rally. Meeting out in front of the big building. A pep talk from Gregorio, and from another leader, a woman who talks about the rewilding of the self. Then she looks away, past the camera lens. Then you hear the noise she must have heard.

Gunfire, a single shot.

Running, with the camera on. Footage jumbled and blacked out in spots. Then shots from a hidden position. Men in trucks. New and shiny black trucks, or deep blue. Raptors, Commanders, a Range Rover. An ancient pickup, redone with a big budget, modified for hunting the most dangerous game. They roll in at high speed, scattering the crowd. Sporadic gunfire, maybe warning more than aiming. People running to hide in the buildings. A few people run for the road.

Blurry shots from there, zoomed. Audio weak, too far away from the things the camera is focused on, too much noise of engines and yelling and wind. And the winded breathing of the woman with the camera. As the others hide, Gregorio stands his ground in front of the main building. The men who approach are not all white, but mostly, not a dozen, but almost. Strong-looking, if a few on the heavy side. Masked, with dark bandannas, some with shades. They are dressed better than you would expect people to dress for a lynching. Not in uniforms, but not in redneck militia wear, either. High-end outdoor gear, mostly, all dark colors. A lot of English-looking stuff—black waxed cotton, thin leathers. German and Austrian gunmetal, Mexican couture shotguns. Gaucho knifes and Guatemalan bespoke machetes, with the notches and the fringe. One guy, maybe the leader, in a suit and tie and snake boots, like a junior version of Judge Elwood.

Gregorio argues with the guys, meeting their guns with

words and resolve. And then you see a guy in a black technical jacket sneak up behind Gregorio and club him in the back of the head with a metal gun butt. That sound registers clearly on the audio, the sound of steel cracking bone.

You see a man, still alive, tied to the hitch of a hundred-thousand-dollar SUV and dragged back and forth over the cracked pavement of the old parking area while his people watch from their hiding spots, tracing an infinity loop of blood and skid marks on the sunbaked asphalt. They haul his body up against the hood of the Range Rover, ask him questions and poke him and prod him and then stab him with their well-made knives to make sure he still has some life left in him. Then one of them holds Gregorio's head up by his famous thick black bangs while another one brings his knife in and slowly severs the head from the body.

You can hear the screams. A woman runs out to intervene and is shot like a rabbit.

They hang the head from the flagpole.

You see people being led out from inside the building at gunpoint, hands tied or over their heads, and loaded in a moving truck.

The last shot is of men coming toward the camera, and then the recording abruptly ends.

42

JUDGE SHEILA JEFFERSON JONES HAD BEEN ON THE BENCH SO
long there were no lawyers left who could remember a time
when she was not. Most could not even remember the president
who appointed her, when she was still a young prosecutor. She
had survived several epochs of political change since then, remaining predictably unpredictable throughout. She had life tenure, and she used it.

In the peak of the post-war reckoning, she had sent three
military officers and one congressman to jail. Donny had worked
one of those cases, and gotten a taste of what it was like to be on
her bad side—and to be in her favor.

They had tried all sorts of ways to get her off the bench,
including one almost-successful public corruption investigation into her finances. But while she liked to live well, famous
for her Cadillacs and expensive clothes, it turned out she had
done it all within the law, from her salary and modest investments, over decades of hard work as a judge who called the
shots the way she saw them—no matter who she might piss
off in the process.

All of which meant she had senior status, and could take
the cases she wanted. The judges in charge of the docket would
have been happy if she had taken none, or at least stayed away
from the domestic counterterrorism docket. But she had her
own ideas about that.

So when Donny heard she had taken his Section 23–2

motion for a rehearing on Xelina's diversion to the denaturalization tribunal, he knew he owed Wendy for taking care of him. Yet, at that moment, he wondered if he might have made things even worse. Judge Jones was as mercurial as she was independent, and you never knew what turn of phrase or ill-considered objection might cause her to turn against you.

But there was no other way through.

"If this doesn't work, we're screwed," he said.

"You might be screwed either way," said Percy. "Broyles doesn't like it when you go over his head."

Donny shook his head. "Especially not to judges he considers embarrassing leftovers from 'a weaker time.' If she punts today, it's over."

"You'll still have the denaturalization hearing."

"Have you seen one of those?"

"No. But I've read the rules, and there's always a way."

He nodded. "Yeah, but sometimes the only way is outside the rules. I suppose we could get the footage on TV. Miles says no network would run it. But Mort Hanauer just offered me some commercial time. We could be our own damn network."

"Why are you assuming people who see it would be on our side?"

Donny hadn't considered that.

"Like my dad always said," added Percy, "people love seeing protesters get their heads knocked in."

"How about when they get decapitated?"

"You know the answer to that."

JUDGE JONES'S COURTROOM was one floor higher than Broyles's. It was bigger, too. She was smaller. Not as small as Xelina, and definitely not as skinny, but short enough that the way the black robes draped off her as she entered the courtroom after the "All rise" almost looked like a kid playing dress-up, or a cartoon character made real. Until she took her seat at the bench, looked over the room of powerful and not so powerful people standing in ritual obeisance to her, waited a long moment, and then hit the gavel with such gravity that you wondered if that was bigger, too. She was like a queen, a matriarch at the top of the metropolis who refused to accede to the rule of the guys who had tried to stop her every step of the way for all of her seventy-eight years.

Hers was the only courtroom in the building without the portrait of the President on the wall. Instead, they hung an official portrait of her, a big oil painting from ten years before.

There's one solution, Trey once joked on the course, to the problem of life tenure. Broyles chastised him for that, even though they were out in the surveillance-free zone of the private club, but then a moment later Donny caught him smiling as he put his putter back in the bag.

"Mr. Kimoe," said Judge Jones, after impatiently going through some administrative and scheduling miscellany. "I have read your motion. Twice. I think I understand your argument. But why don't you give me the condensed version."

"Gladly, Your Honor," said Donny, standing. He was happy not to have to make this argument under the judgmental gaze of his own client, even as he was frustrated they would not let her appear at the hearing, saying it was an unnecessary security risk where her testimony would not be required. "Our client is Xelina Rocafuerte, a young journalist who was found by Judge Broyles, presiding as the Special Emergency Tribunal, to be something other than what she is. She was designated an insurgent combatant and transferred for denaturalization proceedings, when all the record shows is that she was an independent documentarian who recorded footage of Councilman Gregorio Zarate-Taylor's recent occupation of a portion of the Coastal Evacuation Zone. Since the initial hearing in Judge Broyles's court, we have produced new evidence that substantiates what we contend is the real reason for Ms. Rocafuerte's detention and consignment to the administration's new star chamber: that she witnessed the brutal lynching and murder of Mr. Zarate-Taylor at the hands of a paramilitary death squad, and being a documentarian, she recorded video footage of the incident, footage the government wishes to force her to provide them access to so they can destroy it, having successfully suppressed its public release through the press. This afternoon we are seeking your intervention to quash Judge Broyles's order pursuant to the standard of review set forth in Section 23–2 of Burn Barnes, and on Fourteenth Amendment grounds, and release Ms. Rocafuerte. The government would remain free to take their charges to the grand jury, but we are confident they will not, because they know they can't even make the case for probable cause."

"What do you say to the government's argument that Judge Broyles's order is non-appealable, at least at this stage? That a Section 23–2 appeal isn't ripe until the denaturalization board makes its own ruling."

"That's not what the statute says, Your Honor. And even if you were to read it that way, we say that the statute and the decision are both constitutionally defective, primarily in their deprivation of Ms. Rocafuerte's birthright citizenship without due process of law."

"What about the Supreme Court's decision in *Rojo*?"

"Different facts, Your Honor. That case involved a naturalized U.S. citizen. An immigrant. Ms. Rocafuerte was born here in Houston, and that puts her in a very different category for Fourteenth Amendment purposes."

Judge Jones was looking at her benchtop monitor, whose screen only she could view.

"I see you have provided evidence of your client's work as a journalist, and supporting affidavits. Where would the court find the footage you claim the government is trying to suppress?"

"I have that here with me, Your Honor, and would be happy to play it back for you. There is about eleven minutes of legible footage. Shall we set up the big screen?"

"Your Honor," said Bridget Kelly, standing and interjecting herself. "The government objects."

"Hang on," said Judge Jones. "Mr. Kimoe, you're saying you have footage of the incident you claim, that you did not include as part of your motion?"

"That's correct, Your Honor. I was only able to obtain a copy after we filed."

"How did you obtain the copy?"

"I am not at liberty to disclose."

"Well, that sounds a little fishy, but I'd like to review it and decide for myself."

"We object, Your Honor," said Bridget again. "It's not relevant to the issue, and if it were we would need an opportunity to authenticate and dispute. And it's an evasion of the fact that, with all due respect, this court has no jurisdiction to even entertain Mr. Kimoe's very creative but substantively and procedurally defective motion."

"This court has jurisdiction to uphold the Fourteenth Amendment, Ms. Kelly, no matter how much the government wishes to evade its limits. Give the clerk your recording, Mr. Kimoe."

Donny looked back at Percy, who already had it ready.

The courtroom bustled with chatter while Donny gave the memory card to the clerk, and showed him the file to display on Judge Jones's monitor. There were reporters there in the gallery—the *Chronicle,* the *Wire,* and a couple of national stringers. And anything that came out in open court was automatically exempt from the news ban. Bridget was also back there at the gallery now, talking over the bar to a couple of suits, no doubt representatives of her real client. One of them was Donny's new friend from the night before. He looked a little tired today.

Donny sat back down. Percy gave him a thumbs-up, which was rare. He looked at his notes, scanned the proposed order he had submitted with his motion, wondered what he had missed, and watched Judge Jones watch the horror movie, trying to assess her reaction and how it would influence her thinking on the matter at hand.

If she had a strong reaction, it didn't register on her face.

"Ms. Kelly," she said, looking at the prosecution table.

"Your Honor."

"Have you seen this footage?"

"I have not, Your Honor."

"I want the woman who made this recording in here Monday morning."

"That's not possible, Your Honor."

"Why is that not possible, Ms. Kelly?"

"The defendant is being transferred out of this district as we speak, to the temporary insurgent detention facility for further denaturalization proceedings. Jurisdictionally, she is gone, and my office has no further power to produce her."

Judge Jones looked down over her glasses. Then she looked over at Donny. Then she looked up at the ceiling, thinking. And after a long moment, turned back to Bridget.

"I was going to withhold judgment on this until we got further testimony, but I guess you are going to make me do this the hard way. Mr. Kimoe's motion is granted. You are to release Ms. Rocafuerte immediately. I rule that the proceedings of the Special Emergency Tribunal are constitutionally defective under the Fourteenth Amendment, at least with respect to native-born citizens, and all pending cases are hereby stayed. Mr. Kimoe is to bring his client before us here on Monday morning at eleven. Am I clear?"

"You do not have that authority, Judge," said Bridget, her tone suddenly less deferential.

"You are wrong on that, Ms. Kelly, but you are free to try to convince the Fifth Circuit. They are officing downstairs now, if you recall, so it's a short trip. In the meantime, I am ordering the marshals of this court to go fetch Ms. Rocafuerte from Coast Guard custody and deliver her to Mr. Kimoe."

The suits behind Bridget had changed their demeanor, too. One was typing away frantically on his phone, while Donny's pal glared at Judge Jones.

"Have a nice weekend, you all," said the judge.

And when she stood to leave, some of the dudes in Bridget's crew did not rise.

It made Donny wonder what kind of weekend had just arrived.

He sent Clint the good news, but got no response.

Apparently Clint was making his own news.

43

DONNY WAS FINISHING UP HIS CELEBRATORY REMARKS TO THE handful of reporters outside the courthouse when Percy yanked at his sleeve.

"You need to come see this," she said.

"Hang on," he said, turning back to the microphones.

"No," said Percy. "You need to see this. Now."

It was on the TV in the hallway, just past security. A news alert, the kind that preempted whatever else was on.

TERRORIST ESCAPES
DARING DAYLIGHT RAID
SUSPECTS AT LARGE

"Fuck," said Donny.

"It's her," said Percy.

"And him," said Donny, the elation of victory bleeding off as fast as the anger rose, anger at Clint and anger at himself for talking too much. "Damn it."

Onscreen, live helicopter footage. A freeway, one of the toll roads out of town. No cars, just a smoke plume. Grainy zoom of a black armored truck, capsized and burning. Cut to a picture of Xelina's mug shot. Then back to a wide pan, the other direction, traffic backed up for miles.

"What did they say?" asked Donny.

"Ambush, looks like," said Cleburne, watching with them

now. "Two pickups and a motorcycle. Intercepted the convoy. Bike diverted the escort while the pickups got the package."

"You forgot about the bomb," said Cleburne's colleague, the one with the drone eyes.

"Yeah, this wasn't on the news but we just heard it on the squawk," said Cleburne. "Looks like they disabled the truck with an explosion. Must have had inside info on the route. Or else an inside man who planted it on the truck before it left the jail."

"Some boys who knew what they were doing," said drone eyes.

Donny remembered what Clint said, about self-help.

"Anybody hurt?" Donny asked.

"You better fucking hope not," said drone eyes.

"So they were headed south," said Donny, looking at the freeway footage more closely.

"Watch and see if these aren't the same scumbags that killed Turner," said Cleburne.

"There's no way—"

"Cleburne's right," said drone eyes. "I hope you didn't do anything to help these guys."

"We gotta go," said Donny, grabbing Percy to leave through the back door and make a run for her car.

44

SATURDAY MORNING, DONNY TRIED TO SLEEP IN, BUT THE DREAMS wouldn't let him. He woke up before sunrise, in his own apartment. He figured it might be the last chance he had. While yesterday's hearing may have given him a little breathing room, he knew it was only a day or two before they came after him again. And this time, it would be with charges that could stick, no matter who won the election: that he had conspired with his client and her associates to plan her escape.

Maybe it wouldn't happen. Conveniently—maybe too conveniently—the guy who had given him the information he unwisely passed on was now dead. He thought about the bald man. He didn't seem like the type who needed to kill people to get his way. And those goons in the video didn't look like feds. But then neither did the bald man. Not really. At least not a typical fed. More like a guy you'd meet in the boardroom of a big company.

Out the window, the light was coming up behind the towers of downtown. Donny decided to go for a walk, and pay his last respects to Turner.

THE MAYOR DONALD Barthelme Memorial Turnpike was the name of a freeway they had begun building to the design of its namesake, but never finished. People said Barthelme would have liked nothing more than to have his name plastered on a road to nowhere. Some suggested he had planned it that way, knowing they would run out of money. Barthelme had been a local developer, but a uniquely creative one, a patron of contemporary art famous for building projects that took advantage of Houston's laissez-faire zoning laws to let the city's inner freak flag fly. Sometimes his projects incorporated monumental sculpture, like the giant yellow balloon that had floated over his Museum of the Buffalo Bayou for several years before it finally broke free of its tether during the first night of Superstorm Zelda and rampaged over the suburbs until lodging half deflated against a TV transmission tower. Many of the buildings were sculpture as building—the auditorium since renamed as the Diboll Timber Harvesters Arena along the South Loop that looked from a distance like a pyramid designed by aliens or shrooming hippies or both. Mayor B's freeway followed the same logic, or smiling defiance of logic. The idea, he had proclaimed when he first published his crazy sketches, was to build the sort of freeway that you are happy to be stuck on. The freeway itself as public art. There was a cloverleaf that corkscrewed on top of itself like an internal combustion Charybdis, a fork that tripled and rejoined, stretches that skirted the edges of buildings or went right through them. A Texas freeway without straight lines, except when it ended abruptly one hundred feet over a block of old warehouses at the edge of downtown.

Underneath the drop was where Turner had come to rest. They had moved him and his truck by the time Donny showed up, but the crater was still there. Not a deep one, but one in which you could clearly see the F and the R from the grill of his F-300 embossed backwards in the cracked asphalt of an empty lot.

Donny stood there for a while, looking up at the precipice of exposed rebar where the freeway terminus had been slowly crumbling away. He wondered how you could pull such a crazy move unless it was on purpose. The freeway had never been opened to cars. The two entries they completed were gated off, but the thing was such a popular monument to folly that people were always breaking down the gates to walk, ride, or even drive up there, and there were stories that from time to time someone would enter the ramp thinking they were hopping on I-10.

He walked up there himself to take in the view. He peeked over the edge, and quickly stepped back. Then he approached again, more slowly. The air was crisp, and the breeze a little scary without any railing to grab. But the view, if you looked beyond the crater, was kind of awesome. You could see the bayou, and the way the city grew up around it, public space and private space, infrastructure and industry, houses and apartment towers, and the green that was always trying to come back up, especially in the channels cut by water. He saw it for a moment through Xelina's eyes. What it must have looked like five hundred years earlier. What it would look like in another five hundred years, or even fifty. How nature and the city weren't really different things. Or at least they didn't have to be.

"Hey," he said, after taking a minute to remember the number, since the new phone didn't remember for him.

"Good morning," said Percy.

"Sorry if I woke you."

"It's cool. I was going to call you anyway."

"Guess where I am."

"Where?"

He told her.

"That's kind of cool," she said. "But mostly creepy."

"Considering what my client just did, I feel like a bit of a creep. Anyway, I thought maybe I would find a clue. But instead

I got another idea. One I had at the beginning of this deal, and almost forgot."

"What's that?"

"Meet me at the office and I'll loop you in. It's a way to keep our case alive until we find our client. Hopefully before they do."

"It's Saturday, and we just got our ass kicked."

"Actually, we just kicked ass—except for that little client control problem caused by my blabbering lips. All the more reason why we need to keep at it. See you there in an hour?"

Percy sighed. "Okay," she said. "Make it two."

"Thank you," said Donny. Then he pulled a nickel from his pocket, tossed it with his thumb, and watched it shimmer in the light all the way down. Turner always told him they had nickel draws in heaven.

45

THAT EVENING, AFTER THEY FINISHED DRAFTING THE NEW PETITION,
Percy drove Donny to Iowatown.

Iowatown was not the official name of the place. That was
Domestic Refugee Resettlement Center–Houston East. And it
wasn't a tent camp like you see on TV. It was a suburban subdivision that had been evacuated, fenced off, and repurposed as
temporary housing. A gated community meant to keep people
in, not out.

You could see it from the freeway if you knew where to
look, but you had to get a good bit closer to really see the differ-
ences. The security was pretty lax, since the residents were allowed to come and go—the government at least pretended they
were still citizens—but the high fences clearly demarcated the
area, and the streets were policed by corporate paramilitaries
ready to lock it down on a moment's notice. The last big lockdown was after the assassination attempt.

When you got inside, you saw how crowded it was. Rows
of single-family factory homes crammed with three or four
families. The backyards and front lawns filled with improvised
housing for the overflow—shanties made of plywood and
Tyvek, metal panel and cinder blocks, the remains of garden
sheds and backyard playscapes. There were said to be close to
twenty thousand people living in the camp. And yet somehow,
despite the chaos of it, it did not look disordered.

"It's weird how tidy it is, right?" said Donny.

"Yeah," said Percy. "And how white."

"Also true," said Donny, looking out at the gang of corn-fed kids running beside their car as they drove down the main access road.

"This place is seriously fucked up," said Percy.

"I know," said Donny. "But what's more fucked up is how they make these people pay their way."

"What do you expect? This country loves using prisoners as cheap labor. Why would refugees be any different."

"Picking up trash along the freeway is one thing. But those cleanup brigades they send out into the Zone?"

"Yeah, you couldn't give me enough safety gear to do that."

"I guess that means you're not going out there with me."

"You'll be fine," said Percy. "Your body is proven to have a high capacity for poison."

"Very funny. This is our turn, isn't it?"

"Yeah. The place we're looking for should be down the block."

They passed a line of people taking handouts of bottled water and MREs from the back of a truck.

"I think we're gonna need to walk from here," said Percy.

The street came to a dead end, a cul-de-sac with a few houses around the circle. Between the last two houses was a wide, well-worn path, almost the width of a road, that led into a maze of improvised structures that went back farther than you could see.

"That's it," said Percy.

"Down that dirt road? How are we going to find our way around in there?"

"She said there would be a guide waiting for us," said Percy. "To wait at the entrance and they will find us."

Donny gave her a quick doubtful glance as she pulled over,

behind a shipping container that had been parked at the side of the street.

"Come on," said Percy. "It's time."

They got out. Donny turned up the collar of his suit coat, as if it would help him blend in, but it only made him stand out more.

They walked down the path, to the entrance of the maze. Percy led them to a spot where a gas camping lantern hung from a pole.

"We wait here," she said.

People were coming and going, many returning with heavy loads of food and water from the truck. Moms and kids, bent old men, sullen teens, and a few angry-looking young men. A security guard walked by in his dark tacticals with the Texical logo on his hat and shoulder, a small military assault rifle strapped on and held low, in patrol mode. He gave Donny and Percy a long lookover as he walked by. And after he had stepped out of sight, you could hear the crackle of his radio. But you couldn't make out the words.

"Percy?" said a voice from the shadows.

"Yeah," said Percy.

A tall white kid stepped into view. He wore a ball cap with a picture of a deer skull, a black sweatshirt, and work pants covered in patches. His neck was crazy skinny, the skinny of a kid whose weight had not yet caught up with his rapidly growing height, and Donny wondered how it held up his head.

"I'm Jared," said the kid. "Come on."

Without waiting, he led them back into the maze. The farther in you got, the tighter the spaces seemed to get, and the more elaborate the shanties were, some layered two and three stories high. There were a lot of people outside in the alleyways, working on stuff, preparing food to share, or just hanging out.

There weren't any security forces in sight, and you got the sense from the residents that their minders didn't come back in there much. That didn't stop Jared from walking so fast it was hard to keep up. Especially in lawyer shoes.

"Up there," said Jared, stopping suddenly, then pointing at a ladder in the wall to their right.

Donny looked at the ladder, and followed it up the side of a structure that looked like a post-apocalyptic variation on neo-Tudor, with an exposed frame of salvaged timbers and big patches of sheetrock and concrete that looked ill-balanced and maybe on the verge of falling right on top of them. The ladder, which was really just a series of handholds, went to a door about two-thirds of the way up.

"You go first," said Percy.

"Why not," said Donny.

He didn't look back until he reached the little portal, and a woman's hand reached out to pull him through.

"You must be Tara," he said.

She nodded. She was tall, too, with long black hair pulled back, Eurasian features, a black hoodie, jeans, and black work boots. "Where's the lady I talked to?"

"Right behind me," said Donny, as he helped Percy up, and then Jared.

The room was small and the ceiling low. They had painted the ceiling sky blue, as if that would keep you from bumping your head. The walls were covered with a multi-artist cartoon variation on the Garden of Earthly Delights. The floors were covered with carpet remnants repurposed as rugs, the only furnishings some big pillows and a couple of beanbag chairs.

"Thank you for meeting us," said Donny, once they were all there.

"I already regret it," said Tara, sizing up Donny. "But you said I could help Xelina. So let's talk."

She took one of the beanbag chairs, and invited them with a gesture to join her on the floor. The kid stayed standing, alternately watching the door and Donny and Percy.

"Well, here's the deal," said Percy. "Xelina escaped."

"I heard," said Tara.

"And we need to find her," said Percy.

"I can't help you with that," said Tara.

"If we can find her, we can still save her," said Donny.

"You just said she already saved herself," said Tara. "She's probably in Matamoros by now."

"I doubt that," said Percy. "We had to get through four checkpoints just to come here. The city's on lockdown."

"Her and Clint know how to find their own paths," said Tara.

"I bet they do," said Donny. "But they don't need to. We already won her case. Instead, they're in more danger now. The people who came after her the first time will be pursuing her even harder. I'm worried they won't come out of this alive."

Tara considered that. "Those were some scary dudes."

"You were with her when they picked her up the first time?" said Percy.

Tara nodded. "I still don't understand why they only took Xelina, and left me and Bar."

"Maybe they wanted you to tell the scary stories," said Donny.

"Or maybe they needed more evidence," said Percy.

"They didn't seem like the types who care much about evidence," said Tara. "Or warrants. Or even badges."

"Uniforms?" asked Percy.

Tara shook her head. "Street clothes. Like expensive out-door gear. And one wore a suit. Like you." She nodded at Donny.

"Did they say who they were?" asked Percy.

"Yeah, sort of. Called themselves 'the Squad.' But they didn't say who they worked for. They were all young white guys, real clean-cut, in a mean kind of way. Just one of them a little older, with some grey."

"Six of them?" said Donny.

"Yeah. And I think a couple of them were the same guys who were there when they took out Gregorio."

"You sure?" said Percy.

"No, I'm not, because that time they were wearing masks. But I recognized the clothes. And the swagger."

"An extrajudicial lynch mob," said Percy, looking at Donny.

"Exactly," said Tara.

"You saw them kill Gregorio?" asked Donny.

Tara nodded.

"And could you identify these two guys if you saw them?"

"I think so," said Tara.

"Will you testify?" asked Donny.

"No fucking way," said Tara. "Everybody knows that court-house doesn't have an exit."

Percy looked at Donny.

"If they didn't take you when they had the chance," said Donny, "I don't see why they would now. I think I can keep you safe."

"This is so much bigger than Xelina, y'all," said Tara. "Don't you get it?"

"We get it," said Donny. "It's about the elections."

"No," said Tara with a sneer. "The elections are just a dis-traction. Maybe you haven't been out to the Zone."

"Only to the edge," said Donny.

"Then you have no idea. You should see what they're doing out there. I mean, I don't even know what it is, but they look like giant robots. Like something out of a movie."

"Giant robots?" said Percy.

"I've seen it," said Jared. "It's an eviction. To make room for the machines."

"While they corral us behind fences," said Tara. "Make us do the scut work the robots can't do. And then when we're too worn out to do that, they'll probably feed us to them."

"Come on," said Donny, looking at Percy with raised eyebrows. She kept a poker face.

"Tell me you haven't heard the noises," snapped Tara.

Donny considered that.

"They're planning something big out there," said Jared. "The elections won't matter."

"Okay," said Donny. "Maybe we need to check that out. If I promise to do that, will you tell us where Xelina is hiding? I can keep her safe if I can just get her to come back to the courthouse with me on Monday." He held his hand to his heart. "I swear."

"Even after the escape?" said Percy, and Tara looked at them sharply.

"I have a plan," said Donny.

"Maybe we need to make our own plan," said Tara. "And take the fight to them."

"We don't need another action like that," said Donny. "I have one client dead because of that kind of thinking."

"I knew I recognized you," said Jared.

"Yeah?" said Donny, losing patience.

"Yeah. I saw your picture in the news. It's your fault Jerome's dead."

"Thanks, kid. I'd almost forgotten."

"Jerome was my friend, man. He helped us out. Gave us a path out of here."

"I understand. He was my friend, too."

"Well, you let him down, man. Probably because you don't get it. The whole thing was a setup."

"How's that?" said Donny.

"Jerome didn't give Bill and those guys the guns, or the plan. It was these same guys Tara's talking about."

"What?"

"How do you know?" asked Percy at the same time.

"Because I was there. With Bill when he had one of the meetings and I was gonna help, and then later. And I know those were some of the same guys."

Donny processed that.

"False flag?" said Percy.

"Totally," said Tara. "Everybody knows it."

"Nothing quite so convenient as a terrorist emergency when you want to get things under control so you don't lose power," said Donny, as much to himself as anyone in the small room.

"So what are you going to do about it?" said the kid.

Donny looked at him. "I'm gonna get you to help me find those bastards, that's what. But first you are going to tell me where Xelina is."

46

TO GET TO THE HIDEOUT THE NEXT MORNING WITHOUT BEING seen, they had to walk up a paved creek through the secret backside of some subdivision on the far southeast side, in the heart of Gregorio's old Council district and right at the edge of the Evac Zone. The creek was mostly dry, littered with the occasional shopping cart or lost tire, but it went on much longer than they expected. They took a wrong turn at one point and found themselves in a big homeless camp back at the end of one fork of the creek, dozens of tents and lean-tos made from found materials. The people seemed friendly, and when Donny asked directions, they weren't sure what place he was talking about, but they told him where the channels of the creek would go.

As they continued on, a small black dog followed them, first at a distance, then closer, quiet and non-aggressive. Donny tried to shoo it at first but Percy said leave it be. Maybe it will show us the way.

Another forty-five minutes and two more wrong turns walking down in there, as the morning sun started to get hot, Donny wondered if it was a stupid idea to wear a suit. He had honestly thought they were headed to an apartment building, and might end up dealing with the law before the day was out. Now he wondered if he had stepped into some even bleaker future than the one he was living in, and by sundown the suit would rediscover its hunting attire roots as they scrabbled to survive in the ruins. Seeing how many people already lived like that, hiding in plain sight in the ruins of the right now, made you realize how adjacent that reality really was. He imagined himself trapping nutria at dusk, long hair held back by a necktie repurposed as a headband—

"I think this is it," said Percy, interrupting his post-apocalyptic daydream.

She was behind him, pointing at a graffiti tag he had walked right past. There were so many down in this urban canal, and they all looked so similar to Donny, it was easy to miss one.

This one was different, though. It was a stencil. A mastodon in bright red spray paint, its tusks pointed in the direction they were supposed to go. Just like Tara and Jared had told them.

They appraised the path before taking it. It was a narrow trackway leading through tall weeds, up what looked to be a smaller tributary creek. This creek seemed wet, with a trickle of water emptying out onto the concrete channel.

"You go first," said Percy for the second time in two days.

"Okay," said Donny. He looked around for a rock or a stick or something that would serve as a defensive weapon in a pinch, and settled for a broken-off chunk of concrete he put in the side pocket of his suit coat. Percy watched him do this, at once amused and mildly approving.

Donny almost tripped as he walked in there, and looked down to see an old section of chain-link fencing unmoored from its pillars and trampled onto the ground. It had been there long enough that the weeds were growing up through it. He looked forward, then back at Percy.

"Do you think we're going into the Zone?"

She shrugged. "Those kids said it was okay. This is definitely the way. I can tell."

Donny nodded, looked around again, sniffed the air as if he

were more tracker than lawyer. Then he stepped over the fence and walked on in.

Pretty soon the weeds were up to their shoulders, and it did start to smell funny, like some gas from beneath the earth was leaking out. He was about to say they should turn around, when the path abruptly ended and they found themselves staring into the mouth of a huge pipe. It was an enclosed concrete storm culvert that drained out into the creek. Damp, very dark, and a little slimy-looking. There was a small but steady flow of water pouring off. Instinctively, Donny put his hands up to catch it. And then he drank some.

"Are you nuts?" said Percy.

"Maybe," he said. "I just know it's clean. I don't know how."

They looked at the dog, who was lapping the water up where it hit the ground, oblivious to the plastic bottles and other trash that had collected around the puddles.

"This has to be the place," said Percy, still shaking her head. "It's just like they said."

"Yeah, but they didn't seem like they really wanted us to find it."

"They just didn't think we could follow their directions. That we would get lost."

That's when the dog scrambled around them, and soon was standing up there in the mouth of the culvert looking back.

"Look," said Percy, pointing at the tunnel. "You can see it through there."

Donny looked to the far side, into the light. She was right. He climbed up and followed the dog into the storm sewer, which was big enough that you could walk in it only slightly crouched. It was a short distance before it opened back up, and there it was: a big apartment complex behind a chain-link fence covered with dense green vines and flowers that looked like blood orange trumpets. There was an engineered drainage terrace connecting it to the creek, overgrown with weirdly beautiful thirsty grasses coming up through the wire mesh and landscaped rocks of the gabion. Inside the fence was all green, too, with retama and fan palms popping up in a yard gone wild. The building looked abandoned, four stories of beat-up stucco under a mansard roof that had been fighting the elements longer than its designers had in mind, some of the windows boarded up and others broken, big graffiti tags on the walls that looked like a menagerie of fantastic animals and an alphabet of hieroglyphics from the future. But when you watched for a while it looked weirdly like maybe there were people living in there. Donny noticed one nearby window that was cracked open. Inside you could see some furniture, something hung on the wall, a mug on a table. A gun.

Donny looked back at Percy, half-expecting her to be gone, but she was smiling and giving him the thumbs-up.

They climbed over the gabion, under the fence, and into the yard. The foliage was even thicker than it looked. Percy shushed him as Donny led the way through, snapping twigs and stepping on a fallen branch. Then they were through, by an old paved path that led between the building they had seen from the outside and another one that was identical but at a different angle, facing a third path that made a central courtyard with an old playground and an empty swimming pool. The courtyard had been turned into a giant garden. And there were people, two women and some kids.

And then they heard a click, metal on metal, and turned.

"Howdy," said Clint, rifle trained on them.

"Have you heard the one," said Xelina, from behind them, "about what happened to the lawyers who tricked the people?"

47

"YOU'RE HARD TO FIND," SAID DONNY.

"When your attorney lets them lock you up, you have to make your own sanctuary," said Xelina.

"I got that order vacated," said Donny.

"Too late," said Xelina. "Someone more reliable beat you to it."

Clint looked a little sheepish. He also looked injured, with a gash on his face, a bandage over his forearm, and exhaustion in his stance.

"Can you put that down?" said Donny, nodding at Clint's AK-47. "And can we sit down and talk?"

"This place is cool," said Percy, looking around at the complex while the dog guarded her.

"Come on," said Xelina, sizing up Percy and smiling. "I'll show you around."

SABINE WATERS APARTMENTS was the name on the old sign up front at the street, but the people who were squatting there had other names for it, names they didn't tell Donny.

There were forty-three people living there, they said, but Donny didn't see that many. He saw about fifteen people, including the three little kids. But from what they had done with the place, you could believe the energy of a much bigger group than that had been put into it.

The buildings had been put back to use, with dwellings, a little school, a television studio, a group kitchen, and an arsenal, energy provided by solar panels on the roof, water provided by rainwater collection and by the springs they had somehow managed to bring back to life back there by the creek. They showed them the old signal oak that had been bent hundreds of years ago to mark the springs, one of the few trees that had been left when they built the complex, and the way they first knew to look for the springs when they found the place. Now the zone around the springs had been transformed into some relic of a healthier past, a yard gone wild.

"It's so beautiful," said Donny, meaning it.

"This happened on its own," said Xelina. "Wait until you see it after we help it."

"I want to help," said Percy.

Xelina smiled at her. "Good," she said. "You can help us spread it." She reached into her pocket and tossed Percy a small plastic bag. Percy held it up and saw a mix of seeds.

"Those ones go close to the water. I'll show you how to find more, so you can collect them for us. Come on, let's talk."

They sat back there, under the trees, at a table made from an old cable spool.

"Those were a lot of guns back there," said Donny.

"They have more," said Xelina.

"What are you planning?"

"Why should we trust you?" said Xelina.

"I'm your lawyer."

"I fired you."

"You never told me."

"I guess that's true."

"Let me in. Let me know what you want to do, see if I can't help you achieve your goals by lawful means."

"There's no more time for lawyer bullshit," said Clint. "Now is when we fight back, the only way that gets their attention."

"There are still a few levers we can pull without shooting anyone. It just takes some work to find them. Not as much work as finding you all. If you had stuck with me, you would be free. Now Xelina really is a felon, and they have probable cause to round up the rest of you. If we want to build a better future, we need to build it on law."

"If we want to build a better future, we need to take it," said Clint. "Break it, break it down, blow it up, hang some of these Earth-eating fascists from streetlamps like they have their secret squads doing to the people who want to do it your way."

"Sounds like a blast," said Donny. "I'll put my money on the guys with the tanks and drones."

"If you'd ever been on the other side of asymmetrical warfare," said Clint, "you might have a different opinion."

"And if you'd been with me in the room when they executed Jerome Hardy, you might have a different opinion."

"Listen," said Xelina. "Here's the deal. The FRO is a figment of the government's imagination. It never existed, other than as a bunch of different people trying to figure out a way to have an actual future, or just have some fun in the meantime. There is no underground. Or I should say there *was* no underground, until now, until they showed us that we don't have a choice. I was an observer, and they taught me I need to be a participant. If you want to help us, you need to do the same thing."

Donny wasn't sure if it was the words or the thing with her eyes that made him certain she was right, even though what she was pushing on him went against everything he had been taught. He broke her gaze, only to find himself looking at the gun on her hip, as he considered his next move.

Another couple walked up just then. A burly little brown

guy in work pants and a hoodie, and a tall, straight-haired blond woman with a black T-shirt, patched bell bottoms, and goatskin boots, white skin tanned the color of an endless summer, both carrying rifles, his a beat-up Armalite, hers a high-end Italian shotgun with metal inlays.

"Hey, Clint," said the woman. "We may have a problem."

"What's that?" said Clint.

"Listen."

Donny listened with the rest of them, but only heard birds and faraway cars.

"Fuck," said Clint. "Get everybody inside. These idiots got followed. I knew we shoulda just shot 'em."

Percy heard it, and then she pointed at the sky like she saw it.

Then they heard the sirens, outside, a lot closer.

48

THEY WERE BETTER PREPARED FOR THIS THAN DONNY WOULD have expected.

Clint said the stateside drones weren't armed. Not yet.

He said I've seen what it looks like when they aim a Hellfire missile at the middle of a city, and you don't want to see that.

He said everybody get your radios on and go to your spots, just like we practiced.

Donny got winded following them up to the top floor of the building closest to the street.

Percy said I'm going to the basement.

They stepped into an open floor, all the walls torn out, some of the debris still there piled up over to the side. There were holes in the ceiling, and patches where old green carpet was still stapled in, getting greener. Most of the windows had been taped or boarded over, but other viewholes had been punched through. And through them, they could see what was coming: two teams of fugitive-hunting U.S. Marshals and a squad of Coast Guard DOGs, ready to rumble. One of the squads was suiting up in its battle armor, while the snipers took positions, and one tough-looking lady Coastie loaded a grenade launcher. The first drone was already in the air, hovering and watching them right through the walls.

"This isn't as bad as I expected," said Clint, binoculars up against a slit in the wall.

Donny put his hand on the wall. It felt like he could push

right through. A bullet sure as hell could, and they were ready to bring down a lot more than that.

"You think?" said Xelina, looking through a broken window.

"They didn't come ready for the kind of fight we got."

"What are you going to do?" said Donny.

"Soon as they start coming, hit 'em hard from five points. You watch, they won't even send a second wave."

Donny looked at Xelina. "This is nuts," he said. "They're going to shred us."

"You got a better idea?" said Clint.

"Surrender," said Donny.

"Fuck that," said Clint.

"Not all of us. Just let me go talk to them. See if I can get them to take one of us."

"He's right," said Xelina. "We should try it. We didn't plan this very well."

"Yes we did. We are ready to light the fuse."

"I'm not ready to die, baby. I'm going out there with Donny."

"The fuck you are."

"You can stay here and cover me."

"Nope. If you're gonna be your stubborn-ass self then you are going to stay here and watch me go out there and make sure this weasel doesn't give us all up."

"Up to you all, but I'm going," said Donny.

WHITE FLAG HANGING from a top-floor window, Donny hollered the deal, we're coming out, we want to talk, don't shoot. The Texas-twanged robot voice of a loudspeaker said roger that, exit this door, we will send negotiators.

Donny followed Clint down to the ground floor. Clint set his weapons there just inside the double doors.

"I wish I'd never seen you," he said. "But I'm keeping an open mind."

Then he threw the doors open, and Donny stepped through, hands on his head.

That was when he finally saw the sign, out in front of the complex. It had a picture of some big machine that looked like a cross between a drill, a refinery, and a water park. It had a fancy corporate logo. And a legend:

COMING SOON

A NEW PROJECT FROM

NEW FRONTIER DEVELOPMENT GROUP

49

THE FIRST CLASS THEY TAUGHT THEM IN LAW SCHOOL WAS CALLED Property.

The first case they taught them in Property was about how you make the things in nature your property through kill or capture.

The specific example they used to teach this lesson was one about a real estate investor chasing a fox across an empty lot.

Of course it took place in the Hamptons. The Hamptons in 1800, when a rich dude could still roam on horseback across "waste and uninhabited land."

"Waste and uninhabited land" was the New York Supreme Court's term for the commons—land no one owned and everyone shared. Every *thing* shared, if you counted the fox, and its fellow forest creatures that had inhabited the uninhabited land for longer than the humans that were there when the Anglo-American real estate investors showed up.

The dude on the horse was named Lodowick, which Donny thought was kind of an awesome name. Lodowick was new in town, having moved there to buy and sell real estate. When he read cases like that, Donny always got distracted by wanting to imagine what those people were really like, what they looked like, what the details were that the judges didn't think were relevant to their opinions. Donny imagined a guy who looks like a realtor, complete with whitened teeth, dressed up like the opposite of a Pilgrim, riding a horse that's like if horses could be like new BMWs.

What happened was Lodowick chased the fox, and just as he was about to shoot, another guy beat him to it. Lodowick sued, asserting that by initiating the chase he acquired ownership of the animal. The trial court agreed, but the New York Supreme Court reversed, digging out ancient authorities from the likes of Puffendorf, Babeyrac, and Blackstone to explain that the way you make an animal your property is to mortally wound it or get it in a net or a trap.

The rule of capture, as they called it, worked well for other things. Oil, gas, and water, for example. The early Texans used one variant to reclaim the cattle that had strayed from their former Spanish masters and gone feral. Wandering bovines ready to be herded like found money, worth so much dough it was profitable to drive them overland all the way to Kansas, where they could be taken by freight car to the big cities for slaughter and consumption.

Take 'em to Missouri, Matt.

They had sucked Texas and most of the rest of the country so dry that they were working on figuring out ways to suck the water from the deep crust of the Earth. Now they wanted to export the rule of capture into outer space. Donny imagined John Wayne on Mars.

Take 'em to Jupiter, computer.

Donny imagined John Locke on Mars. The guy who really gave the first-generation American judges their self-serving ideas of property. Viewing the recently discovered Americas through the prism of an English gentleman, Locke cooked up a theory of individual ownership of the things we take from the Earth by imagining a "state of nature" that never actually existed, a world of natural bounty to which no prior claims exist. If you own your own body, you own your labor. And when you apply your labor to nature, by carving a piece of wood, or drilling a hole in the ground, or capturing a fox, you become the owner of that, too, because your labor is now embodied in it.

Joyce called that the view from nowhere, the assumption that one's own perspective is neutral and objective, when in fact it is totally skewed by self-interest. Locke's principal example for the state of nature was America as discovered by the English. And thanks to Locke, the English created a fantastic real estate empire, selling off pieces of a continent on the other side of the ocean that had been occupied by others for millennia.

The same kind of theory was how the early American Supreme Court was able to rule that the guy who bought his land from the U.S. government had superior title to the guy who bought the same land years earlier from the Indians who had lived there since before the Pilgrims.

It was how people could capture other people, and enslave them to work the land they had captured on the other side of the planet.

And now it was how these guys thought they could capture water trapped down there so deep it was underneath everybody. Take things that belonged to the whole world, make them your own, and sell them to the poor and thirsty for the highest price you could get them to pay.

The men who invented this system said it was natural law. And it was, in a way, the same way that it was no law at all. It was the law of the apex predator, the creature who takes what nature lets it.

Donny's job, he realized as he sat there buried in casebooks trying to figure out how to deliver on his promise to Xelina after he had saved his own ass by bringing her back in, was to rewire that system, on its own terms. Before there was nothing left to take.

Good luck with that, said the dead white guys on the wall of the law library, laughing their asses off.

Donny thought they didn't know there was a whole army ready to change the law by other means. Then he realized they knew better than everybody. That they had set up the whole system to prevent that from happening. And that if it did, they were ready to show the real power that backs up the law.

PART THREE

Judgment

50

ON HEARING DAYS THEY AIRLIFTED THE LAWYERS TO THE COURT-room. Check-in was at the uncivilized hour of 6:00 A.M. at the Coast Guard staging area, an old auto salvage yard east of downtown where they parked those orange armored trucks that sent people scurrying when they rolled through the neighborhood. Donny arrived late, almost on principle, and because of that it took even longer to pass him through security at the gate and again at the pad. They inspected, scanned, and logged his ID, phone, and bar card, and then they put them in a metal box and told him they would be returned to him at the end of the day. They searched his files by hand, removing and discarding each metal object they found bigger than a staple. They even took his pens, including the old fountain pen he liked to use, the one his mom had given him when he graduated from law school. In their defense, it would have made a decent stiletto in a pinch. As replacement, they gave him two one hundred percent plastic ballpoints to use, with blue ink. He asked them how you could kill someone with paperclips, but they ignored him. Then they asked him a series of weird verification questions they read from a screen, several of which related to motor vehicles he once owned, and two of which Donny declined to answer, to the immense annoyance of the guard. When he finally stepped through the fence lugging his litigation bag, the big chopper was already rotored up and loaded with cranky young prosecutors looking impatiently through the windows at him.

It was harder to read the faces of the Coasties. Donny was old enough to remember when the Coast Guard was not scary, the one branch of the armed forces dedicated to helping people instead of killing them. To most of Donny's clients, the robot bug face of the chopper jockeys was the face of the oppressor, as likely to drown you as pull you out of the water. Their visored helmets were stenciled all over town by the anonymous street artists who tagged the answers to questions real journalists were afraid to ask. Donny had cross-examined his fair share of Coast Guard special operators, successfully revealing their limited capabilities for independent thought when you took their augmented informatics away, and he resented having to bum a ride to work from them.

He knew the feeling was mutual. He could sense it when the dude checked his ID, as if some scarlet designation flashed up on the display. Or when the copilot saw Donny stumbling through the rotor wash with his tie blowing around his neck, and signaled him to hurry the fuck up, thumbing at the open door to the back bay in a way that felt more like the finger and suggested he half-hoped the tie would get caught in one of the blades.

Bridget Kelly was already there, strapped in with her crew. She glanced at Donny as he climbed aboard, then quickly looked away and back at the tablet on her lap, scrolling through her plans to fuck up Donny's day.

"Good morning, Bridget," said Donny, once his headphones were on.

She acted like she didn't hear him. Maybe she couldn't hear him, as loud as it was. Or maybe it was something in the way she looked like the orthodontist had overtightened her entire personality.

Or maybe his case was better than he thought, and it had her worried.

More likely, the heightened profile this case had obtained after the escape had dialed up the pressure to produce the desired outcome. Bridget's career—and maybe more than that—rode on it.

Seeing the stress on her face, Donny wondered if maybe that meant it wasn't too late to work out a deal.

He looked at the guy sitting next to Bridget to make sure they were hearing him over the wire. The guy, whom Donny hadn't worked with before, had the look on his face of a teenager protecting his older sister.

Behind them were the other two helping Bridget on the case, a Coast Guard JAG officer Donny remembered as Lieutenant Wachs and a tall skinny paralegal who went by Rounds.

"I wish I had as good a team as you backing me up," said Donny.

Bridget kept typing.

Donny waited.

"Sorry we couldn't get the clearance for your legal assistant to come along," she said.

"It's okay," said Donny. "She technically works for my co-counsel now, so I wasn't surprised. It's probably better this way. I'll have more freedom without anyone looking over my shoulder."

The airman sitting next to little brother had turned his attention to Donny. Donny had a pretty good idea what the airman's goggles said about him. He turned to little brother.

"Will you help me when Bridget and this guy try to shove me through the hatch and see if I can fly?"

"Don't give me any ideas," said Bridget. You could tell the airman already had the idea.

"You know what they call that, don't you?" said Donny, still looking at Bridget's younger colleague. "'Sending you on a trip to Argentina.' Much more efficient than dealing with lawyers, especially when they just have us acting out a script where everybody knows the ending."

Donny pointed at the hatch, through the window, at the open sea below. The guy looked, and when he looked back at Donny, and saw how the airman was looking at Donny, you got the sense Donny had gotten through.

Donny had heard such stories. They always sounded like urban legend, and most of the people who repeated them were the sort of folks who thought it sounded like a good thing to do, which in a way was even scarier than the stories. An extreme variation on "ship them back where they came from."

The red car stories had sounded like urban legend, too.

Donny looked around the chopper and wondered where they kept the parachutes. And then he looked out the window, at the sea lapping against what passed for a coastline here in this boggy region of subtropical river deltas that had once been underwater for millions of years, and wondered why it couldn't hurry up and get things back the way they were supposed to be.

The chopper banked, and suddenly you could see the tanker formerly known as the *Hungry Sooner* floating there at the edge of territorial waters, which were conveniently marked with a line of buoys blinking as far as you could see in either direction.

Now known as Marine Mobile Holding Camp Hotel Charlie Zero Zero Two, the *Hungry Sooner* had served many corporate masters in its forty years, most recently making inter-American runs for Zapata to and from the fields it had leased after the so-called liberation of Venezuela. Percy had researched its entire history, and generated a report, as they worked every angle to find holes in the legality of the setup. Zapata had leased the

Hungry Sooner to ARTCo, the American Management and Re-training Company, one of the leading U.S. private prison operators. ARTCo in turn worked out a contract to operate the ship as conveniently mobile extraterritorial detention. Now that the offshore wars were all over and the detainees were not foreign nationals, but Americans who'd had their nationality taken away, the ship stayed right here within commuting distance of downtown.

Those were not the exact words Broyles had used when he explained to Donny where the proceedings would be held.

As the chopper came in, you could see the cage city of kennels for humans laid out across the foredeck. The detainees on the deck were all in white jumpsuits, the color issued to the compliant, who got to enjoy the open air. The others were down below, in the former storage tanks that had been converted into holding pens, two for the men and one for the women.

That's where Xelina was. And seeing it made Donny wonder if they could come up with a better strategy of getting her out. And maybe getting most of her shipmates out with her.

Because otherwise, he'd have to risk ending up down in there with them.

51

THE TRIBUNAL HELD ITS HEARINGS ABOARD HOTEL CHARLIE IN A former cargo hold on one of the lower decks. To get there you walked down a long narrow hallway that passed one of the sections that had been turned into detention chambers, and when the buzzers sounded and the door opened you could hear the yelling and screaming.

All part of the show.

They had decided to hold the hearings on the ship rather than endure any more risks of transporting prisoners back to shore. Especially Xelina. The courtroom was improvised, with a desk for the judge up on a wooden platform, tables for each of the prosecution and defense, and two tables set together along the side with chairs for the members of the panel that served the role of a jury. There were a few more chairs along the back and sides for prosecution witnesses and government representatives as needed. The walls were metal, and the furniture and everything else was plastic. A live feed had been set up to pipe back to the room at the federal courthouse where members of the press, victims, family, and others with good cause to attend could watch the proceedings—on a forty-second delay and subject to censoring at the discretion of the security officer.

Donny's table had four chairs, even though they hadn't let him bring anyone along to help him. As he settled in, he looked at the flags they had hung on the wall, the portrait of the President, and the camera over his head that would be recording the lawyers from the court's point of view. The tribunal administrative officer came in to tell them that the audio and video were still not syncing up, and Donny imagined the reporters watching his opening like some badly dubbed character in a Japanese monster movie.

Godzilla was not the Raymond Burr performance he had in mind.

52

YOU COULD SAY THEY WERE MAKING THE RULES UP AS THEY WENT along, but that would give them too much credit for having rules.

The procedural model for this new star chamber was a hybrid of three different types of unfair trials that had been around for a very long time: the immigration and asylum proceedings that were presided over by administrative law judges who worked for the President instead of being part of the independent judicial branch; the treason and espionage trials in which only the prosecution could present secrets in evidence and political motives were excluded; and the military tribunals that had been used to summarily lock up and sometimes execute enemy combatants during the Civil War, the hot and cold wars of the twentieth century, and the more recent conflicts with terrorist insurgent groups in the hemispheric south. There had only been five of these cases taken to trial since the courts were authorized earlier that year, three of which resulted in denaturalization and a sentence of indefinite detention until the government could find a government willing to acknowledge the legitimacy of this proceeding and provide sanctuary to America's most dangerous expatriates. The fourth was a case Miles had been handling, which he had managed to get Broyles to transfer back to regular federal court for a bench trial based on an evidentiary defect that made the outcome-oriented judge a little nervous.

Donny had copied Miles's strategy to get the fifth case diverted as well. That was Jerome's.

Thinking about the hundred or so detainees on the ship waiting their turn, Donny wondered if it was true, that denaturalization was the only sentence worse than death. To be a stateless person in a world of increasingly closed borders, locked in a penal post-American purgatory stripped of rights. Jerome had it worse than Xelina, in the end. But her case was more important, because the outcome would affect not only her future, but everyone's.

That was part of the reason they had moved her to the front of the line, scheduling the trial so fast that the defense would have little time to prepare.

A trial that wouldn't be necessary if Xelina hadn't escaped.

But that was past them now, and the only thing that mattered was what was happening on this ship, in this room, with this judge.

Donny thought about the Broyles he had known as a colleague. About the things he cared about. About the quirks in his personality that could work for you or against you. About the ambitions that still drove him, and the private anxieties about oversight from above that you could sometimes exploit.

Broyles did not look anxious when he arrived through the hatch in the back. Instead, he made Donny nervous, when Donny stood for the "All rise" and saw that Broyles was wearing his old Navy dress uniform under his robes, with brass at the lapels, gold piping down the legs, and campaign ribbons earned through the offshore interrogations he liked to reenact as darkly humorous anecdotes over drinks after work.

"Please be seated," said Broyles, after he climbed up onto the little platform they had built and took his seat. He looked around the room. "Is our video feed up and running properly now, Mr. Hackett? With sound?"

He got the answer he wanted.

"Very well then. Good morning, everyone, and thank you for your efforts in accommodating our new venue here, which is the same court, but a very different room. One designed to provide us a level of what you might call judicial operational security that the mainland does not. For those of you watching our live feed, thank you for your presence as well, and please be reminded that we will be sending you our footage with a delay in the event I or the government's security officers believe there is any need to censor any portion of the proceeding."

Broyles said that last part as if it were something natural. Maybe it was now. And then he gaveled it in.

He started with the lecture for the lawyers. How he wanted to provide two days for the government to present its case, one day for the defense, and the fourth day for closing arguments and hopefully a swift verdict. It would be split over two weeks, with a break for the holiday. When Donny complained about the inequitable allocation of time, Broyles told him he didn't see that Donny would need much more than half a day based on the outline of the case he had provided, but that he would be open to revisiting it later in the week.

With Donny standing there at what was a weirdly close distance between bench and bar, Broyles went on to badger him about why he was still insisting on having a trial in the matter, when the defendant has already inculpated herself with her escape, flight, and standoff with the government. Donny said we admit no such thing, having arranged a partial immunity as a condition of surrender, and we plan to prove why this court must exonerate my client summarily.

Broyles told Donny please don't talk like a TV lawyer just because we are on TV.

Then he summoned the panel.

Instead of a jury, Xelina's guilt or innocence of the predicate charges would be assessed by six uniformed federal officers, five of whom were men.

When they were seated, Broyles called for Xelina.

And when they opened the back hatch to bring her in, you could hear the screaming, even though they had her gagged.

53

THE BONDAGE OF XELINA WAS SO COMPLETE THAT YOU WONDERED how she moved. And the answer was, she barely did—weighted down with the chains, she was partly carried by the guards, one on each arm and another behind her.

Instead of a hood, they had outfitted her with blindfold and headphones to maximize the sensory deprivation.

"Judge, this is outrageous," said Donny.

"Master Chief," said Broyles, addressing the head guard. "It does seem a little much."

"Protocol, sir, for any movement of the prisoner," said the Master Chief. "Now that we're here the eyes and ears can come off. The mouth is up to you."

Donny caught her gaze as she opened her eyes to the courtroom.

"Leave it on for now, until things are settled," said Broyles.

Donny put his index finger over his lips, and then stepped over to his client. As he removed her gag, he dropped the tiny black device he had been wearing as a lapel pin into the small chest pocket of her jumpsuit, where the guards sometimes stuffed the prisoner's paperwork.

"Kimoe!" said Broyles, alarmed at Donny's disobedience but oblivious to his misdirection.

"I heard you," said Donny. "And my client has a right to breathe freely." He looked at Xelina, hoping she understood, and then turned to Broyles.

Broyles watched for a moment with his stern father face on. Xelina leaned on the back of her chair. She looked weak now, not just from the chains.

"Perhaps we can try it out," said Broyles.

"Thank you, Your Honor. Can we lose some of the restraints as well? This is nuts. Way beyond any reasonable need."

Broyles looked at Xelina. Then he looked at the main camera, the one with the red light on.

"We're not ready for that yet," he said. "She has escaped once."

"Welcome to the Harold Broyles Theater of Performative Cruelty," said Donny. "See the live Indians hung from chains."

"Security officer, mask that remark," said Broyles.

"Yes, sir," said Walton.

"Kimoe, are you going to ape for the cameras throughout this proceeding?"

"No, Your Honor. That's not what I'm doing. I am advocating for my client, the best way I know how. And trying to advocate for some measure of actual due process in this so-called court. A goal I would think Your Honor would share."

"I'm watching you," said Broyles.

So were the members of the panel. You could feel the gazes. Feel the weird gravity of judgment. The cameras, and whatever eyes they extended, were more abstract and intangible. The feed was not carried on TV, but the members of the press viewing it back at the courthouse would be reporting on the trial.

"And they are watching us," said Donny. "The people at the other end of the feed, and all the people who will see this in the future."

"They will thank us," said Broyles. "I used to think they would thank you. That we all would thank you."

Donny was helping Xelina get settled into her chair, which

seemed barely sturdy enough to bear the extra weight of the steel with which she was burdened.

"I saw your television interview, by the way," said Broyles.

Xelina looked like she was about to lose it.

"If I find you arguing this case in public like that again I will find you in contempt and lock you up right here with your clients."

"I thought you might say that, Your Honor. But if the government gets to talk about this case in the White House briefing room, we should be able to get our own message out. And help people see that what the government is presenting as an outbreak of 'domestic terrorism' that justifies the imposition of martial law is no more than a crisis manufactured by them to hoodwink the people and perpetuate their power."

"Both sides will refrain from public statements regarding this proceeding until we have a verdict," said Broyles.

"If we get a fair hearing in here, we will keep it in here," said Donny. "Now may I have a moment to confer with my client before we get going?"

Broyles kept talking, but Donny stopped listening.

54

"HEY," SAID DONNY, LEANING IN, SPEAKING IN A NEAR-WHISPER. "It's going to be okay."

Her eyes were raw, ringed with red, pupils wide, and the soul behind them screaming.

"Here," said Donny. He poured a glass of water into one of the ridiculously tiny paper cups and served it to her.

She drank it, and he gave her another.

"This place," she said.

"Tell me."

"The noise."

"Isolation?"

She nodded.

"Do you get out at all?"

She shook her head.

"I just left you something from Percy for when you do," said Donny. "It's in your pocket. She says you'll know what to do with it. Starting with, don't let them find it."

She went to check her pocket, but she couldn't lift her arms high enough.

"It's there," said Donny, looking at her arms. "Did they torture you?"

She looked away. Donny looked over at Bridget, and the ramrod government goons she had lined up to testify for her.

He turned back to Xelina. He moved to put a reassuring

hand on her shoulder, but stopped when he sensed it would have the opposite effect.

"Listen to me, Xelina. It's almost over. I promise."

You could tell she had left whatever remaining hope she had back in her cell.

"I'm serious," said Donny. "We have good news. The Court of Appeals upheld the trial judge's decision in the election case. They appealed to the Supreme Court, but it's all moving super fast and there's a good chance we'll have a decision by the end of the week. So if everything goes according to plan, this whole nightmare could be over in days."

"Days? You want to trade places, Donny?"

"I will, if that's what it takes to get you out of here. But I won't need to. Because even if the election case goes the wrong way, we have a solid strategy to win this case."

"Are you kidding me?" She looked at the panel of uniforms sitting in judgment, and the judge who had already ruled against her once.

"I promise," said Donny, against the evidence before their eyes.

She raised her eyebrows in disbelief. He didn't blame her. But he was determined to show her.

55

"ARE THERE ANY OTHER PRELIMINARY MATTERS WE NEED TO discuss?" said Broyles.

"Yes, Your Honor," said Donny, standing. "We'd like to confirm our agreement that the purported confession earlier produced by the government and obtained through unlawful means will be excluded."

"Ms. Kelly?" said Broyles.

"We've agreed to that, Your Honor. With the agreement from defense counsel that no objections or related actions will be pursued regarding the means of interrogation."

Donny nodded. He knew better than most that challenging the methods they didn't call torture was not a winner. The law was on the government's side now, and so, when people heard about it, was public opinion.

"Very well," said Broyles. "Let's proceed."

"One other thing, Your Honor," said Donny. "The defense would also like to get your ruling on admitting the Zorn deposition."

"Which one is that again?"

"Amanda Zorn, Your Honor. Managing Director at Manaugh Feldman, the investment bankers. Her testimony includes foundation we need for one of the principal witnesses we plan to call. You have our briefing and motion on this."

Broyles looked to his clerk, who handed him copies. He scanned them, then turned to the prosecution.

"Ms. Kelly?"

"Your Honor, I personally have not had time to view this, as one of my colleagues handled the deposition. But my understanding is a protective order has not been worked out for the information discussed in her testimony, and that is the basis of our objection."

"There is no basis for objection, Your Honor," said Donny. "Ms. Zorn is a private citizen. A businesswoman. And all she discussed with us are matters related to her work."

Bridget was conferring with one of her colleagues.

"And how does it relate to this case?" said Broyles.

"It is essential foundation for one of our principal defenses," said Donny, trying to convey confidence in his position without getting into details that might invite more scrutiny than he wanted.

Bridget spoke up again. "My understanding," she said, looking at her colleague for confirmation as she spoke, "is that Ms. Zorn's testimony in fact involves government work. Advisory services related to the Coastal Evacuation Zone."

"Work for the State of Texas," said Donny. "Not for the United States. The government that is prosecuting Ms. Rocafuerte has no legitimate interest in protecting the putative secrets of the government in Austin."

Broyles considered that. He looked to the CSO.

"Mr. Walton?"

Walton shrugged reluctant agreement with Donny.

"Very well. Your motion is approved, we can rely on the general protective order covering this entire proceeding."

"Thank you, Your Honor," said Donny. Then he turned and gave a reassuring nod to Xelina.

She didn't return his confidence.

56

IN THE FIRST SEASON OF THE 1950S TELEVISION SERIES *PERRY Mason,* the title sequence opens with a shot of the judge, a white-haired old white man, sitting at the bench looking over the courtroom with a humorless expression. A lawyer approaches, his back to the camera. He hands a document to the judge. The judge looks it over, unhurried and officious. He kind of nods, and hands the document back to the lawyer. The lawyer turns, revealing his face to the camera, the face of Raymond Burr. Burr looks down at the paper, then, his face hidden from the judge now, looks up to where you can see his eyes. And then his mouth breaks into a subtle but indisputably sinister grin. The grin of a lawyer who has just successfully tricked the judge. Tricked the whole system.

That was the idea.

Donny had never noticed this detail when his grandmother, the first lawyer in the family, used to make him watch the show when he would stay with her. At the time, he just wanted to watch the nature shows and the new westerns that were so popular then. But he knew Grandma had a similar bag of tricks.

Maybe he would be able to live up to her example.

He remembered the scary theme song they gaveled in Raymond Burr with. He wondered what the theme song for this trial would be, if they had one. Maybe the black noise they played at night on the lowest deck, to keep the non-compliant detainees like Xelina from sleeping.

57

THEY HAD CONDUCTED AMANDA ZORN'S DEPOSITION AT THE OF-
fices of her lawyers, Worthington & Hurley. Mark Worthington himself sat in as Amanda's bodyguard. A young prosecutor
named Wesley Wilson attended for the government, and Percy
accompanied Donny.

It was rare to take depositions in a normal criminal case,
but there was nothing normal about this case. It was a summary
proceeding being pursued by a government on a war footing,
expedited far beyond any reasonable norm with no more than a
week to prepare. The court was happy to be lenient in order to
minimize bases for reversal and shorten the list of people who
had to be heard from at the actual trial, especially considering the unique logistical challenges. Donny could also tell that
Broyles and Bridget both assumed this was a sideshow that had
little to do with the real issues in the case.

That, Percy argued, was probably because they were not in
the loop about what was really going on. Donny agreed.

Amanda was definitely not happy to be there.

Donny tried to soften her up by talking about her string of
successes, the deals she had done to literally change the world.
She didn't mind that, but it didn't make her any less cagey when
they got around to the projects she was working on now, right
here in their backyard.

"What is Pallantium Corporation?" asked Donny.

"I don't think I can talk about that," she said. "I'm under a confidentiality agreement."

"That doesn't apply here," said Donny. "Here, everything is secret, and so nothing is secret."

"Just answer what you can," said Worthington. "Stick to what's already public."

"Very well," she said. "Pallantium is a new venture, a sort of public-private partnership set up by community-minded entrepreneurs and the State of Texas. The company pays to help remediate some of the damage that has been done to our coastal region and the industrial foundation on which our economy is based. In exchange, they get to keep any returns on their investment, and operate with a certain degree of autonomy for a fixed period of time."

"How long?"

"Ninety-nine years, I believe."

"How much autonomy?"

"It's relative."

"More than a normal company?"

"Yes."

"As much as a country?"

"Oh, no. It's a tenant, not a sovereign."

"Are you sure of that?"

"Quite."

"Is it bound by U.S. law?"

"That's complicated. You would have to ask a lawyer."

"I thought I was, but I guess you don't practice anymore. Is it bound by Texas law?"

"Yes, by its charter."

"Which says it can make up its own rules, within the leased territory."

"Well, yes. Not much different from a shopping mall in that regard."

"Or a country club. Or a gated community."

She looked bored with him.

"Is it subject to the Accords?"

"I can't answer that."

"Because you're working with them, right?"

"I work with a lot of people."

"So we heard. A lot of very rich people."

"Oh, please, it's not like that at all. I work for your people, too."

"Lucky them."

"You would understand they are, if you knew the alternatives."

"The alternatives to this mass eviction you are helping to orchestrate?"

"It's not an eviction. It's a remediation. A rebuilding. It's not some big conspiracy. It's a bunch of different transactions. I'm only working on a few of them. Not just redevelopment deals, but also resettlement projects. Not just here, but in other parts of the country, especially those ravaged by drought."

"Turning people into refugees and selling the lands from which they've been displaced."

"They're already refugees. Their homes are gone. And those lands are no longer viable, at least not for their former uses. They require massive reinvestment, infusions of capital that will only happen if they come with the right incentives."

"Like political autonomy and freedom from taxation."

"Among other things."

"So what's in it for 'my people'?"

"The same kind of autonomy. More, really."

"Where, exactly?"

She looked at her lawyer. "I'm not allowed to get into those specifics."

Percy handed Donny a document. He handed it in turn to Amanda, while Percy gave copies to the other lawyers.

"Is it this island that Pallantium just purchased?"

Amanda looked at the document. You could see her surprise.

"How did you get this?" said Worthington.

"Through a private information service," said Donny. The "service" was Ward Walker, who had made an expensive trade with one of the younger brokers who had worked on the deal. "But this is public information. It doesn't reveal the price. Just the transfer of title from the prior owner."

Worthington put the document down. "Go ahead and answer," he said.

Wilson objected, but in a setting like this without a judge present, all he could do was preserve the opportunity to argue for its exclusion later.

"Is this where you're sending 'my people'?" asked Donny.

"I'm not sending anyone anywhere," answered Amanda.

"It's not an accident that this is just outside territorial waters, is it?"

"You would have to ask the buyer."

"The buyer didn't give you its requirements?"

"The buyer was not my client in this transaction. But yes, okay, I understood that was part of their needs. We identified several possibilities."

"Several possibilities of places where people could be sent into exile."

"No," she said, growing more impatient. "A place where all the people who have decided they don't want to be part of this country can have a new one. And we are working on a bigger deal, something probably a bit farther out, to meet future needs."

"Does it ever make you feel like a monster?"

"You bottom-feeding weasel. Hard to believe I once considered you a peer. Don't you get it? The world is falling apart. We're all on the *Titanic*. And there are only so many life boats."

58

AFTER THEY SPENT MOST OF THE FIRST MORNING ON PROCEDURAL arguments that tested Broyles's patience, Bridget spent the rest of her two days walking the panel through a much more detailed version of the case she had made in the original hearing. They read the chats, saw the videos, handled the materials collected from Xelina's house, and heard hours of testimony from the investigating agents authenticating every item presented. The CSO blocked much of that from the feed, but not from the defense in the courtroom. Donny was surgical in his cross-examination, spending only what time it took to lay the record for alternate theories of what the evidence showed. Every minute he used on cross was a minute he wouldn't have for putting on his own case.

Bridget closed her case with the escape, which was a smart way to go.

Still, Donny argued it wasn't relevant to the case, and even prejudicial. He was right. This case revolved around the original treason charges. But Bridget said it shows her connection to the network. Donny said what network, but you could tell the panel wasn't buying it.

Bridget's case was one of those prosecutions so important to the government's institutional self-protection that the court, no matter who is on the bench, will bend over backwards to help the government make its case. They do this by providing all the time and evidentiary leeway they want to present every last scintilla of evidence supporting a guilty verdict. Donny had once helped out on the federal prosecution of a state court judge who had been shot and almost killed pulling her Lexus into the driveway of her River Oaks home after a high school lacrosse game. The shooter was a defendant in a felony prosecution before her court, out on bail. They gave the prosecution a month to make their case, with long days of forensic minutiae, every phone call and text message and online search, hourlong trajectories of each bullet, laboratory re-creations and disquisitions about the explosive qualities of different types of automobile glass. The defense took three days. They knew the likelihood of an acquittal had lottery odds or worse, so they focused on evading the death penalty. Which would have worked, had the defendant not also been a radical. That he was also black, and his victim white, did not help. Donny remembered her sitting there in the front row of the gallery in a dress that revealed the deep scar tissue in her left shoulder, guarded by a personal detail of marshals and accompanied by a row of her country-clubbing friends and family, while the prosecution projected cinema-scale mug shots of the defendant's associates on the screen above the defense table. That was the first time Donny understood that the game was rigged, even in a case where the guilt was pretty obvious, one that still went through the motions of providing a trial by jury, even if the jurors mostly looked like they could have been the judge's neighbors.

Watching Bridget get the marshal with the bullet wound in her leg to tell the sad story of what happened, as the attentive panel listened in judgment and the court reporter hammered away at his live transcript, Donny imagined the short day he had coming to make his own case, the evidence he already knew Broyles would preclude, the fate that awaited Xelina if he played the game by the rules they wrote to handicap the outcome. That's when he had the revelation that trials for political crimes were different. That the way to defend them was to attack the politics of the case, to expose the charade, show the wizard's real face. That you needed to figure out a way to do that *during* the prosecution's case. That you needed to make the trial itself part of the defendant's political program. Because after that, it was all over. It was what he had been building toward, without really understanding that's what he was doing.

As he got up to cross-examine Deputy Marshal Garrison, he still wasn't sure if he could do that and get the verdict he wanted.

But it was worth a try.

59

"HOW ARE WE DOING?" SAID DONNY, SITTING BACK IN THE ARM-
chair in Miles's office late that afternoon as Percy brought
in the files to prep for the next day. Bridget had finished her
case before lunchtime, Broyles said he needed the afternoon
to attend to other matters, and the defense was happy to have
the extra time.

"I can't believe you tried to argue that escaping from federal custody through armed violence is a legitimate form of
self-defense," said Miles.

"I think it is, when the custody is unlawful, and I thought
some of the panel were with me. Part of the way at least."

"You talked to that marshal like it was her fault."

"That was good stuff, right? When I made her walk through
each part of the restraints they use, how they decide who gets
what, how arbitrary and punitive it all is."

"It's a loser," said Miles.

"You're crazy," Percy added.

"We just need one member of that panel to see the view
from where Xelina is sitting. And we need to get other people
thinking the same way. People outside the courtroom. That's
what the client wants."

"Well, you're definitely starting to get some coverage,"
said Percy. She turned on the TV Miles had installed in the
wall and cued up a talking head clip. "I burned this from

the afternoon feed." There was a chyron headline across the bottom.

TERROR LAWYER SAYS COP-KILLING IS THE WAY TO THE FUTURE

"You know it's true," said Donny.

"I wish I had gone to Washington," said Miles, shaking his head.

"Were the oral arguments today?" asked Donny.

Miles nodded. "I hear they went well. But you can never tell."

"What do we do if they reverse?" asked Percy.

They all stared at each other. After a long silence, Donny finally answered. "We keep fighting," he said. "One case at a time."

They nodded, but you could tell they weren't entirely convinced.

"And we start by winning this case," he added. "Speaking of which, should we start with the Zorn depo?"

"Broyles's clerk just called about that," said Miles. "Said Broyles already watched it. In camera, with the censor. Evidently he got a call from the CSO's boss, in Washington. He has reconsidered his decision. He's going to exclude it."

"Fuck!" said Donny. "Are we ever going to get a break in this case?"

"Yes," said Miles. "Or maybe I should say kind of. Because the other thing that happened while you were out is the notice came in from the U.N. Court of International Claims. They received your crazy petition. And if you can believe it, they took it."

"Sweet!" said Percy.

"Let's not get ahead of ourselves," said Donny. "That's a

long way off, and the chances of it going anywhere are between slim and none."

"I agree," said Miles. "Let's get to work. You have four witnesses to prep."

They moved to the conference table and started working through files.

They were about an hour into it when Donny got the call.

60

"I DIDN'T EXPECT TO HEAR FROM YOU," SAID DONNY.

"I was feeling guilty," said Joyce.

"Why? I was acting like a freak that night."

"I've been following the coverage. What they'll let out. Not much, and you have to read between the lines, but enough to get an idea of what you've been dealing with."

"My client has it a lot worse than me. So are you in Mexico already? You sound so close."

"No," she said. "Had to reschedule. Needed to wrap up some loose ends here. Should be able to hit the road Friday. Have you thought any more about riding along?"

"I assumed the offer was revoked."

"Why don't we talk about it over dinner tonight?"

"I'd love to, but I can't. I'm in trial. I need to work."

"What if I told you the place I want to take you is the President's election defense fund-raiser?"

"I would not believe you."

"For real. My department head asked me to go. He had to head out of town on short notice, and says it's important we have someone there. And I am up for tenure."

"You're about to flee the country."

"And what better way to make it seem like that's the farthest thing from my mind."

Donny thought about who else would be there. It wasn't just Bridget.

"I'm in," he said.

61

A NEW SUIT WAS NOT IN THE CARDS (SPECIFICALLY THE CREDIT cards), but Donny did put on a clean one for the event, and a nicer tie, silver with black polka dots. He was still underdressed. Most of the other men wore black tie. Some even wore this season's runway versions, with their structured variations on tails and crazy collars, and a few that looked like they were made of those new designer Kevlars. Donny wondered how much it would cost to get a bulletproof business suit, and whether it would produce better or more reckless behavior on his part.

The ladies mostly wore black as well, because it was that sort of crowd. Joyce wore green, because she was not afraid of pissing people off. She said he'd seen the dress on her before, but he said I am pretty certain I would remember it if I had. She let Donny drive her old Mercedes to the event, which elicited only a tiny bit of restrained derision when they dropped it with the valet at the Four Seasons.

"Are you ready for this?" said Joyce, pointing to the sign welcoming them to the event.

INDEPENDENCE PARTY OF HARRIS COUNTY
PRESIDENTIAL ELECTION INTEGRITY
LEGAL DEFENSE FUND
SECURING THE AMERICAN FUTURE

They arrived when the cocktail crowd was at full steam, loitering and hand-grabbing and laughing outside the ballroom. Joyce took him by the arm, except when she broke away to grab two flutes of champagne from a passing server. It was the good stuff, and as they drank it and the bubbles started popping inside their heads, they traded who's who notes on the gathered crowd of power brokers. The Governor's speechwriter, the CEO of Brown Burton Elf, the daughter and sole heir of the water purification inventor John Siddiqui, the partner in charge of the Houston office of McKinsey. Donny saw faces from the newspaper and the bar journals, two members of Congress, one state representative, a radio talk show host, and the Texas Railroad Commissioner, who contrary to what you might think from her job title was in charge of setting the price of oil, and was soon to be regulating the price of water.

The weirdest thing for Donny was that people seemed to be noticing him, something he was sure he was imagining until Joyce made the same observation.

"Everyone's following your trial," she said. "But I don't think they're fans."

That sense of recognition felt good, all the more so that people like these saw him as the enemy. Seeing them here in their private gathering, writing the checks that fed the monster, helped him know they were right. There was no sign of Bridget, which made him second-guess his decision to come to the event when he could be preparing for trial.

"Let's go find our table," said Joyce, pulling at his arm to go away from the crowd.

Donny pulled back, as he saw what she had seen. Amanda Zorn, burning a hole in him from across the room.

Donny looked right back for a long minute, until Zorn turned and grabbed the arm of the man standing at her left. When that guy turned from the group he was talking to, Donny realized that the guy was Trey. Zorn leaned in and said something to Trey, who then looked across the room until he saw Donny, nodded, and pointed right at Donny with a smile that did not seem directed at him.

"Come on," said Joyce. Donny looked at her as she found their seats, and wondered if she was in on the game.

Their table was low-profile, at the edge of the room, shared by others from Rice—a political scientist who had worked in the administration and his husband, the head of development and her husband, and the new provost, who had been recruited from the Institute. They were polite to Joyce, but not friendly.

They ignored Donny.

The speeches started too soon, and went on too long. The Railroad Commissioner gave a punchy one in her West Texas drawl about her plans to confound the world's expectations and make Texas the water capital of the world. She was followed by some well-groomed Hollywood dude who screened a clip of his documentary about how the President was rebuilding the country's strength. Working title: *America Rising.* Where other patriotic visual platitudes would be expressed through landscape shots of open prairie and Western canyons, this guy was all about industry, and armor, with a dark palette and a heavy metal soundtrack.

As extra audience, extra security, and performative presence, a perimeter of private security guards stood around the outer walls of the room, wearing dressier versions of the Texical uniforms Donny had seen on the guards at the camp.

When Pastor Roger Loving took the podium and began his prayer for the assurance of the President's victory through the wisdom of the Justices of the Supreme Court, Trey got up and headed for the exit. Donny thought he had the right idea, and decided to follow him.

62

WHEN HE PUSHED THROUGH THE DOORS AT THE BACK OF THE hall, Donny was surprised to see how many more guards there were out there in the lobby. Watching the doors and stairs, watching the bar staff make each drink, crowding the kitchen to ensure none of the food was poisoned, and watching Donny every step. Trey was there at the bar, getting another round. They would have an audience.

"Hello, Trey," said Donny, joining him at the bar but giving him space.

Trey took his time before he looked over. "Donny."

"I was hoping I'd run into you at this thing."

"You are a real piece of work, pal. I thought Joyce had come to her senses a while back."

"Just friends, Trey. I think she thought I'd benefit from seeing things from another perspective."

"For a guy who can barely get his ass out of bed in the morning you sure know how to fuck a lot of shit up."

The bartender brought Trey two whiskies, and asked Donny what he wanted. He ordered tequila.

When he looked back at Trey, Trey was staring at him. You could see the stress in his eyes.

"Can I talk to you about something, Trey?"

Trey looked at one of the whiskies, picked it up, and drank the whole thing. Then he turned back to Donny.

"What," he said.

Donny pulled the envelope from his inside pocket. He opened it, unfolded the sheet inside, and set it in front of Trey, next to the empty glass.

It was a still from Xelina's footage, the video of Gregorio's lynching.

Trey looked at the image. It was a close-up of one of the guys who led the mob.

"What is this?"

"Crime scene. A political assassination."

"You are so full of it," said Trey, pushing the paper away.

"If you don't recognize that profile behind the mask, you must at least recognize that jacket."

Trey looked again. He picked the photo up and looked more closely. Then he crumpled it up and shoved it in the empty glass.

"I thought maybe you could help me work out a deal," said Donny. "I assume you know about Charlie's little project out in the Zone. The one he needed Gregorio to approve. The one he evidently paid Gregorio to approve, only to have Gregorio welch on the deal after he realized it would burn too much political capital with his young acolytes. The ones whose support he needed to take his political career to the next level."

The red eyes were on Donny now, getting redder. You could tell some of the other eyes around them were watching, too.

"I will assume you didn't know Charlie and his prepster militia pals killed a guy. Or that the murder of Gregorio is only the most recent of the atrocities we can connect them to."

"That picture doesn't prove shit."

"Whatever, Trey. We have recognition analytics that say otherwise. And we have witnesses. We know how far the network really goes. Who really did the dirty work they executed Jerome for. And I don't care about that. We live in scary times, and scary shit happens. I just want it to end."

"That's a sweet dream, Donny. What do you really want?"

"I want them to free my client."

"What makes you think I have the power to do that?"

"You're the most connected guy I know, Trey. Even more than Lou. Even more than Broyles. And the power of a father's love can accomplish amazing things."

Trey was tensing up now, both hands on the bar in front of him, trying unsuccessfully to summon the calm.

"And I'll promise to keep what I've learned quiet, as long as they drop this election fight and let the results stand."

He didn't say anything. Didn't even look.

"Come on, Trey. Peace."

He put his hand on his old friend's shoulder.

The next thing he felt was Trey's fist in his face.

Donny went down.

Ass on the carpet, he felt his face and looked up at Trey. He pushed himself up, and swung back.

He whiffed bad, almost falling back down. But his swing gave the guards permission. They swarmed, taking him back to the floor and beating the crap out of him until Trey said stop.

It took a few minutes.

"No deal, Donny," Trey said, standing behind his guards. "You're too late."

"Suit yourself," said Donny.

Then he straightened himself up and walked back into the party, pocket square under his bloody nose, and suggested to Joyce that maybe they should leave early.

63

THE ANIMAL NIGHT WAS IN THEM WHEN THEY DROVE OFF, AS WAS
the booze, so much so that having the gearshift of the Mercedes between them was too much, and they ended up pulling over into a parking lot and making out right there in the
car, fogging the windows, both tearing off their nice clothes,
and accidentally blasting the radio twice, like a pair of pent-up
teenagers. And when that wasn't enough, and they got back to
her place, she invited him in. They were both hungry for it.

Later, when Joyce was asleep, Donny couldn't even close his
eyes. Too amped up from it all, mind racing about what tomorrow had in store. So he grabbed the extra key and went for a
walk.

Down the block from Joyce's house was a big empty lot
where they had torn down an older building in preparation for
the construction of a shiny new one, just in time for the crash
that dried up the real estate debt markets like one of those barren farms up north. The lot was fenced off and dark, but there
was a spot where the chain link was bent back enough for a human to get through, and when he walked across and checked it
out, Donny could see it was a narrow dirt path, made by who
or what knows.

As he walked that way under the cold light of the city
lamps, he realized how ridiculous his outfit was—a pair of insanely wrinkled suit pants with a small but evident tear in the
crotch, suit coat over a white undershirt that he had sweated

through three times during the preceding eighteen hours, and a pair of dress shoes with leather soles and no socks. He also realized that he didn't give a shit, and almost felt overdressed, like he could feel the memory coded into his cellular proteins of his ancestors who walked without shoes and never wrote a single thing down.

The ambient light of the city seeped into the involuntary park, aided by the arc of the waxing moon, and his eyes quickly adjusted. The path led through a stand of tall ragweed that brushed against him and then opened up into a little clearing of concrete with patches of grass coming up through the cracks. At the edge of the clearing was a shelter made of trash—a big tarp roof made from some industrial package stamped with the logo of a Chinese manufacturer, rope of varying gauges and colors, cardboard boxes, and rotting old lumber. Before the lean-to was a little fire pit made of broken bricks and chunks of concrete debris, still giving off warmth from the coals. There was a beat-up bicycle trailer that had been repaired with duct tape and parked against a scrubby tree. A cheap folding table on three legs and a stack of cinder blocks was between the fire and the shelter, and on it lay a dirty paper plate and an array of found objects in the process of being transformed into secret works of art—the severed head of a pink flamingo, the fins of a model rocket, three sharp shiny rocks, some electrical cable, a very old soda bottle, some blue glass, and the skull of some small fanged mammal, maybe a raccoon. There was a weird beauty to the thing the occupant of that tent was synthesizing from those fragments of other things, and some kind of secret message encoded about the world they came from. It felt like he had just stumbled into the future, a glimpse at the way people would soon live in the ruins conjured by the current generation.

Donny was imagining what a lawyer would do to survive in the post-apocalyptic wasteland when he sensed the stare.

He turned, and saw the coyote there across the little clearing, as still as some stuffed critter you would see in an old museum, but radiating life, the wild life that the city hides in plain sight through the partitioning of time and space. It was no bigger than a medium-sized dog, maybe fifty pounds, kind of lanky. The fur was a weird mix of red, brown, black, and grey, the grey really a silver, almost a quicksilver that picked up the stray beams and shined them back at you like some computer-generated baffling. And when Donny shifted, the coyote broke its gaze and moved, and the way it shimmered as it disappeared made you understand why the people who had lived here before the pavement thought perhaps it traveled across the dimensions. Because really, it did, if you thought about it the right way. It was another visitor from the future—one that portended how green that future would be, as all the life we had crowded out returned to the spaces abandoned by our collapse.

For a moment after the coyote slipped away Donny soaked in the animal's smell, a pungent but elusive musk, and wondered if he would now carry some of that scent with him. He thought that would be okay.

He grabbed two sticks from the pile, squatted by the pit, and started rubbing them together to see if he could start a fire.

By the time he heard the movement behind him, they already had the gun at his back.

As they pulled the black hood over his head, he noticed the matches sitting there.

64

"IS THIS PUNISHMENT OR INTERROGATION?" ASKED DONNY, WHEN they pulled off the hood an hour or so later, after they took him for a ride in the trunk.

He was duct-taped to a wooden chair, in a dark room. There were two men standing there in the shadows. One was Trey's son Charlie.

"We haven't decided yet," said Charlie. He was shirtless, with a golf club in one hand and a bottle in the other. "Moody here's going to flip a coin."

"Can I have my pants back?"

"No, asshole. We're going to torture you."

"Just promise you won't give me the Mary Lou."

"The what?"

"The Mary Lou. Guess you never read the memos."

"I told you we should plug this shyster's piehole," said Moody. He looked weirdly like a young Richard Nixon. The charcoal suit he was wearing only added to the effect, except for the cowboy boots. In Xelina's video he wore snake boots.

"They weren't actually memos," said Donny. "Maybe technically. But more like a manual. A glossary of ways for the government to subject captives to fear and pain without breaking the law. But maybe you guys aren't too worried about that. Because you don't seem like the government types."

"You don't have to work for the government to want to help your country," said Moody.

"You guys take care of the things the memos won't let the government agents do. With no fingerprints."

"Yeah," said Moody, flashing a blade. "We're going to show you what no fingerprints looks like."

"We should pull one of his teeth," said Charlie.

"Jesus!" said Donny.

"Why stop at one," said Moody.

"What do you guys want?" said Donny.

"The first thing we want is for you to stop talking," said Moody.

"Where am I?" said Donny.

"Don't you recognize it?" said Charlie.

Donny looked around the room. He closed his eyes and opened them again, trying to see into the shadows. That's when he saw the face of Tiger Woods, framed on the wall to the side. Then he noticed the map of the course, and the soft glow of the dormant TV screen. And the nine iron in Charlie's hand.

"What the fuck?" said Donny. They were in the men's grill at the Cypress Bayou.

"It's perfect, right?" said Charlie.

It was definitely private.

"He's not a member," said Moody. He was plugging a cord into the wall.

"Tonight's the initiation," said Charlie.

"I didn't know country clubs had hazing rituals," said Donny.

"This one does," said Charlie. "Have a drink."

He pulled Donny's head back by the hair, still holding the gun with the same hand, then poured brown liquor into his gullet until he was choking.

"I don't know if he's gonna pass," said Moody.

Donny spit out what he could, and felt the rush from what he couldn't.

He looked at his laughing captors. "We know you idiots killed Gregorio."

"Dude, you really need to learn to keep your trap shut," said Charlie. "And stop poking your nose around in other people's business."

"The future is not your private property, you little trust fund commandos."

Charlie swung the golf club in the air, like he was warming up to hit a long one. "You could have fooled me," he said. "Why don't you ask Gregorio how that kind of thinking worked out for him?"

"Where's the body?" said Donny.

"You know that water hazard on the seventeenth hole?" said Moody.

Donny knew it. He had put a few balls into that deep black pond.

"Shut up," said Charlie.

Charlie looked pretty loco. But Moody was the one holding the cord. The one that was bare wire at the business end.

"This fraternity sucks," said Donny.

Charlie laughed at that.

"We're just getting started," said Moody. "Hold him down, Charlie."

"Fuck that," said Charlie. "I don't want to touch this weasel." He teed up his club against the side of Donny's head. "We should just bash his skull, and retire him out there with the Councilman."

Donny tried to move his head away, but Charlie just pushed the club harder, right on his ear.

"Ease off, will you?" said Donny. "I'm one of your dad's oldest friends, for fuck's sake."

"You're nobody's friend," said Charlie. "Not anymore. You're on the list now."

"What list is that?"

"The list of problems that need special solutions. The kind we take care of. Like you were saying."

"You guys set up the Refugio Five, too, didn't you?" said Donny. "Set up Jerome."

"Not our idea, but we helped out those friends of Dad's from Washington," said Charlie.

Donny tried to press at his bindings, but they had him tight. He twisted his neck, and found the golfer staring back at him again.

"How old do you think that picture is?" he asked.

"Huh?" said Moody.

"Tiger," said Donny, nodding at the photo. "That photo's been there for eons. And look at him, he looks like a kid. Before the anger started coming out."

They both looked. That's when Donny noticed what was lying on the chair by the wall.

"See that jacket?" he said. "If you reach into the right side pocket, there are some nice treats. If you want to really party."

They looked at him, curious.

"You know Ward Walker, right?"

"Sure," said Moody. "Best hookup inside the Loop. Good shit."

"This is his extra-good shit."

"White-Out?" said Moody.

Donny nodded. "New mix. 'Light Show.' You gotta try it."

Charlie was already in his pockets, fishing around. He pulled out the tin, shook it, and raised his eyebrows. He knew.

"Open it," said Donny. "And if you're determined to fuck

me up, at least let me get fucked up first. One last time. Because you guys and me are a lot more alike than we think, and I've had to stay clean all week for work."

Charlie opened it, sniffed it, touched it with one finger. He showed it to Moody.

"Imagine how much more fun this will be if we light it up," said Donny.

Charlie smiled, and Moody nodded.

"You first," said Charlie.

"Happily," said Donny. "Just give me one hand free, okay? I need to pinch it just right. Ward showed me how."

Moody nodded again, and cut the tape along Donny's right wrist. Then Charlie held out the open tin. Donny deftly broke the ball with a practiced hand into three equal doses. Then he took one and ate it.

Charlie and Moody followed.

Tiger Woods lit up like a Bodhisattva, and pretty soon, he was there in the room with them, playing Texas Hold 'Em with Aaron Burr and Quanah Parker.

GIVING A MILITARY-GRADE performance enhancer to his aggressive young captors turned out to be not as great an idea as Donny thought it would be.

They *did* let him go. More accurately, they gave him a running start. They also let him take the golf club, for good sport.

He did not know he could be that fast, but the abuse he had heaped on his body caught up with him as he huddled in the trees, panting, watching the golf cart come closer. They had let him put his pants back on, but not his shoes.

"I hear you, asshole!" yelled Charlie.

Donny decided to run, before they also saw him. But they

had a big flashlight, and they shined it on him just as he started moving.

He stumbled as he punctured his foot on a sharp stick in the turf, and looked back. Charlie was out of the cart now, coming after him, a blade in hand.

Moody kept the light on, until Donny was able to lose the beam back in the trees. It was when he stepped on the pine-cones that he got a better idea.

But when Charlie got close to where he was, he wondered if he had made himself a sitting duck by climbing the tree.

He heard Moody call for Charlie from the distance. When Charlie replied, he realized Charlie was right there under him.

When he decided to jump, he was no longer thinking, and he didn't even realize he was swinging until he had stopped.

He looked down at Charlie's body, motionless but making the weird sounds of labored respiration, like an animal that's been hit by a car.

He looked up, saw the flashlight a ways away, and heard the sound of the electric motor rolling. He ran in the opposite direction, out of the trees and onto the wide-open fairway, feeling almost in flight.

When he finally stopped to catch his breath at the edge of a green, the bloody nine iron still in his hand, he realized it was the seventeenth hole. He could see the water hazard there. He got up, thinking he could use the club to find the body.

Then he heard the sound of an engine. Not the golf cart. More like a truck.

He saw the fence, maybe a hundred yards away. He dropped the club and ran for it. Gregorio would have to wait.

He was almost there when Moody came roaring down in the cart, hooting and then firing a pistol at Donny with his free hand.

Donny dove for the ground, feeling the lawn chemicals up in his nose as he ate it.

He heard another shot, and then the sound of the cart hitting the chain link.

He looked. Moody was on the ground.

Joyce stood there in the moonlight, her gun still trained on Moody. Her car was there behind her a little farther, idling.

65

IN THE MORNING, BROYLES HIMSELF CALLED BEFORE SUNUP.
Donny only picked it up because he recognized the number.

"I need you to come down here, Donny. My chambers. As soon as you can."

"The chopper doesn't leave until eight."

"No, come to the courthouse. No trial today. Something has come up. That's what we need to discuss."

Donny wanted to ask for more of an explanation, but could tell he wasn't going to get one over the phone.

"Okay, Judge."

He took the extra keys next to Joyce, but this time left a note.

Just in case.

WHEN HE GOT there forty minutes later, it was still dark out. No traffic, no protesters, no Cleburne—just a night shift of two younger marshals manning the entry checkpoint.

The judge's chambers were behind the courtroom, and that was how Donny entered, even though there was a more normal entrance from the hallway around the side and past the secretary's office. The courtroom was empty, and dark, and stepping back into that secret space behind the bench felt like walking into some mountain cave. But the big wooden door embossed with the seal opened without compelling a password.

The chambers were a suite of rooms along a small hallway, with the judge's library, the clerk's office, and a small conference room where Broyles would sometimes summon counsel to bang their heads together in an effort to work out a deal. The library had breached its bounds and spread out into the hall, which was also lined with shelves. The spaces on the wall that weren't crammed with law books were covered with pictures and art—photos of Broyles from throughout his career, consorting with pols, golfing with Supreme Court Justices, presiding over prosecutorial press conferences, a few photos of the young JAG officer in full dress, and one big painting of a cowboy defending himself with a rifle from behind the corpse of his horse as the Indians surround him. Right outside his office was the photo of Broyles shaking hands with the President, when he was just a candidate, a candidate that even people like Donny had thought perhaps could unite the broken country and restore the American future that had been shredded in the wars.

The door was open, and Broyles was alone, hunched over his desk with tie loose and jacket off, reading a document with a sharp red pencil in hand.

"You son of a bitch," he said. Then he looked up, and you could tell he meant it. "You look like shit."

"I just got the crap beat out of me last night." He thought about it. "Twice."

"Good. Sit down."

Donny grabbed one of the two armless chairs Broyles had there in front of his old wooden desk, a desk that had belonged to one of his predecessors in the old courthouse. Broyles kept a tidy office, with rarely a paper out of place and no more books than needed for the task at hand, but it looked a little unkempt that morning, like old Harry was having some trouble keeping it all together. He had four casebooks open in front of him and a stack of old-school phone messages scrawled on red paper. The judge's precious *Oxford English Dictionary* was there on its stand, also open, and Donny wanted to go look through the magnifying glass and see what word it was Broyles had last looked up, but the image of old Justice Korb staring down from its frame on the wall above made him think it better to sit and listen. Even though Korb was smiling in the picture, enough to make his weird beard fan out like the facetail of some exotic mammal.

"What the hell is this?" said Broyles, tossing the document he'd been reading across the desk at Donny.

Donny ducked the interoffice projectile, and picked it up after it fluttered to the floor. He knew what it was before he saw the U.N. file stamp. He had written every word, except for the annotations Broyles had scrawled in the margins, which Donny saw as he laid the pages back in their stapled order.

"Zealous advocacy," said Donny, setting the document down on the edge of the desk. "A forum-shopping flanking maneuver. Just like you taught me."

"I never taught you to go running to courts run by foreigners."

"You told me to give my clients the best defense I could. Looks like it worked."

"You better hope that doesn't work," said Broyles, pointing at the document. "You could do more harm to this country than all your terrorist clients combined. Upend our entire system of property ownership, the roots on which our entire economy is built. To sort out what the consequences would be if you got the remedy you ask for there would take decades. Decades. People would lose their homes, their businesses. We would lose the past and the future."

"That's not my problem."

"Not your problem! You are an officer of the court, Donny. An agent of the state."

"Doing what I am sworn to do, within the bounds of the rules. And sometimes that means testing the rules. Pointing out that the emperor has no clothes. Even if he has soldiers and secret police and kangaroo courts."

"This isn't testing the rules," said Broyles, pointing at the brief. "This is trying to rewrite history."

"No it's not," said Donny. "It's just checking the title. In this case, to a chunk of Texas that your paisanos in Austin want to sell. And like any title, if you go back far enough, you find it was stolen. Taken by force. If you build a legal system on a foundation of theft, you're living on borrowed time. Cooking the books. I didn't expect to get far with this, but I'm glad to see the very idea of an accounting—of real justice—has you rattled."

"Real justice comes from real order, Donny. An order founded on allocation of resources to those willing to make productive use of them. I guess you would rather have us all become nomads, like your free-roving clients. Shall we bring the buffalo back, track them along the abandoned highways?"

"That would be kind of awesome, actually, but no. I just think there needs to be a fresh reckoning that starts with an honest assessment of what right underpins the system. Of who really 'owns' the land and everything in it. Because I do think my clients are correct when they say the system we have is no longer sustainable. We all share this place now—this state, this country, and this planet—and we need to figure out a way to take care of it together and keep it healthy instead of fighting over the last harvest of a fallow field."

"You want us to cry about Indians in the twenty-first century."

"You don't have to cry. Just be honest. And follow your own rules."

Broyles looked at him. He was tired. And you could tell he knew Donny was right. Even as he knew the real right lay with the power.

"Well, I'm not going to cry. But I may get fired."

"You have life tenure."

"Really, Donny? Do you still not get it? Nothing is guaranteed these days. The people you have angered can be very persuasive. And determined to get their way."

"I think I know what they are capable of. They killed my client for something they did."

"We did. It was not an easy decision, Donny. And he was not an innocent."

"Let's not go there."

"Okay. In any event, you're going somewhere else."

"How do you mean?"

"They want you in Washington. To talk about this." He pointed at the brief again. "And some of the other matters you have been rather recklessly sticking your nose into."

"Oh," said Donny. He considered that for a long moment. He looked back at Broyles, and Broyles nodded in agreement at what he could tell Donny was thinking.

"They are making me tell you, because it's part of their way of letting me know they think I screwed up and let things get out of my control."

"That brief is out of your jurisdiction. And you can't control what I do outside your courtroom."

"That's not how they see things. You have been summoned. To the White House."

Those were scary words to hear.

"Is this a one-way trip?" said Donny, all his cockiness of

the moment drained out like a flaccid balloon, suddenly seeking succor from the mentor he had been lecturing moments before.

"That's probably up to you," said Broyles. "They told me they would like to see you. Maybe they want to make a deal. You'll need to decide how you want to play it."

Right before the conventions that summer, as the campaign started to overheat, the President had invited a television commentator who was one of his most colorful and relentless critics to the White House. The guy, Virgil Miller, was never seen again. The White House produced photos of him leaving, and said he had fled the country. Others said he had been killed by Secret Service agents and dumped in Chesapeake Bay.

Donny didn't want to end up like that guy. Or like Gregorio.

"What if I don't want to go?" he said.

"That's not an option," said Broyles, looking at something behind Donny.

Donny turned, and saw Cleburne there, looking down at him with gallows eyes. He hadn't even heard him come in.

"Cleburne is going to take you downstairs now," said Broyles. "We have a driver waiting, who will take you to the airport."

"Come on," said Cleburne, hand on Donny's shoulder.

66

THAT MORNING, WHEN DONNY FLEW TO WASHINGTON, THEY launched the first rocket from the Evac Zone. He could see it through the window as they ascended, close enough that you could almost make out the lines of the upper stages. The burn in the clear morning was so bright and orange, beacon of a right turn in the future. For a minute he thought he could see the corporate logo painted on the side, then he just thought it was a trick of the light. But he knew it was there.

They had kept the plan in stealth mode while they prepared for launch, as best they could despite whispered leaks by guys like Ward. But when Donny landed, the news alerts started popping. The mission was a scout, to an asteroid on a near-Earth trajectory believed to contain massive quantities of water and platinum. The next mission, if everything checked out, would try to capture it. The name on the fuselage was *Pallantium SPX*, explained by the commentators as a joint venture of Texical, privatized elements of old NASA that provided the expertise and IP, and joint venture partners that included Chevron, TI, Blackstar Group PE, and a handful of undisclosed investors.

For all the money and mindpower behind the operation, including the successful maintenance of secrecy, the real geniuses in the deal were the lawyers. They had found an interplanetary loophole in the Accords, one that made the launch legal, a private undertaking on territory that had established sufficient jurisdictional autonomy that the international treaty authorities could not assert control. Donny wondered what sort of back-office financial conduits they had been able to establish on similar lines. And then he wondered what could be done with something like that if it were controlled by the likes of Xelina and her people instead of Trey and his masters.

Maybe in time. Or maybe only in some other timestream.

"What a great day," said the female Secret Service agent who met him at the gate, took his phone and computer for safekeeping, and rode in the back with him while the TV in the seat replayed the same clip of the rocket arcing over the Gulf.

When Donny didn't answer, the other Secret Service agent, a guy who was now riding shotgun while their other colleague drove, looked back at Donny.

"She said it's a great day," he said.

"Fly me to the moon, asshole," said Donny.

"Only parts of you," said the woman, without looking away from the screen. "And now we finally can again."

Donny looked out the window instead of replying. That was when he noticed that there was no way to open the doors from the inside.

As they came up out of the tunnel into the heart of official Washington, Donny remembered the last time he had been to D.C. It was years earlier, when he was working on the war crimes trials and they brought him up here for training. It was a different town back then, free and still full of possibility, locus of a rare historical moment when politics was infused with the same imagination as the arts, and the so-called politicians were practicing a utopian experiment in applied science fiction. The experiment, in the views of most, turned out to be at the expense of the idea of the nation, an experiment that lost a war and caused the hard-held bonds of union to rapidly decay. The futures people were planning were too many, and too divergent. And when it came down to it, especially as the economy cratered, most people were too deeply imprinted with the tribal codes of national identity to be able to stomach a path to the "totally local and totally global" mañana that the current regime's predecessors had envisioned. The only future people could really get their heads around was the one that looked like the glorious past of their imaginations. And the only way to conjure that was with the stick.

So now the scene outside the window as they waited at the first checkpoint at 14th and Constitution was one of holiday lights on razor wire and dark flags flapping under grey skies. There was one group of very angry protesters, but they were confined to a small cordon behind the Washington Monument, barely visible to the cars lined up for the ID checks and bomb scan. They were behind chain link and guarded by uniformed federal police with helmets and assault rifles, the first official contingents Donny had seen of the new consolidated security force they were creating from several existing federal services. The whole zone of museums and monuments along the Mall was fortified by them and some local military battalions. Donny saw one Marine directing tourists there between Natural History and the monument, and the craziest thing was how you could tell the people liked seeing combat-ready soldiers controlling the streets.

They passed through four more checkpoints to get to their destination, which was not even technically the White House, but the adjoining Old Executive Office Building. The intense security reminded Donny of visiting clients in prison, but with a better class of guards. Until they got to the third checkpoint, the one where they pulled his biometrics for the file, which was more like going to the doctor's office. A doctor's office where the nurses carried automatic weapons and handcuffs.

Donny was just happy that they didn't put a bag over his head. Maybe that depended on how he conducted himself in the meeting they escorted him to, down an elevator and into the basements beneath the mansions of state.

The office of Andrew Davidoff, Deputy White House Counsel for Domestic Security Matters, was a lot smaller than you would expect. Smaller even than Donny's vault, not much bigger than a large closet. And Davidoff himself was bigger than Donny expected, maybe because in the photos he had seen, the glasses and unkempt professorial hair suggested something different from the long-limbed guy who got up from behind the desk and looked like maybe he would have to elbow the wall to shake Donny's hand as the escort brought him in.

"Come in," he said to Donny. "And you can please wait outside," he said to the agents.

"Yes, sir," said the woman.

"I appreciate you making the trip," said Davidoff, turning back to Donny and extending his hand. He had a Beltway smile. "It's good to put a face on the briefs."

Donny had wondered on the way up here if he would even shake the guy's hand, the same way he wondered if he would ever shake the hand of the guy's boss in the very unlikely event he ever got the chance. And then it was like, of course you do. And in the process, feel the permanent and irrevocable shift in the aperture of the politically tolerable.

"Likewise," Donny said. "I appreciate the opportunity to meet."

He sensed a presence behind him, and looked over his

shoulder to see a guy in a military uniform and a woman in a business suit blocking the door.

"Let's see if we can all fit in here for now," said Davidoff. "This is my associate Erin Lee, who works on DOJ liaison, and Colonel Shaw from the Guard."

"Coast Guard?" said Donny.

"Not exactly," said Davidoff. "In fact we don't even have a final name yet, but it's looking like United States Motherland Guard is what it will be. Right, Colonel?"

"Correct," said the Colonel. His uniform was Air Force, with drone wings and the silver eye of the surveillance corps.

"Why not Fatherland?" said Donny.

"I heard you were a joker," said Davidoff. "The Colonel's got your whole file here, maybe we can show you some of the highlights when we're done."

Donny looked at the Colonel, who had a thick leather portfolio under his arm. The Colonel returned the gaze with eyes that had already decided what they were looking at.

"Why don't you grab one of those chairs from the hall," said Davidoff, addressing the Colonel, but one of the Secret Service agents was already there with the chair. They put Donny in the corner facing Davidoff's desk, with the Colonel seated between him and the door, and Lee at Davidoff's side next to the desk. She started taking notes on her computer before they even started talking business.

"I've read a lot of your work, too," said Donny, addressing Davidoff. It was true, and he'd even re-read some on the plane. Davidoff was the legal architect of the administration's reconstruction of the American state. He'd spent a decade in academia at the Institute, incubating many of the ideas that were now being implemented, writing books like *The Permanent Exception* and *After Grotius* that few people read and many now wished they had before it was too late. Maybe even more important was his white paper on "Executive Governance of Civilian Populations During Geocrisis." That's the one they always cited in their write-ups of initiatives around insurrection management, domestic counterterrorist operations, resettlement and dissident identification, and the theory of denaturalization that underlay Article Three of Burn Barnes.

"Fortunately for everyone else we're here to talk about your case," said Davidoff.

"Which one?" said Donny.

"We'll get to that," said Davidoff.

"I can guess."

Davidoff had framed photos of the President and Vice President on the wall behind him, above the one of his wife and kids. There was a map of the lower forty-eight on the wall next to him, annotated in dry erase marker to show the zones of heavy weather, mass relocation, and incipient rebellion. It reminded Donny of the map in Amanda Zorn's office, but through the eyes of national security instead of capital. The climate-stressed middle of the country, from Davidoff's vantage, looked like one big mid-continental DMZ.

"We should be talking about where the food's going to come from," said Donny, looking at the map.

"I think we have that covered," said Davidoff. "As long as you don't screw up our access to the water we need to grow it."

"Isn't that what today's launch is about?"

"The Colonel here can tell you better than me," said Davidoff. "But the short answer is no. That's about the water we need to expand our sovereign territory beyond orbit, without having to haul it up there. The water we need to restore the American continent is already here."

"In the Evac Zone."

"Under it, technically," said the Colonel.

"So far down that it's under a lot of countries," said Donny.

"Right," said Davidoff. "Which is why we would like to keep this project quiet as long as we can."

"Do you think you can get it all out of the ground before others join the party?" asked Donny.

"We've been working on this technology for years," said the Colonel. "A production application of scientific drilling. Deep drilling. Now we've started implementing it in the field, and it's working. It's going to save us, and let us turn the tables back where they belong. And it'll be a decade before anyone comes close."

Water is the new oil.

That's what Jerome had said, without even realizing what he had uncovered. Donny was privately pleased to have followed the lead to its end, even as he worried whether it meant his own end would be the same as Jerome's. He felt the sweat seeping through his shirt. And then he thought about where Xelina was, and everyone who was there with her, and decided his own burnt-out life was maybe not the most precious thing there was.

"As long as they don't stop you from doing it."

"We don't think they can," said the Colonel.

"Especially not the way we've set it up," said Lee.

The same logic as the launch pad applied to the new deep-drilling rigs.

"How do you keep the corporations from selling it to people you don't want to have it?" said Donny. "From doing deals with Beijing or whoever?"

"Maybe the same people who control the government control the companies," she answered.

"Let's not get into that," said Davidoff.

"I agree," said Donny. "I figured you wanted to talk about my plea to the CIC."

"We kind of want to talk about all of it," said Davidoff. "Including, yes, your very annoying call for foreign intervention in our internal political economy. But frankly, I'm not as worried about that as others, because I know that even if you succeeded in getting them to throw out every real estate title in the USA, they could never enforce it."

"I don't know," said Donny. "They can do a lot through their regulation of the international financial markets."

Lee nodded. Davidoff looked unimpressed. "What I'm worried about," he said, "is the stuff you haven't filed yet."

"What do you mean?" said Donny. He acted surprised, even as he had an idea of what was coming.

"We have the draft in progress," said Lee. She pulled out a red folder, opened it, and let Donny see a copy of work product that only existed on his computer.

"So much for attorney-client privilege," said Donny, feigning shock. They had taken the bait. The brief laid out not just the threads he had pulled on the legal tapestry that underlay their plans. It laid out all of the facts that he had uncovered—about what was going on in the Evac Zone. And about who Jerome took the fall for, and why.

"This is U.S. national security you are messing with here," said Davidoff. "High-stakes provocation to exculpate one green rebel bitch."

"Are you getting all this in your notes, Erin? Because I may need a good transcript after I file this." Before she could respond, Donny turned back to Davidoff. "I'm not the one who picks the bogus prosecutions to suppress political speech, Andy. And you guys tapping my files is only going to help my case."

"That's not something you are going to be bringing up," said Davidoff. "And that new brief is not one you are going to file."

"Like hell I'm not. I'm filing it this week," said Donny. "And sending copies to the media. Not just the U.S. media. And when what you people have been up to is revealed, and the election is called, we'll see who has to worry about prosecutions."

The room was quiet for a long minute.

"You make some big assumptions about the election, counselor," said Davidoff.

"The Supreme Court is about to rule," Donny reminded them. "And you can bet even they will agree with the Fifth Circuit, and the trial judge. The Governor overstepped his authority. It's over. You guys should start packing your shit."

"The Supreme Court doesn't decide elections in this country," said Davidoff. "The People do."

"And that's what just happened," said Donny. "The vote was clear."

"The vote was a fraud," said the Colonel. "And the country is at risk. The People need to be led."

Donny looked at the Colonel. You could tell the kind of leadership he had in mind. Another one in a long line who thought "We the People" meant *his* people.

"Change is coming," said Davidoff. "And we have enough in our files to put you in a cell where no one can hear you blab. Ever."

"Maybe even a trip to the Island," said the Colonel.

"Or we can work out a deal," said Davidoff.

Donny swallowed.

"I'm listening."

67

CLINT OFFERED TO PICK DONNY UP AT THE AIRPORT, BUT DONNY said you go wait for her, I'll meet you there.

When Donny arrived, Clint was parked at the outer perimeter fence of the Coast Guard operating base, sitting on the hood of his truck. So Donny joined him up there, after throwing the overnight bag he hadn't needed into the bed. Clint said you can explain all this to me after she gets here. So they sat there together in the cool air under the Texas stars and watched the choppers come and go, listening to the bugs sing their night songs between the wind-cutting chops of the rotors, until it was the chopper they were waiting for.

The Coasties wouldn't let them pull the truck in, and they didn't want to let Clint in at all, but after Donny got done talking and Clint put his pistol in the glove box they said they could wait on the civilian side of the last gate before the tarmac.

When the big Blackfoot flew in, painted a blue so dark you could only see the lights until it was there in the arc of the big lamps along the field, it looked like some kind of robot whale. And when they opened the side hatch you could not believe they would use such a huge machine to move such a small person.

Xelina was uncuffed, but still in the red jumpsuit. She didn't seem to care about that. She ran across the tarmac to Clint, dragging a small plastic bag with her few personal belongings, even as the airmen were yelling at her to walk. And when she was done with Clint, she even gave Donny an authentic hug, and a thank-you.

They wanted to talk, but Donny said let's talk in the car. So they sat the three of them side by side on the bench seat of the old pickup, Xelina in the middle, as far to the Clint side of the middle as she could get.

The radio came on as Clint started the car. Radio Ochenta, playing some kind of gringo variation on a revolutionary corrida. Clint reached over to turn it off, and when he moved Xelina grabbed on tighter. That was when Donny realized it was the first time he had seen her free—because even after her escape, that hideout was just a prison of her own making. And as he looked at her in the darkness as they pulled away, he could see that she no longer was fully free. That something she'd had before, even in chains, was gone. Left behind on that ship.

They were all three quiet for a while as Clint drove away from the base, Donny looking off out the side window at the distant flareoffs, until Xelina asked the question she had been holding on to.

"How did you pull it off?" she said.

"I found something they were a lot more scared of than you," said Donny. "It wasn't easy."

You could see the hint of a smile on her face at that.

Clint had one eye on the military trucks lined up in the oncoming lane, but he didn't say anything. None of them did. Instead, Donny kept talking.

"After the way I screwed this up at the beginning, I had my work cut out for me."

"We did our part," said Clint.

"You sure did," said Xelina, holding on to him like they were still on the run. "Not that I don't appreciate it."

"That was pretty badass," said Donny. "I hope you will come get me like that when it's my turn."

"You'll talk your way out of it," said Xelina.

"Maybe," said Donny. "But to answer your question more honestly, to save you, I made a deal with the devil. You know which devil I mean."

"What kind of deal?" said Xelina.

"I agreed to suppress, or at least keep to myself, the evidence I had on who killed Gregorio. Evidence that linked it to said devil."

"We'll get that information ourselves," said Xelina. "And they can't keep us from getting the word out."

"Maybe," said Donny. "We still have your footage, but I'm afraid it needs to stay locked in the archives for now. Part of the deal I cut." He didn't see any need to tell them what happened out on the golf course. Partly because he'd agreed to keep that secret, too, even from his own colleagues, in exchange for immunity for Joyce and him.

"It's okay," said Xelina. "Wait till you see the footage I got inside that ship."

"With that little camera I snuck you?"

She nodded.

"Can you wait a while before you do that?"

"Maybe," she said.

"Because I think I also got *everyone* on that floating prison freed, and I'd like to make sure that actually happens."

"No fucking way," said Clint.

"Wait until you hear the price," said Donny.

"I don't think I even want to know," said Xelina. The light from a passing truck crossed her face, and you could see that dead spot again.

"I do," said Clint. "Keep talkin'."

"Basically, as close to giving the land back to the Indians as you could ever manage. Or at least starting the whole Monopoly game over."

"Well, that sucks," said Clint.

"It does," said Donny. "But the ideas are out there now, anyway. People will keep pushing. And while we can't actually re-write history, we can slowly excise the injustice from the law."

"Assuming there's still any law left," said Clint.

"There will have to be a settling up, sooner or later," said Donny.

That was when Clint remembered to give Xelina her new gun. They had a different idea of how to hasten the settling up.

They drove on for a while longer. You could see the obelisk of the San Jacinto Monument off in the distance, the star the Texans had added to make it taller than the Washington Monument lit up in a way that made it look like it was burning.

"Where're you going, anyway?" said Clint. He was holding Xelina close with his right arm, left hand on the wheel.

"You can drop me off anywhere," said Donny. "I'll find my way home."

"You want some turkey?"

"You made turkey?" said Xelina.

"Yeah, girl. It's Thanksgiving. As of about an hour ago."

"Cool," said Xelina.

"She hates Thanksgiving, you know," said Clint. "Says it's like celebrating the Holocaust."

"It's okay this time," said Xelina. "Maybe we can make our own version."

"Sounds good to me," said Donny.

68

DONNY GOT UP AT FIVE THAT FRIDAY MORNING AND WENT TO MEET Joyce. He still had his overnight bag packed from the trip to D.C., so he just threw in the one swimsuit he owned, which was probably the ugliest and definitely the most colorful thing in his closet. He wore a suit, a blue cotton one that you could throw in the wash if you needed to. It never hurt to wear a suit while crossing borders. He grabbed the small quantities of foreign currency he had in the little wooden tray he kept atop his dresser, which included enough pesos to buy the first round. Then, for like the eighth time in as many hours, including the ones when he was asleep, he checked his phone for the passport app they had issued him in D.C. before his flight home. They could deauthorize it from the other end without notice, and Donny was sure it was just a matter of time before that happened.

He grabbed just one book, the one he had bought at the airport for Joyce.

Then he called a cab. The driver was a middle-aged white guy. Donny got him talking. He had been an actuary in Des Moines, saw the drought coming in his hand-wringing apocalyptic probability tables, and got out before they started closing the internal borders and diverting people to the camps. He said he was mostly living off his investments, and just driving the cab to learn the city. Donny took his word for it.

As they drove down Westheimer headed toward Joyce's

place over by Rice, they passed a convoy of military vehicles headed the opposite way, toward downtown.

"That doesn't look like Coast Guard," said the cabbie.

"No, it doesn't," said Donny.

The convoy must have been forty vehicles. One of those big armored cars led the line with a balaclava-masked dude standing in the turret showing off his black beret, followed by jeeps, troop carriers, a couple of trailers carrying what looked like flat-stacked sections of barricade, and three light tanks. Several of the jeeps pulled little trailers with big loudspeaker systems, and two of them had sonic cannons on the hitch, the ones they used for non-lethal crowd control. Donny looked back at one of the troop carriers as they passed and saw the platoon of soldiers sitting in there in the dim light, dressed for war, gas masks covering their faces and the flickers of augments where there should have been eyes.

"There must be a protest," said the cabbie.

"Or a coup d'état," said Donny.

It was weirdly awesome, Donny thought, even as it was horrifying. Something about the sight of the convoy stimulated his inner eleven-year-old, the sheer wonder of the massive power of the nation-state on display. That shock and awe was how they wanted you to react. But mostly it made him mad. Especially as he realized he had played a key part in it.

Toward the rear of the convoy were a dozen regular SUVs and a few flatbed semis, carrying even more troops. Only they weren't soldiers. They were contractors, in the branded tacticals of Texical and Pendleton-Bolan.

It wasn't a coup. It was a hostile takeover.

"Does this thing work?" asked Donny, messing with the TV embedded in the back of the seat.

"Oh, yeah, sorry, I forgot to turn that on."

What came onscreen was white noise and test patterns. Donny kept tuning, wondering if something was up with the network, until he finally got a live feed from American News Network. The closest thing to an official organ of the government, but it was the only one on. When he saw what they were reporting, it made more sense.

PRESIDENT RE-ELECT DEPLOYS MOTHERLAND GUARD IN FORTY CITIES TO SHUT DOWN TERROR CELLS, read the banner across the bottom. DECLARES NATIONAL CALL TO ORDER.

Scenes of even larger military displays in Los Angeles, Chicago, Atlanta, New York. Miami was already basically one big Coast Guard base, the parts that weren't yet underwater.

"Those motherfuckers," said Donny. "They couldn't even wait for the Supreme Court to decide their case."

"Trust me," said the cabbie. "He's doing the right thing. It's this or chaos. I saw it back home. People, neighbors, fighting over water when the emergency tankers roll up. We need to protect what we have."

"With a dictatorship that sells off the country and evicts its own citizens? I'll take my chances with anarchy."

"Maybe I should drop you off in the Tropic of Kansas and see how much you like that, buddy."

"I'll leave you my card and you can call me when they're done torturing you," said Donny.

And outside the window they were suddenly in the very lovely old residential block west of the Rice campus, where Joyce lived in her perfectly nice little house. A lawn sprinkler kicked on just as they pulled up.

"Sorry," said Donny. "It's been a rough couple of weeks."

"You should be careful," said the cabbie.

"So should you," said Donny. And he did hand him his card. "Call me when you aren't."

As he grabbed his bag to get out of the car, Donny saw a crew in the yellow jumpsuits of Midwestern refugee laborers, preparing to work on one of the neighbors' lawns. He wondered if they knew what was coming.

And then he saw Joyce, standing there at her front door, that beautiful old Mercedes of hers in the driveway, and a realtor's for sale sign stuck in the yard. She was smiling, like she was actually happy to see him.

69

"HEY," SAID DONNY.

"Good morning," said Joyce. Maybe it was the dawn light that made her look so good. Or maybe it was just the way she was holding the door open, the path to something better.

"You look great," said Donny.

"You look like shit," said Joyce. "And yet good. Must be the suit."

"Rough couple of weeks."

"Did you get it done?"

"I think so. It's complicated."

"Tell me," she said.

"I got my client off."

"Well done."

"And I shut down the secret camp."

"Get outta here."

"But to do that, I gave up the opportunity to stop these guys, impact the election, maybe even achieve some meaningful land reform."

She shook her head.

"It was my job, Joyce. And my sworn ethical duty. Not that anyone else cares about that sort of thing anymore."

Joyce laughed.

"And it's not over yet."

"Yes it is," said Joyce. "We're out of here. I just shot a rich kid."

"I know a good lawyer. And that incident is taken care of, too."

"This place is beyond repair. We need to go start our own new country."

"What if we could restart this one?"

"Come on."

"I mean it."

"How long do you think that will take?"

"Four years, at least. Probably more like forty. It's a long game."

"Fuck these people, Donny! They don't want the help. Listen to what they're letting those bastards do." She put her finger to her ear. In the distance, you could hear the sound of orders being yelled over loudspeakers. "They want to be controlled, not liberated." She held out her phone and shook it. "The willing architects of their own enslavement, using their thumbs to beat off their brains while the planet dies."

"You're wrong, Joyce. People are already fighting back. Maybe not in this neighborhood, but they're out there, right now. And I'm fighting with them, right here, the only way I know how. One case at a time."

She gave him a hard look. "I knew you would bail on me."

"I'm sorry, Joyce. I have to. I didn't realize it until I saw those tanks rolling down Westheimer. But now I know it with more certainty than I've had about anything in a long time."

"I just saved your life," she reminded him.

"I know. But I still have to earn it."

He held out his hands. She let him hang there for a minute, before she let up and reached back.

And as they pulled each other closer, and kissed, you could feel the pull. But the house behind her was empty, and the only door that was really open was the car's.

"'In the future, there won't be any borders,'" said Donny, quoting one of Joyce's favorite lines from Brigada. Joyce nodded, and tried to smile. But they both knew he was lying.

Acknowledgments

TEXAS IS A PLACE WHERE LAWYER ADS FLOURISH LIKE PRICKLY pear, and it was a lawyer on a billboard that provided the initial inspiration for this story. I was pumping gas one afternoon on the side of Highway 71 at the outskirts of Austin, looking in the direction of Houston. Staring down at me from above the overpass was a criminal defense lawyer sporting a leather jacket, wild hair, and a trickster's smile—one of those rare lawyers who work to show potential clients they are ready to fight the system, not be part of it. I was working on *Tropic of Kansas* at the time, and while I didn't need a lawyer, my fugitive characters did—a lawyer who would combine some of the frontage road tenacity of a Texas plaintiff's attorney with the political courage of advocates like William Kunstler and Jacques Vergès to help clients navigate the legal minefields of dystopia. Donny Kimoe didn't make the final cut of that book, but his billboard did, and it was enough to make one character pick up the phone for that free initial consultation. My imaginary dystopian defense lawyer would not be possible without the example and inspiration of all the real ones who roll up their sleeves to fight for a dream of justice we all know is rarely achieved outside of fiction, and I humbly hope that this book inspires some others in the same way.

Donny Kimoe practices in a legal system I invented for this book. If you try to look up any of the statutes or cases cited here, you won't find them (with a few exceptions, notably *Johnson v. M'Intosh*, 21 U.S. (8 Wheat.) 543 (1823)). But they are all extrapolations from existing legal precedents, from the military tribunals of Guantánamo and the Civil War to the loyalty laws of the Red Scare and the Cold War and the martial law invocations that occurred with remarkable frequency in the twentieth century, especially before World War II. To develop my jurisprudential variation on speculative fictional world-building, I spent a tremendous amount of time in the Tarlton Law Library at the University of Texas School of Law, taking advantage of its prodigious collection of material, which even includes a section of dusty how-to guides for the domestic administration of military government in times of insurrection or emergency—as well as an amazing collection of law and popular culture ready-made for a writer wishing to decode the deep roots of the American lawyer story. I owe thanks to the librarians of that amazing institution, and to the authors of the many remarkable works I drew from in my research.

The other experience I had while working on *Tropic of Kansas* that had a big influence on this book was my service for several months on a Texas grand jury. Having only ever worked at the margins of criminal procedure over the course of my career as a lawyer, I found it a unique opportunity, and an eye-opener. Unlike a trial jury, which sits as the finder of fact in a specific case, the grand jury hears the government's presentation of each felony indictment it wants to prosecute. The standard it applies is low. And the volume of cases it hears is huge—dozens or more a day, two or three days a week. Our panel was a diverse group of Texans with good bullshit detectors and a strong sense of justice, and we did our job to turn away cases where the standard was not met. But in most of the cases, indictments were issued based on the evidence, and you learned what it feels like to be part of the machine that takes people (many of them young people) off the street, marks them for life, and locks them up. People who may be guilty of the crimes for which they've been arrested, but caught through a process that's rigged—from the decisions about what activity should be criminalized to the decisions about what neighborhoods to patrol to the way the system allocates access to lawyers. Serving on a grand jury, you quickly gain a deeper understanding of how justice is distributed the same way everything else is in this society. That from at least some vantage points, the system is already pretty dystopian, even without distortion through the prism of imaginative fiction. The experience recharged my sense of pervasive injustice in a way that impacted my own practice, especially my pro bono and community work, and led me to pursue the idea of this book. So thanks to my fellow grand jurors for helping me see the law from the perspective of their very different experiences, and to the court for the opportunity.

This story bears the imprint of my own experiences as a working lawyer, sometimes helping people who had no money and sometimes helping people who had too much, and the things I have learned from the clients and lawyers and paralegals I have had the good fortune to work with, from government and non-profit clinics to big law firms and bigger companies. Those people are too numerous to list, but I owe particular thanks to Charlie Szalkowski, who sets the model of professional ethics and can tell you the story of just about every Houston lawyer who ever lived; Melissa Russell, who helped me see the things lawyers hide from each other; Len Sandler, who taught me how to truly listen to a client; and

Steve Bercu, whose example has been more influential than he knows.

A few of those lawyers are also writers, and they proved especially helpful sounding boards as I fleshed out this book. In particular, I owe thanks to Paul Miles for reading various drafts and providing essential election law advice; to Dan Wood for helping me think through my ideas for how to write a legal thriller that was about the law as much as the facts; and to Justin Castillo for helping me vet both my law and procedure, and other insights as well. I also owe thanks to some writers who are not lawyers, including Pepe Rojo, for once again helping me see this country from the other side of the border wall that keeps us in; Kelly Link, for titular affirmation; Jessica Reisman, for being the truest of colleagues and the most trusted of advisors; Henry Wessells, for being the sounding board who always gets it; and Timmi Duchamp, for the engagement and example.

I want to thank my neighbors here in East Austin, with whom I have had the opportunity to work in recent years, especially Daniel Llanes and Susana Almanza, who have helped me see how the injustices of the twenty-first-century city are rooted in the history of the land on which it is built, and Bill O'Rourke, who provided important encouragement and helped me see the city from the streets. Thanks also to Sam Douglas for his documentary filmmaker's tips on where to find Houston's very best lawyer commercials.

Big thanks to my editor, David Pomerico, who saw the potential of this idea early on, and played a critical role in helping me flesh out the concept and make it something much bigger than I initially conceived. Thanks to the rest of the team at HarperCollins, notably cover designer Owen Corrigan for helping to convey the book visually. And thanks to literary agent Mark Gottlieb for helping to guide the project forward and providing insightful advice and counsel along the way.

Finally, thanks to my family, for the love, support, and inspiration. Especially Virginia and Eliseo, for sharing with me some sense of what it is like to live in a country where the government is truly at war with the people. Thanks to Hugo and Ajin, Bill and Sibyl, and Katiti. And thanks most importantly to Agustina, for the partnership that makes works like this possible, and teaching me what it means to love someone from Houston (and learn to love Houston in the process).

After this book went to production, my brother Alex, to whom this book is dedicated, died unexpectedly of a stroke. A painter and hardcore punk pioneer, Alex set a powerful example of how to live a life that stays true to the idealistic manifestos of youth, even in the face of adulthood's frequent calls to pragmatic compromise. He loved secret histories, weird fictions, hidden truths, and golf, and I thought of him often while I was writing this book—not just because we were planning a trip together as soon as I finished it. He lived a rich life, and left a meaningful body of work behind as an artist and musician. Preparing for his memorial service, we rediscovered some of the earliest work he had done—DIY punk zines that grounded their passionate political and social protest in profound empathy and a deep sense of community, and by their very making helped create a new community, one that went on to positively impact the world around it. I'll never know what Alex would have thought of this book, but in his absence I see more clearly how much he taught me about what real justice should feel like, and his deep influence on this book's effort to bridge the gap between the world our youthful selves want to live in, and the one we find.

LOOKING AT THE BRIGHT BLUE SKY FROM THE BACKSEAT OF THE armored truck, which was more like a cell than a seat, Sig could almost believe it was a warm day. But the shackles around his ankles were still cold from the walk out to the vehicle, and when Sig put his head up against the bars to test for faults, he could feel the ice trying to get to him. And winter was just getting started.

"What day is it?" asked Sig.

"Deportation day," said the big constable who had muscled him out of lockup thirty minutes earlier. When he talked the red maple leaf tattoo on the side of his thick neck moved, like a lazy bat.

"Friday," said the Sergeant, who was driving. "December 1. The day you get to go back where you came from."

The thought conjured different images in Sig's head than his jailers might have imagined.

"Back to cuckoo country," laughed the constable. "Lucky you. Say hi to the TV tyrant for me."

The Mounties had nicknames for Sig, like Animal and Dog Boy, but they never called him any of those to his face. They didn't know his real name. When they trapped him stealing tools and food from a trailer at the Loonhaunt Lake work camp a month earlier, he had no ID, no name he would give them, and they couldn't find him in their computers. They still tagged him, accurately, as another American illegal immigrant or smuggler, and processed him as a John Doe criminal repatriation. They did not know that he had been up here the better part of seven years, living in the edgelands.

The memory of that day he ran tried to get out, like a critter in a trap, but he kept it down there in its cage. And wished he had stayed farther north.

He pulled his wrists against the cuffs again, but he couldn't get any leverage the way they had him strapped in.

Then the truck braked hard, and the restraints hit back.

The constable laughed.

They opened the door, pulled him out of the cage, and uncuffed him there on the road. Beyond the barriers was the international bridge stretching over the Rainy River to the place he had escaped.

"Walk on over there and you'll be in the USA, kid," said the Sergeant. "Thank you for visiting Canada. Don't come back."

Sig stretched, feeling the blood move back into his hands and feet. He looked back at the Canadian border fortifications. A thirty-foot-high fence ran along the riverbank. Machine guns pointed down from the towers that loomed over the barren killing zone on the other side. He could see two figures watching him through gun scopes from the nearest tower, waiting for an opportunity to ensure he would never return.

Sig looked in the other direction. A military transport idled in the middle of the bridge on six fat tires, occupants hidden behind tinted windows and black armor. Behind them was an even higher fence shielding what passed for tall buildings in International Falls. The fence was decorated with big pictograms of death: by gunfire, explosives, and electricity. The wayfinding sign was closer to the bridge.

Sig looked down at the churning river. No ice yet.

He shifted, trying to remember how far it was before the river dumped into the lake.

"Step over the bridge, prisoner," said a machine voice. It looked like the transport was talking. Maybe it was. He'd heard stories. Red and white flashing lights went on across the top of the black windshield. You could see the gun barrels and camera eyes embedded in the grill.

"Go on home to robotland, kid," said the Sergeant. "They watch from above, too, you know."

Sig looked up at the sky. He heard a chopper but saw only low-flying geese, working their way south. He thought about the idea of home. It was one he had pretty much forgotten, or at least given up on. Now it just felt like the open door to a cage.

He steeled himself and walked toward the transport. Five armed guards emerged from the vehicle to greet him in black tactical gear. The one carrying the shackles had a smile painted on his face mask.

2

THE PILGRIM CENTER WAS AN OLD SHOPPING PLAZA BY THE FREE-
way that had been turned into a detention camp. It was full.

The whole town of International Falls had been evacuated and
turned into a paramilitary control zone. Sig saw two tanks, four
helicopters, and lots of soldiers and militarized police through the
gun slits of the transport. Even the flag looked different—the blue
part had turned almost black.

No one in the camp looked like a pilgrim. Instead they
wore yellow jumpsuits. There were plenty of local boys in the
mix, the sort of rowdies who'd have a good chance of getting
locked up even in normal times. The others were immigrants,
refugees, and guest workers. Hmong, Honduran, North Korean,
Bolivian, Liberian. They had been rounded up from all over the
region. Some got caught trying to sneak out, only to be accused
of sneaking in.

They interrogated Sig for several hours each day. Most days
the interrogator was a suit named Connors. He asked Sig a hundred variations on the same questions.

Where did you come from?

North.

Where specifically?

All over.

What were you doing up there?

Traveling. Hunting. Working. Walking.

What did you do with your papers?

Never had any.

How old are you?

Old enough.

Are you a smuggler?

No.

Where were you during the Thanksgiving attacks?

What attacks.

Where were you during the Washington bombings last month?

I don't know. In the woods.

Tell me about your friends. Where were they?

What friends.

Tell us your name. Your true name.

They took his picture, a bunch of times, naked and with his clothes on. They had a weird machine that took close-up shots of his eyes. They took his fingerprints, asked him about his scars, and took samples of his skin, blood, and hair. He still wouldn't give them his name. They said they would find him in their databases anyway. He worried they would match him to records in their computers of the things he'd done before he fled.

They made fun of his hair.

THE IMPROVISED PRISON WAS SMALL. A ONE-STORY MALL THAT
might once have housed twenty stores. The camp included a section of parking lot cordoned off with a ten-foot hurricane fence
topped with razor wire. They parked military vehicles and fortifi-
cation materials on the other side, coming and going all the time.

They rolled in buses with more detainees every day. A couple
of times they brought a prisoner in on a helicopter that landed
right outside the gate. Those prisoners were hooded and shackled, with big headphones on. They kept them in another section.

At night you could hear helicopters and faraway trains. Some
nights there was gunfire. Most nights there were screams.

Every room in the camp had a picture of the same forty-
something white guy. Mostly he was just sitting there in a suit,
looking serious. Sometimes he was younger, smiling, wearing
a flight suit, holding a gun, playing with kids and dogs. In the
room where they ate there was a big poster on the wall that
showed him talking to a bunch of people standing in what
looked like a football stadium. There was a slogan across the
bottom in big letters.

Accountability = Responsibility + Consequences

One of the other detainees told Sig the guy on the poster
was the President.

They just tried to kill him, Samir explained. He whispered

because he didn't want them to hear him talking about it. Said people got into the White House with a bomb. Sig asked what people. Samir just held up his hands and shrugged.

Samir was the guy who had the cot next to Sig. He was from Mali. Their cot was in a pen with an old sign over it. "Wonderbooks." There were holes in the walls and floors where once there had been store shelving. One of the guys that slept back there, a middle-aged white guy named Del, said they were closing all the bookstores on purpose. Samir said it was because no one read books anymore. Sig wasn't sure what the difference was.

The women detainees were in a different section, where there used to be a dollar store. Sometimes they could see the women when they were out in the yard.

One day a lady showed up at Sig's interrogation. Blonde in a suit. She said she was an investigator from the Twin Cities. Why do you look so nervous all the sudden, said Connors. They asked him about what happened back then. About other people who were with him. Sig didn't say anything.

Looks like you get to go to Detroit, said Connors.

Sig did not know what that meant, but it scared him anyway, from the way the guy said it, and from the not knowing. He tried not to show it.

That afternoon Sig found a tiny figure of a man in a business suit stuck in a crack in the floor. His suit was bright blue, and he had a hat and a briefcase. Del said there used to be a shop in the mall that made imaginary landscapes for model trains to travel through, and maybe this guy missed his train.

Del and Samir and the others talked whenever they could about what was going on. They talked about the attacks. They talked outside, they talked in whispers, they swapped theories at night after one of the guys figured out how to muffle the surveillance mic with a pillow they took turns holding up there.

They talked about how there were stories of underground cells from here to the Gulf of Mexico trying to fight the government. How the government blamed the Canadians for harboring "foreign fighters," by which they meant Americans who'd fled or been deported. They told Sig how the elections were probably rigged, and the President didn't even have a real opponent the last time. Some of the guys said they thought the attacks were faked to create public support for a crackdown. For a new war to fight right here in the Motherland. To put more people back to work. Del said he had trouble believing the President would have his guys blow off his own arm to manipulate public opinion. Beto said no way, I bet he would have blown off more than that to make sure he killed that lady that used to be Vice President since she was his biggest enemy.

One of the guys admitted that he really was a part of the resistance. Fred said that lady's name was Maxine Price and he'd been in New Orleans when she led the people to take over the city. He said he joined the fight and shot three federal troopers and it felt good.

Sig asked the others what it meant when the interrogator told him he was going to Detroit. They got quiet. Then they told him about the work camps. They sounded different from what he had seen in Canada. Old factories where they made prisoners work without pay, building machines for war and extraction.

On his fourth day in the camp, Sig made a knife. It wasn't a knife at first. It was a piece of rebar he noticed in the same crack in the floor where he found the little man. He managed to dig out and break off a sliver a little longer than his finger, and get a better edge working it against a good rock he found in one of the old concrete planters in the yard. Just having it made him feel more confident when the guards pushed him around.

The seventh day in the camp, as the other detainees loitered in the common areas after dinner, Sig escaped.

He got the idea watching squirrels. The squirrels loved it behind the tall fences, which kept out their competition. Sig saw one jump from a tree outside the fence onto the roof, grab some acorns that had fallen from another nearby tree, and then jump back using the fence as a relay.

Del went with him. Samir said he didn't want to die yet.

They waited until the guards were busy after dinner. Samir took watch. They leaned Sig's cot up against the wall and pushed through the section of cheap ceiling Sig had cut out the night before. They carried their blankets around their shoulders. Del could barely fit when they got up in the crawl space. Sig didn't wait. They followed the ductwork on their hands and knees to the roof access and broke out into the open air. Sig half-expected to get shot right then, but the guards in the tower were watching a prisoner delivery.

He could see the black trucks driving by on the high road behind the mall.

They tossed their blankets so they would drape over the razor wire where the fence came close to the back of the building. Del's throw was good, but Sig's went too far, over the fence. Too bad, said Del. Sig backed up, got a running start, and jumped anyway.

The razored barbs felt like sharpened velcro, grabbing onto his prison jumpsuit in bunches, poking through into his forearm and hand.

Del didn't even make it to the fence.

Shit.

"You go!" said Del, curled up on the ground, groaning.

The sound of Sig's body hitting the chain link like a big monkey got the guards' attention, but by the time bullets came they hit torn fragments of his paper jumpsuit that stayed stuck when he leapt from his momentary perch.

The tree branch Sig landed on broke under his weight, and he hit the frozen ground hard. But he got up okay. Nothing broken. His blanket was right there, so he grabbed it.

He looked through the fence. Del was up on his knees, hands behind his head, hollering at the guards not to shoot as they came around the corner and from the roof.

Sig ran. He heard the gunfire behind him, but didn't hear Del.

They came after Sig fast, but he had already disappeared into the landscaping that ran along the side road. He heard them off in the distance as he crawled through a vacant subdivision of knee-high grass, broken doors, and gardens gone wild. He evaded capture that night moving through cover, the way a field mouse escapes a hawk.

He was glad it took them half an hour to get out the dogs.

He used torn chunks of his prison jumpsuit to bandage his wounds. They were little bleeders, but he would be okay. Then he cut a hole in the middle of the blanket to turn it into a poncho. He thought about where he could get new clothes, if he made it through the night.

Later, as he huddled in a portable toilet behind a convenience store just south of the borderzone, he wondered if what that Mountie said was true. That they had robots in the sky that could see you in the dark, tag you and track you, and kill without you ever knowing they were there. Sig thought maybe if he got cold enough, their heat cameras couldn't find him.

Tropic of Kansas is available in paperback, eBook, and audiobook now.

About the Author

Christopher Brown's debut novel *Tropic of Kansas* was a finalist for the Campbell Award for best science fiction novel of 2018, and he was nominated for a World Fantasy Award for the anthology *Three Messages and a Warning*. His short fiction has appeared in a variety of magazines and anthologies, including *MIT Technology Review*, Lit Hub, Tor.com, and *The Baffler*. He lives in Austin, Texas, where he also practices law.